FACTS ARE STUBBORN THINGS

Richard A. Danzig

Copyright © 2023

By Richard A. Danzig

All Rights Reserved. No part of this book may be reproduced or transmitted in any form or by any means, electronic or mechanical, including photocopying, recording, or by any information storage and retrieval system without the written permission of the author, except where permitted by law.

ISBN: 979-8-852-99189-8 (Soft Cover)
ISBN: 979-8-388-36034-2 (Hard Cover)

DEDICATION

To my son Matthew Daniel Danzig
who enjoyed a good book,
a good joke, and a good life.

Facts are stubborn things;
and whatever may be our wishes,
our inclinations, or the dictates of our passions,
they cannot alter the state of facts and evidence.*

~ *John Adams*

**The Portable John Adams,* Introduction by Jack Diggins, Penguin Classics; First Edition, 2004

PROLOGUE

Six months is not a very long time. That is unless you are a trial lawyer and your license to practice law has been suspended. Then, it can seem like an eternity. After being a successful litigator and a member of a profession I have respected and loved for more than twenty-five years, I am now on the outside of the courtroom and the doors are locked. I envy the lawyers who can still try cases, practice their profession and serve their clients as counselors-at-law.

I deserved to be suspended. I acted unprofessionally and the grievance committee was more than justified in taking my license away. At the end of my six-month suspension, provided I don't do anything else stupid, my license will be restored. I now have plenty of time to try to understand how I lost control over my profession, my life, and my future, based on one case I never wanted to begin with. I made some bad mistakes in judgment, but I always did what I thought was right at the time. I regret the loss of my license, but I don't regret what I have done or why I did it.

I thought it might help to write down what happened. Many things I now know to be true I only learned long after the fact. Had I known all the facts at the time, maybe I would have done things differently. But I doubt it.

CHAPTER ONE
IT'S WHAT YOU DON'T SEE COMING

"Knopfler."

"Knopfler?"

"Yup, Mark Knopfler."

"You mean *Dire Straits?*"

"Nope, Mark Knopfler. Please, Damian, try to pay attention. The topic is the best rock guitarist, not the best rock group."

"So, you are telling me Mark Knopfler is the best rock guitarist of all time?"

"Best guitarist, best composer, and best singer. *Romeo and Juliet* is Shakespearean rock."

I started singing, "And all I do is miss you and the way we used to be; And all I do is keep the beat, the bad company; All I do is kiss you through the bars of a rhyme, Julie, I'd do the stars with you any time."

"Stop. Please! I feel for you. I do. No taste in music, no voice and if you keep this up, no one to have lunch with. You do realize they don't make 45s anymore."

"Don't knock vinyl. Scratches give records character."

"Even assuming rock music ended twenty years ago, when you were still old but not yet senile, what about Hendrix? Page? Clapton? And please, please never sing around me again."

"Sorry, only Knopfler. And my friends think I have a beautiful voice."

"One, you have no friends, and two, you should never sing outside the shower. How about the whole new world of guitarists who know how to shred? Tom Morello? A Harvard graduate, by the way. Angus Young? Or Eddie Van Halen?"

"All bangers. I should have known you're a closet metalhead.

Knopfler now and then. Look up Rock Star in the dictionary and you will see his picture."

"*Dictionary*? Where would I find one of those? I hope I never become a dinosaur like you."

"Dinosaurs ruled the earth."

"Of course, this is all just your opinion."

"No, young Jedi, this is a fact."

"Oh, really? How is it a fact that Mark Knopfler is the best rock musician in the world?"

"Normally, as a trial lawyer, I would say a fact is something I believe is true, based on all the credible evidence. But in this case, it's a fact because my heart and soul tell me it's true."

"Wow! I always wanted to meet a real hippie. Where did you have that revelation? In the mud at Woodstock?"

"I was there but, unfortunately, *Dire Straits* didn't play."

My investigator and IT expert, Damian Pressler, and I have lunch together whenever possible when we are not on trial. We alternate taking turns ordering the takeout food and choosing the "Best Of" category for the day. It's a game we have been playing at lunch for years. Today Damian chose tacos, and I chose Best Rock Guitarist. After Damian and I review our pending cases, we eat and play our game. It's a nice diversion from the practice of law. We have debated "Best Of" topics ranging from movies, foods and sports teams to more revealing and challenging topics like morality, and the law. We rarely agree on who or what is best, but even after ten years of working together we learn something new and interesting about each other.

My office is located on the ground floor of a brownstone I own in the Williamsburg section of Brooklyn. There is a hand-painted sign next to the front door that says: "Chance Cormac & Associates." It still makes me proud whenever I walk down the street. I was very fortunate to buy and renovate it about fifteen years ago, at a fraction of what it would cost today. It is on a tree-lined street down the block from a park that has real grass, a playground, and lots of benches. My neighbors know me and one another. We stop to talk to each other on the street and we watch out for each other. It's a short walk to my favorite coffee shop, bookstore, and restaurants.

Williamsburg is a good mix of the old and the new. Brooklyn is officially known as Kings County in the City of New York. It was named after King Charles of the Netherlands, but is always just called Brooklyn. It is less like the crowded streets and towering high rises of New York City and more like a patchwork of small neighborhoods, each with its own culture and flavor. I am a few subway stops from Manhattan, which we call simply The City.

My office is a converted apartment on the ground floor. The conference room, with a large old oak conference table and bookshelves, was formerly the living room of the ground-floor apartment. It has a working fireplace and a comfortable couch we can sit on to review documents or discuss cases. We eat lunch in the conference room on the big oak table, scratched and scarred from years of being used as a war room for our trials.

We have braided throw rugs on the large plank oak wood floors in every room, similar to the ones on the floors of my childhood home in Yonkers. I kept the kitchen on the ground floor, and I am met by the smell of freshly brewed coffee when I come downstairs in the morning. I have pictures of an eclectic group of people I admire on the office walls, including Thomas Aquinas, Mark Knopfler, Hunter S. Thompson, and Mike Tyson.

The offices are wired with quality Bose speakers and there is always music playing. I keep a scrapbook on my desk containing letters from clients thanking me for my help and how much it changed their lives. Those letters mean more to me than the size of any verdict.

My home is on the second floor, where I live with my best friend, a pooch named Tort, a mixed breed Lab and Australian sheepdog. I walk Tort at the park down the street and bring him to the office each day when I go downstairs to work. I talk to him and believe, without a doubt, he understands everything I say.

This arrangement works out perfectly for both of us. I have fully integrated my personal life, to the extent I have one, with my professional life. Tort and I have a good life together.

I consider Damian a good friend. We enjoy working together and being in each other's company. Damian is thirty-eight, nine years younger than me. He is a graduate of Annapolis, but after graduation, instead of accepting his commission, he chose to become a Navy SEAL. After completing basic training he completed advanced training in covert ops at The Naval Special Warfare Center. Based upon Damian's leadership ability he quickly became a platoon leader and served for two tours of active duty in the Middle East. After his tours were completed, Damian attended the Naval War College and became a specialist in Naval Intelligence and Cyber Security. Damian never speaks about his engagements, but I know he received the Naval Medal of Honor for valor in combat in recognition of courage and bravery under fire.

He has only one tattoo, barely visible on the wrist of his right hand: "The Only Easy Day is Yesterday." That tattoo says all you need to know about Damian. He is disciplined, determined and loyal. If a friend is someone you can call in an emergency, day or night, no questions asked, then Damian is that friend.

Like most SEALs, he carries himself in a way that is calm and yet somehow intimidating. When you meet Damian, who stands five-foot-ten, you feel his presence before you notice his muscular build and chiseled features. His blond hair is still cut in a Navy buzzcut and his posture is always perfect.

He is centered in a way certain people are, who carry themselves with complete confidence in their skill, judgment, and ability. There is always a thoughtful pause before Damian speaks or acts, as if he is considering the full meaning of his words or actions – a habit I am sure served him well in combat. If you shake his hand and feel his iron grip, or confront his steely gray eyes, you understand what a physical force of nature he is.

More importantly, Damian is the most skilled and talented investigator I have ever worked with. There are no longer paper trails to follow in investigating a case. They have been replaced by digital footprints, cloud memory, and encrypted messages protected by virtual private networks. In the new digital age, every case is inevitably won or lost based on digital data and IT expertise.

Damian has the skills, and access through his Naval Intelligence experience and relationships to explore the dark web and uncover facts most people never want to be discovered. Even better, Damian continues to consult for Homeland Security and has high-level security clearance. I don't ask how he accesses the confidential government documents that are invaluable in investigating our cases and he never reveals his sources.

I was fortunate to have been introduced to Damian by a client who ran a cyber security firm. Damian was looking for a job where he could use his cyber security and investigative skills. I felt certain he would be a valuable addition to my practice. It was a perfect fit. I appreciate every day how lucky I am to have him on our team. Hiring Damian is probably the second-best decision I ever made. The first was hiring my paralegal office manager, and my first true love, Sally McConnell.

At the end of our lunch, I told Damian, "I want you and Sally to sit in with a new client tomorrow morning. Are you free?"

"Yes," he replied. "What kind of case?"

"It's a matrimonial."

He gave me a puzzled look. "What? I thought you swore you would never take another divorce case."

"I did, but the wife is the daughter of a good friend of Roy Brown's. He asked me to do him a favor. You know Roy. He is a poker buddy and corporate lawyer who refers a lot of commercial litigation work to us. I was introduced to Roy by Judge Donovan, the judge I clerked for in law school. Roy and the judge are old friends. They were in the same class at Harvard Law School and sit on a number of bar association committees together."

"Got it. Sally is not going to be happy. Have you told her?"

"Not yet."

Damian laughed. "Well, good luck with that! Now it's my turn for a riddle. You know what they say in combat?"

"No good deed goes unpunished?"

"No. It's what you don't see coming that can hurt you."

CHAPTER TWO
BROKEN PROMISES

I waited a few days to speak with Sally. We were enjoying the afterglow of our success at a recent trial, and Sally was buried in doing the post-trial cleanup. I wanted the dust to settle before telling her about Roy Brown's request.

When I thought the time was right, I went into Sally's office, moved a stack of files off a chair and sat down. I smiled at a new picture on her desk of her daughter Melody with my dog Tort. I'm Melody's godfather and she is like a daughter to me.

I said casually, "You should really get Melody a dog."

"Oh, sure, and are you going to walk the dog when I'm trying to get Melody out the door to school in the morning? I'm warning you, you better not make trouble. What's up?"

"I'd like you and Damian to sit in with a new client tomorrow."

Sally always got excited when we were retained by a new client. It's the prospect of a great new adventure we will all share together. A blank page in the law books we get to write on. Our clients become part of our lives and the history of our firm. But I was careful not to mention it was a matrimonial case.

"Great! I've almost finished the clean-up from the trial. Who's the client? What kind of case is it?"

I deliberately evaded Sally's question about the nature of the referral. "It's the daughter of a friend of Roy Brown's. I'm doing Roy a personal favor. I doubt we will take the case."

Sally isn't a big fan of Roy's. She knows him well from past referrals and has often sat in on conferences with him and his clients at our office. She feels he is too impressed with himself, his prestige, his white-shoe law firm, and his country club life. But Sally understands the benefit of our business relationship and is always cordial and professional.

I hoped she would assume the new referral was more corporate litigation. Unfortunately, Sally is just too sharp and knows me too well. She gave me a quizzical look. "Right." Her green eyes flashing danger, she added more forcefully, "But I didn't ask you who referred the client, I asked who the client is and what kind of case it is."

I knew the game was lost but still tried to put off the inevitable. "I'm not sure what's involved, but it's only a consultation. It's a favor to keep his good will and I don't expect we will be retained."

"Right," she replied again, "but now what I would really like to know is why you don't want to tell me what type of case this is."

Knowing it was hopeless, I gave up. "It's a divorce."

"Don't do it!" she replied angrily, more as a warning than a suggestion. "You promised me you would never take another divorce after the Foster case."

Now, ten years after the Foster case, Sally held up three fingers, one at a time. In a barely controlled voice, she ticked off the reasons. "One – you don't need the work. Two – you don't need the brain damage. Three – I expect you to keep your word. I won't get involved. Not a prayer. Refer her to a good matrimonial attorney. Roy will understand."

Of course, she was right, but despite my success, I understood the law is both a business and a profession. Lawyers, particularly solo practitioners, keep a running ledger in their heads of billings, collections, and expenses. The truth is, I owed Roy and he had never asked me for a personal favor before.

I tried to appeal to Sally's professionalism and business sense. "I know what I said. I intend to keep my word. I owe Roy the favor of at least meeting with his client. I can handle the meeting alone, but you know how much I rely on you when we interview a new client, especially in a divorce case. You give them a comfort level and trust neither Damian nor I am capable of. If you will just sit in, I promise you I will refer the client to another matrimonial attorney after the consultation."

Sally looked away. "You're the boss."

That pretty well summed up the full extent of her anger and disappointment.

CHAPTER THREE
THE LAST DIVORCE

A few days later, Damian and I were sitting down to lunch in the conference room when he asked, "So, did you discuss the new divorce case with Sally?"

"Yup."

"How did it go?"

"Somewhere between a disaster and a train wreck."

"I'm not surprised. So, you never told me, why was this last divorce case such a nightmare?"

"You really want to spoil my lunch, don't you? All right, you asked for it. Actually, it might be helpful for you to know the history anyway, to understand Sally's reservations about divorce cases before we meet with Roy's client. The last divorce we handled ended shortly before I made the mistake of asking you to join the firm."

"Best mistake you ever made."

"Agreed. So, as you know, I'm not a divorce lawyer. Not anymore, anyway. When I opened my office, to survive, I had to take any case walking in the door. I ate what I killed."

"Got it. In the SEALs we say when the lion's hungry, he eats."

"Exactly. And this case was a beast. Abusive husband, unethical lawyer, *and* corrupt judge."

"Now, I'm really intrigued. Sounds as bad as it gets."

"Worse. Are you really sure you want to hear about this mess?"

"Yes. I don't know if I ever mentioned it, but my parents are divorced."

"I'm sorry to hear that. How old were you when they got divorced?"

"I had graduated high school and I was already appointed to the Naval Academy. I think my parents wanted to make sure I was on my path in life before they separated. There was never really any acrimony. They just drifted apart. I never heard them say a bad word about each other. They came to my graduation together and I am still very close to each of them. It puzzles me how people who once loved each other, and had children together, can be so consumed with rage, they only want to hurt the person they once loved."

"I respect your parents. Some people just need someone to say they are not to blame. They think a judge will decide who's at fault. Of course, that never happens in a divorce. The court could care less who the good guy or bad guy is. Divorces are about broken marriages and broken people who are in crisis. No one wins, everyone loses."

"Except the lawyers. They get paid – win, lose or draw. Right?"

"Always. Anyway, when Mary Foster was referred to me, she had suffered physical and emotional abuse at the hands of her husband for many years. Her marriage was one where she held her breath, never knowing what would provoke her husband. She was in and out of different ERs, always making excuses for her injuries and bruised face. When we served her husband with divorce papers, he threatened to kidnap their seven-year-old daughter and kill her."

"Nice guy." Damian grimaced, shaking his head.

"As soon as he retained an attorney, he cut off all support for Mary and their young daughter. You don't need to know all the sordid details, it's enough to know he was not a good guy. And his lawyer was a politically connected gunslinger."

"Got it. A bad guy getting bad legal advice."

"Exactly. She was lucky to find a good therapist. It took a few years of therapy before Mary had the courage to retain a lawyer. I told her I understood how difficult it was for her to walk through the front door of my office. I immediately made an emergency application for an order of protection and temporary support. Mary was terrified and I assured her the motion should be routinely granted, based on the history of abuse by her husband and the threats to her life and her child's life."

"I guess it's a fine line between being a lawyer and a therapist."

"You have to be the rock in the stream. Anger and fear drive divorces. On the return date of our motion, Sally, Mrs. Foster, and I sat in the cavernous Supreme Court of Kings County courtroom, at the large wooden table designated for plaintiffs, and waited for the judge to take the bench. Mary was terrified when she saw her husband, but she did her best to keep her composure in front of the judge. Mr. Foster's attorney was

Conrad Dumbrowski, who had a reputation for his scorched earth litigation tactics."

"A real credit to his profession."

"Right. A land shark who dressed the part. He was in his mid-forties, lean from daily workouts with a personal trainer. He had dark black hair, probably two shades darker than it should be. He dressed impeccably for court in a Brioni suit, with a silk pocket square, a custom shirt with his initials on the cuffs, and an imposing Audemars Piquet on his wrist. The watch cost about the same amount as the S-Class Mercedes he drove. He had a habit of dramatically shooting his cuff back to draw attention to the watch and his engraved gold cufflinks. He is the type of person my father would say, if he shook your hand, you better count your fingers."

"A silk purse made out of a sow's ear."

"Exactly. Anyway, on my first day in court with Dumbrowski, I couldn't resist, and when I caught his attention, I slowly pulled up the sleeve of the left arm of the plain white cotton button-down shirt I always wear to court. Dumbrowski finally noticed my watch. He shook his head in disgust and snorted derisively when he saw the Mickey Mouse face and Mickey's arms telling the time."

Damian laughed. "I always wondered about your watch. I thought maybe Goofy would have been a better choice."

"Thanks a lot. Sally gave it to me as a gift when she joined the firm, as a good reminder not to take myself too seriously. It never leaves my wrist. Every time I look at Mickey's hands I think of Sally and I smile. Also, I often see smiles on the faces of jurors when I try a jury trial and they notice it."

"Who doesn't like Mickey?"

"Right. Anyway, Dumbrowski and Mr. Foster sat at the defendant's table. Dumbrowski made a big show of setting out his files and documents in front of him and his client, pouring himself a cup of water, and shooting back his sleeves in a gesture of total confidence. Foster stared at his wife in a menacing way, with clenched fists."

"It's easy to be a tough guy when your victim can't fight back."

"True. A real coward. We all rose when Judge Granger, the assigned judge, shuffled slowly into the courtroom, as if his black robe was a heavy weight on his back. He walked with great difficulty and struggled to step up to the bench. At sixty-five, he looked much older. He was bald, heavyset, and very bent over. He sat hunched over the bench, a scowl on his face. He kept his head down, often with his eyes closed, and rarely showed the attorneys or the litigants the respect of looking at them when he addressed them. His demeanor made it clear, sitting on the bench was now a burden, not a privilege."

"I guess judges burn out, too."

"Too often, especially in the matrimonial part. Anyway, the need for a protective order and the removal of Mr. Foster from the marital home was overwhelming. Temporary support and counsel fees were routinely granted in order to maintain the status quo in cases like Foster's. Mary sat rigidly between Sally and me, afraid to even glance at her husband. I had assured her our application would be granted and she had nothing to worry about but she was still very nervous. The judge, without looking up, said, 'Mr. Cormac, I've read your papers. Quite frankly, I am shocked and very concerned about what you have alleged.'"

"That sounds pretty promising. What happened?"

"Like you, I thought the judge was acknowledging the seriousness of Mr. Foster's misconduct. I felt confident he would afford my client and her daughter the protection they desperately needed. I said, 'Thank you, Judge. I am sure you appreciate the exigent circumstances and the urgent need for temporary relief in this case.' Without hearing any further argument, or addressing the overwhelming evidence of abuse, the judge, without looking up, said in a stern voice, 'I am denying your application, with prejudice.'"

"What?"

"I was blindsided. Like a punch I didn't see coming. Even worse, he raised his head for the first time to stare at me and with a half-smile on his face, he said, 'I know the defendant's attorney, Mr. Dumbrowski, very well. He is an excellent and experienced matrimonial attorney. Mr. Dumbrowski has appeared before me on many occasions, but I don't believe you have appeared before me prior to today. I don't know if you practice matrimonial law, but it is evident you are not aware of my court rules and how I conduct my matrimonial cases.'"

"Nice to know he had such high regard for your adversary."

"Yup. In just one sentence, he praised Dumbrowski, denigrated my experience and legal ability, and attempted to undermine my client's confidence in me. Of course, I had handled many divorce cases and was fully familiar with the applicable state and local court rules. The judge was letting me, and my client, know he was bent and the playing field was not level."

"Hmmm. It sure sounds like the fight was fixed. A least when I fought, I knew who the enemy was. They never wore black robes."

"Wait, it only gets better. After the judge beat me up, Dumbrowski jumped right in. 'Judge, I will be happy to provide Mr. Cormac with copies of your court rules if he is unfamiliar with them.' The judge, with a smirk, said, 'Mr. Dumbrowski, thank you for your courtesy. I think that would be very helpful.'"

"It must have been real comforting to know that your adversary wanted to be so helpful."

"Not the help I needed. Addressing me and my client, the judge continued in the same threatening voice. 'Since you appear unfamiliar with my rules, let me tell you how things work in this courtroom. My overriding concern is for the well-being of the children in a divorce. They are the only innocent parties, and I will always consider their best interests first. It is clear to me these are both loving and concerned parents. I will not tolerate one party making false and defamatory statements about the other spouse as a strategy to gain some advantage in this divorce.'"

"Now I'm beginning to understand why Sally was so upset," Damian said.

"The judge was just getting started. He wanted to make it clear that the playing field wasn't level. 'I applaud Mr. Dumbrowski and his client for not responding in kind by attacking your client. However, I must admonish you and your client, if you continue to proceed in this fashion in making salacious allegations against Mr. Foster in an attempt to undermine his relationship with his child, I will strongly consider awarding Mr. Foster sole custody of his daughter and imposing sanctions against you and your client. Also, if you were at all familiar with my rules, you would be aware it is premature to even consider making an award of temporary support or counsel fees at this time, without full financial disclosure. I will excuse your conduct this one time. I hold you, not your client, responsible. But should you continue to violate my rules, I will not hesitate to take swift and appropriate action.'"

"What did you say?"

"Nothing initially. I looked over at Mary Foster, who was completely distraught and shaking uncontrollably. Justifiably, she felt betrayed by both the judge and me. Sally was outraged and looked at me in disbelief. I deliberately put my head down and took a deep breath before I finally addressed the judge. 'Judge, may I be heard?' The judge held up his hand. 'You can answer my question, nothing more. Have I made myself clear, Mr. Cormac?' I looked up slowly. I waited until I had the judge's full attention. I stared into his eyes and said, 'Everything is crystal clear to me now, Your Honor.'"

"I'm really curious; how could you protect your client? The husband's attorney was unethical and had a corrupt judge in his pocket. Sounds like you were standing in a deep hole."

"Dumbrowski, and the judge, made a mistake in judgment. They underestimated me. When the judge left the bench, I put together my file. As I got ready to leave the courtroom with Sally and Mrs. Foster, I felt a strong grip on my arm. It was Dumbrowski, holding me back. He said, 'We should talk.'"

Damian put his sandwich down and smiled. "This should be good. What did you do?"

"Nothing. I turned my back on him, and started to follow Sally and Mrs. Foster toward the courtroom exit. Dumbrowski came up behind me and grabbed my arm again, saying, 'I can help you.' I stopped and told Sally, 'Please take Mrs. Foster outside and wait for me in the hall.' I turned to face Dumbrowski in the empty courtroom. 'Counselor, that's twice you have put your hands on me. I would suggest you don't do it again.'"

"Did he back off?"

"Nope. He said, 'Sorry, I didn't know you were so sensitive. You know, we are on the same team. It's us against them. We need to protect each other. You got beat up today in front of your client, but the judge actually did you a favor. Your client is terrified and you can cut a quick deal and exit this mess. Your client obviously has no ability to pay you and my client will make a generous contribution to your fees as part of the settlement. It's a win-win. For you and me. C'mon, these people deserve each other. If it was really so bad, she would have left him a long time ago. She probably gets off on the rough stuff. It's like foreplay.'"

"A real bottom feeder."

"The very bottom. I moved in close and said, 'You know, I trained as a boxer when I was a kid in Yonkers. I was pretty good, but more importantly, I had a great coach. He felt there was nothing wrong with the sport if both boxers wanted to be in the ring, were in the same weight class and there was a neutral referee. What he called a fair fight. This case is not a fair fight. It would be like you going into the ring with me. You would be badly hurt.'"

Damian smiled again. "The gloves came off."

"Dumbrowski jumped back. His slick composure was gone. He stuttered, 'Are… are you threatening me?' I said, 'No. Not at all. I'm simply returning your favor. You offered to help me and I want to help you by explaining the rules I live by, in or out of court. Tell your client if he touches Mrs. Foster again, my only mission in life will be to visit him in the Tombs. Good day, Counselor.'"

"Nice. I like the Clint Eastwood touch. Very persuasive. You know, I could show you how to use three fingers and strike a quick blow to the throat. Mr. Dumbrowski wouldn't be speaking, much less gaslighting the court, for at least a few years."

"Thanks. I missed that course in law school. Believe me, I'm not easily provoked, but the judge and this guy tested the limits of my patience. Heard enough?"

"No way. I bought a ticket and I want to hear how the forces of evil were defeated by truth, justice, and the American way."

"Okay, but this fairy tale ended a little differently. When I left the courtroom, I found Sally sitting with Mrs. Foster on a bench in the empty hall. Sally had her arm around our client, who obviously had been crying. Mary looked up at me, shook her head and whispered, 'I can't do this. You told me not to worry. I'm too scared. I'm not strong enough. You don't know my husband. He will hurt me. Badly. He will take everything from me. I couldn't live without my daughter.' I replied, 'Let's just sit here for a minute. Mary, I will do anything you ask me to do, but first I would like to talk about what happened in there. Will you give me five minutes before we make a decision?' She didn't answer right away. We sat on the hard wooden bench in silence for a few minutes. Sally was furious but said nothing."

Damian said, "Got it. I'm beginning to understand why she was so upset."

"When Mary finally looked up, I said, 'I understand why you are frightened. I apologize. There is no excuse for what happened in there. Believe me, I'm very upset and embarrassed. Not because of what the judge said about me, but because he has no integrity and dishonors our profession. But I need you to trust me so I can represent you to the best of my ability. We can always discontinue your divorce action at any time. Before you make any decisions that will affect you and your daughter for the rest of your lives, allow me to file an immediate appeal to reverse the judge's decision. If the appeal is denied, I will do anything you want me to do. Is there a safe place you can go to with your daughter for a few days?'"

"Did she take your advice?"

"She did. She said, 'I could go to my sister's house. But you must give me your word I will not lose my daughter. Promise me.' I assured her, 'I will do everything in my power to protect you and your daughter.' She said, 'I trust you. File the appeal.'"

"I hope the appeal was granted."

"Yup. The judges sitting in the Appellate Division are appointed on merit, not elected, and are the great equalizer for parties who are victims of a miscarriage of justice. Mrs. Foster was granted temporary custody of her daughter and Mr. Foster was ordered to vacate the marital residence. An order of protection was entered directing Mr. Foster to stay away from his wife and daughter, pending a hearing. In addition, Mrs. Foster was awarded temporary alimony and child support and Mr. Foster was directed to pay me a retainer in an amount equal to what he had paid Dumbrowski."

"Ah, justice prevailed."

"For a while. The case played out over the next year and was no less acrimonious. Mr. Foster still stalked his wife, sitting outside her house in his car or tailgating Mary when she drove to the store. He sent letters addressed to Mary with no return address, containing articles about children kidnapped during divorces, or wives murdered by their husbands. He didn't pay support most months and always brought his daughter home late on his visitation days, causing Mary great distress."

"Some people just never learn."

"Only the hard way. Well, Dumbrowski played his usual games during discovery and succeeded in delaying the case with the help of the good judge."

"So how did you get to the finish line?"

"The case finally ended, as most contested matrimonial cases do, when the parties ran out of money. Mr. Foster simply stopped paying Dumbrowski's fees. Dumbrowski immediately withdrew from the case and sued Foster for his outstanding bill. Foster retained a new lawyer, who had no hook with Judge Granger, and who quickly realized there was no upside for him or his client in continuing with protracted litigation, which his client couldn't afford."

"Got it. If there's no war chest, there's no war."

"Exactly. When Dumbrowski withdrew, the judge no longer had a horse in the race and became disinterested in the outcome. We settled shortly thereafter. Mrs. Foster got sole custody of her daughter. Mr. Foster was allowed supervised visitation as long as he participated in an anger management program. Mary Foster received a favorable financial settlement, including possession of the marital home, permanent alimony, and child support for her and her daughter. Mr. Foster was also ordered to pay all of Mrs. Foster's legal fees."

"Hey, congratulations. I say well done. I consider that a real victory. I don't understand why Sally doesn't appreciate justice was served. She's smart enough to know the system isn't perfect. It's only as good as the lawyers and judges who sit in the courtroom. The plaque on her desk says: *It could get ugly.* Mary Foster was lucky to have you guys represent her. As you know, sometimes it gets very ugly and you still lose a case, or even worse, people die."

"I was happy with the result. I don't mind playing hardball. I've been in the ring with fighters who hit below the belt. Unfortunately, as it turns out, it was a short-lived victory. I got a call from Mary Foster less than six months after the divorce judgment was entered. She was calling from her driveway and crying uncontrollably. The tires on her car had just been slashed. It was starting all over again. It seems Mr. Foster fell off the wagon, lost his job and stopped paying support. He blamed Mary for all his problems. He was again threatening to kidnap their daughter and make sure Mary never saw her again. The second act is not uncommon in acrimonious divorces. Mary pleaded with me to help her again."

"I'm sure Sally was not very happy."

"When I told her, she said, 'Chance, no way. I can't do this again. The system's broken. Her husband is an abuser, his attorney had no conscience, and the judge was corrupt. There was no justice. No one was held accountable. They just ran out of money, got tired of playing the game, and walked away. Now it's starting all over again.'"

"She felt the system was broken?"

"Yes. She was frustrated and very angry. She said, 'In divorces, it's all a game and nobody plays by the rules.' I said, 'Listen, Sally, I understand how you feel. We obtained a favorable settlement, notwithstanding Dumbrowski's tactics or the judge's bias. I reminded her of what Professor Connelly, my torts professor often said, 'You get justice in the next world; in this world, you have the law.'"

"Did she accept that?"

"No. She gave me an ultimatum: 'Chance, never again. Not this case, or any divorce case. I want you to give me your word you won't do any more matrimonial work. Not now. Not ever. Promise me.'"

"Got it. And you promised?"

"The truth is, it was an easy promise to make. I no longer had the need or inclination to continue to do divorce work, due to the success of my commercial litigation practice. I referred Mary to another divorce attorney I respected."

"Good story. Lots of drama. I learned in the service, sometimes you have to fight the same battle over and over. So, tell me, are you going to keep your promise?"

I wish I had just said yes. But instead, I said, "I hope so."

CHAPTER FOUR
MARRIED TO THE LAW

They say the law is a jealous mistress. It demands your attention and devotion. Once you fall in love with the law, it will possess you and at times break your heart.

I'm pretty much married to the law. If I wasn't, I would have married Sally a long time ago. We met during the first year of law school. We were in a study group together. Sally is an all-Irish beauty with endless blond curls, just the right amount of freckles, and those green eyes can fill you with joy or dread. She is smart, sassy, and passionate about life and the law. Her beauty shines from within.

It may have been love at first sight for me, but it took a lot longer for Sally to even notice me. She had worked too hard to get into law school to be distracted from her dream of becoming a lawyer by someone like me. I had good grades but hers were better. I tried flirting with her by using my best jokes, but all I ever got was a shake of her head and a comment that we had a lot of work to do.

Finally, after a semester of trying to get her attention, I got a laugh and a date by telling my best Irish joke: "Bono and The Edge walk into a bar in Dublin. The barman exclaims, 'Not U2 again!'"

At dinner we got to know each other. Sally opened up and told me about her childhood and her family. "I'm an only child. My dad died when I was six. I have memories of him playing the piano and singing to me, but not much more. My mom is my hero, role model, and best friend. She worked as a secretary during the day and as a cashier at a local supermarket at night to support me. She sacrificed a lot to make her dream that I would go to college come true. I was lucky enough to attend St. Mary's parochial school, where the good Sisters gave me an excellent education, a love of literature, and a strong moral compass. I still go to Mass every Sunday. Does that surprise you?"

Nothing Sally said surprised me. It was like we had known each other our whole lives. I said, "You are remarkable. We are cut from the same Irish linen. You know we were meant to meet. I was raised in an

Irish Catholic neighborhood in Yonkers. I am the only child of Francis Xavier Cormac and his young bride, Didi Marie."

Sally laughed when I added, "I've always believed a face without freckles is like a sky without stars." When she laughed, her hazel eyes lit up and she glowed. I felt the warmth from across the table. I was enchanted.

She wondered how I got the name Chance. I explained I was named Chance because my mother's blood type was RH negative and my father's was RH positive, so it was a miracle I was born. My mother's doctor told her that it was one chance in a million that I would survive. She couldn't have any more children, but it didn't matter to me because the kids on my block were more brothers and sisters than I could hope for.

I inherited my love of music and literature from my mother. My love of puns and bad jokes comes from my father. My father was famous for his sayings, which he called truisms. He claimed there is more truth in one time-honored proverb or saying than you could find in all the works of Plato. He always seemed to know the right saying to answer any of life's problems. His favorite saying was "facts are stubborn things", a quote he lived by.

He taught me to accept life's challenges head-on. Confront the facts. Change the things you can and accept what you can't. Be honest with people, but more importantly, be honest with yourself."

I shook my head and said, "Sorry, I must be boring you. As you can tell, I don't go on many dates."

Sally said, "Thank you for sharing your life with me. I'm glad you kept telling me your stupid jokes and asked me out."

Outside the restaurant, Sally gave me a warm embrace and a kiss on the cheek. Her eyes sparkled when she said, "You know, if you can think of another good Irish joke, I might consider going out with you again."

That was everything I hoped for. Soon we were inseparable. We studied together, ate together, and made love together. I had never been so happy. I couldn't remember what my life was like before we met.

Unfortunately, it didn't last long enough. Early in the second semester, Sally's mother was diagnosed with ovarian cancer. The prognosis was not good, and the treatment would be expensive. Sally immediately withdrew from law school and went home to help care for her mother. She was suddenly gone.

I missed her gentle smile, warm embrace, and her scent in my bed. We kept in touch, but with the demands of law school and Sally's commitment to her mother, we drifted apart. Sally never returned to law school. After her mother passed away, she eventually became a paralegal at a large law firm.

CHAPTER FIVE
ENGLISH, PHILOSOPHY, AND A RIGHT HOOK

I attended Yonkers High School in Westchester County, a wealthy suburb of New York City. But Yonkers is a far cry from the bucolic tree-lined neighborhoods of Westchester. It has more in common with the hard streets of the Bronx. My high school was very much an inner-city school.

I got both a great academic education in the honors program from my teachers, and some real-life lessons about how to survive in the boys' room when no teachers were around. I was never a team player and didn't try out for any high school sports.

Once, when my father saw me come home from school with a black eye, he only said, "You know the key to self-defense is to believe you are worth defending."

I thought about what he said and started training at a local boxing gym after school to learn discipline and self-defense. I loved the feel and smell of the old gym and soon felt at home in the ring. The sound and rhythm of gloves hitting bags and boxers jumping rope were music to my ears.

I was taught by Patsy "The Irish Shamrock" McCormick, a former professional middleweight, who was known to everyone as Coach. Coach told us he gave himself his boxing nickname because he would rather be lucky than good.

Every day, summer or winter, Coach wore the same sleeveless sweatshirt with a shamrock on the front. He taught me the importance of posture, balance, and anticipating a punch before it was thrown. I learned to take a hard punch and still move forward. I came to appreciate confidence and courage were as important as talent in the ring. All-important skills that benefit me today as a litigator.

I was a middleweight and relied more on speed and strategy than power. I always wore head gear to try to protect what my mother claimed were my boyish Irish good looks. My confidence grew with my boxing skills. I competed in local boxing matches and did well in my weight class.

My favorite combination was a jab, jab, uppercut, then a right cross. If it was thrown correctly, you never saw the right cross coming. When I started competing and won a Golden Gloves competition for my weight class, Coach warned me, "Chance, be a professional, but never a professional boxer. Make a living with your mind, not your fists."

I graduated from Yonkers High School *magna cum laude* and went to college at Fordham University in the Bronx. I double majored in, of all things, English and philosophy. The Jesuits instilled in me a passion for critical thinking and the belief a life must be examined to be worth living. I learned God is in the details and you must be willing to do the heavy lifting to master a subject.

After graduating from college at the top of my class, I decided to attend law school. I thought the law would be the perfect fit for me. I could put to good use the lessons taught to me by the Jesuits about critical thinking and respect for a higher law in order to achieve a just result. Ironically, English, philosophy, and boxing were the perfect preparation for my legal career. Litigators are wordsmiths who have to know how to throw and take punches.

I was lucky enough to have Professor Connelly as my first-year torts professor. He was heavyset, with thick gray hair and had a strong Brooklyn accent. He wore the same faded grey sweater to class every day. He was a prominent personal injury lawyer, who after a successful career with record verdicts in the Bronx and Brooklyn courts, decided to teach at Fordham Law as an adjunct professor for a few years. He paced the lecture hall, as he must have paced in front of countless juries, challenging students to confront his interpretation of a case or statute.

Torts is a favorite course of first-year law students, whether they want to be litigators or not. Torts involve cases based on assault, battery, trespass, and negligence. These cases are real-life dramas, like we watch on TV crime shows. Only the tort verdict spells money, not guilt or innocence.

I was captivated by Professor Connelly's practical approach to the law, his sense of humor, and his war stories about jury trials. He had office hours in the afternoon after class. After I did well on his first exam, I felt confident enough to make an appointment. He invited me to meet him in his small office on the tenth floor, overlooking Lincoln Center Plaza.

I knocked on his door and when I entered his office, I noticed there were no books, no papers, and no computer. He was reading the *New York Law Journal.* He put the paper down and got up to shake my hand. He gestured for me to sit across from him at a small round conference table.

I looked up and saw two plaques hanging on his office wall. One said:

MAN'S LAWS. IF YOU CUT THEM DOWN, DO YOU THINK YOU COULD STAND UPRIGHT IN THE WINDS THAT WOULD BLOW?
~ *St. Thomas Aquinas*

The other said: SEMPER UBI SUB UBI

This made me smile, because I understood it was Latin for "always wear underwear."

The professor said, "Good afternoon, Chance. Thanks for taking the time to meet with me. I noticed you looking at my plaques. Have you studied Aquinas? Do you speak Latin?"

I laughed. "Yes. Great advice. I always try to remember to wear underwear. I was an English and philosophy major in college. The Jesuits made sure we studied Aquinas. I am not very religious anymore, but I can still recite the Baltimore Catechism. I was fascinated by Aquinas and his thoughts on a life well lived."

"You know, Chance, you may be more religious than you think. 'Religious' is Latin for careful – the opposite of 'negligent', which means careless. Aquinas was full of concern for humanity and would have made a great lawyer. He said, 'Nothing can be known save what is true.' Chance, let me ask you, what do you want to achieve as a lawyer?"

"I want to do more good than harm. I would like to make a difference in people's lives. I would like to be a trial lawyer, like you."

"Some noble aspirations. Let me give you the benefit of my forty years of experience as a practicing lawyer. Very few lawyers are equipped to be litigators. Even fewer who call themselves litigators can actually try a case. I believe, although I am sure many lawyers would disagree with me, the trial lawyer is the highest calling in the law, just as a surgeon is the highest calling in medicine."

The professor's tone, for the first time, became very serious. "The trial lawyer must be fearless and committed to his clients. When you are on trial, no matter how many other cases you have tried, you will never feel adequately prepared. You will doubt the merits of your case and your ability to present it. To the extent you sleep at all, you will wake up with a start in the middle of the night, tormented by the questions you asked a witness, or the questions you didn't ask. Many trial lawyers turn to alcohol or drugs to cope with the pressure. Have I dissuaded you?"

"No. Not at all."

"Good. Then let me tell you, when a jury renders a verdict in favor of your client, it is the best feeling in the world. It is the validation of all your hard work and dedication, but more importantly, it is a validation of the legal profession you have dedicated your life to. I never doubted, once, my decision to be a litigator."

I was convinced that this was the career I wanted.

"Now, listen carefully, I'm going to give you the best advice I can. If you want to become a trial attorney, as often as you can, sit in on any jury trials being conducted in the state and federal courts. You are fortunate to have some of the best litigators trying cases in the best courts in the country a subway ride away. Skip classes if you have to. What you will learn in the courtroom is more important than anything you will be taught in a law school class. Good luck to you, Chance."

As suggested by Professor Connelly, I began visiting the majestic marble federal and state courthouses in lower Manhattan, which remind me more of churches than office buildings. I sat silently in the back of the courtrooms where jury trials were being conducted, often the only spectator. It didn't matter what kind of case was being tried, I was fascinated by the skill, expertise, and drama of lawyers in presenting evidence and advocating for their clients.

I saw which lawyers were best prepared and had a mastery of the law and the facts. I learned how jurors responded to how lawyers conducted themselves during a trial and how they addressed the jury. I saw the slight smile, frown, or smirk on a juror's face in reaction to a lawyer's conduct or arguments.

I learned the best trial lawyers were teachers who respected the intelligence of the jury and wanted them to come to the right verdict based on the facts. The juries were judging not only the character of the witnesses but of the attorneys. I loved the adrenaline rush I got, even as a spectator, when a verdict was rendered. Professor Connelly was right, it was the best education I got during law school.

In my second year of law school, Professor Connelly recommended me to Judge Dennis Donovan, a highly respected state court trial judge in the New York County Supreme Court. I clerked for him until I graduated. The judge was a skilled and compassionate jurist. I learned how he saw a case from the bench, what arguments were persuasive, and how to write a well-reasoned and just opinion based on the facts and the law.

I put what I learned watching trials to good use. I won some national moot trial competitions and received an award as the best oral advocate at graduation. When I graduated, Professor Connelly gave me a gift. It was a copy of the *Summa Theologica*, the seminal work of Thomas Aquinas. He inscribed the inside of the cover:

To Chance,
To one who has faith, no explanation is necessary.
To one without faith, no explanation is possible.
Be true to yourself and your beliefs.
I know you will be a superb trial lawyer and a credit to our profession.
Fondly, your friend, Bill Connelly.

That book sits today on the corner of my office desk. Professor Connelly passed away many years ago, yet I often think kindly about him and the generous advice and wisdom he imparted to me as a young law student.

CHAPTER SIX
GOING SOLO

After I graduated from law school, *cum laude* and with strong recommendations from Professor Connelly and Judge Donovan, I was offered what is every law student's dream job: a position as an associate at Cooper Conners, a large prestigious NYC law firm.

These firms used to be called Wall Street firms, but they are no longer located in the narrow canyon of office buildings in downtown Manhattan. Cooper Conners has three floors in a luxury building on Fifth Avenue overlooking Central Park. Their conference rooms are bigger than my parents' home in Yonkers. There is more marble in the waiting area and conference rooms than in St. Joseph's Church, where I went to Mass as a kid.

As a first-year litigation associate, I was paid the firm's going rate, which was much more than my mother and father ever made, combined, in all their years of hard work. I celebrated my good luck at a firm reception for new associates, held on a yacht sailing around Manhattan, where we were served a four-star dinner. After dinner, the yacht sailed slowly up the Hudson River with the lights of the New York skyline shining in the background. Outside, under the stars, we were welcomed to the firm by a senior partner. He congratulated us for being the best and the brightest of our class, who were fortunate enough to join one of the premier law firms in the world. I felt very proud. All my hard work and education paid off; I had grabbed the golden ring.

Of course, it was all a big mistake. I was a poor fit for a large firm. I realized immediately I had made the decision to join Cooper Conners for all the wrong reasons. I never played well with others to begin with. I soon learned that my performance, and value to the firm, were being judged solely by the number of billable hours on my time sheets at the end of each day. The other new associates never spoke about their legal work but only bragged about how they were on track to bill 2400 hours a year, the magic number to become a partner someday.

I worked under a senior associate and was relegated to reviewing documents, doing legal research, and proofreading citations. I had no contact with clients. It was made clear, under no circumstances, as a first-year associate, was I ever to speak to or email a client directly. I made no appearances in the majestic courtrooms where I had spent endless hours observing trials as a law student.

There was no prospect I would try a case for many years, if ever. I also learned, while I respected many lawyers, I didn't really like most of them as people. I simply didn't fit. After a few months, I began dreading the thought of another day at the office, billing time by the tenth of the hour. So I jumped. I thanked the firm for the opportunity of working with them, and with an enormous sense of relief, I resigned.

At my exit interview, I met – for the first and last time – with the managing partner of the firm. He welcomed me into his large corner office with views of the park. He shook my hand, smiled and said, "Please sit down." He sat behind his polished teak desk and asked, "Chance, what's going on? I understand you are a talented lawyer. Why would you give up this golden opportunity after only a few months?"

"I appreciate the opportunity, but I just don't think I'm a good fit for a large firm."

"Son, let me give you some advice. Becoming a lawyer is a process. It is just as important to learn how to work with your colleagues as it is to try a case. It takes patience, discipline, and sacrifice. I think you are making a big mistake you will soon regret. It will not look good on your resumé to resign after such a short time. You should be aware, we have a strict policy of never rehiring associates after they leave. I think you should seriously reconsider your decision."

"Thank you for your concern. But my mind is pretty well made up."

Now the smile was gone and there was an edge in his voice. He interlaced his fingers as if in prayer and said, "Chance, you know we have invested a great deal of time and money in bringing you on as an associate and training you. It doesn't appear you appreciate that investment or our efforts on your behalf. You must realize it will be difficult for the firm to give you a good recommendation."

I paused, took a deep breath, and looked the managing partner in the eyes. "How much did the firm invest? Maybe I can just write you a check."

The managing partner turned red and stood up abruptly. "Okay, wise guy, clean out your desk. Now! Return your phone, laptop, and firm ID. I would suggest you review your employment agreement carefully, don't even think about contacting any clients or suggesting other associates leave with you."

It was the best decision I ever made. I rented a furnished office in downtown Brooklyn on Court Street and hung out my shingle. I was flying solo and couldn't have been happier. I never looked back.

I have now been a solo practitioner for more than twenty-five years. My firm is Chance Cormac and Associates. I am very content to control my own destiny in my own small office with the help of Damian and Sally. We are a good team, and we take good care of each other.

I always feel great pride and satisfaction when I walk downstairs from my apartment to my office each morning to practice a profession I still enjoy and find exciting, despite the often overwhelming challenges of being a trial lawyer. I'm lucky and I know it.

I struggled early in establishing a solo practice. Like the Foster divorce, I took the cases no one else wanted, often on a contingency where my fee was based upon the amount of a recovery. I succeeded because I am a trial attorney who actually tries a lot of cases to verdict and gets very favorable results for my clients.

I learned quickly which cases large firms will not accept because they are either viewed as unworthy of the firm or present potential conflicts with their corporate clients. The large firms will not touch criminal or matrimonial cases (too messy), legal or medical malpractice cases (too unseemly), or any cases where a client is suing a bank, financial institution, or Fortune 500 company (all of which are either existing or potential clients of the large firms).

After winning some big verdicts, my reputation and practice grew. I cultivated relationships with large firms, like the one I couldn't work for. These firms were happy to refer me the work they had no use for, knowing their clients would be well represented. As a result, I have very little overhead, and now have the luxury of picking the cases and clients I want to represent. I must admit, I also take great satisfaction in the fact I now earn more than most of the partners my age at large firms like Cooper

Conners.

After I opened my own office, I immediately thought of Sally. I tell my clients Sally works with me, and not for me, because she is as capable as any practicing attorney. She not only does legal research and drafts legal documents, but she also does my trial prep and manages the firm.

My clients love Sally. Her legal skills, rapport, and attention to detail have earned their trust and confidence. As I like to say, she leads with her heart. She has a strong moral compass I rely on when the line between the law and justice gets blurred. More importantly, Sally is also a trusted and close friend.

Neither Sally nor I have ever been married. We have great affection for each other and have been tempted over the years to renew our love affair, but we have been smart enough not to complicate our lives and careers with a romantic relationship. We can be honest in ways most married couples can't be. Or won't be.

After I opened my office, I had a few relationships with women that never lasted long. Sally's comment after each relationship ended badly was always the same: "Not a good fit."

Seven years ago, Sally's daughter Melody was born. After too many failed relationships, Sally knew the clock was ticking. She was considering in vitro fertilization and asked me for my thoughts.

I told her I thought it would be the greatest gift she could give herself and the world. She was lucky and became pregnant quickly. Melody entered our lives nine months later. The biological father is anonymous and not part of their lives. I was proud to be asked to be Melody's godfather and am lucky to have Melody and Sally in my life. Melody has her mother's smarts, curls, and beautiful green eyes. I know what you are thinking; but Sally never asked and I am not the donor.

Sally, Melody, and I have dinner together every weekend at the office or at Sally's apartment. Sometimes I babysit for Melody at my office in the evening if Sally has an appointment or goes out with a friend. Neither Sally nor I date much anymore. We each have a few good friends whom we occasionally spend an evening with, but we do not have the time or inclination to commit to a serious relationship. We're happy to just sit and be in each other's company with Melody and Tort running around.

Melody is all Sally needs in this world. You cannot find a more devoted and loving mother. We're our own little family. We love each other.

CHAPTER SEVEN
IT COULD GET UGLY

Next to pictures of Melody, Sally has two plaques on her office desk. One says: "My Mind is Made Up, Don't Confuse Me with the Facts." The other says: "It Could Get Ugly."

These plaques are good reminders when litigating a case, it is sometimes difficult to accept that the facts are often not quite what we would expect or want them to be and that litigation is not always pretty.

The week before Roy asked me for the favor of meeting with his new client, we had just finished a grueling three-week jury trial in a commercial fraud case Roy had in fact referred to me. I didn't consider Roy a close friend but I valued our relationship. He had been very good to me in referring clients and I was happy to do him a favor if I could.

In fact, when Roy reached out to me I was enjoying the afterglow of a successful trial where I represented a corporate client referred to me by Roy's firm. Our client had been awarded a very significant verdict, which made them very happy and made me even happier because I had a blended fee arrangement where the firm got a percentage of the recovery.

This latest trial verdict was a particularly satisfying victory; my small legal team was pitted against three major law firms representing four different corporate defendants, including my old firm, Cooper Conners. They didn't have enough chairs at the counsel tables for the defendants' lawyers, paralegals, and IT teams. They were spread out across the courtroom.

The writing was on the wall for the defendants by the time the jury started deliberating. The judge was amused when the jury forewoman sent out a note requesting some flowers for the jury room table so their deliberations would be more pleasant. I laughed. It was the perfect reminder that jurors are just human beings performing a civic duty. The jurors felt they deserved to be treated with some respect and courtesy.

The judge said, "I want each of you attorneys to reach into your thick wallets and give the clerk five dollars as your contribution toward a nice bouquet for these fine jurors. Bill it to your client as a disbursement if you want. It's the best investment you can make in this case."

As the jury continued their deliberations, the partners who were the lead trial attorneys for each defendant packed their bags and left before the verdict was rendered. They wanted to avoid the public embarrassment of losing the case and, even worse, losing it to a solo practitioner. With the partners gone, the senior associates were left to do the mop-up. My fee from this recovery alone covered my nut and overhead expenses for the year.

The defendants recognized an appeal would be futile, and the judgment was paid in full shortly after it was entered. When our contingency fee was received, I was happy to give large bonuses to Damian and Sally. I recognize they are just as deserving as I am to share in the fruits of our hard work and success.

We all celebrated a job well done at our favorite Italian restaurant, Ida Rose, which is two blocks from the office. It is everything you want in an Italian restaurant. It has a brick front, with a red neon *Ida Rose* sign over the entrance, red tablecloths, large blocks of aged Parmesan and Romano cheese in the window, and a great red house wine. You feel like you are having a family meal with a large Italian family when you sit down to eat.

Melody was staying at a friend's house, and we walked over from the office on a beautiful fall evening, reliving the high points of the trial on the way. Ida Rose greeted us with hugs and already had a bottle of the house red and three glasses on a back table she had reserved for us.

Before dinner, we each made a toast. I said, "Here's to truth, justice, and big verdicts."

Sally toasted, "Here's to the good guys and gals, who are all at this table."

Damian raised his glass and made the toast he'd always made in the SEALs after successfully completing a mission: "*Chin Don!*"

We didn't need menus. Ida Rose brought out every house specialty appetizer and signature dish, one after the other. With each dish she said, "*Mangia! Mangia!*" I rarely drink, but we polished off two bottles of the house red. When we couldn't eat or drink any more, I left cash for twice the amount of the check, we each gave Ida Rose a hug goodbye and we walked back to the office.

It was a crisp night and there was little traffic. The streetlights cast long shadows on the sidewalk. We walked in silence, breathing in the cool night air, savoring our victory and our celebration dinner. When we got back to the office, I said goodbye to Sally and Damian. Sally gave me a warm embrace and a long kiss on the cheek before catching a cab. Damian raised his eyebrows and smiled before he got on his motorcycle and shot up the street.

Some people just fit perfectly when they hug, hold hands or walk down the street together. They are like two pieces of a puzzle completing a larger picture. They are made for each other. That was the best part of a perfect evening. Everything felt just right.

That night as I lay in bed, I thought about Sally's warm embrace, the feel of her touch, and the smell of her hair. I thought about her intellect and beauty and the good thing we'd had together in law school. I thought about my love for Melody and my desire to have a real family.

More and more, I regretted losing what we had so long ago. I knew I would be a fool to miss another opportunity for happiness. But something was holding me back. Maybe I was afraid I would end up losing the special thing I already had with Sally and Melody. Maybe this was one case where I was afraid of what the verdict might be.

CHAPTER EIGHT
ALL IN

The same five players, with limited exceptions, play in our poker game every Friday. In addition to myself, the regular players are Roy Brown, Dennis Donovan, the judge who I clerked for during law school and who is now the administrative judge in Manhattan, Spencer Bradbury, my accountant, and Gus Guerrera, a client and the owner of a successful carting and recycling company.

Before our weekly poker game, Roy asked to sit down with me about a new client. He suggested that we sit down after the game to discuss the case. The recent verdict was on my mind and I was excited about the prospect of another big case. I told Roy that I would be happy to meet after the game but joked he shouldn't expect me to let him win any big pots just because he referred cases to me.

I'm the host, so whether the other players like it or not, I always get to select the songs for the music playlist. It is a friendly game with three and five dollar small and big blinds as antes. Everybody wants to win, but nobody plays too seriously and with small blinds, nobody gets hurt. There is a lot of joking, banter, and off-color jokes. Tort gets everybody's attention. He sits with the group, gets petted between hands, and is fed lots of food under the table.

About a year ago, we started using a friend of Damian's, John Reynolds, a former SEAL in Damian's unit, to deal the cards, work the bank and distribute the chips. John, known simply as JR, was from Tyler, Texas. He was lanky, with dark hair and a beard. He was quiet, very likable and had a slow Texas drawl.

Before JR became our dealer, we were taking turns dealing ourselves. It was incredible how five accomplished professionals could screw up the antes, misdeal the cards and slow our poker game to a crawl. JR also worked part-time for me as a clerk, making copies, filing documents, and serving processes.

We were happy to have JR deal and he was happy to make some cash and meet some interesting people. JR quickly became a skilled dealer and with his down home humor, he became a welcome part of our game.

Poker, especially the game we play, called no-limit Texas Hold'em, is a lot like litigation. You have to read the cards, the players, and the odds. The game is won or lost based on discipline, patience, and experience. Some say it has a lot to do with luck, but luck in poker comes from not only being dealt the best hand but knowing how to play it. What may seem like luck is often good intuition.

In poker, like the practice of law, it is what you see out of the corner of your eye that is as important as what is right in front of you. The ability to read people, assess risk and evaluate the hand you are dealt is a poker player's, and lawyer's, greatest skill. There are tells in both poker and litigation. A person's posture, gesture, or remark can signal when a player or lawyer is overplaying his hand or bluffing. The good poker player, or lawyer, learns from experience how to tell how strong an opponent's hand or case is.

When the players arrived, I lit a fire in the conference room fireplace. Everyone got themselves some snacks and drinks from the kitchen and sat down at the table. JR collected $300 from each player, which was the buy-in. As JR handed out a stacks of chips to each player, the judge said, "JR, make sure you deal the cards off the top of the deck tonight."

JR drawled, "Judge, ya know, with all the excitement, sometimes I forget which way is up. I find big tips help my memory."

The Judge laughed. "JR, you have the makings of a good lawyer."

Roy said, "JR, maybe we should have you give us a urine sample before each game to make sure you aren't using any substances that might affect your shuffling ability."

It wasn't a particularly funny joke. JR didn't say anything but I noticed how he stiffened and looked disturbed. I knew JR had some problems after he was discharged from the SEALs, but didn't know the history. I made a mental note to speak to Damian and find out more about JR's past. I liked JR and didn't want Roy making any more clumsy jokes at his expense, so I quickly changed the subject. "Gentlemen, you have a rare treat in store for you tonight. My playlist is even more special than usual."

After a lot of groans, Spencer, my accountant, said, "Please, anything but *Dire Straits*."

"Thank you, Spencer, for suggesting *Dire Straits*. They are always a good choice. But tonight, the theme is lawbreakers. The attorneys and the judge are familiar with this topic because they know how people break the law. Spencer knows about it because he helps his clients break the tax laws. And people in the carting business know about it, well, because they are in the carting business. If you look up criminal in the dictionary, you will find Gus's picture next to the definition."

Gus said, "Lucky for you, with the fees you charge me, which is a crime in itself."

"For your listening pleasure, the playlist tonight includes, among others, *I Shot the Sheriff*, both the Marley and Clapton versions, *Sympathy for the Devil* by the Stones, *I Fought the Law and the Law Won* by Mellencamp, *Take the Money and Run* by Steve Miller and, of course, *Lawyers, Guns and Money* by Warren Zevon."

The way each player in our game plays his hand reflects his personality. The judge and Roy Brown are very conservative and if they bet, you know they are holding a high pair or better.

Spencer is very analytical and plays the odds. He keeps track of the cards played and knows the percentages of each player having a hand better than his.

Gus is a wild card. He chases straights and flushes and bluffs with abandon. He taunts other players by showing his hole cards after he takes a pot on a bluff.

I slow play. I never raise when I think I have the best hand until the river. I like to have other players raise and think when I call their bets I am chasing a hand. It keeps the other players off balance as to the true strength of my hand. In poker and court, I like my winning hand to be a surprise.

As JR was shuffling the cards, I said, "Okay, everyone put a chip in the center. The contest tonight is the best lawyer joke. JR is the judge, and the winner takes all."

Each player threw a chip in the pot. Everyone knows a good lawyer joke because we are such easy targets.

Spencer went first. "A Mafia Don, accompanied by his attorney, meets with the Godfather's former accountant. The Godfather asks his accountant, 'Where is the three million dollars you embezzled from me, you thief?' The accountant doesn't answer. The Godfather asks again, 'Where is the three million you embezzled!' The lawyer interrupts and says, 'Don, this man is deaf. Fortunately, I know sign language and can interpret for you.' The Godfather says, 'Well, ask him where my goddam money is!" The accountant uses sign language and asks the accountant where the money is."

I interrupted him. "Spencer, you know there is a time limit. Especially on bad jokes."

"You're just trying to kill the timing of my punch line. Now where was I? Oh yes, the accountant signed back, I don't know what you are talking about. The attorney interpreted the sign language for the Godfather and said, 'He doesn't know what you are talking about.' The Godfather pulls out a nine-millimeter pistol, puts it to the temple of the accountant, and says, 'Tell him this is the last chance to tell me where my money is.' The attorney signs to the accountant, 'You better tell him where the money is.' The accountant signs back: OK! OK! OK! The money is hidden in a brown suitcase behind the shed in my backyard! The Godfather asks, 'Well... what did he say?' The attorney interprets for the Godfather. 'He said fuck you. You don't have the guts to pull the trigger.'"

There is a polite round of applause and I said, "Nice how you defamed both accountants and attorneys in one joke. Also, as a bonus, you included one of Gus's relatives as the client."

Of course, in truth, Gus's carting and recycling companies are pristine, environmentally sound, and fully comply with all state and federal regulations, but this doesn't stop me from mailing my invoices to him in care of Tony Soprano.

Gus told the next joke: "A lawyer buys a farm as a weekend retreat. While walking around his new property he looks down and sees his feet stuck in the middle of a huge cowpie. The lawyer starts yelling, 'Oh my God! Help me! Somebody help me!' His wife comes running out and asks him, 'What's the matter?' The lawyer points at his feet and screams, 'I'm melting! I'm melting!'"

JR was beside himself laughing, and it looked like Gus's joke was a strong contender to win the chips.

The next joke was told by Roy, and was clearly aimed at his friend the judge. "Taking a seat in chambers, a judge faced the opposing lawyers on trial before him. 'So,' he says, 'I have been presented with a bribe from each of you.' Both lawyers squirm uncomfortably. 'You, Attorney Cheatem, gave me $15,000. And you, Attorney Slyly, gave me $10,000.' The judge reaches into his pocket and pulls out a check. He gives it to attorney Cheatem. "Now, I'm returning $5,000 to Attorney Cheatem and we're going to decide this case solely on the merits.'"

Most of us saw the punch line coming but laughed politely anyway. The judge, stacking his chips, said, "I wouldn't trust a judge who showed the poor judgment of refunding one penny to either side."

It was my turn. "A lawyer, a priest, and a social worker are on a ship that hits an iceberg. The social worker says, 'Woman and children first.' The lawyer says, 'Screw the children!' The priest says, 'Do we have time?'"

I got mostly groans and Gus said, "Hey, you can joke about lawyers but the Church is off-limits!"

The judge went last. "What does a lawyer get when you give him Viagra? ...Taller."

Everyone broke up. JR loved the joke and immediately declared the judge had the winning joke. It was short and hit the mark, just like his legal opinions. No one objected. JR gave the chips in the middle to the judge and started dealing the cards as Bob Marley sang about shooting the sheriff but not the deputy.

The game broke up at about eleven. JR cashed in the chips and helped me clean up. I paid him for dealing and he received a nice tip from Roy, who was the big winner. After everyone left, Roy stayed behind to discuss the new case he wanted to refer to me.

We took two cups of coffee and went up to the roof top terrace of my brownstone to talk. It was cool and clear out. The dark starless sky gave us a distant view of the lights of the Brooklyn Bridge and the city skyline. We sat in two Adirondack chairs I kept on the roof. Roy took out two expensive Havana cigars and gave me one.

I rarely smoke. It had been prohibited by my boxing coach and I never developed the habit but, as a courtesy, I accepted the gift. Roy cut off the tips with a flourish and lit up the cigars with an expensive silver butane lighter that had his initials on it and worked like a small blow torch. We sat quietly, smoked our cigars, and admired the skyline that looked like a movie backdrop.

After a few minutes, Roy turned to me. "I brought these to celebrate your big verdict! A remarkable victory for you and our client. I'm glad I was able to refer that case to you."

I ignored the backhanded compliment, which was meant to remind me of my debt for the referral. That was just who Roy was. I said, "Roy, we were very pleased with the outcome. You know how much I appreciate all your referrals."

"Happy to help. You always make me look good, Chance. Now I need to ask you to do me a great personal favor. I have a close friend, Randolph Gault, whose daughter, Courtney Malone, is getting divorced. I am very fond of Courtney, as well as her husband, Jackson, and their twin girls. Randy and I are both members of the Westchester Country Club and we play each week in a regular golf game."

I didn't mind Roy's comment about making him look good. If my work for his clients made him happy and he continued to refer new cases to me, he could take all the credit, for all I cared. I was puzzled though by his reference to a divorce case. He knew I was not a matrimonial attorney.

"By the way, Chance, if you like to golf, I would love to have you up to the club as my guest. It's a beautiful course and the clubhouse is like a hotel. We could have lunch in the Men's Club overlooking the eighteenth green. It has a spectacular view of the course and a great buffet. You could see how the other half lives."

"Thanks, Roy. That's very kind of you, but I don't play golf and I think the members would only confuse me with one of the waiters."

"Not true. I think we let our first Irishman in as a member last year. Of course, he can only play after dark."

I laughed and Roy took a long drag on his cigar and blew the smoke up into the night air, obviously pleased by his own joke. "Anyway, after a recent round of golf, Randolph asked me to have lunch with him at the Men's Club. He told me he was upset about Courtney's divorce and was very worried about her and his grandchildren. Courtney and Jackson have adorable seven-year-old twin girls. My wife and I have known the girls since they were born. We see them at family parties at Randolph and Adelaide's house in Scarsdale. The girls call me Uncle Roy."

I said nothing and puffed on the cigar. I was wondering where Roy was going with all this.

"I don't represent Randolph; his wife inherited great wealth and he uses her family's old-line attorneys. He was, however, kind enough to refer Courtney's husband, Jackson, to me when Jackson started his own tax consulting business. Jackson is a very successful CPA and tax consultant and over the years he, and his consulting firm, have become very good clients. Although we don't normally do matrimonial work, Jackson trusts me and asked if our firm would represent him in his divorce."

I thought it was odd that Roy's firm would represent a client in a divorce. Large firms like his have strict policies to stay away from matrimonial cases. Way too messy. If you lose the case you often lose the client.

"Jackson told me separating was a very difficult decision for him to make. He doesn't want to hurt Courtney or the girls. He wants the divorce settled quickly and wants to make sure Courtney and the children are well provided for. I tried to persuade him to reconsider for the sake of the twins but, when he said his mind was made up, I finally agreed and my firm was retained by Jackson."

"Roy, it's kind of you to help your friend, but it's not clear to me how I can help you."

"Randolph is happy we are representing Jackson because he knows he can trust me to make sure Jackson does the right thing for his daughter and the twins. It's important to him and Adelaide that the divorce be settled as soon as possible in a non-adversarial fashion. He wants to spare Courtney and the twins any unnecessary pain or hardship. With that in mind, he asked me to recommend an attorney to represent Courtney, someone I have a personal relationship with and we can trust. He wants someone who will cooperate with our firm and quickly negotiate a fair settlement agreement."

"So you recommended me? Why?"

"I told him you're a good friend and the most capable and trustworthy attorney I know. I know you used to do matrimonial work. This will be a plain vanilla divorce. My partner, Clay Campbell, will handle it. Of course, I will stay involved and oversee the case every step of the way, to make sure there are no problems. You can always reach out to me if there is an issue. Even better, Jackson will pay all your fees. You can charge any amount you like. It's a blank check."

I took a puff on the expensive Havana cigar before responding. It was starting to leave a bitter taste in my mouth. This was not the favor I expected. There was no way I intended to break my word to Sally and take another divorce case. Also, my experience was, notwithstanding Roy's hard sell and the best intentions of the parties, things were seldom as simple as they seemed in a divorce case.

I thought about how best to refuse Roy's request and decline the case without offending him.

"Roy, I'm flattered you would recommend me to your friend. You have been very good to me and my firm and I am happy to do you a favor. I would like to help you, but I would have some concerns about representing Courtney. First and foremost, I am not a divorce lawyer anymore and have not handled a matrimonial case in more than a decade. I am sure there are many more qualified matrimonial attorneys, who practice with a conscience, you could refer Courtney to."

Roy stopped puffing on his cigar, sat forward and stiffened.

"Also, I am concerned there might be the appearance of impropriety and a possible conflict of interest for both me and your firm in representing these clients. Our relationship, and your past referrals to my firm, might make it appear you are steering a client to me in order to benefit your client, which would be improper."

Roy shook his head. "Chance, honestly I'm pretty disappointed. I have never asked you to do me a personal favor before. This is very important to me. I assure you, there is no conflict for you, me, or my firm. I would never ask you to do anything improper. In fact, we want you to represent Courtney so you can assure them any settlement is more than fair and equitable to her. If anything, my referral to you and my involvement in the case will help Courtney, not prejudice her."

Roy realized the soft sell wasn't working.

"Chance, I can guarantee you Jackson will be more than generous. It would be a great favor to me, but more importantly to Courtney and the twins, if you would represent her." He paused, blew out some smoke, and gave me a hard look. "It would embarrass me now if you didn't at least meet with Courtney. I think you owe me that courtesy, after all I've done for you and your firm."

There it was. The carrot and the stick. I wondered how if someone *owes* someone a favor, is it really a favor at all? Also, I didn't understand why it was so important to Roy I represent his friend's daughter. After thinking about it, I convinced myself there was no harm in at least meeting with Courtney as a favor to Roy. It didn't mean I had to take the case.

Against my better judgment, I made a business decision in order to preserve my economic relationship with Roy's firm. A business decision is made simply by weighing the economic risk against the reward. It may be a good way to conduct a business, but I have found it is a bad way to practice law. I still consider the law a profession, not simply a commercial enterprise.

I put out my cigar. "Roy, of course, I value our friendship and if it is that important to you, I will be happy to do you the favor and meet with Courtney. I can't promise we will represent her, but we can make that decision after we meet. Have her contact the office and arrange to come in next week."

Roy stood up and his expression changed immediately. "Chance, great! Perfect! I really appreciate this. I knew I could count on you. I won't forget this favor. I am confident, after you meet Courtney, she will retain you. I look forward to working together to help these good people."

We went downstairs. Roy shook my hand with both of his, thanked me again, and said good night.

I put Tort on his leash and we went for a long walk. The night had gotten chilly, and the cold air helped clear my lungs from the stale cigar smoke and clear my head from the conversation with Roy. I said to Tort, "Tort, never get married and never agree to do any personal favors you know you will regret."

He wagged his tail and barked. He obviously agreed.

I was thinking about Roy Brown as I walked Tort down the deserted street to the park. Roy lives a very good life. He has a large co-op on Park Avenue in the City. He also owns a house in Scarsdale, another Westchester town but a world away from Yonkers, where I grew up. He travels around the world first class, drives a new S Class Mercedes, and belongs to a premiere golf club with an initiation fee more than most people's salary for a year. His children go to the Riverdale School, a highly competitive private school in Manhattan, and his wife sits on many charitable boards.

Roy has a large corner office on the 45th floor of his building, located in Times Square. He is a partner in a 250-man corporate law firm and is known as a rainmaker. Rainmaking is not my idea of practicing law, even if most attorneys would sell their souls to have his job. Rainmakers originate clients, which is legalese for deep sea fishing and hooking "whales" the firm can feed on for years. Rainmakers are envied by every partner who has to actually bill time for a living.

To the extent Roy practices law, it is limited to overseeing the corporate work performed for his clients by other lawyers at the firm and making sure his clients are happy. His calling is to secure relationships, not verdicts. Roy's clients are mostly large corporations or high-net-worth individuals. He never has to be confrontational, get his hands dirty, or do much law work, for that matter. He leaves that to the partners and associates in the trenches.

He is obviously highly compensated, but my instinct is that despite his income Roy must have some independent wealth to support his increasingly extravagant lifestyle. Even by large firm standards, his homes, club memberships, private school tuitions, and lavish vacations seem excessive. Roy sits on many bar association boards, including the NYC Corrections Commission, the Parole Board, and the Disciplinary Committee for our judicial district.

At first, Roy had his firm refer only some small litigation matters to me, but, over the years, after achieving some very favorable verdicts for his clients, Roy started referring larger cases to me on a regular basis. He never requested a referral fee or any other consideration, other than his clients be well represented. In turn, I refer clients to Roy's firm, at least those who can pay the freight, for advice on corporate matters, trust and estate planning, and mergers and acquisitions.

Some years ago we needed another poker player, and the judge suggested we invite Roy. I couldn't picture Roy as a poker player, but I was happy to accommodate the judge and invited him. I'm not sure Roy loves playing poker. Although he still wears a tie and jacket to our games, he seems to be able to drop his big firm pretensions when we play and join in the fun. I think he does enjoy getting away once a week to socialize with people other than clients or family.

Roy and I are very different people, still, he is now a welcome part of our group and a regular in our game. We have very different practices and live very different lives, but we are both lawyers who have succeeded in our own ways in our profession. I respect him for that.

CHAPTER NINE
TOMORROW IS HARDER THAN TODAY

A few days after the poker game, I was having lunch with Damian, and I told him about Roy's joke about having JR take a urine test and his reaction.

"I know JR's a good friend of yours and you served together. I also know you helped him after his discharge. Other than that, I don't know much about his background or how he ended up here in Brooklyn. I'm interested, if you want to share his story."

"You're right, I consider JR a friend, but more than that, he is a comrade-in-arms. That makes our bond even deeper. Maybe there are some things I should have told you about JR before he started clerking for us and dealing in your game. I wasn't hiding anything, but I felt uncomfortable talking about certain things in his past without his knowledge. I don't think he will really mind, and I appreciate that as his employer you are entitled to know what road brought JR here. Just let me ask him if it's okay first. It was a rough road and it's his story to tell."

I respected Damian's discretion and didn't think any more about it. But a couple of nights later I was working on a file I had spread out on the conference room table when I heard the office door open. It was Damian. JR was with him. I said, "Look what the cat dragged in."

Damian laughed. "We're SEALs, not cats. Cats can't swim. If you have a few minutes, JR would like to tell you how a Texas boy ended up in Brooklyn."

I said I would like to hear the story but JR shouldn't feel any obligation to tell me about his past.

JR said, "I'd just ask that this just be between us. My daddy taught me that lettin' the cat out of the bag is a lot easier 'n putting him back in."

I laughed. "Very true. But enough talk about cats. Be assured I won't repeat anything you tell me without your permission."

"Thanks. If you're busy we can always talk another time. It's a sorta long story. Damian's heard it all before. He can help me if I lose my way."

"Now is a perfect time. I've been looking for an excuse to close this file away. Why don't we get comfortable. It's a nice night. We can talk up on the roof."

We took some snacks and bottles of water and went up to my roof terrace, where it was private and peaceful. We got comfortable and sat back in the Adirondack chairs.

There was little traffic on the street and JR looked up at the dark evening sky. "Ya know, this is the first time I looked at the stars since I come up North. Some folks say the sky in Texas is too big. For me any other sky is just too small. I guess Damian's right, I'm still a country boy. I'm from Tyler. It's a Christian town with a large Walmart in the center and still has blue laws prohibiting the sale of alcohol. My parents were simple folk. They taught me the important things in this life are family, friends and country. We had a flagpole in the front yard and we proudly flew the American flag. I liked the sound of the flag flappin' in the Texas wind."

"JR was the youngest of five kids," Damian added. "Don't let that Texas drawl fool you, he's as smart as a whip."

"I'm not so sure 'bout that, Damian, but I do know I wish I'd paid more attention in school. One teacher told me, 'Son, you give me a headache because I shake my head so much every time you come to my class.' I enjoyed goin' to church more than school. My family went to the Baptist Church, all our kin did. I wasn't sure I much believed in God, but I liked bein' in the warmth of the church with my family and our neighbors on them cold, windy Texas days. My full God-given name is John Reynolds."

"He's a junior," Damian explained. "He was named after his father and was always called JR, which conveniently stands for both his initials and John junior."

I said, "JR, do you know, some of the largest verdicts of record against Fortune 500 companies come out of two little towns in Texas? One of them is your home town Tyler. The juries are fiercely independent and believe in protecting the rights of the little guy."

"Knowing JR, it doesn't surprise me," Damian said. "He's a real Texan. Truth, justice and the American way. He was raised in a modest ranch house sitting in the middle of acres of woods on the outskirts of town. Your dad taught you to hunt, right, JR?"

"Yup. As a young boy I hunted with my daddy and my older brothers in the woods behind our house. When I was ten, for Christmas, my daddy gave me my own rifle and a high-powered scope. Boy, that was the best present I ever got! My daddy taught me to respect and maintain my rifle."

"I've never shot a gun," I admitted.

"Well, I don't 'spect there's much hunting in Brooklyn."

Damian said, "It soon became apparent JR had an uncanny skill as a marksman. He and his father would set up targets in the backyard and compete to see who could hit more bullseyes. Soon, JR never lost."

"My daddy kept moving the targets further and further back. One evening, he took me to the deserted local high school football field and set up a target in one endzone. He sent me to the other endzone with my rifle and a box of bullets."

Damian said, "Very few trained snipers can hit a target three-hundred feet away. It's a crazy distance."

JR said, "I could barely see the target but I took aim through the scope and took ten shots."

"He hit six bullseyes," Damian said. "He was twelve years old."

"My daddy said, 'Son, I never seen nothin' like that. You could shoot the wings off a mosquito!' I was bustin' with pride. When I got home. I told my oldest brother about the shots and showed him the bullet holes in the target. My brother said, 'Oh, sure. Ya know, JR, I once hit the moon. Perfect bullseye. Beat that!' I didn't mind the kidding. I framed the target and kept it on the wall in my bedroom."

"I guess you have a special gift, JR," I said.

"It is a gift," Damian said. "There was no question about what JR wanted to do after high school. Serve his country just like his father did. He was a Navy veteran."

"I signed up two days after graduation. After basic training, I went to Great Lakes, Illinois to be trained as a Navy SEAL."

"His superior marksmanship made him a natural to qualify as an elite sniper," Damian said proudly.

"From there, I trained at the Navy Sniper School in Indianapolis. I learned a lot. The science and variables behind the perfect shot – wind, temperature, barometric pressure, degree of latitude, bullet velocity and the earth's rotation. Although I was never good in science classes in high school, I ate that stuff up."

Damian explained, "His weapon of choice was not a semi-automatic sniper rifle but the bolt action Mk-12. It reminded him of the rifle his father gave him as a boy. The bolt action forced him to make each shot count."

JR smiled. "Ya know, the scope on my sniper rifle was a state of the art Bausch & Lomb 10x. The target appeared so close I felt I could touch it before I took a shot. They trained me harder than a backwoods hound dog. I learned to hit targets under the toughest conditions, like after sprinting 500 yards, or after climbing ten flights of stairs, or after swimming long distances. I trained twelve hours a day for months until every shot I took was instinct. I got my certification as a SEAL sniper. It was the proudest day in my life. I was immediately deployed to the Middle East."

"I was the leader of the platoon JR was assigned to," Damian said. "JR was one of my best. Maybe the best. We learned to trust and respect each other in combat and soon became close friends. Throughout our tours of duty, we were engaged in many missions together in places we're still not allowed to talk about. He always had long hair, a beard wore a black bandana on his head when we were on a mission. He looked more like a member of an outlaw motorcycle club than a SEAL."

"I guess discipline takes more than a shave and a clean uniform."

JR nodded. "It made no difference to the enemy how long my hair was or how I dressed for combat. In sniper school they taught me truth comes out of the barrel of a gun."

Damian said, "SEALs are taught discipline is being calm and focused when your life is on the line. In his role as a sniper, JR was always the point man when the platoon entered a hot zone. He would establish a camouflaged advance position and assess the risk to the platoon before we engaged. It was his responsibility to take any proactive steps he felt necessary to minimize the risk to our platoon. I knew I could rely on him to do what was required to protect our platoon."

JR sat back. He looked proud as he let Damian tell me about his skill and courage in combat.

"When he was in the mix, JR had to make split second life and death decisions through the lens of a scope and the squeeze of a trigger. He never hesitated. If he saw an imminent threat and an enemy's life had to be sacrificed to protect his platoon, the decision was an easy one. In war people die. He always took two bolt action head shots, but the first one was all he ever needed. His skill saved many more lives than he took. No one ever questioned his judgment."

JR looked down and shook his head. "That is until I started questioning myself. Then the questions never stopped."

"I was never in the service so I can only imagine the disconnect in trying to return to civilian life from combat duty," I said. "Our politicians talk a good game, but do little to support our vets in making the transition."

"I was lucky," Damian said. "I had skills, a good education and opportunities. Few combat vets do."

"I weren't so lucky. I didn't know which way to turn so I just dragged my tail back home to Texas."

"I was able to come north, to New York City," Damian said, "to pursue a career as a cyber security analyst and was lucky enough to meet you, Chance. I kept in touch with JR by email and Facetime, but, as often happens with comrades-in-arms, we drifted apart. We were still good friends, but our friendship was based more in the past than the present. I regret now that I wasn't there for JR when he needed me."

"Damian, you've done more for me than I deserve. Out of the service, I was like a catfish out of water. Couldn't get a job. Without the discipline and direction of the SEALs. I was plum lost. Started askin' myself some hard questions about the purpose of life. The longer I drifted, the more these painful questions began to live in my mind like a burr in my combat boot. Soon, it was all I thought about. I had a dream I was on a boat driftin' out in the Gulf of Mexico and I had lost my oars."

"It was the enemy he couldn't defeat," Damian said.

"A poor reward for your service and sacrifice. I think, throughout history, the countries with warrior kings were the most noble. They had leaders who actually led their men into battle. It's way too easy for someone who has never made any sacrifice to risk the lives of our soldiers."

"Warrior king, I kinda like that," JR said. "I sure would like see our President risk his own life by leading a platoon into a fire fight. We'd have fewer wars, that's for sure. Anyway, I was lost and drifting without an anchor. About six months after my discharge, I was alone in my apartment. There was no warning, it just hit me like a Texas tornado. I couldn't breathe, I couldn't move. I couldn't talk. I was in agony and felt like my body was disintegrating. Never had any fear of dyin' in combat but now I'm terrified."

JR seemed to have run out of steam. Damian helped him along. "You told me you were convinced that you were dying."

"Yup, that's true. Scared to death. Worst feelin on earth. I didn't know what was happening or what to do. I sat dead still, my head between my knees. I suffered for what seemed like an eternity. Without even thinkin', I started saying' the Lord's Prayer over and over, like I was a little kid, sittin' with my parents, safe in church."

"Sounds horrible. If this is too difficult, JR, we can always talk later."

"No. I'm okay. Thank God, the attack finally passed and I realized I'm still alive. I'm terrified to move or talk, out of fear it was gonna come back. I sat on my bed for probably another hour. I slowly started to feel sorta normal."

Damian said, "You told me you read out loud from a newspaper to prove you were still alive and had the ability to read and speak."

"Yup. Crazy as it sounds, I did. I was convinced I had a fatal disease. Finally got the nerve up to drive myself to the emergency room at the local VA hospital."

"Were they able to help you?"

"They tried. I sat in the waiting room on an orange plastic chair, shielding my eyes. I felt dizzy and off balance 'cause of the glare of the antiseptic white walls and fluorescent lights."

Damian said, "I've learned that certain bright lights, or total darkness, can trigger anxiety attacks. Light or dark, the monster is hiding right behind you."

"I felt god awful. But tormented as I was, I still felt guilty when I seen the other vets with serious physical injuries needin' emergency treatment being brought in on gurneys by paramedics and ambulance drivers. I think, *man, you're a poor excuse for a SEAL, you're not even hurt.* I waited forever. Finally, I'm brought to an examining room. This young Black ER doc, Dr. Thomas, takes my history. The doc ordered a barrage of tests."

"I'm sure you were worried."

"Worried as worry could be. I'm layin' down on the tissue paper of the examining table, closed my eyes, waitin'. I'm afraid to move because I'm sure it would trigger another attack. I'm focusing on every breath that I'm takin', afraid that if I didn't I would stop breathing altogether. When the doc finally returns, he pulls a chair over in front of the examining table. I open my eyes see the doc reading my test results. I slowly sit up and hold on to the examining table with both hand. I look at the doc, 'spectin' to hear the worst. He says, 'Good news. I've reviewed your test results. The tests are all negative.' I say, 'Doc, that can't be right. I almost died this morning!'"

"You didn't believe him."

"Not for a minute. But he said, 'There's no mistake. You have no physical illness. I believe you have all the symptoms of a panic attack.' I said, 'Of course, I panicked. I almost died!' He said, 'You didn't almost die. Your body reacted to overwhelming anxiety.'"

"Unfortunately, it's a common anxiety disorder," Damian said. "Many servicemen suffer from it when they return home from active duty. But hearing that doesn't make it any easier, does it, JR?"

"Nope. I said in a whisper so nobody else could hear, 'Doc, are you tellin' me I'm goin' crazy?' He told me I wasn't going crazy, that panic attacks are not classified as a psychiatric disorder. That's his words. He asked me, 'Did you watch the first season of the Sopranos? Tony Soprano, a mob boss, suffered from panic attacks.' I said, 'Doc, with all due respect, what the fuck? I was deployed and in the mix for two tours. We didn't watch TV shows. I'm aguessin' you never served in combat. I'm real sick and you're talkin' about a TV show.'"

"The doc told me, 'Mr. Reynolds, I appreciate your combat service. I am equally proud of my service as a VA doctor. I'm sorry about talking about the Sopranos. I wasn't making light of your condition, I just wanted to reassure you this kind of anxiety disorder is widespread and can be easily treated with medication and behavioral therapy.'"

"Did you feel relieved?"

"Nope. I didn't feel no better. I was confused and upset. The doc gave me two scripts, one for an anti-depressant and the other was a referral to a VA staff psychiatrist. I stared at the scripts, still not convinced I wasn't dyin'. I put the scripts in my pocket, walked out, and filled the one for the pills at the VA pharmacy. Outside the hospital, I ripped up the other one and threw it away."

"You wouldn't see a psychiatrist?"

"No way. I was humiliated by the doc's sayin' I had a mental problem. SEALs don't see shrinks. We don't go into therapy, we go into battle. I was angry. I thought the doc sure as hell had no understanding of who I was and what combat was all about."

Damian said, "We were trained to never panic in battle. JR had the skills to deal with the turmoil and stress of war on his own. He would never admit to his fellow SEALs, much less a shrink, how scared and confused he felt when he suffered a panic attack."

"I took some of them anti-depressant pills and felt like crap so I stopped takin' 'em. Now I'm anxious all the time. I'm worried sick about havin' another attack and stopped going out in public unless it was absolutely necessary. I ordered everything online, I'm livin' confined to my small apartment. I can't sleep. I start dreading the day and the night."

"He was a prisoner. Only he couldn't figure out how to escape his own mind."

"Finally when I couldn't stand it no more, I called Dr. Thomas, the ER doc, and told him how I was suffering and couldn't sleep or eat. I begged him for help. Dr. Thomas agreed to call in a prescription for oxycodone to help me sleep, provided I agreed to start seeing a therapist."

"Did you agree to start therapy?"

"Yup. I agreed, but I had no intention of ever goin'."

"Unfortunately, JR," I said, "I think I know where this is going. From bad to worse. Oxy is a very slippery slope. I feel bad for what you've gone through."

"You know, Chance," Damian said, "there but the grace of God, that would have been me if I didn't have my degree and training. I was very lucky."

JR said, "Damian, you weren't lucky. You deserve everything you've gotten in life. Anyway, ol' oxy put me out at night and dulled the pain during the day. It made me feel nothin', which was better than the pain and anxiety. I pop pills day and night. She was my best friend. Didn't take long before we're hitched."

"JR soon became dependent on oxy and very quickly he ran out of his stash of the prescribed pills."

"Chance, I'm not proud, but you guessed right about how hard I fell. When you're scared, you're stupid. Doc Thomas wouldn't renew my prescription, I start trollin' the local doc in the boxes to get new scripts. I run out of docs, I'm on the Internet buying oxy scripts on the black market. For a price, I got scripts, mostly forged, under fictious names with fictious dates of birth. I was careful never to go to the same pharmacy twice. I was a real Jesse James. Only I was the dumbass being robbed of my integrity and health."

JR closed his eyes and was breathing heavily. He opened his eyes and took a drink of water. He looked exhausted.

I said, "JR, you look beat. Why don't we call it at night. You can tell me the rest another day."

"Chance, it's funny, I've told this story a million times but it never seems to get any easier. Damian knows the rest. He can tell you how this Texas boy finally ended up in Brooklyn."

"JR started traveling hours each day to feed his habit," Damian said. "He stopped bathing and washing his clothes. His appearance became emaciated and ragged. He looked like what he had become: an addict. Eventually a suspicious pharmacist concerned about JR's appearance realized the script JR gave him was forged. He asked JR to wait while he pretended to fill the prescription and called the local drug enforcement hotline number on the wall of his office. When JR left the pharmacy with a bottle of placebos, two Texas DEA agents were waiting for him. He was cuffed, read his rights and put in the back of a squad car."

JR said, "And you know what? I felt relieved. When you plum hit bottom, the only way is up."

"JR was charged with a number of felonies, including possession of a forged instrument. By the time he was arraigned, JR was going into withdrawal. Fortunately, Judge Johnson, the presiding judge, was a former Marine. He was aware of JR's service and that this was his first arrest."

"Most defendants arrested for oxy related offenses are victims, not criminals," I noted.

"This judge released JR on his own recognizance with the condition that JR immediately admit himself to an inpatient drug rehabilitation program at the VA hospital. He warned JR, if he did not complete the program, he would be remanded to jail. The judge adjourned the case for two months to allow JR to get clean."

"The judge was a good Christian man," JR said. "Reminded me of our preacher back home."

"As part of the rehabilitation program, JR had to write letters, not emails, to friends and family and tell them about his addiction and ask for their help. JR finally wrote me a long letter detailing everything he just told you and asked me for my help. As soon as I read it, I was on the next plane down to Texas. I visited JR often during the next two months."

JR said, "I'm proud to say I did real good. Facing my demons was harder than trainin' to become a SEAL. I completed the rehab program with flying colors. I was prescribed the right anti-depressants and I learned though therapy the skills I needed to control an anxiety attack if I have one. When I feel a panic attack coming I have learned to focus all my attention on a song, a book or a picture, knowing that it will always pass. It's funny because in some ways it's the same way I focused as a sniper just before I pulled the trigger. I would look through my site and focus my whole being on the target. Nothing else existed. How upside down is that? Anyway, in group therapy, I faced the demons of combat with other veterans who were also suffering from PTSD. I slowly begin to feel in control of my anxiety. And my life. I'm a lucky cowboy."

JR looked at Damian, now completely exhausted, and Damian told the last chapter. "After JR successfully completed the rehab program he was placed on parole. The conditions of his parole were for JR to continue to attend AA meetings, not be arrested for any other offenses, not use any illegal substances and take urine tests and report to his parole officer monthly. I helped JR get disability benefits from the VA and suggested JR move up to Brooklyn and start a new life. He quickly agreed."

JR nodded. "Yup. Damian's my best friend. Today and tomorrow, no matter how hard the next day is."

"About a month later, JR got permission to relocate and his parole was reassigned to a parole officer at the Department of Corrections in New York City. He moved into a nice studio apartment I found for him in Brooklyn. He was healthy and happy, looking forward to his new life. When he moved up here, that's when I asked you if you would consider hiring him to work part time as a clerk for us. You were kind enough to do me the favor, no questions asked."

"I never thought I would be talkin' real kindly about some northern lawyer with an office in Brooklyn. But, Chance, I have to thank you. I lucked out, clerkin' for you and dealin' at your poker games."

"JR, thanks for sharing your story. I'm glad to hear about your recovery and happy that we can work together."

"I'm real glad to hear you say that. I'm hopin' you don't feel I took advantage of you by not tellin' you about my past. I'm sure sorry if I did," JR said.

"You have no need to apologize. Damian is not just my investigator, he is my friend. I trust him. JR, I have only one question: are you still clean?"

"Yup."

"Great. This conversation never took place. JR, I'm sure you appreciate the favors Damian has done for you. You're lucky to have him as a friend."

"Not favors," Damian said. "Obligations. He's a brother SEAL."

CHAPTER TEN

THE FAVOR

The day we met with Courtney Malone, the divorce client Roy Brown asked me to meet with as a favor to him, was just another Monday.

My typical weekday morning routine is always the same: I wake up at 5:30, I feed Tort, and look at my emails and texts to see if there are any fires that have to be put out. Then I turn my phone off until I get to the office.

When Tort is fed, fat and happy, we sit side-by-side on the bedroom rug and I meditate. When I started practicing meditation early in my career, I quickly appreciated why it has been practiced by millions of people for more than 1,500 years. It is not, as many people believe, a discipline related to any religion.

There is nothing mystical or magical about meditation. It is quite the opposite. It is the practice of suspending any thought, belief or emotion. The key to meditation is to stop the world, center yourself in the moment and simply breathe. There is no one way to meditate or need for a magic mantra.

I first relax the muscles in my jaw, my shoulders and my arms. Once relaxed, I take a long cleansing breath and focus on my surroundings. I try to see colors, hear sounds and focus on a nearby object, like my pen or legal pad. Greater clarity and perspective always seem to follow becoming the rock in the stream.

I always play music while I meditate. I choose artists whose music I believe is transcendent, like Keith Jarrett, George Winston or, of course, one of Knopfler's soundtracks like *Local Hero*, *Princess Bride* or, appropriately, *Last Exit To Brooklyn*.

I have also learned to use meditation techniques in court. When trying a case and my adrenalin is flowing, I use the same techniques to regain my composure and focus.

Trying a case is like carrying a thousand-pound rock on your back all day and sleeping with it on your chest at night. Just when you think you have balanced the weight, something happens that shifts your balance and undermines your stability. Meditation helps me carry that weight. I know attorneys who try to ease the pressure and pain of litigation with alcohol or drugs. It never works for long and always ends badly.

Each morning, after finishing my meditation, I work the heavy boxing bag hanging in my bedroom. There is a very different play list for banging the bag – Springsteen, Mellencamp or the Stones. Boxing is actually just another form of meditation, a moving meditation. The key is to have your mind and body act as one.

When Damian learned about my morning workout on the heavy bag, he was amused. He does the 100s every day: a hundred sit-ups, a hundred pushups and a hundred squats.

He said, "Rocky, you do realize, boxing is a useless form of self-defense, don't you?"

"Really? And why is that, Mr. Miyagi?"

"Because by the time you throw three combination punches, the fight is already over, and you are on the floor."

"And what should I be practicing? Wax on, wax off?"

"No. That wouldn't work because you don't even own a car. It's very simple. In any form of combat, you always use a weapon, not your fists. Even cavemen knew to pick up a rock or a stick to defend themselves. In today's world you don't need a gun or a knife, you can use anything within reach – a glass, a book, your iPad. Your keys."

I smiled. "Fascinating. Tell me, exactly how does that work?"

"Move in as close as possible and use your home-made weapon and violently attack the eyes, the throat or the groin. Don't stop until there is a complete submission or retreat. Then you can go do Pilates or yoga or whatever you middle aged men do after menopause."

"Damian, I am sure that would be very effective. I do have a paper weight on my desk for unruly clients. But I have mastered a very different art of self-defense."

"Really? What is that?"

"I run. I run as fast and as far as I can away from trouble until I am out of harm's way."

Damian shook his head and laughed. "Got it. That also works."

Tort always waits patiently while I complete my morning routine. I shower, shave every other day, and put on a pair of blue jeans, an open-collared white Oxford shirt, and my Mickey Mouse watch. This is how I dress, without exception, unless I am going to court. I have no need to wear a suit and tie in my office. There is no one I need to impress with the clothes I wear. I like to be comfortable. Maybe I'm just getting old.

I take Tort to the park for his morning walk. He runs with his friends while I sit on a bench, look at the trees and sky, and say hello to the other early dog walkers who have become my friends over the years. I feel at peace and appreciate the gift of another day doing what I still love to do. Then we go to the office.

Little did I suspect that morning, things would never be quite so routine again. When I arrived, Sally and Damian were already in the conference room. Sally had set up the conference room table with pads, pens and bottles of water. To her credit, even though she wanted no part of this divorce case, she placed a big box of tissues in the center of the table. She knew from past experience, even the angriest spouses often break down and shed tears when discussing their broken marriages with an attorney.

Sally wore a smart black dress and a matching jacket. Damian, wearing his usual black jeans, a tight black tee shirt and a brown leather jacket, was sitting at the conference room table, already working intensely on his laptop, searching the web for background information about Courtney and her husband, Jackson Malone.

It is my practice to greet new clients in the waiting area of my office when they arrive. I meet them at the front door, introduce myself and shake hands. I like to sit with clients in the waiting area for a few minutes. I invite them to sit down on the soft cushions of one of the four old, comfortable, brown side chairs near the entrance so we can talk before going into the conference room, which is a more formal and imposing setting.

I take the opportunity to get to know my clients in this informal and non-threatening setting. I know how hard it is for a client to walk into an attorney's office for the first time, especially in a divorce case. It is often a difficult and gut-wrenching experience. I let clients know I appreciate the courage it takes to retain an attorney, especially for a divorce.

It is important, especially in a divorce case, for me to build a mutual trust and respect at my first meeting with a client. We have to be honest with each other, so we can make difficult decisions together that will affect not only the outcome of their case but the rest of their lives. I need them to feel comfortable in a very uncomfortable situation.

I understand many clients are only hiring an attorney because they have no choice. They never wanted a divorce to begin with and have no desire to go down the black hole of litigation. They don't care who wins or loses, they just want the case to be over and for their lives to go back to normal.

Roy had called and texted me a number of times early in the morning before I got to the office. I saw no benefit in speaking with him until after my meeting with Courtney. Roy's last text said: "Thank you for seeing Courtney. I consider it a great personal favor. She needs your help! Best regards, Roy."

I saw Courtney Malone coming through the front door of our brownstone office with a well-dressed older man and woman, whom I assumed were her parents, Randolph Gault and his wife.

Courtney wore a simple black dress that looked comfortable yet elegant. She had long auburn hair, striking features and the posture of a ballerina. She had a soft and open countenance you notice right away with people who are gentle and kind. She wore no makeup or jewelry, except for a gold wedding band and a simple gold cross on a gold chain around her neck.

I always notice when someone is wearing a cross. I hope it is a sign they believe in a higher authority and have the humility and courage to show their belief. I also know sometimes it's just a nice piece of jewelry.

Courtney's father had on a high-quality knitted sports jacket, an open-collared blue cotton polo shirt and a gold Rolex. He was trim and had a thick head of manicured gray hair. He looked like he would be at home in the boardroom or at the country club.

Courtney's mother was extremely thin and had a great resemblance to Courtney. She was very well kept and could easily have been an older sister instead of Courtney's mother. She wore an elegant black pantsuit and lots of expensive jewelry, including a large diamond engagement ring and a beautiful necklace, also with a gold cross. Courtney's parents were clearly very comfortable with their wealth.

As I always do, I met Courtney and her parents at the front door, shook hands and introduced myself. "Hi, I'm Chance Cormac. I am a friend and colleague of Roy Brown. Roy asked me to meet with Courtney and help her if I could. I assume you are Courtney and these are your parents?"

Before Courtney could say anything, her father took over the conversation. He looked around, obviously disappointed with my small office and modest waiting area. He said, "My name is Randolph Gault. This is my wife, Adelaide. I am Courtney's father. As you know, Roy Brown suggested I meet with you. To say the least, your offices are a little different from what I expected when Roy referred me to you. I'm puzzled. Are you a solo practitioner?"

Randolph's blunt question and hostile tone surprised me. With great relief, I thought this might be a short meeting after all. "Nice to meet you, too, Mr. Gault. To answer your question, no, I have a legal assistant and investigator. We work on all cases together."

"But you are still just one lawyer, right?"

"In my experience, one good lawyer is all a client needs."

"I'm not convinced that's true, Mr. Cormac. Regardless, I'm here only because Roy went out of his way to recommend you. Quite frankly, I was disappointed Roy's firm would represent Jackson without the courtesy of speaking to me first. Roy apologized but assured me he was very fond of both Courtney and Jackson and his firm took the case only on the condition it would be uncontested and Jackson would be very fair and generous with Courtney and the twins. He insisted I meet with you before retaining anyone else. He said you are his close friend and the best divorce lawyer he knows."

I didn't like Roy's hard sell of me as a divorce lawyer. Also, it immediately struck me as odd that Roy had told me Courtney's father was the one who had asked him for a referral, not that Roy had gone out of his way to steer Courtney's case to me. It's possible I misunderstood what Roy had said, but I didn't think so. I made a mental note to speak to Roy about this later.

Mr. Gault looked around again, shaking his head. "Honestly, Mr.

Cormac, I'm not very impressed by your firm or your offices. Have you tried many divorce cases?"

"Not recently. I haven't handled any matrimonial cases in over ten years."

"Mr. Cormac, is this some sort of joke? Why are you, and Roy, wasting my time? I want my daughter to have the best legal representation possible. You obviously are not that attorney."

"Mr. Gault, I couldn't agree with you more. There are many other more capable and experienced divorce lawyers. I suggested the same thing to Roy. I would be happy to refer Courtney to some reputable divorce attorneys. Or you should use one of the firms you have already interviewed. Roy told me he wanted me to meet with Courtney because you are friends and he has known Courtney since she was a young girl. He is concerned about her, and he believes he could trust me to advise her as to what is in her best interests."

Gault gave me a blank stare. His wife looked uncomfortable and Courtney was near tears.

"I am a commercial litigator, not a matrimonial attorney. I do believe the economic aspects of divorce are in many respects identical to the dissolution of any partnership, but divorce is no longer my area of specialty. Roy assured me this would be an uncontested divorce and his firm would be representing Courtney's husband, who, as I assume you are aware, is an existing client of his firm."

Randolph said, "I know all of this already. I don't care about what Roy says or Jackson wants. My only concern is for my daughter."

"I understand. But I do believe Roy only wants to help. He also assured me Jackson would be more than fair and his partner representing Jackson would have marching orders to negotiate an agreement in good faith. I fully expected to meet with Courtney as a courtesy to Roy, give her some guidance and refer her to a more experienced matrimonial attorney. Rest assured I do not expect to be retained by your daughter."

Randolph had heard enough and loudly interrupted me. "Don't worry, you won't be representing my daughter. Jackson is a selfish prick! He's broken all his marriage vows. He has hurt my daughter and my grandchildren. I want him to pay dearly for the suffering he has caused my family. I don't know what Roy was thinking. I want someone who will take no prisoners, not be conciliatory. Thanks for your time. You can send me your bill."

So much for the "plain vanilla divorce." I hid a smile and was very relieved when Courtney's father turned to go back out the front door. I didn't enjoy getting beaten up by a client's father about a case I didn't want to begin with, but in this case it was a gift. I had now done Roy the favor of meeting with Courtney, and, best of all, I didn't have to find an excuse for why I would not be representing her. Even better, I could now keep my promise to Sally.

As Courtney's father opened the front door to leave, Courtney finally spoke in a soft but firm voice. "Daddy, wait. I appreciate your help, but Roy Brown recommended Mr. Cormac. He has taken the time to meet with us and I would like to at least hear what he has to say."

Courtney's mother gently took her husband's arm. Randolph pulled his arm away. Giving Courtney a disapproving look, he reluctantly turned around and came back into the office. He closed the door with a bang. Glaring at me, he addressed his daughter. "Courtney, if that's what you want, since we are here, I'll buy an hour of this guy's time. Mr. Cormac, does this office have a conference room or do we have to keep talking out here in the open?"

"We have a very nice conference room. Mr. Gault, why don't you and Adelaide sit here and make yourselves comfortable? I can offer you some coffee or water. We will be no more than an hour."

"My wife can wait here. I'm coming in with Courtney. Jackson is a born liar and a poor excuse for a human being. He has no concern for Courtney or the twins. He moved out and hasn't seen his children in weeks. He specializes in tax shelters and wealth management. I have bought and sold more businesses than you can count. I understand these finance guys and the tricks they use to manipulate their assets and income. Courtney is out of her depth, and I am here to protect her. I intend to be present and involved every step of the way, starting with you and what happens in that conference room today."

I took a deep breath, focused, and said, "Mr. Gault, Courtney is lucky to have parents who love and support her. I know your business and finance experience will be a great benefit to her in planning a future for her and your grandchildren. Unfortunately, you can't be present when I meet with Courtney. Everything Courtney and I discuss is privileged and confidential. We can never be compelled to disclose any attorney client communications. My staff are afforded the same privilege. That privilege is critical to my representation of her as a client. Your presence would destroy that privilege and you, or I, could be forced to testify against her interests."

"Mr. Cormac, please spare me the lecture on how many angels can sit on the head of a pin. It's simple. My company will also retain you for the hour. I will have my own privilege as your client and the benefit of writing off your fee. It's done all the time."

I was impressed by Gault's proposed tactic to skirt the law. He clearly was someone who didn't care if he crossed the line if it benefited him.

I said, "I appreciate the suggestion, but I don't think it would be appropriate or benefit any of us. First, your privilege argument would be suspect in a matrimonial case. Second, I would not be rendering services to your company, and it would be unethical, and possibly a tax fraud, for me to disguise Courtney's legal fees as a corporate expense. Maybe you are right, and Courtney would be better served by being represented by another firm you are more comfortable with."

Courtney faced her father directly and now said in a much louder voice, "Dad, stop! I'm going to meet with Mr. Cormac by myself. Please don't make this any more difficult than it already is."

Mr. Gault glared at his wife. He started to object, but instead he slowly sat down in one of the waiting room chairs. Adelaide sat down next to him and was speaking softly to him as I showed Courtney into the conference room.

Sally was sitting at the conference room table, looked at her watch and gave me a puzzled look. I just shook my head and introduced Courtney to Sally and Damian. They both stood and shook her hand.

Although I was confident we would not be retained, I still treated Courtney like any other prospective client. I explained to her that we worked as a team and if she ever had a question or concern, she should feel free to contact any one of us at any time. We gave her our business cards, with our personal cell phone numbers.

I sat Courtney next to Sally on one side of the conference table. She is always a great comfort to clients and I wanted Courtney to be comfortable during what I was sure would be our first and last meeting.

Damian and I sat across the table from Courtney and Sally. I never sit at the head of the conference room table when meeting with a new client. I want the client to feel we are all rowing together to reach a common destination. I don't take any notes. I try to sit still with my hands folded and focus on what is being said as well as what is not being said. A client's body language, facial expression or tone of voice can reveal as much as a thousand words.

Courtney looked relieved. With her father outside, she seemed much calmer and more composed. She looked at the pictures on the conference room wall and smiled for the first time since she arrived at my office. She said, "You have a Ralph Steadman poster of *Fear and Loathing in Las Vegas*? I'm guessing not many attorneys have Hunter Thompson pictures in their conference rooms."

I smiled back. "No sane attorneys do. Have you read any of Hunter's books?"

"It might surprise you to learn, despite my appearance, I am a big Hunter Thompson fan. I even have a signed copy of *The Curse of Lono*, which is one of my prized possessions. I think Hunter was in his heart a journalist and a reporter. He wrote the most amazing letters and articles. He was really quite romantic. He spoke from his heart and always reported the unvarnished truth as he saw it."

I was intrigued. My first thoughts about Hunter were always the drugs and his fear and loathing of the establishment, not romance. He certainly was not a big fan of the country club set.

"Sometimes," Courtney continued, "what he wrote was absurd, sometimes it was ugly, but it was always true. I think the alcohol and drugs were just props Hunter used, like a top hat and magic wand waved around by a magician. When I was teenager, he made me want to be a writer."

Against my better instincts, I was beginning to like Courtney more and more. "Courtney, I'm very impressed. It's too bad Hunter's gone. We need his voice now more than ever. I don't want to keep your parents waiting too long. How can we help you?"

"You have to forgive my father. He loves me and the twins very much. He is just used to getting what he wants."

I nodded but didn't interrupt.

She looked me in the eyes and continued in a very strong and firm voice, "I just want this over. The only thing I care about is protecting my twins, Sophia and Claire. I know my marriage is over. I have denied that truth for a long time because a divorce is the last thing I ever wanted. I believe in my marriage vows, but I accept Jackson should be free to live the life he wants."

I looked over and saw Sally shaking her head. She wanted no part of the pain and hardship of another divorce involving young children.

"Jackson has not really been part of our lives for a long time. The children and I are very well provided for. I don't care about more money, a bigger house or any of his businesses. He worked hard for his success, and he deserves to enjoy it. I don't want to fight with him, or my father. I just want to move on and be able to start a new life for myself and the girls."

I knew that Sally was thinking about Melody, who was about the same age as Courtney's twins. Despite Sally's reservations, I knew that Courtney's concern for the wellbeing of her children would strike a chord in her heart.

Courtney told us about her relationship with Jackson, how they fell in love in high school and their married life. She didn't know much about Jackson's wealth management and consulting business, other than the fact he was very successful and had clients all over the world. Courtney had been a nurse practitioner, caring for babies suffering from cancer. She loved caring for critically ill children, but decided to stop working when the twins were born, at least until they were older.

The hour went quickly. I told Courtney I admired her strength and commitment to her children. I informed her, as I advise all divorce clients, that who the good guy or bad guy is in a divorce has little impact on the rights of the parties, other than in regard to parenting. "There's no verdict on who's at fault in a failed marriage. No winner or loser."

Courtney said, "I'm not trying to win anything. I don't want to fight with Jackson."

"Good, because going to war rarely affects the outcome of a divorce. It only made the lawyers rich. Most good divorce lawyers know how a case will be resolved within an hour of first meeting with a client. Roy has assured me that your husband wants to be fair and with Roy's firm representing Jackson your case should be settled quickly and without any litigation."

As I always do at the end of an initial consultation, I asked Courtney if there is anything else she felt was important we should know. I was surprised when Courtney suddenly froze, and her face was stricken with fear. She began sobbing uncontrollably and couldn't stop.

Sally gave me a quick glance and moved closer to Courtney. She put her hand on Courtney's arm and gave her some tissues from the box on the table. After some time, Courtney tried to compose herself and took a sip of water. She looked down, clasped her hands, and said in a pleading voice, "You can't tell my father! You can't tell anyone! No one must ever find out!"

Sally placed her hand on Courtney's shoulder and spoke softly to her, trying to console her. Finally, I said, "Courtney, on my oath as a lawyer, we would never repeat anything you tell us to anyone."

I waited and Courtney, without looking up, struggled to say what she obviously had kept secret for a long time. "It's the pictures! The horrible, obscene, unspeakable pictures!"

"Tell me, what pictures are those, Courtney?"

She took a sip of water. Still sitting rigidly, staring straight down at the table, she said, "Jackson had been home for a few days about a month ago. He was no longer staying at the house, but he stopped by to visit the girls and pick up some personal items. He was packing for another lengthy business trip. Before he went upstairs to pack, he unlocked his laptop and was playing with the twins, a horse riding video game they love to play. After a few minutes he left the girls giggling and playing the game, and told them he had to pack but would be right back down to say goodbye. The girls were sitting side-by-side on stools at the kitchen counter both staring at the laptop screen when I heard the giggling suddenly stop."

I knew then that the rest of the story was not going to be pretty.

"I asked, 'Girls, is everything all right?' Claire called, 'Mommy, come look!' I went over, stood behind the girls and put my arms around their shoulders to see what they were looking at. It was like a punch to my stomach. On the screen were dozens of pictures of girls in their early teens, completely naked. I closed the laptop. Claire said, 'Aren't the girls pretty, Mommy? Can we show Daddy?' I composed myself the best I could and said, 'Daddy is in a hurry to catch a plane.' I said let's have a snack and wait for Daddy to come down and say goodbye. I wasn't about to let them out of my sight."

Sally nodded but was obviously upset.

"I was frantic. I didn't know what to do. I was shocked and repulsed, I didn't want to believe what I'd seen." Courtney stopped talking, holding the gold cross between her fingers and tried to collect her thoughts.

It was very difficult for her to speak about this dark and disturbing secret she had kept. She understood, once the words were spoken out loud, it was a harsh reality she would have to confront.

I recognized Courtney's dilemma and tried to minimize the impact of the pictures. "Courtney, maybe it was just a porn site your husband opened by mistake. Porn is a billion dollar industry. They send computer generated emails phishing for new customers all the time."

Courtney looked up and steeled her eyes at me. She shook her head and said forcefully, "No! You don't understand! I finally told the girls to go to their rooms and I opened the files on his laptop again. They all contained the most vile and obscene pictures and videos of young teen girls. My husband was in all the videos! He was having sex with these young girls, sometimes two or three at a time. There was page after page of these video files. One more disgusting than the next. Oh my God! What have I done? Please! Please! Please! I have never told anyone except you about these pictures. I shouldn't have said anything. You can never tell anyone!"

"Courtney, I would never disclose anything you tell me without your consent. But you understand those files exist and sometimes facts can take on a life of their own. Hiding a fact doesn't hide the truth. The truth exists whether we want to deny it or not. The hard question is what to do now."

There was dead silence. Courtney was bent forward, tightly gripping the edge of the conference table, as if to keep her balance. Sally moved closer to Courtney, leaned over and again talked softly to her. I looked at Damian. He was sitting perfectly still, staring at his laptop and not moving a muscle except for his jaw, clenching and unclenching.

I took a deep breath and waited for Courtney to look up into my eyes. I asked the question that had to be asked. "Courtney, are you concerned about your husband being alone with your daughters?"

She looked up and said, "Oh, God! Don't even think that. He loves the girls. If I thought that for even a moment, I would never forgive myself for marrying him."

The hour was over long ago. I wanted Courtney to have some time alone with Sally so she could compose herself before seeing her parents. I said, "Courtney, thank you for your courage and honesty. Be assured, your secrets are safe with us."

I got up. "I am going to go out and speak with your parents for a few minutes. Of course, I won't tell them anything about what we discussed in this room today. It's up to you if you want to share with them, or anyone, your concerns. When you find the right attorneys to represent you, you should trust them to help you. I will see you before you leave. Damian, why don't we leave Courtney with Sally for a few minutes."

We left the room together and once outside Damian started to say, "You know we have to-"

I cut him off before he could complete the sentence. "Damian, not now. I need some time to think this through. Please, dig deep into this guy. I want to know things about him even he has forgotten."

"Got it."

Damian went into his office, and I returned to the waiting area. Mrs. Gault was sitting alone in one of the armchairs looking at her phone. When she saw me, she put her phone down. "My husband got tired of waiting and went for a walk. He will be back soon. I want to thank you for taking the time to meet with our daughter. I apologize for the things my husband said to you. When he is angry, he says things he often regrets. He is very angry at Jackson, and he should not have taken his anger out on you. Is Courtney all right?"

"Courtney is fine. We had a good meeting. She is just finishing up with my paralegal. Adelaide, there is no reason for you to apologize. Be assured, I don't take the things your husband said to me personally. I understand his anger and frustration. It comes from his love and concern for your daughter and your grandchildren. I still view my profession as a counselor-at-law. In divorce cases I often have to be more counselor than lawyer. If you like, I'll be happy to help you find an attorney to represent Courtney."

Just then, Mr. Gault came back though the front door. He said, "Where's Courtney? We're not going to pay you for more than an hour of your time for this consultation. In fact, I'm going to give you a check right now, so our business will be concluded. Don't worry, I will tell Roy you were great, brilliant even, but it just wasn't a good fit for Courtney."

Randolph took out his checkbook and quickly wrote out a check he thrust at me. I looked at it. It was made out to my name in the amount of $1000, much more than my hourly rate.

I said, "Mr. Gault, thank you. This is very generous, but I can't accept it. First of all, this consultation is a professional courtesy for Roy Brown, and I wouldn't accept a fee under any circumstances. Second, even if I was to be retained by your daughter, which seems highly unlikely, there are strict rules in matrimonial cases regarding legal fees. I cannot charge a fee for legal services unless I have been retained in writing and the client has been provided with a client bill of rights, neither of which has happened here."

Mr. Gault shook his head, taking the check back. "Even better. I guess you're getting paid what you are worth." He ripped up the check and gave the pieces to his wife. "Mr. Cormac, I hope to God we are finally done here. Will you kindly get my daughter so we can leave. I've wasted all morning here and have much more important things to do."

I headed to the conference room. I felt badly for Courtney, but very happy that we were not going to be involved in what appeared to be a very ugly divorce case. As I was walking back, my phone chimed, and I read another text from Roy: "Please call me as soon as you have finished your meeting with Courtney."

I found Courtney still sitting and talking to Sally. She had recovered her composure and seemed at peace.

I asked, "How are we doing?"

I was surprised when it was Sally who answered. "We're doing pretty well. Courtney wants to retain our firm to represent her."

I was taken aback and wasn't sure how to respond. I had already made up my mind, for any number of reasons, it was a case I did not want under any circumstances. I certainly didn't need it and was convinced it would be a big mistake. Not only had I promised not to do any more divorce work, I was concerned about Courtney's father's hostility, Roy's agenda, and the evidence Jackson Malone was a sexual predator of young girls. It was a bad hand I didn't want to play.

I frowned and gave Sally a hard stare, but before I could say anything, Courtney said, "I want to thank both of you. It has been a great relief and comfort speaking to you and Sally. I trust you to help me and more importantly help my children. I understand why Roy Brown referred me to you and I want to retain your firm. I have only one question, can you guarantee me my children will be protected from all this?"

Without discussing with me what was best for the client or our firm, Sally had put me in the difficult position of now either accepting Courtney's case or coming up with a credible excuse why we couldn't.

I ducked the question and tried to hedge in order to buy some time to think things through.

"Courtney, I still think you would be better served by retaining another attorney. Someone who can protect you and your children. We don't do matrimonial cases anymore. Also, before we could even consider representing you, we are required to do conflict checks to make sure we have not represented any of your husband's businesses or any of his clients."

"I understand. But I've decided. I don't want another lawyer. Roy Brown recommended you. I trust Roy. I trust you and Sally. Can you do your conflict checks right away?"

"Yes, but honestly, I am also concerned because your farther has strong feelings as to who should represent you, and it isn't us. He's not wrong to want a lawyer who specializes in divorce law. It might be easier for you if he supported your choice of counsel."

"Mr. Cormac, my father still likes to think of me as the little girl he has to protect. I am no longer that little girl. I'm married and have my own family. I was a nurse, caring for critically ill children for many years. Babies died in my arms and I consoled parents who lost the most precious gift in their lives. I have raised my own children mostly on my own. I am very capable of making my own decisions about who will or will not represent me. My father will have to accept my choice."

I still had no intention of taking the case but said, "I respect your decision. I will contact you after we do our conflict checks, to set up another meeting to discuss our possible retention and how best to proceed. It's been a pleasure meeting with you."

I walked Courtney to the door, saying goodbye to her and her parents without any further discussion.

As a courtesy, I called Roy Brown. "Roy, it's Chance. I met with Courtney and her parents."

"Great! What did she say? Did they retain you?"

"You know I can't disclose any discussions I had with Courtney. She indicated she would like to retain us. What I can tell you is this, I still have some serious reservations and don't think we should represent her. Her father feels strongly Courtney should not use us. I told her we would do a conflict check and meet with her again to discuss our possible retention. I did you the favor of meeting with her and now I think you should refer her to another firm."

"Good. Very good. What I'm hearing is, she wants to use you, as I knew she would. Let me handle Randolph. Courtney is like a daughter to me. Considering our history together, Chance, I will be disappointed for Courtney, and for myself, if you don't take her case. Very disappointed."

There it was again. That veiled threat. "Roy, you know I will be happy to do you a favor if I can. I just don't understand why this is so important to you. Also, I'm confused about something."

"What's bothering you?"

"I thought you told me Courtney's father came to you and asked you to recommend a lawyer for Courtney."

"That's correct. He asked me for the best lawyer I know to represent Courtney. I told him that's you."

"Well, I'm confused because Randolph was pretty adamant he did not ask you for a recommendation. He said he already had consulted other high powered firms and it was you who insisted he and Courtney see me. He seems to want to go to war – not resolve this dispute."

"That's not true. He's probably just upset and doesn't recall our conversation. We were at lunch at the club. He asked my opinion as to who should represent Courtney. What does it matter how Courtney was referred to you anyway? You never question how any of my other referrals come in your front door or the fees they generate. I know you will represent her to the best of your ability."

I said, "Okay, Roy. Let me give all this some thought. I will inform you if we are actually retained."

I thought about what Roy was saying. Maybe I was being too sensitive about why this referral was made. It's true, I didn't question Roy's referral of other commercial cases to me. If Courtney retained me, I knew I wouldn't be influenced by Roy, Courtney's father or anyone else. But some things still troubled me. Roy knew I was no longer a matrimonial lawyer, much less the best divorce lawyer he knew. There were plenty of other honest and more skilled lawyers to represent Courtney, especially in an uncontested matter. Why me?

It was true Roy and Randolph were members of the same golf club, but I got the feeling they weren't particularly close friends. Randolph's son-in-law Jackson, not Randolph, was Roy's client. That's whose interests Roy's firm should be protecting.

Maybe it was just the bad taste in my mouth from Roy's repeated reminders about what I owed him for the cases he had referred to me and the large fees I had been paid. The truth is, I was very ambivalent about taking a case I knew I shouldn't only to preserve an economic relationship. My boxer's instinct told me it is never good to be forced into a corner in the ring.

After I got off the phone, I asked Sally and Damian to come into my office. I sat at my desk and Sally and Damian sat in the side chairs facing me. Sally didn't wait for me to say anything. She said, "The husband is a very bad guy. We have to report the child porn and possible statutory rape. He's a predator and has got to be put away."

Damian was nodding in agreement. "In combat, if the enemy raped a child, we were trained to make sure it would never happen again."

I said, "Slow down! Both of you! Sally, you know I'm not happy with you. First, I don't need to remind you, it was you who made me promise I wouldn't take Courtney's case. The next thing I know, without even consulting me, you are discussing with her the possible retention of our firm. So, maybe you can somehow explain to me how things got turned so upside down in there."

"Chance, I still don't want to take another divorce case but I'm also angry and upset. I think Courtney needs our help to make sure she and the twins are protected. We talked at length while you were out with her parents, not about her case, but about our lives as single parents of young girls. I couldn't help but think about Melody and how I would feel if I couldn't protect her. Courtney told me she has lived her life under the control of her domineering father and then the control of her husband."

"I get it. I understand why you want to protect her. But it's way too much brain damage, I think we should pass."

"I understand what we agreed to and your concerns, but she's scared to death. She is a very kind and generous person. A good, loving mother. She devoted her career to helping children with serious medical problems. Now she devotes her life to her children. I think her husband is dangerous in ways we don't understand."

"Very dangerous," Damian agreed. "You don't keep those pictures on your laptop unless you are convinced you are above the law."

Sally said, "There is something very wrong here and she needs our help. If I was in her situation, I know you are the only one I would turn to."

"I understand your empathy for Courtney and your desire to help her. It's who you are. But spare me the accolades. I'm no superhero. I agreed to see Courtney for all the wrong reasons. I wanted to preserve a relationship benefiting us economically, not because I'm the best lawyer for the job. I did the favor and met with her. I had no intention of taking the case. I have serious concerns about her case and why Roy referred her to me."

Damian said, "I agree. One hundred per cent. It's a case we don't want or need."

"As to the pictures, they are reprehensible. Sexual predators should be eliminated. Not in the way Damian is suggesting. But they are animals and should be put in a cage for the same length of time as their victims have to carry any memory of the abuse they endured. If that's for the rest of a deviant's life, even better. But no matter how outraged we are, whether we are retained or not, before we report the husband we have to consider our professional responsibility to Courtney."

Sally said, "So what are you saying? We put blinders on and Jackson just gets to continue to abuse these young girls and destroy their lives?"

"What we have to do is think like her lawyers. Lawyers representing the best interests of a client, whether Courtney ends up being our client or not. We are not part of law enforcement. Or social services. So, what are the facts? The facts we actually can prove. Courtney and her husband have separated. They will be divorced. Courtney expressly directed us, as her attorneys, not to reveal her secrets to anyone. Not to Child Protective Services, not to the police, not to the DA. No one. Even if we could report her husband, we have no evidence of a crime, other than pictures Courtney claims to have seen on Jackson's laptop, which is not in her possession."

"But didn't the twins see the pictures too?"

"Yes, but think about it. Under no circumstance would I involve the twins. A criminal investigation would traumatize them far more than the pictures they didn't understand to begin with. So that leaves us with no other witnesses to corroborate the pictures. Jackson has not threatened her or the children. He will deny the pictures exist and claim Courtney is fabricating a false claim to gain some leverage in the divorce action."

"I don't like it but I understand what you are saying. So what do you think we should do?" Sally asked.

"I need time to think through this mess over the next few days. Damian, I want you to go down the wormhole and find out what this guy does when no one is watching."

"Got it."

"Sally, I want you to research our legal and ethical responsibilities to report knowledge of what may be criminal conduct we discovered committed by someone other than our client."

"On it."

"What I don't want is this case, which we agreed not to take, to become a distraction to our practice. I still want to exit gracefully. We have an important appellate brief due in Federal Court in two weeks. I would like you to review the record and have a draft for my review by the end of next week, Sally."

"Not a problem."

"Also, we are being consulted by a potential client looking for a firm to represent his hedge fund as the lead plaintiff in a large class action case. I am very, very interested in this case because it has a very high profile defendant and I believe strongly in the merits of the claims."

As Damian left my office, Sally got up, closed my office door and sat down again. "Chance, I'm sorry. You're right. I acted unprofessionally and put you in a difficult position. I just don't understand how men can act like such animals. I'm sickened by the thought of the girls looking at those videos of their father. I just kept thinking about Melody, when Courtney described those pictures."

"I knew you were thinking about Melody. I did too. Don't worry about it. I'll do my best to unwind this and still keep Roy happy. You know I appreciate your support of Courtney. You made her feel safe. I'm glad she confided in you. In regard to your question about men acting like animals, I think we forget, essentially, this is what we all are."

"Is that the excuse?"

"Not an excuse, an explanation. Our problem is, as opposed to other animals on this beautiful earth, the human species has, for better or for worse, developed the ability to ignore the laws of nature. We don't act instinctively or according to natural law. We have the ability to choose before we act. It's a gift and a curse. We can act out of love and generosity or commit the worst atrocities imaginable."

"The best and worst of human nature."

"Yes. Except there are no rules of nature we must follow. It is why we practice religions. It's why we live under the rule of law and recognize a higher order. But even when people act without any regard for the life of another, I believe in the truth of what Thomas Aquinas said when he wrote that all men know the difference between good and evil and are accountable. That is also part of our nature. That's why I believe in justice and why I became a lawyer."

I smiled. "Sorry for the speech. My altar boy roots are showing. It's been a long day for all of us. Are you and Melody still coming over for dinner on Saturday?"

I got a broad smile. "We wouldn't miss it."

Later that evening, I didn't feel any better about anything. I fed Tort and got into my sweats. Tort looked up from his bowl when he heard the sound of Zeppelin's *When the Levee Breaks* coming at full volume from my bedroom speakers. He was confused because I was hitting the heavy bag at night. I pounded the bag, throwing wild haymakers to the rhythm of John Bonham's thundering drum beat and Robert Plant's shrill pleading vocals:

If it keeps on raining, levee's going to break,
If it keeps on raining, levee's going to break,
When the levee breaks, I'll have no place to stay.

As I threw punches, I thought about Jackson and the pictures. I thought about the innocence of his young twin daughters. I thought about Sally's concern for Melody and how I wanted to protect my goddaughter from the dangers of living in a world with men like Jackson. I thought about being manipulated by Roy. And Randolph's distain for me and my firm.

As I pounded the bag, I lost track of time. When I was exhausted and drenched in sweat, I took off the gloves and noticed that my knuckles were bruised and bleeding.

I looked down at Tort. "Okay, buddy, I feel better now. Let's go for a walk."

CHAPTER ELEVEN
A GOOD PROBLEM

The next morning, I had scheduled a meeting with my accountant, Spencer. We needed to review my estimated tax payments based upon the windfall of the recent verdict.

I took the subway a few stops to his office in Brooklyn Heights. I always enjoy walking around the Heights, one of the most exclusive areas of Brooklyn and one subway stop from Manhattan. It has a beautiful promenade not far from Spencer's office that overlooks the East River and the surreal landscape of the towering buildings of lower Manhattan. Each new building looks like it is in a competition to be taller than the one next to it. A real life Legoland.

Brooklyn Heights still has cobblestone streets and beautiful townhouses dating back to the early 1800s. The Brooklyn Bridge was built in 1883 and its beautiful architectural spans stand today as they did when the Heights was first connected to the City. Brooklyn Heights has a mixture of wealthy Hassidic Jews, who can walk to the local synagogue, and prosperous young professionals who work in the financial district that used to be known as Wall Street. The old and the new living in the shadow of the big city.

Whenever I meet with Spencer, I leave time to pick up hummus, tabbouleh and falafel at my favorite Middle Eastern restaurant on Atlantic Avenue. I also pick up a box of rugelach at the Brooklyn Height's Deli on Henry Street to bring to his office.

Spencer is ten years younger than me. He went to college on a tennis scholarship, and he is still fit enough to compete in regional matches against the college kids. He has boyish good looks, blond hair, blue eyes and an easy smile. Similar to me, Spencer worked for one of the Big Eight accounting firms before he went out on his own. His clients are now a mixture of successful finance guys, small business owners and young professionals.

As he does in our poker games, Spencer exercises the right amount of caution and risk in advising his clients. He never plays "audit roulette" by being too aggressive, but he knows all the loopholes and the flexibility in the tax code to maximize deductions and minimize taxes without drawing scrutiny. His clients are well served, never audited and he has a thriving practice.

When I go to his office, I always bring him, and Julia, his assistant, cups of their favorite blends of Starbucks coffee with the box of rugelach and bag of Middle Eastern food. I make it a practice to come early to say hello and flirt with Julia, who sits up front outside Spencer's office. She was a former model and is drop dead gorgeous. She always thanks me for the ruggis and coffee with a big hug and kiss. The truth is, I don't really have to meet with Spencer in person to go over my taxes, but then I wouldn't get to see Julia and bask in her glow for a few minutes before Spencer and I sit down.

Neither Spencer nor Julia are married. I never asked Spencer about his relationship with Julia, and he's never volunteered. Hey, more power to him if he can bring his work home and that work happens to be a beautiful woman.

Julia brought me into Spencer's office, and I sat down in front of his desk. I looked at the tennis memorabilia on his walls, including autographed pictures of Serena Williams and Roger Federer. He keeps an unopened can of Wimbledon white tennis balls on his desk, next to a plaque that says: "Love Means Nothing to a Tennis Player."

"Thanks for the coffee, Chance. It's worse than heroin. I'm up to about eight cups a day, especially during tax season."

"You're welcome, Spencer. There are worse vices. By the way, I want you to be the first to know, Julia and I are getting married."

"She is a wonder. The whole package: looks, smarts and a sense of humor. But I don't think she is looking for a father figure. I hear AARP has a new dating site for people your age."

"Ouch! That really hurts. I guess I should return the engagement ring."

"So, you have a good problem. I love when my clients make too much money. I can raise my rates and not feel guilty. I did a *pro forma* of your projected income and estimated taxes, based upon the recent verdict you somehow fooled a jury into awarding you."

"Okay. Be gentle. How much is the pain?"

"Nothing you can't afford. You can pay the safe harbor amount, based upon last year's income taxes, and pay the balance in April when you file, or pay the full estimated amount now and not have to worry about paying the cash later. We have some time before the next estimated payment is due. I will give you the projections so you can think about it."

"No need. I have more money than I need to meet my expenses. I would rather pay the full amount now and not have to worry about coming up with a chunk of change next April. Just send me the amounts needed for the estimated payments. I already have the cash set aside. Also, I have to thank you. The pension plan you created for me is a wonder."

"You must have a good accountant. Are we on for poker Friday?"

"Yes. You better be there."

"Wouldn't miss it."

"Can you bring Julia?"

"You wish."

Before I left, I said, "Spencer, I have a new client who may need your help."

"Great. Who's the client?"

"It's someone Roy Brown asked me to represent. The daughter of a friend of his. He asked me to represent her in a divorce."

"What? Now you're a divorce lawyer? Why don't you just poke a stick in your eye instead?"

"Believe me, this is the last thing I want to do. I'm still trying to duck the case, but Roy has a relationship with the family and is putting a lot of pressure on me to help as a personal favor to him. It looks like a large asset divorce, and I think she may need your advice on tax planning in the future."

"That's odd. Roy knows you don't do matrimonial work. How can I help?"

"Her husband is an accountant with his own wealth management and tax consulting firm. His name is Jackson Malone. His firm is called Checkmate Consulting. Ever hear of them?"

"Nope, but there are more accountants in the City than even a CPA can count. Let me check his website."

Spencer looked at Jackson's website. "Not much here. He was with a big firm and jumped. It looks like Checkmate is in the offshore tax shelter business, which normally means he's walking a tightrope. I would be careful, if he falls, he might bring your client down with him. Good luck. If the wife needs my help, feel free to call me."

When I left Spencer's office, I hugged Julia goodbye and I thought about how I always felt better after I met with Spencer than before I walked in his office. I realized, as a client, this is the true sign of a good professional.

I also thought about Spencer's comments about Jackson walking a tightrope. I knew I didn't want to walk it with him.

CHAPTER TWELVE
THE COMMANDMENTS

I got back to the office after my meeting with Spencer around lunchtime. I stopped in to see Sally and find out how she was coming on the appellate brief. As I expected, she had things well in hand and would have a draft in a few days, way ahead of schedule.

Damian and I had planned to have lunch together. It was my turn to get lunch, and I ordered eggplant parm sandwiches, to be delivered from Ida Rose's. When the lunch came, we sat down in the conference room. We dug into the delicious sandwiches and enjoyed just eating together in silence. Eventually, Damian wiped his mouth. "So, what's your decision?"

"If you are talking about Courtney's case, I haven't made up my mind. Roy's putting the pressure on me. I am curious about what your thoughts are?"

Damian took another bite of his sandwich, and, as usual, thought for a while before he replied. "As you know, I don't like the case. I don't understand why it even came in the front door. I've been in battles and I've experienced the worst things people are capable of doing to each other. Few things shock me, but I want you to know I am very, very disturbed by the videos of child abuse. Jackson Malone has a dark soul. Sure, we can help her, but so can ten other lawyers. Why is this so important to Roy? I think if you take the case, you will regret it."

"Damian, I have all of the same reservations. To be honest I don't want the case but I don't want to lose Roy's firm's referrals, if I can help it. It wouldn't be fatal, but it would eventually hurt our bottom line. As troubling as the pictures are, I'm not at all sure we need to address them to settle the case. Courtney has directed us not to go there. Also, of all things, I now have Sally who is suddenly gung-ho to take the case. I will sit down with you and Sally before I make a decision. Where are you in vetting the husband?"

"I will have a preliminary report done by the end of the day. I can always dig deeper if we are retained."

"Great, that will be very helpful. Okay, what's the Best Of topic for today? I got these delicious heroes, so you better have a good topic ready."

"The Best of The Ten Commandments."

I put my sandwich down. I was surprised. Damian had never discussed his religious beliefs with me. I said, "Damian, what a great topic. You know you are up against a Jesuit-trained lapsed Catholic, right?"

"That's why I picked the topic, Chance. I did some things I'm not proud of during my service. There are no rules in warfare. It is existential. You either kill or you will be killed. We buried both our enemies and our mistakes. The good soldier is stripped of all humanity. I will tell you something I have never told anyone before."

I listened closely. People keep secrets for a reason. Whenever someone says that to me, it's inevitably about something they find very troubling.

"I never went to church as a kid, except maybe on Christmas. My family wasn't very religious. But after one unspeakably brutal fire fight, I just couldn't find myself. One of my SEALs saw I was obviously distressed and, without saying anything, he gave me a plastic card with the Hail Mary prayer written on it below a picture of the Virgin Mary. I read the prayer and was suddenly at peace. I still have the card. I memorized the prayer. Before every battle, I said silently to myself the last part, 'Holy Mary, Mother of God, pray for us sinners now and at the hour of our death. Amen.' I'm not even Catholic. I don't know if there is a God. But it gave me great solace to believe the mother of Jesus would forgive sinners, like me, at 'the hour of our death'. Who else would forgive me for the unspeakable things I was about to do?"

I was moved by Damian's story. It reminded me of the power of prayer in my own life. How just reciting certain words gave me strength and hope even after I stopped going to church.

"Do you think that, for a nonbeliever like me, saying the prayer before battle was wrong?"

"No, Damian, it wasn't wrong at all. I think if we can somehow keep our sense of right and wrong in the worst of circumstances, it's the best we can do. I was taught we're all sinners and we all want to be forgiven for our sins. That's what the Bible teaches. It shows you believe in the value of each person's life. Thank you for sharing this with me."

"Thanks for listening."

"Okay, now I'm interested, what's your choice for the Best of the Commandments?"

"My instinct is to say, 'Do unto others as you would have them do unto you,' but it's not even one of the Ten Commandments, is it? I think it should have been the first and only Commandment. It's an easy rule to remember, even if it's not always so easy to follow. Think of this world if we all just followed that one proverb. No hatred, no war, no crime."

"Damian, I agree. That proverb has existed in one form or another in every culture throughout history. It is not part of just one religion or culture. It is a recognition we are no better than how we treat our friends, strangers or even our worst enemies. Now how about picking one of the big ten actually on the hit parade?"

"Fine. As to the actual Ten Commandments, the one I believe is the best and most important is Thou Shalt Not Kill. Life is precious. Once you take a life you can't give it back. You live with that sin for the rest of your life."

I realized we were no longer just playing a game. Damian was revealing some very deep and personal feelings about his service and the sacrifice he had to make.

I respected his honesty. "I agree, life is precious, and 'Thou Shalt Not Kill' recognizes the sacredness of other people's lives, not just our own. You may be interested to learn the original translation was 'thou shalt not murder'. It recognized there are circumstances when it is necessary to kill to protect life. A just war is certainly one of those circumstances. The irony is that the bloodiest wars throughout history were 'holy wars', mostly waged by or against the Catholic Church."

"Chance, you know I always believed that I was fighting for the right reasons to protect my country. Your turn. What's your choice for the best Commandment?"

"It's a tough choice, but I think I would choose 'Thou Shalt Not Steal'. If you think about it, that Commandment somehow incorporates almost every other Commandment. You shouldn't steal someone's property. You shouldn't steal someone's life. You shouldn't steal another man's wife. You shouldn't steal someone's reputation by bearing false witness against him. It is, in many ways, the basis of all secular civil laws."

"I never thought of it that way, but I see how many things in life can be stolen."

"But whichever Commandment is best, I believe if we were to just simply follow the Ten Commandments, there would be no need for the countless other laws in the lawbooks. No need for lawyers, for that matter. I guess it's lucky for us there is never any shortage of sinners, or we would be out of a job."

When we got up after lunch, Damian and I were both drained from our heartfelt conversation. I put my arm around his shoulder. "Damian, you are a good man, but I think we have to find a game that's more fun to play at lunch."

He laughed out loud. "You know, I was just thinking the same thing. Maybe we should play Go Fish. But when you think about it, it's sorta the same game. You never really know what cards the other player is hiding."

CHAPTER THIRTEEN
THE NEW CLIENT

Before we made any decision on taking Courtney's case, she called the office and asked to make an appointment to come back in as soon as possible.

Roy had texted me twice, asking if we had been retained. I knew, as a courtesy, we owed it to Courtney, and Roy, to at least meet with her again, whether we accepted her as a client or not. Sally scheduled an appointment for late the next day.

I told Sally and Damian I wanted to meet with them and make a decision about Courtney's case before she came back in. I needed Sally to give me her research on the issue of reporting the suspected child abuse and Damian to give me some more detailed background on Jackson and his consulting business.

I texted Roy and told him Courtney had scheduled another meeting with us. He texted me back three smiley faces.

The next morning, we cleared our emails and calls, and sat down at the conference table. Sally had bought in a pot of coffee and our coffee cups.

Once we had each poured ourselves a cup of coffee and got comfortable, I started. "Okay, team, Courtney is coming back in this afternoon. I have to make a decision about her case before we meet with her. I would like to find out what your research disclosed and then get everyone's thoughts. Sally, do we have any legal or ethical obligation to report the suspected child abuse?"

"I researched the issue and I don't think as Courtney's attorneys we have any mandatory reporting requirement under New York Law. There is a New York statute mandating certain professionals, including nurses, teachers, police officers and childcare workers must report suspected abuse or neglect to the state hotline. Attorneys are not included."

"Any ethical considerations?"

"Ethically, the overriding concern is to protect the confidentiality of lawyer-client communication. Even though we have not been retained, the privilege still applies under New York Law to our meeting with Courtney in contemplation of her retaining our firm. There is no exception under the attorney-client privilege for suspected criminal activity by a third party. Courtney, of course, could waive the privilege and consent to our reporting her husband's suspected abuse anonymously to the state hotline."

"However," I said, "not only has she not consented, she has directed us, in no uncertain terms, not to disclose the information."

"I know. As a mother of a young girl, I want him hung. I'm not happy about it but it appears we are not required to report and we, in fact, can't report without Courtney's consent."

"Thanks, Sally. As usual, very helpful. Damian, where are we with Jackson Malone?"

"I did a preliminary background search on all the standard databases and social media sites on Jackson and his firm, Checkmate Consulting. He was an honors student and some sort of chess whiz in high school. He majored in finance, graduated at the top of his class at Columbia and is a CPA. He worked for a year or two at a major accounting firm. A number of years ago, he formed his own consulting firm, which is an off-shore corporation, specializing in tax planning, tax shelters and succession planning."

"That's consistent with what Roy told me."

"Got it. For a high-end consultant, his firm's website is pretty unimpressive. It has his bio, his contact information and a brief description of his firm's services. It indicates he has experience in both domestic and international tax planning and tax shelters. It doesn't list any employees or representative clients. It is interesting to note he is not on any social media sites, like Facebook, or business sites, not even LinkedIn."

"That's odd," Sally said.

"Agreed. I did a credit search. His credit is impeccable. Very little debt. No judgments or liens. He has a leased Mercedes 500 and a Range Rover I assume is Courtney's car. The NYC co-op where Courtney now lives with the twins is owned by both of them and has no mortgage. They have leased different homes in the Hamptons during the summers and enjoy the good life. Maybe too good."

I asked, "Why? What's wrong with the picture?"

"Their lifestyle just seems pretty rich, even for a successful tax accountant. Once I get his personal and business returns, I can take a deep dive through more sophisticated search engines into his finances. If it wasn't for the pictures on his laptop, I would think Roy is right, and this is a pretty vanilla divorce, if everyone cooperates. It appears there is more than enough here to make everyone happy."

"Great. A good start. If we go forward, we can serve a document demand, asking for copies of the husband's personal and business tax returns, bank statements and financial statements. Now let's make a decision before Courtney comes back in. Here are my thoughts. I don't want this case. I think it's a mistake to take it. I hate to break a promise I made to you, Sally, and myself for a very good reason a long time ago. Having said that, I think we should do Roy the favor and represent Courtney."

At the same time, Damian shook his head and Sally nodded.

"We can get by without his firm's business, but I would rather keep the relationship if we can. Tell me what you guys think."

Damian said, "So we take the case and just ignore the pictures?"

"I don't like the pictures, but we don't really know what they prove. We don't know who took them or where they were taken. We don't really know how old these girls are. Courtney looked at them only briefly and, understandably, she was very upset and disgusted by what she saw. She could be mistaken about the ages of these girls. A young-looking eighteen-year-old could look sixteen. Every divorce has an ugly secret. If we represent Courtney our responsibility is to make sure that she and the twins are protected and well provided for after the divorce."

"How do you expect to protect them if this bad guy has a get out of jail free card?"

"By cutting him loose as quickly as possible. I think he will pay a price for his sins eventually. I want Courtney divorced and protected before he takes a fall. If criminal proceedings are brought against Jackson as a sex offender, it will be the end of his career and his reputation. Not only Jackson, but Courtney and the twins would pay a big price. They all would suffer shame and humiliation as well as the loss of their financial security."

"That makes sense. Cut a quick deal that protects Courtney and let Jackson sink on his own," Sally said.

"Exactly. If Jackson is not a threat to his family, for all I care he can live with his demons until after they are divorced. Then he can burn in hell." I turned to Sally and said, "So, it's a real nightmare divorce. Do you still think we should represent Courtney?"

"I do. You know my original feelings, but I changed my mind when I met Courtney. I understand the responsibilities of being a single mother. I can empathize with her concern for her daughters and their futures. I understand the fear she is feeling, losing her marriage and learning very troubling things about the father of her children. This guy frightens me. You have to make sure no one, especially the children, will be hurt."

"You know I will do everything necessary to make sure Courtney and the children are protected. Damian?"

Damian was clearly still not on board. He took his time before speaking. "We shouldn't touch this case. Apart from the fact that we don't need the work, I'm uneasy about why Roy referred it to us. I don't like the veiled threats he made if you don't do him this favor. I'm not sure what his agenda is, but I know you don't ask for a favor and then demand it to be done. Don't fool yourself, Courtney was a pediatric nurse. She knows how old the girls in the video were. That being said, I'm part of this team and I will be guided by both you as to what you believe we should do. I will support your decision. But, for the record, my instincts tell me it's a big mistake."

"Okay, I don't disagree but I don't want to waste any more time on this. I'm still very ambivalent, but I've made a decision. Sally, draft up a retainer agreement and client bill of rights for Courtney to sign when she comes in. We need a large retainer. Her husband can afford it."

Sally said, "I'll get right on it."

"Also, we haven't done a divorce case in a while. Sally, make sure the retainer forms are up to date. Also, give me a memo on any relevant changes to the Domestic Relations Law we should be aware of. Damian, put together a schedule of preliminary discovery we need to complete our due diligence. Sally, I would like you to sit in on the conference with Courtney this afternoon. Damian, you can gear up after we are retained."

Damian said, "Got it."

Courtney came alone to our second meeting. She had on jeans, a simple red sweater and the same shining gold cross. I noticed she still wore her wedding band. Today, it was Sally who met her at the front door and Courtney gave her a hug when she came in. They walked into the conference room together and sat next to each other across from me. Courtney seemed anxious and her fingers absently rubbed the cross hanging around her neck.

I said, "How are you?"

"Everything is about the same. Jackson has now rented an apartment near our co-op. He continues to pay all our bills and sees the girls when he is in town, which is less and less often. I have been very anxious to meet with you again and find out if you will be my lawyer. I can't stand treading water any longer. I feel like I'm sinking."

"Well, I have some good news. We have done our conflict check and there are no conflicts we are aware of. We would be happy to represent you if you would like to retain our firm."

"Thank God! I've been a wreck!" She grabbed Sally's arm. "I was worried sick you didn't want to take my case. I want to retain you immediately and get on with my life."

"Courtney, before we go forward, I'm just wondering, have you had any discussions with your father about our representing you? He had some pretty strong reservations about me and that we aren't the right firm for you."

"Don't worry about my dad. I told him it is my decision and my mind is made up. Besides, I think Roy spoke to him after our meeting and persuaded him you're the right lawyer for me."

I wasn't convinced Courtney's father was on board. Also, I wasn't thrilled about Roy communicating with my client's father when his firm was representing her husband.

I kept those thoughts to myself. "Great. We look forward to working together with you. We will use our best efforts to resolve this case quickly and in a favorable fashion. Roy has assured me the partner from his firm representing Jackson will negotiate in good faith. I don't expect any litigation. If we can finalize a separation agreement, we can file for an uncontested divorce, and you will never have to step foot in a courtroom other than for a preliminary conference, early on."

"What about the twins? You know that's all I care about."

"Roy said your husband recognizes you should have physical custody of the girls. It's not really much of a concession. As the primary caretaker, you would be granted custody by the court anyway. Unless you object, Jackson would have the right to be consulted regarding major decisions affecting the girls and he would be entitled to visitation on a regular basis."

"Of course. I want him to be involved in the girls' lives. He's their father."

"If there is no issue as to custody and parenting, all the rest is about money. We will get all of the financial information necessary for you to make decisions as to a fair property settlement and your right to support under New York Law. I don't foresee you or the girls will ever be in need or have to make any financial sacrifices for the rest of your lives."

"I'm so relieved. How soon can I be divorced?"

"I would like to see you divorced as soon as possible. As soon as you and your husband sign a separation agreement, we can submit the uncontested divorce papers. You should have a divorce judgment within a month after the papers are submitted. Has your husband agreed to pay your fees?"

"My father said he didn't want me to ask Jackson for anything until we have a deal. He wants to pay my legal fees."

"That's very generous, and your father should feel free to give you and the girls any gifts he wants to, but for a number of reasons I would prefer your husband gives you the funds to pay your own fees. You should both be on a level playing field. Also, as I already discussed with your father, I don't want there to be any suggestion he is retaining our firm."

"I understand."

"Great. If you're comfortable, we would like to start by learning more about the history of your relationship with Jackson and your marriage."

Courtney paused. "Fine, but I don't want to talk about the pictures."

I said, "No pictures."

She looked relieved. She said to Sally. "Good. It's a long story. We were high school sweethearts."

Sally said, "Take your time. We like love stories."

Courtney smiled sadly. "Funny you should say that. In the beginning it was a real love story. We were both raised in Mamaroneck, but on different sides of the tracks. My family lived in a big colonial home on the sound and Jackson lived in an apartment his parents rented in an area called the flats. I was an only child and had everything you could dream of. I was an honors student and a cheerleader."

"Sound's perfect," Sally said, even though I sensed Courtney's childhood was not really a fairy tale.

Courtney's eyes teared up.

Sally gave her a glass of water and pushed the tissue box over to her.

"Thank you. The truth is, my childhood was anything but perfect. You saw my father, he is very domineering and volatile. He loves me and my children and has been very generous to us, but both my mother and I have always been frightened of him. When he becomes angry, especially after he has been drinking, he becomes extremely abusive and threatening. He drinks every day."

Having met Randolph, I wasn't surprised. "It must have been tough for you."

"We never knew when the explosion would come. My mother was the target and I was the peacemaker. I thought I had to be perfect to keep the peace. We lived with the uncertainty of stepping on a land mine that might set him off. Books were my escape and refuge."

"I'm sorry," Sally said. "I'm sure it was hard to be perfect and invisible at the same time. Listening for your father's footsteps and never knowing who would show up."

"You can't imagine. Do you know what my father does for a vacation every year?" She asked me.

"I have no idea, but my guess would be a golf outing."

"No. He goes to a ten-thousand-acre ranch in Argentina and shoots doves."

"I don't understand. He shoots *doves*?"

"They breed doves by the thousands and the guests at the *estancia* go out with their shotguns and shoot hundreds of them."

"Why?" Sally asked.

"The thrill of competing to kill the most doves. It's reprehensible. He takes pictures of the doves he kills."

"I don't really know what to say. I'm not sure I understand the psyche of a person who kills defenseless doves with a shotgun for sport. I'm sorry you suffered such unhappiness growing up."

"Thank you, Mr. Cormac."

"Please, just call me Chance."

"Chance, I'm sure many kids had it much worse, but for me it was a nightmare. Anyway, I don't know why I am talking about my parents, other than maybe to explain I have lived my life under the influence of very strong and domineering men. You must think I'm very weak not to stand up to my father or Jackson."

"Just the opposite. I have seen you stand up to your father at a time when it would be very easy to let him take over. He wants to punish Jackson, but you are determined to do what's best for you and your children. That takes real courage in a divorce."

"I hope I can be strong, but sometimes I have no idea what to do or where I am going. I'm really lost. I am so relieved to have you and Sally here to help me. Anyway, Jackson and I were always in the same classes but didn't start dating until the end of senior year. All I knew was that he was bright but a loner. I had heard he had won some chess tournaments."

"So he was your first love?" Sally said.

"He was. I dated some kids from our country club, but never had a serious relationship before Jackson. Somehow during the winter of our senior year we were on a class trip to a Broadway show in New York City and ended up sitting together on the crowded bus on the ride home. It was warm and cozy on the bus and we started talking like we'd known each other our whole lives."

Sally smiled and nodded encouragingly.

"I had never been so comfortable with anyone before. He was just so smart, confident and attentive. He made me feel like he understood me just by looking in my eyes. I told him of my love of literature and how JD Salinger was one of my favorite authors. How I dreamed of being part of the Glass family and a sister of Holden, Franny and Zooey. As dysfunctional as they were, they led exciting and romantic lives."

Sally said, "Everyone loved Holden. The lost, sensitive soul."

"Jackson won me over when he said, 'Do you remember Holden's first girlfriend, Jane? Her stepfather was an abusive alcoholic. Holden loved her and wanted to protect her in his own way. I remember they played chess together. Maybe you need someone to love and protect you.' I was touched. I said, 'I do. Jackson, I heard you're a genius at chess. Will you teach me to play?' Jackson laughed. 'I'll be happy to teach you, but I won't be able to keep my eyes on the board.' I said, 'You better not let me win!' And then I don't know why but I told him about how my father was an alcoholic and how miserable my life was."

"You trusted him with your secrets," Sally said.

"I did. He understood me. He said, 'You have everything money can buy except happiness. I have none of those things but am equally unhappy. Maybe somehow we could find the things we need together.' Nobody had ever really understood me before. By the time we got off the bus, we knew we were made for each other."

Sally smiled sadly.

"My parents were furious when we started going steady. My father, in one of his rages, called Jackson a born loser from a loser family with no future. But it didn't matter what he said. We were in love. I don't know what happened, I don't know what changed. Jackson has everything he ever wanted but now it's not good enough. I'm sacred he's spinning out of control."

"Hopefully he still cares for you and the girls and wants to do the right thing. Courtney, tell us, how did you decide to become a nurse?" Sally asked.

"When we applied to college, I still had dreams of being a writer and wanted to apply to a liberal arts college and major in English. My father forbade it. He said an English degree was worthless and his daughter should be a professional. I didn't have the resolve, or financial ability, to fight him. I gave up my dream of becoming an author and attended NYU to become a pediatric nurse. I love children and knew I would be a good nurse. My father wasn't happy with this choice, either. He said nurses were only good for changing bed pans, but he eventually gave in and paid for it."

"Where did you practice?" I asked.

"When I graduated, I became a pediatric nurse at Sloane Kettering Hospital, caring for children with cancer. Later I became a Nurse Practitioner. I loved my job and became very attached to my patients. Parents thanked me for sitting in bed with their frightened children and singing or reading to them after my shift was over. As hard as it was, I always attended the funerals of my patients who we lost."

"Your patients were lucky to have you as their nurse," Sally said.

"And Jackson?" I asked. "We know he went to Columbia and was originally with a big accounting firm in the City."

"Jackson got a full ride and majored in finance. Without my parent's knowledge, most of the time I lived with Jackson in his apartment, not my dorm room. I never felt so free. When Jackson graduated, he immediately got an offer to join a prestige firm. He worked long hours and sat for his CPA exams, which he said were a breeze. With CPA after his name, Jackson became more acceptable to my parents, but he was never made to feel at home with my family."

"And he proposed?" Sally asked.

"Yes. Jackson wanted to elope but I couldn't do that to my parents. We had an elaborate wedding and lavish reception at the Westchester Country Club. It was really a vanity project so my parents could impress their friends at the club. They made Jackson and his family feel like out-of-town guests at his own wedding. You know, maybe that's the one insult he could never forgive them for."

Courtney was quiet for a few moments and changed the subject. "When the twins were born, I couldn't work with terminally ill children anymore and stopped working. Their suffering was now too close to home."

"When did Jackson start his own firm?"

"He left after three years at the CPA firm. I'm sorry to say I know very little about Jackson's business or our finances. He told me the firm didn't appreciate his talents and that he could do much better on his own. He was concerned at first because under his employment agreement, he couldn't take his clients with him."

"He had a covenant not to compete?"

"Yes, that was what he called it. He consulted a number of attorneys, who advised him against violating his agreement. They said it would be illegal and unethical. He would be sued and his reputation would be ruined. Finally, he sat down with my father. My father had no problem with Jackson stealing the firm clients. He told Jackson, 'Screw the firm. A client should be free to choose who he wants as an accountant.' Dad suggested Jackson speak with Roy Brown. He told Jackson that Roy had a reputation as an attorney who gets deals done."

"Is Roy Brown a good friend of your father's?"

"I wouldn't say so. Roy is not my father's attorney. They golf together on occasion and we see Roy and his wife at club functions. Roy and his wife were invited to our wedding, but so was almost every other member of the club. At any rate, Jackson met with Roy and was ecstatic. Roy told Jackson everything he wanted to hear. He said he admired Jackson for having the courage to go out on his own. He said most lawyers and accountants make poor businessmen because they can't stand risk."

"Wasn't Jackson afraid the firm would come after him?"

"No, Roy assured him that if it was done the right way, the firm wouldn't confront him for stealing their clients. Roy said it was too much of an embarrassment for a large firm to create a dispute involving a former client. I remember Jackson telling me that Roy said, 'Business is purely existential. There is no right or wrong. Only profit or loss.' I guess he was right, because Jackson's old firm never went after him. Roy helped Jackson form Checkmate on an island somewhere and he now has clients all over the world. He became very successful. I don't know much about his clients, or what Jackson does for them."

"There's no reason you should."

"I do know Jackson pays Roy both legal and consulting fees and Jackson doesn't make any business decisions without consulting Roy. Jackson likes to say kiddingly he and Roy are partners in crime. I am sure Roy could tell you much more about Checkmate and Jackson's clients. You must think I am pretty pathetic not knowing more about our finances or my husband's business."

"Not at all. You had no reason to be concerned about those things. You relied on your husband to provide for you and your children, and he did. You have been very helpful. Don't worry about the finances. We will investigate Jackson's income and assets in order to arrive at a fair settlement proposal. Roy promised to cooperate fully. The good news is, you are very lucky your husband is successful, and you and your children will be well provided for after your divorce. Do you have any other questions for us today?"

Courtney hesitated. "Before I leave, is it possible for me to sit with Sally for a few minutes. There are a few things I would be more comfortable discussing with her alone."

"Of course. Stop in my office before you leave."

About twenty minutes later, Sally and Courtney came into my office. Courtney thanked me and I told her we would be in contact with her shortly after I spoke to Roy in order to discuss how best to proceed.

After seeing Courtney to the door, Sally came into my office, shut the door and sat down.

"Anything I should know?"

"Courtney didn't feel comfortable discussing certain things with you in the conference room. She feels embarrassed and guilty. But I could use your male perspective."

"I'm glad she could confide in you. Exactly why I rely on you. Did she give you permission to discuss with me what she told you?"

"Yes. She wants you to know. Neither she nor Jackson had ever had an intimate relationship before they started going out at the end of high school. They were both naïve but they were soon making love whenever they could find some privacy. After they got married, they had a pretty good sex life and Jackson was very loving. Things changed after the twins were born. When the twins were a few months old, Jackson started revealing to Courtney some of his sexual fantasies. He told her when he was in high school, he used to think about the white panties and bras under the young girls' dresses and pleasure himself in bed at night thinking about them."

"Pretty adolescent fantasies."

"If you say so. Except he then started asking Courtney to play out these sexual fantasies by dressing up like a schoolgirl. Plaid miniskirts. White panties. Pigtails. He asked Courtney to sit on a chair and spread her legs while he pleasured himself in front of her. Courtney was very uncomfortable with these requests but didn't know how to say no. Soon, the only way he would have sex with her was if he penetrated her anally. He claimed she wasn't 'tight enough' after the babies were born. Finally, when Courtney felt dirty and found these requests too disturbing, she refused to engage in his fantasies. After that, they rarely had any relations at all."

"She stood up for herself."

"Yes, but Courtney now feels guilty. She wonders, if she had accommodated her husband, might he not have lived out his fantasies with the young girls on the videos? She has been too ashamed to speak to anyone about Jackson's sexual demands or their failing marriage until now."

"I'm glad she spoke to you. What did you say?"

"I told her I am not a therapist, but my personal belief is consenting adults can engage in any sexual activity they want as long as both parties consent and no one gets hurt. I said she was justified in not agreeing to engage in sexual activities she found disturbing. Jackson's need to fulfill these fantasies with other people was his decision. If he abused underage girls to satisfy his urges, he is a deviant and a criminal. I said she was not responsible for his needs or actions. I suggested she speak with a good therapist to resolve these issues."

"Sally, you are a real gift to our clients. I am glad she opened up to you. No male perspective is needed. This guy's a creep. He was damaged goods before they ever met. But, that said, unless she tells us differently, we are going to try to keep the abuse allegations out of the divorce."

"I agree. Let's get her to the finish line and get this guy out of her life."

After Sally left, I called Roy. "I thought you would like to know we are being retained by Courtney Malone."

"Chance, that's great news! Just great! I knew I could count on you. I really appreciate the favor. As you are aware, Clay Campbell will be handling Jackson's divorce case for our firm. He has his marching orders to cooperate and negotiate not only a fair but a very generous settlement for Courtney and the children. If at any time there is any problem with Clay, feel free to call me and I will help resolve it right away."

"Roy, thanks, but I don't think it's necessary for you to be involved."

"I want to help. By the way, I was consulted by the general counsel for a large hedge fund that apparently is considering using you for a major class action. I gave you a stellar recommendation. I told them you are good friend and the best trial lawyer I know. I didn't know you're interested in doing some class action cases. Of course, we would be happy to keep you in mind for class action work in the future. Now let's get this divorce case settled."

There was nothing about the conversation with Roy I felt good about. Roy was now somehow taking credit for the class action client he had nothing to do with originating. He wasn't a "good friend" and wasn't acting like one. I took a breath. "Roy, thanks for the recommendation. I look forward to working with your partner. I am sure we will have some questions about Jackson's consulting business you will be able to help us with."

"Absolutely. Anything you need to know. See you at the game Friday night."

CHAPTER FOURTEEN
THE GOOD BOOK

I had lunch with Damian after the second meeting with Courtney and brought him up to speed.

I said, "Guess what Randolph Gault likes to do?"

"Other than yell at you, I'm not sure."

"He likes to shoot doves."

"What? Like shooting pigeons in the park?"

"No. He goes to a luxury ranch in Argentina that breeds doves and shoots hundreds of them with a shotgun."

"Why in the world would he do that?"

"It's a sport. He tries to kill more birds than the other guests."

"It's not a sport unless the doves shoot back. That's a pretty twisted hobby."

"Yup. Unfortunately, that sort of sums up Randolph Gault and the type of father Courtney grew up with. She suffered because he's an alcoholic and was often abusive when he drinks."

"This is the case that just keeps on giving."

"I know. My concern is not what it gives but what it will take. I need to focus on this new class action case. I need you guys to carry the load on Courtney's divorce until after I meet with the new client. Sally is preparing a net worth affidavit for Courtney, and I want you to start investigating Jackson's assets and his consulting business."

"Got it. Do what you have to do."

I was finally free to prepare for the meeting with the new client. Class actions are big business for lawyers. Some of the largest judgments ever recorded are in class actions. The fees for representing the plaintiffs can be staggering. The only problem was, I knew nothing about class action law and even less about trying a class action case.

I wasn't worried about trying the case. A trial is a trial. What I had to do was some heavy lifting in a short amount of time to research the law on class action claims and understand the procedural requirements for certifying a class. I didn't mind. I'm a quick study and I was pretty sure I would be up to speed as to how these cases were litigated before the meeting. I was looking forward to the challenge of learning something new about the law at this stage in my career.

Why would I even meet with a potential client looking for an attorney to handle a very substantial class action when I have no experience in that area of the law? The reason, believe it or not, is simply because I love to read books. I don't watch TV, except cartoons with Melody. I rarely go to movies, plays or a museum. Instead, I read books. I read to relax, escape and learn things about how different authors see our world.

I will only read new hardcover books. Real books printed with ink that can sit up straight on a shelf. I like the feel of the paper as I turn a page and the ability to dog-ear a corner to keep my place. I will read almost anything but my favorite books, as you might suspect, are about the law, lawyers, and criminals.

I have read anything and everything written by Michael Connelly, Cormac McCarthy, Elmore Leonard, George Pelecanos, and Don Winslow. Of course, I also have read all of Hunter Thompson's many *Fear and Loathing* books chronicling the political corruption of this country. My problem is, every time I add a new author to my reading list, I have to read every book they have ever written. One would think that the last thing a lawyer would want to do is read books about the law in his spare time, but I can't get enough of it.

I had just finished a fascinating book, *Bad Blood* by John Carreyrou, in one sitting a few months before I got the call about the class action case. The book is non-fiction, but read like a Sherlock Holmes mystery. The author is a reporter for the *Wall Street Journal*. He first wrote an exposé about a company called Theranos and its founder, Elizabeth Holmes. He later expanded his articles into a bestselling book.

I was fascinated because the book is a real life crime story that reads like a fairy tale with an evil, baby-faced princess who casts a spell on her followers. It's about a magic box invented by the evil princess and her Svengali, who sell their souls for fame and fortune. The story is about selling high-tech snake oil that defrauded investors and jeopardized the health and lives of thousands of people.

In the end, it is the same old morality tale about the evils of greed, gluttony and deception, set in the modern world of bio-tech. Like a good trial lawyer, Carreyrou meticulously built a case against the corrupt CEO, avaricious lawyers and a gold plated board of directors who were happy to turn a blind eye to a massive fraud for their own personal gain.

Thanks in large part to the relentless investigation by the author and his exposure of the criminal fraud committed by Theranos, the last chapter of the book was written by a federal court judge. The founder, Holmes, was convicted in Federal Court of four counts of criminal fraud. So was her Svengali lover. They will both serve hard time. The stock of the public company became worthless, and the investors lost all their money. A multitude of civil actions are pending against the company, the founders and other responsible parties. Just like all good fairy tales, the wolf in sheep's clothing met her well-deserved fate.

Sometime after the conviction of the CEO, a representative of a group of hedge funds who had invested in Theranos and were defrauded contacted me to discuss my possible representation of the group in a potential class action.

I was surprised but intrigued by the possibility of adding my own chapter to the book that was already written. I like cases where the defendants already wear black hats. The hedge funds understood I was not a class action attorney, but they were impressed by my large jury verdicts in fraud and corruption cases. They wanted a litigator, not a class action attorney. Someone who could and would actually try the case.

Theranos was insolvent and any recovery would have to be recovered from the founder, her paramour, the board of directors and the attorneys the book disclosed intimidated witnesses and helped perpetrate the fraud.

I knew I would be in a dog fight from the first round until someone was knocked out. Just my kind of case. I was excited by what could be a very high profile case, the righteousness of the claims and, of course, the potential large fee. Even better, the hard work and script for the claims were already written in crayon in *Bad Blood*.

The criminal conviction of the founder made a civil verdict against her and the company almost a certainty. Ironically, the company name,

Theranos, was a combination of "therapy" and "diagnosis" but when the same word is spoken in Greek, it means "death". I looked forward to having the founder and her company pay for their sins. It was a case I wanted.

A conference on the potential class action was scheduled at our office with Dylan Moore, the managing partner of Constellation Partners, the lead hedge fund, and Bob Balaban, his general counsel.

Sally and Damian were preoccupied with Courtney's case and I told them I didn't need them to attend the meeting or gear up in the class action unless we were retained. They knew I was excited about the case but because of my lack of experience it was a long shot we actually would be retained. Just before the meeting, I went into Sally's office. "Well, wish me luck. I know just enough not to totally embarrass myself."

Sally said, "Go work your magic."

I laughed. "It will have to be a real good trick because I don't know the first thing about class actions."

Constellation was a five billion dollar hedge fund. They had invested a total of $100MIL in Theranos though the A and B private equity funding rounds and the IPO when the stock went public. They were the single largest hedge fund investor and had been authorized to act as the representative for other hedge funds to explore legal remedies for the group. The total amount invested by their group of hedge funds was in excess of $250MIL.

As usual, I met Dylan and his counsel at the office front door. Dylan was trim, average height, and looked very unassuming. He had jet black hair, a stubble beard, and very intense brown eyes. He was dressed in blue jeans, a black tee shirt, a zip up UNTUCKit sweatshirt and Adidas running shoes. Dylan exhibited a quiet confidence and was obviously unconcerned about impressing people with his appearance even though his fund managed billions of dollars.

In contrast, his counsel, Bob Balaban, wore a blue pinstripe suit, a white shirt and a red Zegna tie and pocket square. After our introductions, Dylan immediately went over, bent down and gave Tort a good scratch behind his ears. I liked him already. People who are kind to my dog are my kind of people. We all got some coffee in the kitchen and went into the conference room, where I had started a fire.

I had checked the Constellation website and learned Dylan was thirty-two, had gone to Harvard undergrad and later received an MBA from Harvard Business School. He was a whiz kid who was named managing partner for Constellation at the age of thirty, due to his superb finance and management skills.

After we sat down, he said, "Cozy office you have here, Chance. I have been trying to convince my partners there is no longer any need for our firm to maintain any physical offices in high-rise luxury buildings in cities scattered around the world. The future is people working remotely from home in New York, Bangkok or Bali. All that is needed is good Wi-Fi reception. The economic advantages are all too obvious, decreasing overhead, improving productivity and morale. I did some of my best trades from my dorm room in college. I hear you live upstairs so it appears you are already ahead of the curve."

"It works very well for me, and it makes it easy for me to walk Tort, who you met outside. Also, I don't play particularly well with others. How can we help you?"

"Chance, I never get emotionally involved in our firm's investments. We make money and we lose money. Fortunately, we make more money than we lose. A losing investment is part of doing business, but this case is different. I take my fiduciary obligations to my investors very seriously. When you lose your own money, it is one thing, but when you lose other people's money in a company built on smoke and mirrors it is gut wrenching."

Dylan's counsel gave a weary nod but said nothing.

"We have very sophisticated systems and a matrix in place to assess risk before we invest. A primary consideration in making a private equity investment is the expertise and integrity of the management team. We rely on them to do what is best for the company and the investors. Of course we vet them heavily. But it turns out, the CEO and management team of Theranos, despite their pedigrees, were very bad people. They have no conscience and no shame. We were lied to and defrauded, but even worse, we have been publicly embarrassed by failing to protect our investors. We can exercise poor judgment, but we can't be made to look like fools."

His counsel folded his hands and just nodded again.

"But they made a serious mistake in judgment by underestimating me and my firm. I know they are wounded but we want them put down. Not only the CEO, but every culpable party has to be held accountable to the investors. I want them to feel the pain and humiliation of a public civil trial exposing their corruption. They must be held responsible for their misconduct. We want them to pay, and pay dearly. It is important to our investors. It's important for our firm's reputation. It is important for my reputation."

"Dylan, I get it. You made a bad investment in bad people. I was fascinated when I read *Bad Blood*. It's an amazing job of investigative reporting and the bible for your case. The criminal conviction goes a long way in establishing liability in your class action. The fraud and criminal conduct by this CEO and her company was egregious. They defrauded investors, but even worse, they put people's lives at risk to live the rock star life. But I wouldn't beat myself up if I was you. Your firm was not the only one deceived. You were in good company with $4.5BIL in Theranos stock now worthless."

"Chance, that all may be true, but we're not some yahoos fresh off the bus. We have the most sophisticated bio-tech guys in the world at our firm. It is inconceivable Holmes created a company that was just a house of cards and we were completely suckered in. We were made to look like clowns with our pants down around our ankles. We failed to do the necessary due diligence. We should have known better than to get snowed by amateurs with an unproven technology and an inexperienced CEO. We made real rookie mistakes. What the fuck, this wasn't our first rodeo."

"Dylan, I appreciate your frustration. It's always easy, in hindsight, to see what appears obvious now. But remember it took years of investigation by a relentless reporter before this fraud was uncovered. The truth is, this con was very elaborate and not easily detected. First of all, the CEO had good credentials. The company had clinical trial results conducted by what appeared to be independent labs confirming the efficacy of the equipment and test results. She had a gold plated board of directors including Henry Kissinger, George Shultz, William Perry and the former Director of the CDC, who shilled for her. She had not one, but two, national drug store chains who contracted to do blood tests in their stores using her product. Imagine that for one minute."

"It's shameful. Chance, they were doing blood tests on patients with a device that was no more effective than a box of tissues."

"The idea was good," I said. "Unfortunately it was too good to be true. The invention didn't work. It never did. The technology and the blood tests were all faked and worthless. She endangered the lives of everyone who relied on the test results from her equipment. There was an elaborate cover-up and when the truth was eventually revealed by disgruntled employees, the company attorneys threatened and intimidated the employees to keep quiet, like mob enforcers. Of course, like most good conmen, or in this case conwoman, the founder was a sociopath. She is the best kind of swindler, but the worst kind of human being. She had one good skill, she was an accomplished liar. You guys made a mistake, but it was understandable. Be assured, I would be happy to put a stake in the heart of everyone responsible when a jury renders its verdict."

"Chance, that's exactly what I wanted to hear. I am very impressed by you, your knowledge of the case and your track record in securing large verdicts from juries for your clients. I know you are not a class action attorney, but my group wants this case tried. We want these people cross examined and exposed in open court. I want them to be publicly humiliated and go down for the count. My understanding is you might be willing to structure your fees on a blended structure, with a reduced hourly rate and a contingency payment upon recovery."

"I like to have skin in the game. Especially in a case like this. Of course, in a class action the court has final authority to approve my fees at the end of the case."

"Great. Bob has a few questions, but I would like you to send me a fee proposal I can review with our investor group. We are interviewing a few other firms, but I like you and am going to strongly recommend we retain you."

Bob asked me the same logistical questions I am asked by every potential client in a big case. How can we litigate against a large 500 man firm? How can we handle discovery and massive document production? What happens if I get sick? Who would try the case? Do I have any other cases that would preclude me from focusing my attention on this matter?

I told Bob I was healthy and planned to devote my full attention to their case if I was retained. A large firm has no advantage because in my opinion one seasoned trial attorney, a paralegal and an investigator are worth ten large firm associates. Most class action attorneys have never tried a case in their lives. We use sophisticated online companies for discovery support and digesting documents. In the end it is more productive and cost efficient. I have the best investigator and IT expert in the business.

Bob seemed satisfied. I gave Dylan and Bob my business card, which had my cell phone number on it. Dylan looked at the card. He turned it over as if he was holding an ancient relic and laughed. He said, "I like it. Very old school. But just what am I supposed to do with this since I haven't carried a wallet since I bought my first iPhone?"

I laughed and thought maybe Damian was right. I had become a dinosaur.

On the way out, I thanked Dylan and Bob for giving me the opportunity to meet with them. I told them I looked forward to working together. I introduced Dylan and Bob to Sally and Damian on the way out. Before he left, Dylan bent down on one knee and gave Tort another scratch behind the ears. On the way out the door he said, "Good pooch."

It was a nice morning and, after sitting in a conference room for over two hours, I decided to get some fresh air to clear my head. I put Tort on his leash and, before going out, stopped to speak with Sally. I knew she was interested in how the meeting went.

Sally said, "So did you work your magic?"

I said the case was a monster, but I thought the meeting went reasonably well. Sally, sensing my excitement, said, "Enough with the false modesty. You were in there for over two hours. Are they signing us up or not?"

I laughed. "They would be fools not to!"

I asked Sally to email a proposed retainer agreement, leaving the names of the clients blank for the time being. I told her to include a blended fee structure with a reduced hourly rate and a 20% contingency on any amount recovered. I said to ask for a $100,000 retainer, which I knew was nothing more than a rounding error for these hedge fund guys.

Also, before we could be retained, I needed Sally to get from Bob the names and contact information for all the investors who Dylan was representing and would be named as plaintiffs so we could do a conflict check.

Next, I went into Damian's office and told him about the meeting. I said I didn't think we had to set up a war room just yet, but he should anticipate we would hit the ground running in a week or so if we were retained. He said, "Got it. I'll be locked and loaded when you need me."

As Tort and I walked to the park, I took a deep breath. My area of Brooklyn has a smell to it that is all its own. It is a mixture of fresh coffee, exhaust fumes, drying pavement and the aroma of food being cooked in every kind of ethnic city restaurant and store. As we walked down the street, I heard the sounds of the late city morning – the horns and sirens, music from store speakers and children laughing and playing in school yards.

Lost in my thoughts, I looked down and noticed Tort was trotting quickly just to keep up with me. I was more excited than I realized. I wanted this case. It was an opportunity to try a class action, teach some bad people a lesson and generate significant fees for the firm. The case would get a lot of media attention and elevate our firm's prestige. I just hoped I had hooked the whale.

As we walked, I started singing Steve Miller's *Kow Kow Calculator* out loud to Tort.

Kow Kow Calculator
Sure was a smooth operator
Had himself a pet alligator
Kept it in a chrome elevator, yeah

I'm not sure what the lyrics mean, but they felt right. Tort strutted down the road next to me. His tail was wagging in time to the music. At least he seemed to enjoy my singing. I said to him, "Who needs a pet alligator when you can have a dog like Tort?"

***

Early the morning after my meeting with Dylan and Bob, I got up still thinking about the potential big case. I meditated to John Mayer's haunting version of *Last Train Home*. Mayer is perhaps the most underrated rock guitarist in the world. In my mind he would be on the list of the Ten Best Guitarists. His solo on *Last Train* is transcendent and was a perfect background for my meditation.

When I finished meditating, I put on the light twelve-ounce gloves. Boxing gloves come in different sizes. They typically weigh between twelve and sixteen ounces. The heavier the glove is, the bigger it is. You wouldn't think a few ounces would make much difference, but if you threw 100 punches with fourteen ounce gloves your arms would fall off. In heavyweight championship fights, the boxers negotiate the size of the ring and weight of the gloves. Ali loved to fight with light gloves and a large ring so he could throw his lightning-fast jabs and dance away from his opponents.

I have two sets of gloves, one twelve ounces and the other fourteen ounces. The heavier, padded gloves give more protection to my hands and wrists but slow down the speed of my punches. The twelve-ounce gloves permit me to double up on my jabs and uppercuts but leave my hands swollen and sore for a day or two.

I felt the need to be fast and light on my feet today. I turned up the volume and put on the best of ABBA, which I knew would have amused Damian to no end. You can call them pop, but all their songs are the perfect rhythm for double-time jabbing. I smiled as I threw the first punch. My life was pretty good. I said, "Hey, Tort, who's luckier than us?"

After my workout, I walked Tort, and went to the office. I smelled the coffee and saw Sally sitting at her desk in her office. As I knew she would, she had sent out the proposed retainer agreement to Bob the night before.

Immediately after I sat down at my desk, I got the email I hoped for from Bob. He said the investor group had decided they wanted to retain me for the class action. He said the terms of the proposed retainer were acceptable and attached to his email was a PowerPoint containing the contact information for all the investors in the group they represented. He asked me to complete a conflict check and mail him a final draft of the retainer agreement by that afternoon for execution.

They would sign the agreement on behalf of the hedge funds they represented and wire the retainer upon receipt. They wanted me to file the class action as soon as possible. I closed my eyes, centered my mind and enjoyed the moment. I knew we would soon be in the eye of the hurricane for a long time.

We were. Just not the storm I expected.

I went into Sally's office, a big Cheshire Cat grin on my face, and sat down on a chair in front of her desk.

Sally said, "Okay, hotshot, what's up? You look like you just swallowed the canary."

"We got it! Bob emailed me. They want to retain us. He said if I had such an intelligent and beautiful legal assistant we must be a good firm."

Sally laughed. "Flattery and a big bonus will get you everywhere. Congratulations!"

"Congratulations to all of us. Bob gave me the list of investors and I need you to do the conflict check and finalize the retainer agreement. When Damian comes in, I want to sit down with both of you and gear up. You guys have to bring me up to speed on Courtney's divorce. I don't want it to become a distraction, especially now. Let's complete discovery and finalize a separation agreement as soon as possible. I'm going to rely on you and Damian to carry Courtney's divorce as much as possible because now I have to give my full attention the class action. I have to actually learn enough to pretend I know what I'm doing."

Later, I met with Courtney and Damian in the conference room. They had completed Courtney's net worth affidavit and document demands requesting the financial information we needed about Jackson and his consulting firm.

Sally told me Roy's firm had filed a summons and complaint in the Supreme Court, New York County, where Courtney and Jackson resided, seeking a divorce on the grounds of irreconcilable differences.

A preliminary conference had been scheduled by the court for the next week. The administrative judge, after being criticized for letting matrimonial actions languish for years, had set up strict guidelines to monitor and expedite divorce actions. As added incentive, the matrimonial part judges were required to report to the administrative judge regularly as to the progress in every divorce action.

I asked Sally to contact Courtney and arrange to have her meet us at our office early on the day of the preliminary conference so we could discuss what to expect and go to court together. I told Sally to block out the morning of the court conference because I wanted her in court with us.

We discussed the class action briefly.

I told Sally and Damian, after we were retained by the hedge fund, and I completed my research, I would be in a better position to give everyone their marching orders.

After Sally and Damian went back to their offices, I sat at the conference room table for a few minutes more. I looked around, took a deep breath and enjoyed the moment. I was very proud of our firm's reputation and success. When my phone pinged, I thought "Okay, snap out of it, you have a lot of work to do."

CHAPTER FIFTEEN
THE INNOCENT PARTIES

The following week, Sally and I met with Courtney early in morning on the day we were scheduled to appear in court for the preliminary conference in the divorce action. I explained to Courtney the appearance was just a formality to set dates to keep the case moving forward and she would not have to address the court.

Courtney was nervous because she had never appeared in court before. She was relieved to learn Sally would be coming with us and I would be doing all of the speaking.

It was raining heavily as we shared an Uber to the courthouse. The city traffic was a bear and the Brooklyn Bridge was backed up going into Manhattan. I wasn't worried because I always make it a practice to leave early and arrive at court well before a calendar call.

I have seen some judges, especially if they have a heavy calendar of cases, instead of putting a case over to a second call if an attorney fails to appear on time, simply proceed in the absence of the missing attorney. There is nothing more embarrassing for an attorney than having to try to explain to a client why he didn't get to be heard because he didn't show up in court on time.

We went through the metal detectors and walked across the large granite lobby that had the faint smell of disinfectant from the night cleaning crew. We entered a crowded elevator to go up to the courtroom.

The elevator was dead silent. There were mostly attorneys in the elevator with their game faces on anticipating their appearance in court. Even seasoned attorneys know the uncertainty of a court appearance where a judge can decide a case based upon what he or she had for breakfast.

I left Courtney and Sally in the hallway outside the courtroom and went inside to sign in with the court clerk. We were the tenth case on a long calendar and the assigned judge was the Honorable Maria Gonzales. Judge Gonzales had spent eight years sitting as a Family Court judge before being elected to the Supreme Court. She had earned a good reputation as a fair but tough judge who demanded the attorneys and litigants show proper respect for each other and the court. She got her message across with equal force in English or Spanish.

In New York, the Family Court is the court of last resort for domestic violence, juvenile offenses, neglect and abuse, child support and maintenance. Ironically, the Family Court has no jurisdiction over divorce cases, which must be filed in the Supreme Court. The Family Court handles the most shocking cases of family violence and dysfunction that exist in the poorest parts of the city. Judge Gonzales had paid her dues.

After I checked in, I went back out to the hall and saw Courtney was at the far end of the hall in deep conversation with someone who I assumed was Jackson Malone. I looked up and was surprised to see Roy Brown standing next to Sally and another attorney who I assumed was Roy's partner, who would be handling the case for his firm.

Sally looked very uncomfortable. I gave her an inquiring look and she said, "I'm glad you're back. Mr. Brown suggested our clients talk. I asked Courtney to wait until you came out, but Mr. Malone insisted it was important he speak with his wife before the case was called. Courtney said she would be fine."

I touched Sally's arm to reassure her she had done nothing wrong. "Thanks, Sally. No problem. It always makes me happy when a husband and wife can keep a dialogue going even though they are going through a divorce. Hello, Roy. I'm surprised to see you here."

"Chance. Good to see you. This is my partner, Clay Campbell, who will be handling the divorce for us. Clay is well aware of my great affection for Courtney and my close friendship with you and Jackson. I am here to help in any way I can. Before we go in, Clay just wanted to discuss some ground rules on discovery."

I shook hands with Clay. He looked more like a corporate attorney than a litigator. He said, "Chance, nice to meet you. I have what Roy likes to say are my marching orders and you can be assured there will be full cooperation and transparency on our side. I'm confident we can resolve this matter without any unnecessary litigation. You will be supplied with any and all financial documents you require from our client or his consulting firm. We will be happy to answer any questions you may have."

Before I could respond, he continued. "We have only one request.

As I am sure you can imagine, the names of Jackson's clients, and their investments are highly confidential. We would request you, and your client, enter an appropriate non-disclosure agreement and agree the names of Jackson's clients and their individual investments will not be disclosed. That information would be redacted from any documents we supply to you."

I wasn't overly concerned about the proposed NDA. I knew if Jackson was diverting assets or income, the court would not be persuaded by the niceties of an NDA. I said, "Clay, that sounds reasonable as long as everyone plays nice. I will discuss your request with my client, but I don't think it will be a problem. I will recommend we enter an appropriate NDA. We are not interested in disclosing the identity of Jackson's clients or any of their personal financial information."

I noticed Roy seemed particularly happy with my acceptance of the proposed stipulation. I wondered what he knew and why he appeared to be so concerned about the identity of Jackson's clients. He rubbed his hands together. "Great! Excellent! Now let's get this divorce over with!"

Courtney came back to where Sally and I were standing. When we were alone, I asked Courtney how her conversation with Jackson went.

She said he just wanted to reassure her he would take care of her and the children and she had nothing to worry about.

I told Courtney about the proposed non-disclosure agreement, and she said she had no problem with it. She had no desire to know anything about Jackson's clients. As we went into the courtroom, I reminded Sally and Courtney to turn off their cell phones.

We sat down in the crowded courtroom on one of the long wooden benches that always remind me of pews in a church. The hard oak wood and straight backs of the benches always make me sit up straight and pay attention. Good habits to practice in court or in church. Finally the clerk called our case. "Number ten on the calendar: Malone v Malone."

We stood and went up to the trial tables in front of the bench. Jackson, Roy and Clay Campbell stood at the plaintiff's table on the right, closest to the jury box. Courtney stood between Sally and me at the defendant's table on the left. The clerk said, "Please note your appearances for the record."

After we noted our appearances, the judge said, "Please be seated. Good morning. This is the first appearance on this matter. It is on for a preliminary conference. I would like to address the parties directly before we proceed."

I heard Courtney take a deep breath.

"Mr. and Mrs. Malone, my job is to help you resolve this dispute. I can do it in one of two ways. I can work with you and your attorneys to negotiate a fair and equitable settlement agreement which will set forth your rights and obligations after you are divorced. You can be sure it will be fair because I will not approve it otherwise. The other way I can resolve this matter is that I will render findings and a judgement after a trial."

I gave Courtney a reassuring look.

"If I am forced to try this case, my order will be final, and I fully expect neither of you will be happy with my decision. However, be warned, I believe the only innocent parties in this proceeding are your children. I don't care who you believe the good guy or bad guy is in this divorce because I am not here to protect you. I am here to protect your children because they can't protect themselves."

She paused and looked around at the attorneys. "I see you have some high priced attorneys with you in court today. So I suspect no one will be in financial need after this divorce. I believe with great privilege comes great responsibility. Mr. and Mrs. Malone, have I made myself clear?"

Courtney and Jackson both nodded and said, "Yes, Judge."

"Good. Now, Mr. Campbell, where are we?"

"Your Honor. First, I would like to thank you for your guidance and offer to assist the parties in resolving this dispute. It is our intention and expectation to come to an amicable agreement without any protracted litigation. The parties will exchange net worth affidavits and discovery demands. We will submit a proposed preliminary conference order agreeing to all critical discovery dates."

"Very good. Is custody in dispute?"

"No, Your Honor. Mrs. Malone will have physical custody of the girls. The parties intend to submit a proposed parenting stipulation."

"Excellent. Anything further, Mr. Campbell?"

"Just one other matter, Judge. Mr. Malone is a certified public accountant and financial planner. The information about his clients and their investments is highly confidential. I believe the parties have agreed to enter a non-disclosure and confidentiality agreement. All client names and investment information will not be disclosed and will be redacted from any documents we produce."

The judge said, "I can understand why plaintiff's clients' financial statements and tax returns might be confidential, but why shouldn't the identity of his clients be disclosed?"

Campbell said, "Judge, the retainer agreements entered with Mr. Malone's clients have very strict confidentiality provisions. He is prohibited from disclosing their identities, and if compelled to do so, he must give them advance notice so they can seek to enforce the agreement. Any attempt to disclose their identities will create needless litigation and compromise Mr. Malone's relationship with his clients. Those relationships benefit Mrs. Malone as much as the plaintiff. We are happy to supply all requested financial statements with the clients' names redacted."

"Mr. Cormac, would you like to be heard?"

"Thank you, Your Honor. We will rely on Mr. Campbell's representations that there will be full disclosure. We will agree not to disclose the names of Mr. Malone's clients or their investments as long as we are provided with all requested financial statements. The defendant consents to enter the non-disclosure agreement."

"Fine, submit the agreement to me and I will so order it as an order of the court. Mr. Cormac, any interim issues regarding support or visitation?"

"No, Your Honor. The parties have separated but Mr. Malone has continued to support his family and pay all their expenses. The children are residing in the marital residence with Mrs. Malone. Mr. Malone has full access to the children and visits based upon his availability."

"Great. I congratulate the parties on their cooperation. Let's keep it up. If you need my help, please contact my chambers. I will set this matter over for a month. At that time I would like discovery to be substantially completed. Thank you."

After we left the courtroom, Roy asked to speak with me in the hall for a minute. We stepped away from the clients. He could barely contain himself. He seemed overly excited and extremely pleased.

He said loudly, "Chance. Thank you! Thank you! I knew I could count on you to help these people. We will send over the NDA today. When do you think we can have a draft of a proposed separation agreement?"

"Roy, there's really no need to thank me. I'm just representing Courtney as I would any other client. As soon as we have reviewed all the financial documents, we should be in a position to discuss the terms of an agreement. I will give this my full attention."

"Perfect. Perfect. I won't forget this favor."

Outside the courtroom, Courtney again went over to talk to Jackson in the hall. Sally had heard my conversation with Roy. She gave me a puzzled look. "What's up with him? Too many happy pills?"

"I don't know, but he is pressing me hard to cut a deal as soon as possible. You would think *he* was getting divorced."

Sally quipped, "Maybe Roy wants to marry Jackson."

"Funny. But maybe they are already married in some way we just don't know about."

As we were leaving, I saw someone standing silently and staring at me from the far end of the hall, down from the courtroom. I asked Sally to go down in the elevator with Courtney and told them I would meet them in front of the courthouse.

I walked down the hall and said, "Hello, Randolph. What brings you here?"

"I wanted to give you the benefit of the doubt and see what would happen in court today. I watched your little dog and pony show in the courtroom and Roy's celebration in the hall. I heard you were an amateur boxer. Did you throw a lot of fights? Don't you have to at least throw a punch to make it look good? What did Roy offer you to fix this case? Another big client? A big payday if you went down without a fight?"

It wasn't true, but somehow it still stung. I was representing a client for the wrong reasons and still had real doubts about my decision. "Randolph, I'm going to ignore the insults. You don't know me well enough to make any judgments about my character. I can assure you I am representing your daughter as I would any other client."

"What a shame for all your other clients then," he scowled.

I ignored the insult. "As you are aware, I tried to convince Courtney to use another attorney, but she insisted she wanted to retain me. I will do what's in her best interest, regardless of my relationship with Roy. Now, if we're done, I have to get downstairs. My client is waiting for me."

I decided not to mention my conversation with Randolph to Courtney. I was sure she would know her father's feelings soon enough.

CHAPTER SIXTEEN
THE LAW OF THE JUNGLE

When we got back from the court appearance in Courtney's case, I returned a few emails and went in to talk to Sally in her office. She said, "I thought that went well. Everyone seems to be playing nice."

"Maybe. Courtney's father was in the courtroom."

"Really? I didn't see him."

"He must have been in the back. I spoke to him in the hall after you guys left. He accused me throwing Courtney's case for Roy. I ignored the insult but, in truth, I'm still concerned about Roy's interest in all this. My instinct is there is a backstory we don't know. I need you and Damian to keep your eyes wide open."

"I promise there'll be no sleeping on the job. I have good practice because by the time Melody gets to bed at night, there's no sleeping at home either."

"I'm glad you mentioned my favorite goddaughter. I know Melody's birthday is coming up soon and her godfather would like to take her out on the town to celebrate. Sorry to say, but Mom is not invited. I got two tickets to *The Lion King* on Broadway for next Saturday evening. Great seats. We'll do it right. Take a limo, go for a horse-drawn carriage ride through Central Park and find a good pizza place before the show."

"She would love that! Just tell me what time she should be ready."

On the day of the show, I pulled up to Sally's apartment building in the early afternoon in a stretch limo I had rented for the evening. Melody answered the door to their apartment and could barely contain her excitement. She was dressed in a beautiful red velour dress, white stockings and black patent leather shoes. Sally had braided her hair and there was a gemstone beret on the side.

She jumped into my arms and squealed, "Let's go! Let's go! Let's get this show on the road!"

I laughed. "Who is this princess? What did you do with Melody?"

"I'm Melody, silly."

Sally said, "Chance, this is so nice of you. It's all she's been talking about for days. We have now watched *The Lion King* movie more times than I can count. She knows all the songs by heart. You really spoil her."

"Of course. It's my job to spoil my goddaughter. Don't wait up."

Sally gave Melody a big hug. "Have a great time with Chance. Be a good girl and listen to him."

"I will, Momma. I love you."

Sally said, "I love you, too, honey." She came up to me and gave me a warm embrace. "I love you, too, Chance. Have fun!"

The feel of Sally in my arms, the touch of her embrace and smell of her hair brought back all the strong feelings I have been struggling with. I knew I wanted Sally and Melody in my life, not just on weekends, but all the time. I told myself I wouldn't wait any longer and would tell Sally how I was feeling later that night, after I brought Melody home.

When we went outside and Melody saw the black stretch limo she jumped up and down and screamed, "No way! A limo! A limo! I'm a rock star!"

We sat next to each other in the big leather seats all the way in the back of the big black car. I let Melody press all the buttons. She turned on the stereo and the TV at the same time. She found a channel with a music station she liked. As she was dancing in her seat, I opened two bottles of Coke, which she is never allowed to drink at home. I poured us two glasses of soda. "Don't tell your mom!" Melody pretended to zip her lips and throw away the key.

It was the perfect fall evening in New York City. The afternoon sun and bright blue sky framed the tall buildings, making a different postcard out of each city block we drove down. The air was crisp but not too cold. I let Melody open the sunroof in the back of the limo so we could smell the air and look straight up at the sky.

As we drove up to the entrance to Central Park, the reds, oranges and greens of the changing leaves were like a blanket laid out over the park. We stopped at the 59th Street entrance, where the hansom drivers waited with their horses and carriages.

When we got out, I told the limo driver to wait for us and we walked over to see the horses. I said to Melody, "You pick out the most beautiful horse to take us for a ride through the park. Take your time. Make sure you find out their names so we can get to know them."

She walked slowly down the line of horses and carriages, talking to the drivers, who tipped their hats and said, "Good evening, young lady."

Melody finally made her choice. "I like this horse. Her name is Zoe."

"Great. Why do you like Zoe?"

"Because her eyes are kind and gentle, like Tort's."

We snuggled in the back of the carriage with a warm plaid blanket over our legs. The driver said, "Get up, Zoe!" and we rolled into the park. He turned around and tipped his black top hat to Melody, "Who is this young princess? You know my carriage turns into a pumpkin at midnight?"

Melody looked at me wide-eyed. "Really?"

I said it's true but, luckily, we would be long gone by then. As we floated through the park to the sound of the horse's hoofs echoing on the pavement, it was like we had left the city and entered a magical kingdom. The driver serenaded us with some Irish tunes in a deep tenor voice. Melody sat silently, as if in a trance. She moved closer to me and held my hand. Some moments in life are perfect.

When the ride was over, Melody hugged Zoe and kissed her on the neck. We thanked the hansom driver for what Melody said was the best ride in the world. We got back in the limo to drive to one of my favorite pizza joints in Times Square.

We opened the sun roof and looked up. The huge digital billboards of Times Square were lit up like Vegas with their brilliant video advertisements flashing in the night sky. Every night is New Year's Eve in Times Square. We ate our pizza and got to the theater early.

The lobby of the old Broadway theater where *The Lion King* was playing is warm and inviting. A beautiful red carpet covers the floors like a tapestry and the walls are covered with a velveteen floral wallpaper.

Melody was immediately drawn to the posters of the characters in their costumes and, of course, all the souvenir dolls, tee shirts and programs. She picked out a baby Simba toy as a birthday present and held it tightly throughout the show. We bought some candy and went to our seats. The seats were perfect and the show was a miracle of music, dancing and colorful animation. Melody squealed when the performers walked down the aisles in their amazing animal costumes. She knew all the songs by heart and sang out loud with the performers throughout the show.

After the show, we went for ice cream at the last Jahn's Ice Cream Parlor in New York City. We ordered the "Kitchen Sink", knowing we could never eat all the ice cream. They brought out a big tub of different flavored scoops of ice cream, covered with fudge sauce, with birthday candles on top.

The waiters joined in, and we all sang Happy Birthday to Melody. She made a wish and blew out the candles. Before we started on our sundaes, Melody paused and looked at me with concern. I asked, "What's wrong, honey?"

She said, "Chance, we forgot to take a picture of me blowing out the candles for Momma. Momma loves those pictures."

Of course, she was right. I called the waiters over one more time. They joined in the fun and told Melody, "We just sang Happy Birthday to a girl who looks just like you."

Melody laughed and we relit the candles and sang Happy Birthday all over again. This time I got the perfect shot of Melody blowing out the candles on my phone.

After we ate as much ice cream as we could possibly eat without exploding, I asked Melody, "How did you like the show?"

"It's the best time I ever had in my life!"

"What part did you like the best?"

"I liked when Simba became King. But, Chance, some things made me sad."

"Really? What made you sad, honey?"

"I was sad when Simba's father was killed."

"Yes, it was sad."

"Chance?"

"Yes, honey?"

"Why do animals kill each other?"

"Well, some animals kill and eat other animals to survive. It's called the law of the jungle. The survival of the fittest."

"But is it right for them to kill a weaker animal?"

"I don't think they have the ability to distinguish between what is right and wrong. They live by their natural instincts."

"But we know the difference between right and wrong. Right?"

"Yes, as humans, we know the difference."

"But why do we kill and eat animals?"

"Some people eat meat. They don't seem to think about the animal that was killed. It doesn't make it right."

She thought about what I said and asked, "Why do people kill other people?"

I paused. The hardest questions are often the most innocent. I was thinking about what Sally would want me to say to Melody. "Melody, you are a smart and caring person. There is no excuse for one person to kill another. It is a sin. I know when you grow up, you will make a difference and help all of us to do what's right. Now, let's just finish our ice cream."

As we drove home in the limo, Melody fell asleep in the back seat holding her toy baby lion. As I put my arm around her, I realized she was more perfect at age seven than I could ever hope to be. The love I felt for her was overwhelming. She was a gift I was grateful for, but didn't feel I really deserved. I wanted to be her real father, not just her godfather. I wanted to care for her and protect her. I was ready and anxious to discuss these feelings with Sally.

I carried Melody, who was still sound asleep, up to Sally's door and Sally took her from my arms. She whispered, "Thank you," and before I could say anything, closed the door.

My conversation with Sally would have to wait. I'm not sure why, but for some reason I felt both disappointed and relieved.

CHAPTER SEVENTEEN
THE LAUNDRY BUSINESS

My father would say, "Some people are too smart for their own good." My instinct was, Jackson Malone was one of those people.

I told Damian it was time to find out more about Jackson and Checkmate. I explained the NDA prohibited the disclosure of Jackson's clients' names and accounts but didn't prohibit us from investigating Jackson and his consulting business. I told Damian not to leave any digital footprints if possible.

Damian said, "Got it. I'm a ghost."

Damian started digging in the dirt. Our suspicion was that Jackson, through Checkmate, was not only in the business of helping his clients evade taxes but helping to launder their undisclosed income.

Damian knew he had to first learn how the game was played before he could understand Jackson's moves. He researched tax havens and how money was laundered. He would use all the sophisticated search engines at his disposal to investigate Jackson and Checkmate. He learned the biggest problem with tax havens for tax evaders was always the same – the possibility of the discovery of the hidden accounts and the identity of the owners.

Money still had to be deposited and withdrawn. There was always an electronic paper trail of these transactions. That's why assets that were hidden and not declared were considered "dirty." Dirty money inevitably has to be "laundered" to come out smelling clean and fresh.

Damian discovered people historically used pretty clumsy and obvious schemes to launder money. They bought gold bullion, fine art, racehorses, vintage wine, stamp collections and jewelry. Anything that could be physically moved, bartered or exchanged on the black market without any evidence of the transaction, or the parties involved.

Of course these schemes were cumbersome and risky because you had to actually buy all these expensive things and transport and hide them. It was hard to hide a racehorse. Also, valuable things are stolen all the time. You can't insure what doesn't exist.

Next came the offshore tax havens with laws enacted for the sole purpose of protecting depositors from any possible disclosure of their accounts or the source of their income. Places like the Isle of Man, Switzerland, and Luxembourg had no income tax and strict confidentiality laws to protect the owners of anonymous LLCs and shell corporations.

I laughed when Damian told me that Alaska, of all places, was a tax haven for foreign investors who wanted to launder money right here in the USA. It was ironic Alaska was considered offshore, not only because of its remote location but because it had the same laws protecting the identities of criminals and tax evaders as the most remote islands in the Caribbean.

Damian explained the biggest risk with all these traditional money laundering schemes is that you can never control all the parties to a transaction. There were too many moving parts. There was always the chance secrecy laws could change, or when pressure was brought to bear on someone in the criminal food chain, they might cave under the threat of prosecution and cooperate with the authorities.

We knew Checkmate had large international clients. We were confident Jackson was well ahead of the curve and in all likelihood had created a new and highly sophisticated money laundering scheme. But Damian hit a brick wall. He was shocked when he was unable to access any data on Jackson, Checkmate, or their activities. There were no government files or investigations of record. He was unable to access any bank accounts, financial statements or tax returns.

Damian found that the Checkmate files were impenetrable. The firewall around Jackson's files was highly sophisticated. He had virtual private networks that changed automatically every day.

Damian was very impressed. But like most brick walls, he was confident, eventually, he would go around it or go through it. I had no doubt he would.

CHAPTER EIGHTEEN
GOD'S GIFT

Despite Damian's best efforts, it wasn't until much later we discovered the full facts about Jackson's business, the clients he served and Roy Brown's true involvement in Checkmate.

What we learned was that when Jackson established his consulting company, in violation of his employment agreement, he took with him almost all of his former accounting firm's high net worth clients. They were happy to jump with Jackson because they were very impressed with his aggressive strategies for tax avoidance.

As suggested by Randolph Gault, Roy was very skilled in helping Jackson steal his clients without the accounting firm's knowledge. He counseled him about how best to surreptitiously divert the clients' files and contact them without any scrutiny by the firm before he gave notice of his resignation. Roy set up the offshore companies to be used as tax havens by Jackson. Roy had no reservation about Jackson's legal and ethical obligations to his accounting firm. As Courtney told us, Jackson was fond of saying that he and Roy were "partners in crime".

It is a fine line between tax avoidance and tax evasion and soon after Jackson established Checkmate, he was advising many clients on how to simply evade taxes altogether and not get caught. Once the reputation of Jackson's skill and sophisticated techniques for evading taxes grew, he had a whole new client base who didn't want tax advice, because they didn't pay any taxes.

They needed help in structuring their offshore accounts and laundering their money so it could be spent without scrutiny. Jackson at first employed traditional money laundering schemes, like investing in cash businesses, papering bogus loans, and employing internet banks chartered offshore. These schemes worked, but were time consuming and always left a troubling paper trail. Then God created cryptocurrency.

Jackson immediately understood it was the greatest gift ever bestowed upon drug cartels, tax evaders and money launderers. It provided absolute anonymity in a digital world with no names, addresses or digital footprints. It was paradise, not just for the drug trade, but for the wealthiest people in the world. Jackson easily mastered the skills necessary to launder his clients' money in the anonymous crypto universe.

***

In the same way he succeeded in chess tournaments, Jackson was thinking about the next two moves and was way ahead of the curve in setting up the perfect secure offshore crypto money laundering operation. He was no longer just a professional, he was now a professional criminal.

Jackson became very careful not to ask who actually owned the money he was laundering or where it came from. It protected both him and his clients. As his reputation grew so did his clients' deposits. Within a year after forming Checkmate, he was managing in excess of $1BIL in his clients' crypto accounts.

In order to hedge the volatility of the crypto market, he diversified the cryptocurrency accounts and used derivatives to protect the principal amounts invested. To effectuate his trading strategies in real time, and assure his clients would never be implicated in his money laundering schemes, he set up secure crypto "wallets", which he alone controlled. He had sole authorization to trade the crypto accounts for his clients.

Only Jackson knew the blockchain identification numbers and the passwords necessary to trade the accounts. He gave clients encrypted monthly statements of their account balances, and nothing more. He transferred cryptocurrency anonymously as directed by his clients. He was successful because he gave his clients the security and protection they wanted. Jackson had gained his clients' trust. He also now had complete control over their assets.

Checkmate was paid management fees in the amount of three percent of the value of the funds on deposit annually. Of course, Jackson took his management fees in cryptocurrency and deposited them into his own offshore accounts. His clients were more than happy to pay his fees. It was cheap compared to what they were used to paying to launder their money.

The $30MIL in annual management fees earned by Checkmate gave Jackson the ability to buy anything his heart desired. It reminded him of a

TV game show called Supermarket Sweeps he watched as a child. The contestants ran up and down the aisles of a department store with a shopping cart and filled it with everything they could until their time ran out. He dreamed that one day he would be able to push that cart. The dream came true but he didn't have to run up and down store aisles in an old department store with a shopping cart to quickly grab the things that were of no value to him. There was no time limit. No need to rush. His cart was never full. It contained everything his heart desired. The world was now his store, and his life was a game show he always won.

Of course, like many dreams, when they came true, they weren't quite what Jackson imagined and not nearly good enough. Everything wasn't enough when others had more. Jackson soon realized the volatility of the cryptocurrency market created another big opportunity. Not an opportunity for his clients but for him. Why shouldn't he enjoy the same wealth and privilege his wealthiest clients enjoyed? It was only fair he should profit off the wealth he created for them.

The clients would be none the worse. They were not interested in his trades or making any return on the money being laundered. They weren't investors. They were just ordinary criminals with enormous wealth who only wanted secrecy, security and protection. He studied his crypto trading algorithms carefully and realized there was an opportunity for him to systematically divert fractional shares of his clients' cryptocurrency to his own accounts and not be detected.

Jackson created a trading strategy permitting him to increase the frequency of his derivative trades and to margin client accounts to maximize the profit on their accounts based upon millisecond fluctuations of the value of a given cryptocurrency for his benefit. He created a new software program that made instantaneous high frequency trades based upon market conditions.

The trading platform automatically traded the accounts based upon his algorithm and deposited any profit he made not into the client's account but into Jackson's own cryptocurrency accounts. On the rare occasions when the value of the client account dipped, he simply transferred back the amount necessary to keep the client's principal balance constant.

If successful, he could now print money day and night. He tested the software and the trading platform, and it worked better than even he could have imagined. Jackson calculated, based upon the first month's profit that had been automatically diverted into his account, he could skim in excess of $100MIL a year from the clients' accounts.

He laughed out loud when he decided to call his trading scheme "Skim Milk", because he skimmed money and milked his clients at the same time. Of course, the money he stole was in addition to his management consulting fees. Better yet, the more money deposited with Checkmate to be laundered, the greater the skim became. Skim Milk worked like a charm. He was now the king and controlled the whole board.

After the Skim Milk trading platform was in place, Jackson knew he had to make some decisions about Roy. Jackson had been paying Roy individually, significant "consulting" fees, in addition to his firm's legal fees, which he knew Roy did not disclose to his law firm.

Jackson originally felt indebted to Roy, who was instrumental in helping Jackson divert his accounting firm clients and setting up the off shore money laundering operation. But, more and more, Jackson didn't feel any real appreciation or gratitude for Roy's help. He began to believe he really didn't owe Roy anything for his loyalty or the valuable legal advice Jackson had relied upon in growing his money laundering operation. In hindsight, he rationalized any lawyer could have done what Roy had done for him. He felt there was nothing special about Roy Brown or his legal advice.

Jackson was the one who had the skill, the ambition, the one taking all the risk. However, Jackson was also smart enough to appreciate Roy knew where all the bodies were buried. He needed to ensure Roy's cooperation and silence in the event there were any client or governmental inquiries into the offshore companies Roy had created for him. Jackson knew, to buy insurance, you always had to pay a premium.

In the end, he made his own business decision. He decided it was in his best interests to handcuff Roy by having him participate in the profit from Skim Milk. Jackson wondered, however, if this might be the breaking point, when Roy might actually draw the line and, as an attorney, refuse to participate in the outright theft of funds from their clients.

Jackson approached Roy and told him he wanted to have a confidential conversation with him as his client. After Roy agreed their conversation would be privileged, Jackson described the Skim Milk operation to Roy. He told Roy, in appreciation for all his help, he would pay him 10% of the profit he was skimming as an additional consulting fee, which would be deposited by Jackson directly into Roy's offshore crypto accounts.

It turned out, Jackson had nothing to worry about any legal or ethical reservations Roy might have. When Roy was informed of the amount of the crypto being diverted, he was ecstatic. He had no concerns whatsoever about the fraud and theft being perpetrated on their mutual clients. He congratulated Jackson on his brilliant scheme and trading algorithm, which he called "genius". He joked he would only drink skim milk from now on.

Roy quickly calculated his share of the projected skim would be over $10MIL a year in undisclosed income. Roy could now live like the wealthiest members of the Westchester Country Club, who he felt had never really accepted him as a peer. Roy was more than happy with the arrangement and the crypto treasure trove he would own. Jackson was happy because he now owned Roy.

The skim worked almost too well. Jackson had more crypto than he knew what to do with. Now, he had the same problems encountered by his wealthiest clients. A mountain of undisclosed income doesn't do you any good unless you can spend it. Of course, Courtney had no knowledge of Jackson's business activities, his cryptocurrency accounts or his newfound wealth.

Jackson knew it was important to maintain a reasonable standard of living at home and avoid extravagant purchases in order to avoid any possible scrutiny from the government or regulatory agencies in the US. This wasn't true however when he took "business trips" to visit his clients in Hong Kong, Moscow, Singapore, Beijing, or the Emirates. He left no paper trails regarding these trip expenses, as everything was paid for with crypto from his offshore account.

He flew by private jet, stayed in the penthouse suites of the best five-star hotels and dined in the private dining rooms of the best restaurants.

He was given VIP treatment at nightclubs, casinos and shows. He drank bottles of vintage wines so rare the price listed on the menu said *price upon request*. He joined the international Core Club, where he enjoyed the exclusive club recreation and social amenities in locations throughout the world.

Of course, there was no real need for Jackson to travel and meet with his clients in person to conduct his consulting business. It was just a convenient excuse for Jackson to travel and enjoy his wealth. His clients were more than happy to accommodate Jackson, make sure he was well taken care of and lacked for nothing he desired.

Eventually they introduced Jackson to the most exclusive escort services catering to world leaders, rock stars and the Royal families. Women who were smart, cultured and would do anything to satisfy his sexual fantasies. Things he would never ask or want his wife to do.

Jackson's sexual fantasies were based upon his earliest adolescent dreams and desires. What he wanted most, and was denied, when he was young, were the young teenage girls he'd fantasized about when he pleasured himself as a young boy. He still had the same need to touch the firm thighs, young breasts and white panties he desperately desired in his youth.

His clients in Bangkok, Moscow and Singapore were delighted to accommodate Jackson. There were no silly Western taboos in these cities. They supplied him with an endless supply of young, petite teenage girls so he could live out his wildest childhood dreams he had harbored for so long. They found nothing wrong with his desires.

His clients could care less about Jackson's sexual predilections. They were happy to meet his needs and know his secrets, which they could now us to their advantage. As Courtney had seen on the videos, before long Jackson regularly enjoyed sleeping with two or three young girls at a time, although they rarely slept. The girls were happy to service him, and their families were well paid. Their tight young bodies gave him an ecstasy and release he had never experienced before. He started videoing his exploits so he could enjoy them over and over again. The same videos his twins had inadvertently seen on his laptop.

He stopped dating the older escorts. He felt they were worn and used and could no longer fulfill his sexual needs. He felt no guilt or remorse. He assured himself his desires were perfectly natural and shared by men like him throughout history. Priscilla was fourteen when she dated Elvis. Juliet was fifteen when Romeo consummated his love for her. Mary was fourteen when Jesus was born. Perhaps some of his girls were younger, but he felt assured he was in good company.

Jackson soon realized his marriage was over. He loved his children and Courtney for being a good mother. But men like him had no use for marriage. He was successful and enjoyed enormous wealth. He lived by his own rules like all powerful men. He met with Roy and said, "Roy, I want a divorce."

Roy said, "What? No, you don't."

"Why not?"

"Well let's see. Let me count the most obvious reasons. First of all, you have a wonderful wife and family. Second, it is obvious you need some stability in your life. But lastly, and most important, you are a criminal who is laundering money and embezzling from your clients. A divorce will cause close scrutiny of your business activities, a risk neither of us, or your clients, can afford."

"Your firm can represent me. I am confident that you will take all precautions to protect both of us and the Checkmate clients. Courtney trusts you. I want you to get it done."

"Jackson, we don't do divorce work. Also, have you thought about how Randolph will react if he finds out you are abandoning his daughter."

"Roy, you can handle Randolph. He's your friend. This is important to me. I don't think I am making myself clear. I'm not asking you, I'm telling you – get it done."

Roy shook his head. "Fine. I'll see what we can do. But I think it's a decision you will regret."

CHAPTER NINETEEN
BACK IN THE USSR

The CIA dossier on Dimitry Kafelnikov was very detailed.

When Damian eventually became aware of Dimitry, it didn't take long for him to access a copy of his dossier from his intelligence contacts. Dimitry was born in Russia. Both his parents were high ranking members of the Politburo until it was disbanded upon the breakup of the Soviet Union and they became elite members of the Russian Federation.

Dimitry was an only child, raised in St. Petersburg and vacationed in a beautiful dacha. owned by his parents. He enjoyed the wealth and privilege that went along with the high-ranking government positions held by his parents. They traveled the world and vacationed for a month every summer on the Baltic. He attended private school at the International Academy of St. Petersburg and from an early age spoke fluent Russian, German and English.

After graduating high school, Dimitry matriculated in the School of Foreign Service at Georgetown. He immediately felt right at home in Washington, with its massive stone government buildings, reminding him of St. Petersburg and Moscow. Upon graduating from the School of Foreign Service, he attended Georgetown Law School. While in law school his parents secured him a position as a junior attaché at the Russian Embassy in Washington.

Dimitry was soon recognized by the Russian Ambassador for his intellect, charm and diplomatic skills. He was also recognized by all the female clerks for his good looks, athletic physique and hand tailored suits. He was admitted to the bar in DC and New York, but he knew he would never practice law in the traditional sense.

He viewed his law school education as just a useful tool to advance his career as a diplomat. He learned, although Washington was the diplomatic capital of the world, it was Wall Street and the world of finance that actually controlled government decisions. He had no intention of ever returning to his homeland.

Upon graduation from Georgetown Law, he was immediately

offered a position as a full-time attaché at the Russian Embassy in Washington. His parents were very proud and sent Dimitry an expensive snow globe depicting St. Petersburg in the winter he kept on the desk in his office. He would often shake the globe and think about how far he had traveled from his home.

Dimitry was quick to learn the real-life skills needed for diplomacy not taught in the classroom. The importance of discretion, of keeping secrets which are the currency of his craft, and how to understand the unspoken messages communicated with a slight smile, frown or the nod of the head.

He learned to tell half-truths with full conviction and without hesitation. To dissemble facts and reassemble them to meet the needs of his government. He learned the secret to the art of deception was to always have enough credibility in constructing a lie to avoid detection and permit him to plausibly deny it after the fact.

With his excellent diplomacy, lawyering and social skills, Dimitry was soon given special assignments to help resolve sensitive problems experienced by Russian diplomats or government officials while on US soil. He was a natural.

It could be as simple as fixing a speeding ticket or making sure an arrest for DWI or soliciting a prostitute, after a night out drinking vodka, disappeared without a trace. It was more of a challenge when prominent Russians were charged with assault or were involved in a car accident where someone was seriously injured or killed. The highest priority, however, was defusing charges of counter-espionage, spying, wiretapping, intercepting emails, or election interference.

To fix these problems required a special talent to bake a cake with the just the right amount of persuasion, bribery and coercion. Dimitry excelled at handing out "Get out of Jail Free" cards to prominent Russians and enjoyed his new role as what Americans called a fixer.

The ambassador was very pleased with Dimitry's success in saving him, and his superiors, from unwanted scrutiny and embarrassment. He rewarded Dimitry by giving him the title of Special Liaison to the Russian Embassy. He was given great flexibility and unlimited resources to make any troublesome problems go away. He was also given access to what the

CIA recognized was now his greatest asset – the SVR, the former KGB.

There was rarely a problem Dimitry couldn't fix with just the right amount of motivation, money, or muscle. As Special Liaison, he had complete autonomy to take such steps as he felt appropriate to put out diplomatic fires without any prior approval.

In fact, the ambassador, as an experienced politician, understood the less he knew about Dimitry's activities the better. Plausible deniability was also the key to the ambassador's longevity. Although Dimitry wasn't considered a foreign agent by the US intelligence community, he was close enough to have his activities closely monitored.

Dimitry was married to Tatiana Petrova. They met at an embassy event and fell in love. Petrova means "rock" and she soon became the one thing in the world he could hold on to when the currents of his diplomatic world became turbulent. Tatiana was a Russian beauty, born in America. Her father was a prominent Russian petroleum trader who split his time between his offices in Moscow and DC.

Tatiana was an elementary school teacher for minority children in an inner-city DC public school. Dimitry loved her dedication to a profession that simply did good. Her honesty and transparency seemed to be the perfect balance to his world of dark secrets and half-truths. She was the ideal wife, mother and lifetime companion for a member of the Russian diplomatic corps. They now had two boys, Gregor and Sasha, ages eight and ten, who were American citizens.

They enjoyed a very good life in America. They lived in a beautiful brick townhouse they owned in Georgetown. Their boys attended the Sidwell Friends School with the children of other prominent politicians and dignitaries. They ate at the best restaurants on M Street and attended DC balls and embassy events with the DC inner circle.

Tatiana understood Dimitry's embassy work was highly confidential and never asked about his work or spoke about her husband's profession, other than to say he was a diplomat. Dimitry was very content to work his craft in the dark shadows of the embassy as long as he could come home to the comfort and joy of his wife and family at night.

After Jackson started the divorce action, the CIA intercepted a conversation held between Dimitry and the Russian ambassador outside, at a park a few blocks from the Russian Embassy.

Early one morning they met on the embassy steps and walked without saying a word to a secluded area of the nearby park. They sat down close together on an isolated bench. The ambassador looked around and said quietly in Russian, "Turn off your cell phone and speak only in Russian."

Dimitry did as he was told and waited silently for the ambassador to speak.

The ambassador put his hand over his mouth and, in a hushed tone, said in Russian, "Dimitry, I have an important matter of the utmost urgency that needs your attention. This is highly confidential, and you must handle it discreetly and outside the embassy. We never had this conversation."

Dimitry replied, also in Russian, "Understood, Ambassador."

"You can use your discretion as to how best to fix this problem. Under no circumstances can there be any electronic or paper trail of any kind leading back to me or the embassy."

"Completely understood."

"I have been contacted by a senior official from the SVR. They have become aware the financial accounts of some of our highest government officials and their strategic partners have been compromised. If this information was to be made public, it would prove embarrassing and undermine public confidence in our leadership."

Dimitry kept his head down and listened carefully.

"The accounts compromised are certain offshore accounts which were formed and are managed by an Isle of Man wealth management firm called Checkmate. The principal of Checkmate is an American named Jackson Malone. He is a CPA and money manager who services his clients out of an office in New York City. He is going through a divorce in New York and it is believed the leaks occurred because of an investigation instigated by his wife's attorney. Start with Jackson, Checkmate and Jackson's attorney, Roy Brown."

Dimitry instinctively committed the names to memory.

"See if they can put out the fire and build a better fire wall. If not, you must eliminate any risk of disclosure by anyone by any means possible. The full resources of the SVR are at your disposal. Igor Badenov, a senior officer at the SVR will assist you personally. After today, the only communication I want to receive from you is that the problem is fixed.

"You can count on me, Ambassador."

CHAPTER TWENTY
THE RUSSIANS ARE COMING

Jackson was on his laptop drafting his monthly PowerPoint summary of the value of his clients' offshore accounts and the fees generated by Checkmate, both on and off the books.

He was happy. Very happy. He was secure in the knowledge that he was the only one with access to this information. His laptop was state of the art and incorporated the cyber security protections utilized by governments for homeland security. All data was encrypted and only he could access the files though his fingerprint.

His client accounts and, more importantly, his fees from Skim Milk had increased exponentially as he had anticipated. Even better, the clients never scrutinized the investments or his fees. They were only interested in laundering large sums of money, not "investing". He smiled as he saved the data and closed all open applications. His laptop was his private safe and only he knew the combination. His closed his eyes for a few minutes, savoring the moment, but his reverie was disturbed when his laptop pinged.

He saw he had a text from someone he didn't know. "My name is Dimitry Kafelnikov. I represent the interests of certain of your Russian clients. It is urgent that I meet with you and your legal counsel. I will be in NYC this Saturday. I will notify you of a time and the location of a safe house for our meeting one hour before we meet."

A *safe* house? Jackson was confused and concerned. He had no idea who Dimitry was. He had a strict policy never to meet with his foreign clients on US soil. It was an unnecessary risk for the client and for him. He texted back and asked Dimitry who he represented.

When he got no response, he texted Roy, telling him a Checkmate client had requested to meet with both of them tomorrow in New York City at a time and place to be made known.

Roy texted back. He said he had a golf game on Saturday and it would not be convenient for him to attend the meeting. He asked who the client was and why they would want to meet with him. Jackson said that

Roy shouldn't send any more texts but should call him immediately.

Jackson and Roy were not aware that after Dimitry's text to Jackson, they were also now persons of interest to the CIA and all of their emails and calls were also being be monitored.

Roy called Jackson from his cell. There were no pleasantries. "Jackson, who is this guy and why does he want to meet with me?"

"All I know is, I got a text this morning from someone named Dimitry Kafelnikov, who said he represents a Russian client and wants to meet with us. I did a search, and he works for the Russian Embassy in D.C. The Russian accounts are all whales."

"But why would he ask to meet with me? Does he know my name?"

"No, he asked to meet with me and my attorney. I suspect the investors are some of the most powerful people in Russia. Their crypto accounts with Checkmate total in excess of $500MIL. They have never asked to meet with me before. I'm not overly concerned, but I don't like surprises. I can't plan my next move if I don't know who is playing the game and what pieces are on the board."

"Jackson, stop right there. There is no way in hell I am going to jump through hoops to meet with some Russian we don't even know at some secret location on a Saturday. I have nothing to do with your business or management of the cryptocurrency accounts. Why do they want to meet with me? I'm your lawyer. Nothing more. I don't want to get involved in your intrigue. You told me there would be no trouble. Wait a minute! Do they know about Skim Milk? Tell me that they don't know about my crypto accounts or the payments to me! Am I in some sort of danger here?"

"Roy, calm down. I'm well aware that you are my lawyer. I know because you have been very highly compensated for your services. This has nothing to do with you. The amounts we skim, both of us, are undetectable. I control all the crypto accounts and they are completely anonymous. No one else has access to them. Any distributions to you are paid in crypto into your offshore account."

"If the accounts are undetectable, why is this Russian demanding to meet with us? With me? You go. Leave me out of this."

"You don't exist as far as these accounts are concerned. But make no mistake, you are very much involved. There are at least ten million good reasons for you to make yourself available. If you refuse to attend the meeting, it will appear that you are not cooperating. It would be the wrong message to send to them. It would be the wrong message to send to me."

There was a long silence. Finally Roy said, "I will be there. But only in my role as your attorney."

Jackson texted Dimitry and confirmed that they were available to meet with him.

Dimitry flew up to New York on the embassy's private jet on Saturday morning. He wore a fine blue wool suit he had hand-tailored in London, a custom-made white shirt, red tie, gold cufflinks with the embassy insignia on them and a gold Patek Philippe watch. As a diplomat he didn't have to go through any of the security protocols when he landed. He was met at the airport by an embassy limo with diplomatic plates. Igor Badenov, the high ranking SVR officer who the ambassador had arranged to accompany Dimitry, was in the back of the limo when Dimitry got in. Igor was built like a middle-weight boxer. He had a square head, square jaw and closely cropped hair. He wore a black leather jacket, a black shirt, wool pants and Timberland combat boots. On his wrist was a Russian Vostok Komandirskie tactical military watch with a steel band.

In Russian, Dimitry asked the limo driver to put up the glass partition between the front and back seats. On the ride over to the safe house, Igor, in Russian, told Dimitry what the SVR had discovered.

Dimitry ordered the driver to stop the car four blocks away from the brownstone safe house where the meeting would take place. He instructed the driver to continue driving around, and come back to a location Dimitry would text to him when the meeting was over.

Once inside the safe house, Dimitry texted Jackson and gave him the address and time to meet. Jackson and Roy met on the sidewalk outside the brownstone at the appointed time and waited. After a few minutes, the door opened and Igor came out. He did not introduce himself and without asking permission took pictures of Jackson and Roy with his phone.

Igor asked Jackson and Roy to give him their drivers' licenses and phones. Roy started to object, but Jackson gave him a sharp look and he thought better of it.

Igor went back into the safe house and left Roy and Jackson waiting on the sidewalk. Roy said, "I'm giving them five minutes and then I'm getting my license and phone back and leaving. I have a tee time this afternoon and there's no way I'm missing it for these clowns."

Jackson said nothing. He knew Roy wasn't going anywhere.

The door opened and Igor motioned for Jackson and Roy to enter. He didn't return their licenses or phones. He asked them to put their hands over their heads. He searched them thoroughly and used a metal detection wand to scan their bodies.

Igor escorted them into a small elevator, and they silently went to a windowless room on the top floor. When they were seated at a conference table, Igor opened a large metallic case that looked like a sophisticated router, put it on the floor and plugged it into a wall outlet. Roy looked at Jackson and just shook his head.

Dimitry entered the room and Igor closed the door. Dimitry said something to Igor in Russian and Igor walked over and took a position with his back to the closed door with his arms crossed.

"Gentlemen, thank you for meeting with me on such short notice. This is my associate, Igor Badenov. I apologize for all the precautions, but this room is now secure. I would appreciate it if you would remove your jackets, shirts, pants and shoes and place them on the table."

Roy immediately stood up. "Okay, enough's enough. This game is over. I don't know who you guys are or why I'm here, but I'm a prominent attorney and I have better things to do. If Jackson wants to stay here and undress, that's up to him, but I'm leaving."

Dimitry looked at Igor, who didn't move a muscle but opened his jacket just enough to expose the Glock 9MM pistol in a holster on his hip. Roy stood still, realizing that there was no way he was going anywhere with Igor blocking the door.

Dimitry said, "Roy, we appreciate your coming to meet with us. We mean no disrespect. Igor finds that it is always best to proceed with an abundance of caution. Once we are assured that there is no possibility of any surveillance, we can speak freely and I will be happy to answer any of your questions."

Jackson and Roy looked at each other. Jackson slowly took off his jacket, shirt, pants and shoes and put them on the table as directed. Roy realized that he had no choice but to do the same. Igor picked up the clothing, searched everything and returned to his position, standing with his arms crossed in front of the door.

Sitting in their underwear, Jackson and Roy felt exposed and humiliated. They realized that these Russians were very serious people and that they had lost all control of the meeting before it started. Jackson tried to defuse the situation. "Dimitry, I agree that you can never be too careful. Why doesn't Igor join us and we can all discuss your concerns." Igor didn't move.

Dimitry said, "Thank you, Jackson. But Igor is fine standing. He will make sure that we are not interrupted. Now we can properly introduce ourselves. I am Dimitry Kafelnikov and I represent the interests of some of our mutual clients. You have already met my associate, Igor."

Jackson introduced himself and Roy. Roy sat silently, staring down at his clothing sitting on the table in front of him.

Dimitry said, "It is a pleasure to meet both of you. Roy, it my understanding your firm represents Checkmate and also Jackson in a pending divorce action. Is that correct?"

Roy finally looked up and replied curtly, "Yes. I do the corporate work and my partner is representing Jackson in a divorce action. We can't disclose any confidential information about our clients or the divorce action. That would be privileged."

"Roy, I am very impressed with your concern for your client's privacy. Privacy is very important to my clients as well. That is exactly why I am here. You should know I am also an attorney, but I have never practiced law, like you. My recollection from law school is that Jackson can waive any privilege, which he has the right to do. Jackson, if I give you my word to keep our conversations confidential, would that be acceptable to you?"

Without looking at Roy, Jackson said, "Yes. We will be fully transparent. I don't know why we are here but I have nothing to hide from my clients. May I ask who you represent?"

"Excellent! Excellent word *transparent*. Do you know the Russian word for transparent means not only clear but also obvious? Be assured, my clients are your clients. We have the same mutual concern for their wellbeing. They include some of the wealthiest and most powerful people in Russia. Their interests are the interests of the Russian state."

Jackson said, "Please, tell me what you are concerned about. We are here to help."

"What has become transparent, or, as we say, obvious to us is that the identities of our clients and their investments with your firm have been compromised. As you can imagine, this is of great concern to them, personally and politically. You guaranteed that their accounts with your firm would be kept strictly confidential and would never be disclosed."

"Dimitry, I have no knowledge of any accounts being compromised. We have the most secure networks and encryption tools available. The accounts are all deposited in cryptocurrency investments in offshore companies that are anonymous. Even I have no knowledge as to who the actual Checkmate investors are. What accounts do you believe have been disclosed? How were they accessed? Are you sure that there has been a breach?"

Dimitry spoke to Igor in Russian and then said, "Igor says that the SVR is certain that our clients' accounts have been compromised. Apparently, they were accessed on the Checkmate computers shortly after your divorce action was commenced."

"That's not possible."

"Unfortunately, not only possible, but true. A sophisticated search engine on a supercomputer was used to circumvent your encrypted virtual private network. The search engine utilized is linked to the internet protocol address of one of the largest private investigation firms in the world. They rival the SVR and CIA in cyber security capability.

Jackson was now very worried. "How do you know this private investigation firm accessed the accounts?"

"Igor has a relationship with a former KGB agent who now works for that investigation firm. The agent was not able to identify the client, but he confirmed that the data was in fact accessed and retrieved. This is a big problem. For us. For you."

Jackson frowned and thought about who might be investigating him. "Dimitry, no one appreciates more than I do how important it is that these accounts be kept secure. I have taken every precaution to prevent them from ever being discovered. I am shocked that they might have been compromised. If true, this is not only a serious problem for our clients but a very serious problem for me personally. When the divorce action started, we went to great lengths to make sure that my clients and their investments would remain confidential."

Dimitry asked, "And exactly how did you do that, Jackson?"

"Roy hand-selected my wife's attorney, who has a close relationship with him, and they agreed that my clients and their investments were strictly off limits. We entered a confidentiality stipulation in the divorce action, which was so ordered by the court, directing that no one could have access to these accounts or the identity of my clients. My wife's attorney would have no incentive to violate the court order or jeopardize his relationship with Roy. Even better, he owes Roy and is in our pocket."

"Jackson, I am happy to hear that you are taking this matter seriously. The first thing we want you to do is to transfer all the assets of the clients I represent to a firm I will designate in Moscow. They will contact you and take immediate control over the cryptocurrency. Any information about these accounts or the identity of our clients must be purged from your records. If this problem goes away, our clients will consider resuming their business relationship with you. Is that acceptable?"

Jackson said, "Yes. Of course."

"Good. Now Roy, I need you to immediately dissolve all the offshore companies that were used as depositories for these assets."

Roy said, "Dimitry, I want you to know that I, and my firm, have nothing to do with any of this. I don't even know why I am at this meeting. I feel very uncomfortable with everything I am hearing. Jackson is my client, not you."

Dimitry said something to Igor in Russian and Igor laughed. To Roy, he said, "You formed the offshore companies and did the regulatory work for our clients, didn't you?"

"Yes."

"I can understand why I might be very uncomfortable if I were in your position. Roy, the fact is, the people I represent are very much your and your firm's clients, but I seriously doubt your firm is aware of the services you are rendering to them. Am I right, Roy?"

Roy remained silent.

"It would be unfortunate if I had to report to our clients that, for some unknown reason, you refused to cooperate and help resolve this problem. It might raise some suspicions as to your trustworthiness. It might make Igor uncomfortable. Now, Roy, can we count on your cooperation?"

Roy, feeling Igor staring at him, looked down and nodded.

"Good. After the offshore companies are dissolved, I need you to meet with your good friend, Chance Cormac, who is representing Jackson's wife. It is comforting to know, as Jackson just assured me, that he is 'in your pocket'. Meet with him, without disclosing the source of your knowledge, and tell him that the Checkmate client accounts have been accessed. Find out what he knows about these leaks."

"I will contact him right away. I'll find out what he knows."

"Good. But you must be discreet. Meet with him in person. Don't discuss any of our concerns on the phone or in emails. We are confident that one way or the other this is related to the divorce. Impress upon him the seriousness of this problem. If you are convinced that he doesn't have any knowledge of who is behind this, we will help you to motivate him to find out who does."

Roy nodded again.

"My clients are reasonable people. They will be patient and wait a reasonable period of time to see if you can clean up the mess, which both of you made. There will be no communications of any substance between us by phone or the internet. Periodically, I will come up to different safe houses in New York, which I will designate at the appropriate time, to discuss your progress.

Jackson said, "Dimitry I can assure you that we can fix this. Tell your clients not to worry."

"I am sure they will be glad to hear that. But you should be aware that if there is no progress, or if there is any dissemination of our clients' information, with the help of Igor, we will take proactive steps to resolve this problem ourselves. Igor's solution to most problems tends to be very simple. Have I made myself clear?"

Jackson said, "Absolutely."

"Gentlemen, thank you for your cooperation. Now, our meeting is over, so please get dressed."

After Jackson and Roy put their clothes on, Igor gave them back their licenses and phones and opened the door to permit them to leave.

As they were walking out, Dimity said, "By the way, Jackson, we need you to focus your full attention on this matter. I would stay away from the little girls. They can be a distraction."

Jackson turned deep red.

Igor laughed. "*Koshka.*"

Roy looked at Igor and then at Dimitry. "What little girls? What did Igor just say?"

"Igor actually has a pretty good sense of humor. He said the Russian word, which translated loosely as 'young kittens' or 'little pussies'. I'm sure Jackson would be happy to tell you about all his pets. Good day, gentlemen."

Outside on the sidewalk, all Roy said as he walked away was, "I missed my tee time."

CHAPTER TWENTY-ONE
NO GOOD DEED

My father liked to say, "No good deed goes unpunished." I knew when I took Courtney's divorce as a favor to Roy that it might be one of those cases. Unfortunately, I also knew that my taking the case was not in truth a good deed. I took the case to do good for myself and the firm, not for Roy or Courtney.

On the Monday after the birthday celebration with Melody, Sally came into my office. She said, "Thanks a lot. Now all I hear from Melody is about the best day in her life she spent with you."

"It was the best day in my life, too."

"I want to thank you for the pictures of her blowing out the candles. I heard about how you had to do it twice. I'm sorry for the trouble."

"No trouble. It was my bad. I'm not really good at doing all the things a mom would do. She was thinking of you, and she straightened me right out."

"She has a way of doing that. She can get her Irish up. I'm working on that with her."

"She does remind me of someone I know. By the way, are you guys coming over next weekend? I want to talk to you about a few things that I have been thinking about."

"Sounds serious. We'll be there. Is everything all right?"

"Everything is just about perfect. Now let's get to work."

We were engaged full bore in the class action lawsuit. After being retained by Dylan and his investor group, we filed a complaint in federal court and requested that the class be certified by the court. We anticipated an onslaught of litigation by the defendants. They immediately filed multiple motions to dismiss which were stacked in a mountain on my desk. I also knew that when the defendants answered the complaint, as a tactic, they would file frivolous counterclaims seeking damages against my clients we would be forced to defend.

My plate was full, and I was relying on Sally to complete the discovery in Courtney's divorce action so we would be in a position to make a settlement proposal. I needed everyone to focus on the big case, not the divorce. That's when things started to go sideways.

I got a call from Roy. There were no pleasantries. In a barely controlled voice, he said, "Chance, we have a big problem. I need to see you today. I'm going to come to your office."

"Roy, I'm up to my neck in alligators with the class action. Can we discuss it without sitting down? What's the problem?"

"No! I can't talk on the phone. I have to meet with you. Today!"

"Okay, I have to finish reviewing some motion papers this morning. How about early this afternoon after lunch?"

"I'll be there at one. No later."

I told Sally about the frantic call from Roy and asked her if there was anything going on in Courtney's case I should be aware of. She said nothing she could think of, and that discovery seemed to be proceeding without a hitch.

At one p.m. sharp, Roy arrived. Without saying hello, he frantically motioned upwards. "Let's talk up on the roof."

I sat down on one of the Adirondack chairs. Roy was too agitated to sit down. He paced back and forth as he spoke down to me. "Chance, what the hell are you doing?"

"Roy, why don't you sit down and tell me what this is all about?"

"I don't want to sit. You are making a big mistake. A mistake that will cost you and your client dearly."

"Roy, calm down. I have no idea what you are talking about. What is the problem?"

"We had a deal. A court ordered NDA. Jackson's clients and their investments were strictly off limits."

"Roy, I'm well aware of the NDA and the order. We have fully complied with it."

"Spare me. Immediately after you were retained and started discovery, Jackson was contacted by certain clients and informed that their accounts have been accessed and compromised. These accounts are protected by the most sophisticated firewalls and virtual private networks. This has Damian's fingerprints all over it."

"Roy, I assure you, I have not obtained any information about

Jackson's clients. And neither has Damian. Why would we do that?"

"Come on. You want to gain some leverage in negotiating an agreement in Courtney's case. It's in your DNA to better the deal. I should have known better than to trust you."

"Okay. Before we both say something we'll regret, I will confirm with Damian that we don't have any confidential information. If we inadvertently got something in violation of the NDA we shouldn't have, we will purge it from our records. Who are the clients?"

"You know I can't tell you that. What I can tell you is that Jackson's clients are very important and powerful people. They know their accounts were accessed. They are dangerous. Very dangerous. You have to convince them we can put the milk back in the bottle. If not, I can't protect you or Courtney."

"Roy, what's going on here? Protect us from what? We're no threat to Jackson or his clients. How are you involved in all this?"

"I'm involved as your friend and Courtney's friend. Chance, listen to me carefully. Fix this before it's too late!"

After Roy left, I was puzzled as to what was going on and why Roy was so upset. I went into Damian's office and told him about my meeting with Roy and his not so veiled threats. I asked Damian if he had somehow accessed any of Jackson's clients' accounts or discovered their identities by accident.

He said, "No way. I never searched for the clients' accounts."

I said that's what I told Roy. "The question is, if it wasn't you, who was it?"

I wasn't overly concerned about the threats. Threats are made all the time in matrimonial actions in the heat of the moment but rarely acted on. Usually it's one spouse threatening the other, but sometimes its third parties who don't want to be involved in the drama of someone else's divorce or have their own dirty laundry aired in public.

This was becoming just the distraction I didn't want or need.

CHAPTER TWENTY-TWO
A FATHER'S HELPING HAND

I called Roy and told him that I had spoken to Damian and confirmed that we had fully complied with the court order and NDA. I assured him we didn't have any records regarding Jackson's clients or their identities.

Roy was not happy. He said that if we didn't access the accounts, then it was up to me to discover who did. When I asked Roy how I would do that, he said it was my problem. A problem he guaranteed would only get worse if the records were ever disclosed.

Who would want to hurt Jackson and his clients? It suddenly occurred to me I hadn't heard anything from Courtney's father since our confrontation in court.

Courtney continued to assure me her father was on board with my representation of her, but after Randolph's accusations made in court, I knew better. I called Randolph and told him that I would like to meet with him privately to discuss some issues regarding Courtney's divorce off the record.

I thought it would be best if we met alone, without Courtney being present. He was surprised to hear from me but said he would come to my office. He was playing golf the next day and was willing to drive down to Brooklyn and meet with me in the late afternoon.

He arrived around five. He was still dressed in a white polo shirt with the Westchester Country Club logo on it, checkered golf pants and a Westchester Country Club Patagonia sweater vest.

Despite our confrontation in court, he was outwardly cordial. We shook hands. and he followed me into the conference room. We sat down at the conference table and I asked if he wanted anything to drink. After he declined, I said, "Randolph, thanks for coming down. Not a fun drive during rush hour. How did your round of golf go?"

"I shot an eighty-seven and won a few dollars. Do you golf?"

"No, I don't have the time or patience to be a good golfer. What's the expression? Golf is a good walk spoiled?"

"Only if you lose. Enough pleasantries. Doesn't look like you have done much with your office since our first meeting. I'm surprised after our last conversation that you would want to meet with me."

"I'm hopeful we can work together to help Courtney. We are making good progress in her case. I believe it can be resolved quickly and fairly. I can't discuss anything that might be deemed privileged, but I wanted to speak to you about an issue that came up during discovery."

"What issue is that?"

"We are in the process of reviewing the financial statements produced by Jackson and his firm. His lawyers seem to be cooperating with all our requests. I know you are aware we entered a non-disclosure agreement that was so ordered by the court, protecting the identity of Jackson's clients and their investments."

"I'm well aware of that and not happy."

"I know. That's why I wanted to talk to you. I've been informed someone may have violated the agreement and order. By any chance, do you have any knowledge of who that might be?"

"Chance, before we have any further conversations, I need you to give me your word that anything I tell you will be kept strictly confidential unless I say otherwise. Not a word. Not to Courtney, not to Roy, not anyone. I can't have you undoing all my hard work."

Reluctantly, I agreed. "Fine. Exactly what hard work is that, Randolph?"

"I am aware of the NDA and order. You know I'm very unhappy about it. If I was representing Courtney I would never have consented to it, but that doesn't matter. My attorneys have informed me the confidentiality agreement and order don't apply to me. I'm not a party to the agreement and the court order only applies to the parties."

"Okay, let's assume for purposes of our discussion that may be true, but I would advise you that if you are found to be acting as an agent on behalf of your daughter, the court might have a different opinion."

"Chance, this has been my problem with you, from the beginning. Instead of worrying about how to bring Jackson to his knees, you worry about how to protect him. I've been forced to use my resources to protect my daughter and my grandchildren."

"What resources are those, Randolph?"

"As I told you, I know how to play hardball. I understand corporate espionage and intrigue. I hired the best investigation firm in the world to do a deep dive into Jackson's clients and their investments. I did the heavy lifting you refused to do."

I didn't like what I was hearing. "What is it you think you have discovered?"

"More than I hoped for. His clients are a who's who of billionaires, oligarchies, political leaders, movie stars and expatriates. Their investments are all in crypto accounts in the names of offshore companies. The information I have is evidence of massive tax evasion and money laundering. I have my foot on Jackson's throat."

I took a deep breath and shook my head. It was one thing for Damian to discreetly try to investigate Jackson's assets and income, it was another for Randolph to try to blackmail him and his clients. "Randolph. I know you are very smart and extremely successful. Far more successful than I will ever be. I'm sure in the world of corporate M&A, you are a master at negotiating and getting deals done."

"I'm the best."

"Fortunately, and I do mean fortunately, in this case we don't need any leverage or dark secrets to protect your daughter or the twins. It's not because I'm afraid of a fight. I try more cases to verdict than any lawyer I know. There is just nothing to fight about here. I understand your anger and frustration. But the reality is Courtney and Jackson will be divorced. Jackson is more than willing to generously support your daughter and your grandchildren. Courtney will have custody of the twins, who will continue to live with her. They will never be in need. Both Courtney and Jackson just want to get on with their lives."

"That's nowhere good enough. Jackson has to pay for what he has done to my daughter, my grandchildren and to me."

"Randolph, please listen to me. I've learned, once you win a case, you stop arguing, close your file and go home. If you hurt Jackson, or his clients, you will only be hurting Courtney and the twins. If the court discovers the order was violated, they will hold Courtney in contempt, not you. If Jackson goes down, the family suffers. You're putting your daughter at risk. Can't you see that?"

"I can only see that you have caved, and that Courtney is lucky that I am here to protect her and see she gets what she deserves."

"Randolph. Do me a favor. More importantly, do Courtney a favor. Please call off the dogs and have your people destroy any confidential files that they may have obtained."

"No can do. We're just getting started. Remember, I have your word you will not to repeat any of this to anyone."

"I get it. I only hope you will reconsider before it's too late."

After my meeting with Courtney's father, I felt bound to contact Roy in good faith and tell him that I was now aware that he was correct, Jackson's clients' confidential information had been compromised.

I called Roy and started to tell him I had some information about Jackson's clients' accounts I wanted to share with him. He cut me off and shouted, "Stop! I can't talk about this on the phone." Without even asking if I was free, he said, "I'm coming right over."

When Roy arrived, I went out to meet him. He didn't shake hands or say anything. He shook his head, put his finger to his lips and motioned repeatedly for us to go up to the roof. Once on the roof, Roy stood close to me, his voice muffled. "You're not recording our conversation, are you?"

"Roy, what are you talking about? Why would I record our conversation? What's going on here? Are you in trouble?"

"Chance, we're all in trouble. Big trouble. Please, tell me what you found out."

"As I told you, Damian did not access any information about Jackson or his clients. We don't have any of that information in our possession or control."

"Good. Do you know who does?"

"Yes. I am informed that someone did access the information without our knowledge or consent."

"Who is it?"

"I can't tell you."

"You can't tell me? For Christ's sake, why not?"

"Because it was told to me in confidence and I agreed that I would not disclose the source."

Roy could barely control his rage. "Chance, listen very closely to what I am about to tell you. This is not a game. This is the real world. The people involved make their own rules. This is not a legal problem. They don't care about your promises or ethical concerns. If they are put at risk, they will eliminate the risk with any means at their disposal. They will be the judge, jury and executioner. Wake up! We're all in danger."

"Roy, how can I help you if I don't know what is going on? Why don't you tell me the whole story? I will be happy to help you in any way I can."

"You can help me by making this all go away. Convince whoever has this information that it has to be destroyed and all records purged today. If that doesn't happen, I won't be responsible for what happens next."

"Roy, I'll do my best, but it may take some time."

Roy, in a defeated voice said, "I'm sorry but we don't have time. Remember I tried to warn you. I'm not responsible. There's nothing more I can do. This is on you."

***

Roy took a black town car back to his office. His head felt like it would explode. As he feared, Jackson's divorce was becoming a nightmare. He knew that his license, practice and comfortable life would vanish if it was ever disclosed that he was engaged in money laundering and skimming money from his clients' accounts. But his biggest fear was what Dimitry and Igor might do if he didn't make their concerns go away.

He was a fool to have trusted Jackson and to believe Jackson could protect him from any risk. It was a mistake to bring Chance into the case and pretend that he controlled him. It was all spinning out of control. Roy realized he had to protect himself. No one else would.

He decided not to tell Jackson or Dimitry about his conversation with Chance. There was no benefit to anyone to disclose that Chance knew who accessed the clients' information but refused to tell him.

Dimitry would only hold Roy responsible and demand that Roy obtain the information from Chance. Roy knew that if Chance refused,

Dimitry would have Igor persuade him. Roy decided not to dig the hole any deeper. He knew that in the end he would only be digging his own grave.

***

The next day, I was still thinking about my rooftop conversation with Roy and how best to convince Randolph Gault to do what I knew was in his daughter's best interests.

I would normally have reached out to Courtney and asked her to speak to her father, but felt bound to keep my conversation with Randolph confidential. I considered since Randolph was not technically a client, I might not be ethically bound to keep my word. It was a weak rationalization and in the end didn't pass the red face test.

I went in to see Damian. I wanted to bring him up to speed on my last meeting with Roy. I also had some motion papers I needed JR to file. "Hey, Damian. Well, you were right. This divorce is becoming a bear."

"Hmmm. I'm not surprised. I remember someone saying, 'Don't take the case' but I just can't remember who. I think it was a good-looking investigator. Now, how can I help put the bear back in its cage?"

"Courtney's father, without our or her knowledge or consent, used a high-powered investigation firm to access information about Jackson's clients and their accounts. He refuses to unwind what he has done or stop the investigation."

"Not good."

"Not good at all. I felt compelled to tell Roy I had confirmed that the accounts had been compromised but that I could not disclose who had violated the NDA because the information was confidential. I assured him we had none of the information and would not use it for any purposes in the divorce action. Roy went ballistic and threatened if we didn't put the milk back in the bottle, there would be serious consequences for Courtney and us. Roy seems very frightened but won't tell me how he is involved or what he is scared of."

"Why don't you just tell Courtney to ask her father to back off? Have him purge any information in his files?"

"I told Randolph I wouldn't say anything to Courtney without his permission."

"Don't the interests of your client come first? What happens if you don't warn her and somehow she gets hurt by all this intrigue?"

"That's what I'm struggling with."

"Do you want me to try to go in through a back door and find out what Randolph has discovered?"

"Thanks, but that would only make things worse. I don't want our fingerprints on this. We would be violating the NDA, the court order and my agreement with Randolph. I will give it some more thought and circle back with you. It's the case from hell that just keeps on giving."

"What would you say? No good deed…?"

"Thanks a lot. I deserved that. By the way, is JR here? I need him to file some motion papers with the court for me."

"No. He is at his monthly appointment to get his urine tests done so that the results can be sent to his parole officer to show he is clean before their next meeting. He told me he would stop by the office late this afternoon after he is done."

"Okay. He can file the papers tomorrow. How are things going with his PO?"

"JR says he is a good guy. He actually enjoys their meetings. JR sees him more as a counselor than a PO."

"Great. He deserves a break."

CHAPTER TWENTY-THREE
GENERATION OF SWINE

I wasn't going to go back on my word to Randolph but I felt that I had to speak to Courtney. Maybe she could help talk some sense into her father without knowing about his investigation. I called her and left a message asking her to call me back when she was in a position to talk.

She called. "Hello Chance. The kids are out. What's going on?"

"I just wanted to check in with you. How are you doing?"

"I'm angry. I'm tired of being the victim. I don't deserve this."

"I agree. I would be angry, too. How can I help?"

"Maybe you can explain some things to me. I have tried to live a good life. I chose a profession where I could help children who were suffering. I was a devoted wife and mother, Why am I being punished? How could I be such a fool? My father was right about Jackson all the time."

"You are not a fool. You loved and trusted someone who in the end is not trustworthy. You are a good and remarkable person. You have your whole life ahead of you."

"When I read Hunter Thompson's books about what he called a 'generation of swine', I never really understood the men he was describing. Now I do. They have no morals or sense of right and wrong. They are sociopaths who say whatever is convenient with no regard for the truth. They have utter contempt for anyone who can't help them achieve their goals. And yet they all succeeded. They are rewarded with wealth, fame and power. Jackson is one of those people. He used me. He betrayed me. I hate him. It's horrible to say, but sometimes, I wish he was dead."

"I think you know there was no happy ending for many of those people Hunter exposed. They learned humility in prison. Jackson's death wouldn't help you or your children."

"I know. I'm sorry. I don't really mean what I said. I just don't know how this all will end. Chance, you must think I'm some sort of helpless wife, enjoying the good life, blind to the realty of who my husband is. Of course I suspected something was very wrong. The offshore companies, our sudden wealth, and his trips abroad were all signs he was spinning out of control. In truth, I wasn't really that surprised when I saw the videos of the girls on his laptop."

"It's not easy to confront someone when you know you and your children will be hurt."

"No. But that's still no excuse. The truth is I was never strong enough to confront Jackson. I have always been dependent on my father and then Jackson. I enjoyed the things he provided for me and the girls. I'm to blame. I have never had the courage to stand up for myself. I'm a coward and now I'm paying the price."

"Courtney, my father used to tell me courage isn't having the strength to go on – it is going on when you don't have strength. You don't have to fight Jackson. That wouldn't be a fair fight. You have to just trust me to protect you and your girls. Can you do that?"

"Yes. I trust you. Did your father really say all those things?"

I smiled. "Well, most of them."

"That's what I thought."

I laughed. "You know, you're the first person to ask me that question."

"Too bad you're my lawyer. I think we could be good friends."

"I am your friend."

There was a pause and Courtney said, "Chance, can I ask you a personal question?"

I hesitated. "Sure."

"I was wondering, why aren't you married?"

"Good question. I guess I made a hard choice when I became a litigator. My profession demands too much. I wouldn't make a good husband."

"Hmmm. I'm not sure I buy that."

Courtney sensed that I was beginning to feel a little uncomfortable and when I didn't say anything she said, "Sorry, I didn't mean to pry. Anyway, how can I help you with my case?"

"Do you talk to your father about your divorce?"

"*He* talks to me! He calls and asks me what's going on and whether

I am happy with you. I tell him I am very happy and that we hope to settle soon. Why?"

"He wasn't happy when I was retained. I want to make sure he is not doing something we're not aware of to try to hurt Jackson that will make things more complicated."

"He wouldn't do that but I'll call him anyway and ask him not to interfere."

"Thanks. That might be helpful. It would probably be best if you didn't tell him we spoke."

"No problem, Chance. Thanks for calling me. I feel much better now. You make me feel safe."

"You're welcome. You should feel free to call me anytime."

For some reason, I felt a little embarrassed and off balance after my conversation with Courtney. I had done nothing wrong, yet I couldn't help thinking about Courtney's suggestion that we could be friends.

Divorces are tricky. Clients are in crisis and start seeing their attorneys as their therapist and best friend. If you are not careful, it can quickly get complicated for a lawyer who has a smart and attractive client.

My head started aching. This is exactly why I stayed married the law.

CHAPTER TWENTY-FOUR
A DIPLOMATIC SOLUTION

Jackson got the text about another meeting from Dimitry late on a Friday afternoon: "Meeting at location to be designated. You and Roy Brown. This Sunday 10 a.m."

Again, Dimitry didn't ask if Jackson and Roy were available. There was no request they confirm that they could attend the meeting. It was assumed they would do as they were told.

Jackson and Roy received another text early Sunday morning with the address of the new safe house. They met at the address outside a different non-descript brownstone a few blocks from the Russian Consulate on Saturday morning at 9:45. The safe house looked much like the first one. It was a large townhouse on a block where similar homes were owned by very wealthy New York families.

Roy did as he was told but was not happy. In a sharp tone, he asked Jackson if there was anything new he should know. Jackson said he had no information, but he hoped, since all the Russian crypto accounts had been transferred by Checkmate as requested, the concerns about the security breaches had gone away. Jackson knew, however, this was just wishful thinking.

Igor came out. He was dressed in the same outfit that he wore at their first meeting, except this time the Glock was immediately visible under his leather jacket. They went through the same drill of being photographed and surrendering their licenses and phones. They were again left waiting on the sidewalk, only this time for much longer.

Finally Roy said, without much conviction, "I've had enough of this silliness. For Christ's sake, I'm a prominent lawyer. This is humiliating. My patience is worn out. As soon as I get my license back, I'm leaving. If they want to see me, tell them to make an appointment at my office, like any other client."

Jackson didn't say anything. He wasn't impressed by Roy's tough guy act. He knew that Roy wasn't going anywhere unless Dimitry told him to.

Roy was a corporate lawyer up to his neck in alligators and making more money than he could have ever imagined by skimming from the accounts of his clients. With good reason, he was very frightened of Dimitry and the threat that he could lose everything.

Jackson and Roy were both in a dangerous situation with people who obviously operated outside the law. They had nowhere to run or hide.

When Igor came back, they were searched and brought into another windowless room in the brownstone. The room again had bare walls, no windows, and long fluorescent lights on the ceiling. In the center of the room was a long metal folding table with some bottled waters on it and six black folding chairs. This room felt more like an interrogation room than a conference room. The metal box was already plugged in on the floor.

Jackson and Roy were still standing when Dimitry came into the room. Igor locked the door and once again stood in front of it with his arms crossed.

Dimitry was dressed impeccably in a Zegna fine wool blue sports jacket and an open collar white shirt with azure cufflinks. He said, "Gentlemen, so good to see you again. Thank you again for coming. You remember Igor, don't you?"

Jackson said hello to Dimitry. Roy said nothing.

"If you don't mind, please remain standing and take off your shoes, jackets, pants, and shirts. Igor insists that we take these precautions again today."

Roy said, without much conviction, "Wait a minute. We were already searched downstairs. I'm not undressing for you. This is totally unnecessary. Why don't you guys undress? You're just trying to embarrass us."

"Roy, I have found that it is often a wise thing to do things that are not strictly necessary but are still prudent. This is for your protection as well as ours. I assure you that you will be very comfortable."

Roy understood that they had no choice but to do what they were told. They were once again in a locked room in a Russian safe house with an armed SVR agent. Nobody knew where they were.

Igor searched their shoes, jackets, shirts and pants and once again assumed his position with his back to the door, saying in Russian,

"Dimitry, nice touch making them undress. Totally unnecessary, but certainly effective."

Dimity smiled and replied, "*Spasibo.*"

Dimity said, "Gentlemen, thank you for your cooperation. Now, please sit down and make yourselves comfortable. Can I offer you some water or perhaps another beverage?"

Jackson and Roy each took a bottle of water and sat down. Roy nervously gulped down half the bottle of water.

Jackson decided to speak first and try to do some damage control. "Dimitry, I'm glad you contacted us. We have been anxious to meet with you again. I think we are making some real progress. As you are aware, all the cryptocurrency accounts have been transferred to the Russian firms pursuant to your instructions."

Dimitry just sat silently and waited for Jackson to finish.

"Roy has dissolved all the offshore corporations as directed. We have purged the Checkmate computers of all records regarding these accounts and Roy has deleted all files maintained at his firm regarding your clients. I would hope this satisfies your concerns about any possible future disclosure of your clients' identities or accounts."

"Jackson, that's a good start, however, although your efforts may avoid any further compromise of our clients' information, unfortunately, it does not secure the information that has already been accessed. We don't need what you call progress, we need a solution. We want to know who accessed this information and why? We believe the answers can all be discovered somewhere in your divorce."

Roy finally spoke up. "I met with Chance Cormac, Jackson's wife's attorney as you requested. I told him that Jackson's clients' accounts had been compromised in violation of the court order. I warned him, without naming any names, that some very powerful people are very upset and intend to do whatever is required to secure the information."

"Does he know who accessed the accounts?"

"No. He assured me his firm has fully complied with the order and he has no information about the identity of Jackson's clients or their accounts in his possession. He said he would investigate to see if he could discover who might have violated the order. For what it's worth, I believe him."

It was at best a half truth. Roy was careful not to inform Dimitry, or Jackson, that Chance had, in fact, discovered who had accessed the accounts and had informed Roy of his discovery. He was confident that Chance would never speak to Jackson directly about their conversation or the identity of the confidential informant. He had done what he was asked to do. Roy was thinking, *if they're such smart guys, Dimitry and this SVR thug can figure it out for themselves.*

"Roy, thank you for meeting with Chance, but I'm not sure you have his attention. When I attended the School of Foreign Service at Georgetown, I took classes in diplomacy and was taught all the academic techniques for achieving a diplomatic solution to international conflicts. I was taught that the goal always is to find a peaceful solution to a conflict."

Roy was in no mood for a lecture but he knew Dimity was telling this story for their benefit.

"The academic techniques included finding a commonality of interest, provide economic incentives, and avoid the risks of war. We were taught to never assume anything about what the real interests are of the other side. We learned to actively listen, and decipher what was really being said behind all the political rhetoric. But do you know what I learned as a diplomat in the real word, Roy? Do you know the real key to a diplomatic solution?"

"No. I don't."

"Fear. Fear, Roy, is the only reason treaties are entered and wars are avoided. Fear of loss of life, loss of land, or loss of face and standing in the world. The greater the fear, the more favorable the terms that can be negotiated. Of course, there can be fears on both sides. The art of diplomacy is to discover what the greatest fear is for the other side and use it to your advantage. Do you understand?"

Roy said, "Yes. But if we don't even know who the other side is, how can we create fear?"

"But, Roy, we do know who the other side is. It's obvious. This dispute is about Jackson's divorce. Our adversaries are Jackson's wife, her lawyer, the lawyer's investigator and possibly the judge. They are the other side. It doesn't matter who actually accessed the accounts. If we understand the greatest fears of those people, we can apply the right pressure and they will make this all go away. First of all, Courtney is much too comfortable about the divorce."

Jackson looked nervously at Roy. He was concerned about Dimitry's veiled threats.

"Roy, I want the gloves to come off. I want Courtney to be afraid of losing the things that are most important to her. I want the divorce to be the last thing she thinks about at night before she goes to sleep and the first thing she thinks about in the morning. I want her to demand that Chance Cormac do whatever it takes to end the divorce and solve our problem."

Jackson was concerned when he heard Roy say, without hesitation, "That should be no problem. I can do that."

"Good. Next, I want to motivate your friend Chance Cormac to help us solve this problem. Chance is a high profile litigator. I doubt he is concerned in the least when you tell him that powerful people are upset. He litigates against powerful people all the time. I want to focus on the weakest links in his firm."

"Who? His paralegal?"

"Not only his paralegal, but his clerk. We have discovered JR Reynolds is on probation and has a substance abuse problem. He is vulnerable and unstable. Let's prey on his worst fears. Once we have his cooperation, we will have access to all the information we need about the divorce from the inside of the firm. Also, if necessary, I think JR can be helpful in other ways we don't have to discuss at this time."

Roy said, "I think I can be very helpful in that regard. I sit on the NYC Parole Board. I can get access to JR's probation records and his PO, to make life difficult for him."

"Excellent! That's what I want to hear, Roy! Next, we are also aware that Mr. Cormac had a romantic relationship with his legal assistant during law school and is her daughter's godfather. He may not care about stepping on the toes of powerful people, but he does care a great deal about them. He will do whatever is necessary to protect them. Igor will take the steps necessary to put them in harm's way and get his attention."

Jackson said, "Wait a minute. What do you mean by harm's way? I don't want anyone hurt. I won't be part of it."

"Jackson, wake up! Many people have already been hurt because of you. You have been reckless and indiscreet. Your wife has more than good and sufficient reasons to divorce you. You have been dishonest and broken all your marriage vows. Not only your wife, but your clients, have paid a price for your indiscretions. However, if we can make, as you say, some real progress, there will be no need for anyone to get hurt. We will assist you in motivating JR, Chance and Courtney to help us. But we must act quickly."

Dmitry turned to Roy, who sat silently but suddenly now seemed overly eager to help Dimitry with his tactics. "Roy, I want you to focus immediately on JR and Courtney. Igor will get Chance's attention. There is a very short fuse on all of this. If there is no diplomatic solution in the near future, Igor will not hesitate to do what he does best and simply eliminate the problem. Thank you for meeting with us. I think this was what you would call a very productive meeting. We will be in touch with you in the near future."

Jackson and Roy got dressed and left the safehouse in total silence. They said nothing to each other as they went their separate ways down the street. They understood all too well Dimitry's lesson about diplomacy and fear was a cautionary tale meant first and foremost for them. There was nothing diplomatic about the meeting.

CHAPTER TWENTY-FIVE
MISDEAL

JR had been meeting with his parole officer in New York City once a month since he moved to Brooklyn a year ago. They met in lower Manhattan at One Police Plaza, located far downtown by City Hall. JR took the subway from Brooklyn to Manhattan. It took some time for JR to get used to the subway maps, the screech of trains entering a station and the frantic rush of riders getting on and off a train before the doors closed. The gang graffiti on the dirty subway walls was a reminder that the underground world had its own rules.

JR saw the effort New Yorkers made to not interact or look at one another on a subway train. They kept their eyes down and earplugs in to protect themselves against any possible confrontation with another passenger. He recognized the fear in their faces. It reminded him of how when he was deployed and the locals saw his uniform they averted their eyes as if he was the real enemy. He realized people never really feel safe around strangers no matter where they live.

One Police Plaza is a large, imposing fourteen-story white office building off Park Row at the very tip of Manhattan, a stone's throw from the Brooklyn Bridge. It is the nerve center for the largest police department in the country. It also houses the Corrections Department and the Parole Office that JR reported to.

JR always checked in at the reception desk in the lobby, where a uniformed officer confirmed his appointment and give him a name tag that said PROBATION in large letters and his probation floor number. He was required to clip the name tag on his jacket and wear it at all times while in the building.

When he walked to the elevators, he was surrounded by a sea of blue uniforms worn by New York's Finest. He knew that when they read his nametag, and destination they automatically thought only one thing: convict.

His rehab counselor taught him to always be humble, but sometimes he still felt embarrassed and angry. He was careful during his monthly visits not to make eye contact or speak unless he was spoken to. Sometimes, he felt like he was watching a movie of someone else's life. He couldn't believe he was a convict on parole.

When he went to the elevator bank, he was required to take off his shoes and belt and walk through a metal detector. When a guard read his name tag and destination, he was always frisked before he was allowed to get into the elevator.

There was one elevator bank specifically for non-law enforcement visitors. A guard punched the button for the floor number for probation department and the elevator only stopped at that floor. JR was thankful he didn't have to ride up in close quarters with police officers.

JR felt very lucky his parole office was Garrett Jones. Garrett was a 250-pound Black man built like a linebacker. Garrett had been an MP in the Army and when he found out about JR's service, they immediately developed a good rapport.

Garrett had been a PO in NYC for ten years. He supervised many parolees who had serious felony convictions, including the big three – rape, robbery and manslaughter. Most of his parolees were hopeless recidivists, and Garrett knew he was only babysitting them until their next stretch at a maximum-security prison.

Garrett liked JR and respected his service as a SEAL. He knew that JR had no priors. He was not impressed or concerned about JR's conviction for the use of oxycodone. He viewed these parolees more as victims of war than convicts. They often suffered from PTSD or other psychiatric disorders. He understood how they started using drugs, usually prescribed to begin with, to keep the demons at bay. Garrett's only concern at each monthly meeting with JR was to confirm that JR was staying clean and attending his AA meetings.

JR actually came to enjoy his meetings with Garrett, and, after answering the routine questions about his parole, they spent time exchanging stories about serving as enlisted men. They debated about which branch of the service was best and who would win the Army Navy football game that year. JR soon considered Garrett not only his PO but his friend.

It was a bitter cold, gray afternoon just before Christmas when JR took the subway from Brooklyn to the City Hall stop in Manhattan for his scheduled meeting with Garrett. The homeless people were forced onto the subway platforms in order to keep from freezing to death. They were found sleeping over subway hot air vents in layers of ragged clothes, or lying on the hard plastic benches in the subway trains with all their worldly possessions in black garbage bags.

The stench of a homeless person always greets you before you see them sitting on a subway train. No matter how crowded the train, riders keep a distance of at least ten feet away from the sight and smell they want to avoid. JR always thought, "There but the grace of God goes me, if I had not gotten the help I needed in time." He always held his breath and put a few dollars in a homeless person's hand before he got off the subway.

On the wide sidewalk in front of One Police Plaza, there are no buildings to block the wind and it blows fiercely in the winter months. The frigid air cut right through JR's leather jacket, and he clenched his teeth as he jogged to the revolving entrance door. The wind blew hard in Texas but nothing like this.

JR stomped his feet and clapped his hands together to get warm. He smiled because inside his jacket he had a small Christmas present for Garrett, an inexpensive replica of an antique British officer's walking stick. He thought Garrett would get a kick out of walking around with the stick under his arm in his office as if he was in an old army war movie.

When he put the walking stick in the basket before going through the metal detector, the guard looked at it carefully and asked JR what it was. He explained that it was a gift that he was giving to his PO, not a weapon. The guard laughed. "That's probably the only Christmas present your PO ever got from a convict."

When JR entered Garrett's office he smiled and handed him the walking stick. "Merry Christmas, Garrett! I was thinkin' that you could use this when you have to get tough with your parolees."

JR immediately sensed that there was something wrong. Garrett looked angry and immediately handed JR back the present. He said in an official tone, "JR, you know I can't accept this. I'm your parole officer. I can't accept gifts from a parolee. It would be totally improper."

JR was stunned. "I'm real sorry, Garrett. I sure meant no offense.

It's just a small Christmas gift. I just wanted to thank you for all your help."

"JR, I'm not here to help you, I'm here to make sure you don't violate the conditions of your parole. Do you mind if I record our conversation instead of taking notes today?"

JR hesitated. "Garrett, I'm a little upside down here. Are you mad at me? Is there a reason I shouldn't want to have our conversation recorded?"

"Not if you have nothing to hide."

JR was confused by Garrett's sudden hostility, but he trusted him and agreed. "No problem, Garrett. You've always been a straight shooter with me. If you want to record our conversation, I have nothing to hide from you."

Garrett spoke to his iPhone: "Siri, record this conversation. Keep the date and time. JR, are you still working part time for the lawyer?"

"Yes, sir. Chance Cormac, I do some clerking and filing for him on a part time basis."

"Is there any other work you do for Mr. Cormac or anyone else?"

"No, sir. Just the clerking. I still get my VA disability benefits. Garrett, did I do something wrong?"

Garrett ignored the question. "You know if you give me false information, it's a violation of your parole, don't you?"

JR's mind was racing. He didn't know where Garrett was going with his questions. He just knew it wasn't good. "Garrett, I am being truthful. I got no reason to lie to you. I'm just wonderin' what this is all about. Should I be worryin' bout something?"

"Do you deal cards and work a money bank for the players at a cash poker game held at Mr. Cormac's apartment?"

"Oh. Is that it? Sorry, I don't hardly think of it as work. Chance asked me if I wanted to deal at a weekly poker game he holds in his apartment with his friends. Chance hosts the game, and the same players play every week. He thought I could use the cash and I might like to get to know his friends. They are all mighty interesting professional people. Heck, even a judge plays. I've been dealing for about six months. I do enjoy it. I've become friends with the players. Did I do somethin' wrong?"

"Are you paid for dealing?"

"Paid for dealing? No sir. But I do get some tips. Each player gives me twenty-five dollars and the winner usually gives me somethin' from his winnings. I might put in my pocket about two, two-fifty in tips on a good night."

"Do you declare that income on your tax returns?"

"Tax returns? I never gave it any thought. If you think I should, I'll be glad to."

"JR, I will be referring your case to the DA with a recommendation that you be formally charged with violations of the conditions of your parole. Once charged, you will be given forty-eight hours to surrender to the local police precinct or you will be arrested."

JR was blindsided. He didn't know what to say.

"If it is determined that you violated your parole, your original prison sentence will be reinstated. In addition, you may be charged with additional crimes based upon your conduct. I would suggest you consult an attorney."

"Garrett, can you hold your horses. Just wait a minute. I'm real confused. I was asked to deal. The players are lawyers, an accountant and a state court judge playing a friendly game of poker. I sure never thought for a minute I was doing anything wrong. If you think it's a problem, I promise will never deal again. My record is clean. Give me a second chance. For the love of God, Garrett, it's Christmas."

For the first time, Garrett looked JR in the eyes and showed some regret. "I'm sorry, JR. I have a family to think about. It's not my call."

"No? Well then, whose call might it be?"

Garrett just shook his head. "We're all done. You can leave now."

As JR walked back to the subway station, he felt totally numb, but not from the freezing weather. He didn't ever notice the frigid air and wind blasting through the wind tunnels formed by the tall buildings.

He realized he was still holding the walking stick he'd bought as a gift for Garrett. He laughed at his own stupidity, cracked the stick in half over his knee and threw it in a dumpster. His mind was racing. He knew he needed help. He called Damian.

Damian answered. "JR, how are you? How did your PO like the

Christmas present?"

"Damian, I'm in all sorts of trouble. I need to see you and Chance."

"JR, what happened? Are you all right? Do you need me to come pick you up?"

"No. I just need to meet with you and Chance right away. I'm sorry as sin to bother you, but can you please make that happen?"

"JR, slow down. I'm here in the office. I think Chance is still here. I'll track him down. We will both be here waiting for you. There's no rush. Take a deep breath. Whatever it is, we'll figure it out together."

***

Damian came into my office and told me about his conversation with JR. He explained that JR was in some sort of trouble and needed to see both of us immediately. I said that I would be happy to wait and sit down with JR whenever he got there. I asked what was going on. Damian said he didn't know but JR didn't sound good. Damian started a fire in the fireplace in the conference room to warm up the office and put on a pot of coffee. He sat down at the conference room table and repeatedly checked his phone with a concerned look on his face.

JR got to the office an hour later. He took his usual subway train but was so angry and confused that he missed his stop and had to walk ten blocks back to the office. He entered the front door to the office, and without warning, was crippled by an agonizing panic attack. He was paralyzed with fear and couldn't breathe. He made it to one of the waiting room chairs, sat down and put his head between his legs.

He hadn't had a panic attack since he'd moved to Brooklyn. He tried to use the techniques that he had learned in therapy to lessen the agony. He knew that his attacks never lasted more than ten minutes so he forced himself to look at his watch so that he could gauge how much longer he would be in pain. He tried to distract his mind by silently singing the same song over and over again with his eyes closed. He had found in the past that the lyrics of *Peace Train* by Cat Stevens gave him solace and helped him tolerate the pain.

Damian had heard the front door open and came out to see if it was

JR. He found JR doubled over in the chair in the waiting room and immediately ran over to him. JR raised his hand and signaled for Damian to hold on. Damian realized what was happening and sat silently in the chair next to JR, waiting for the attack to pass.

After another five minutes, JR slowly sat up. He was pale and his voice was shaky. "Sorry, man, gimme just a minute."

"JR, take your time. Don't move. Just sit there. Tell me, what I can do for you. Do you want to go to the ER?"

"No. Some water would be good. I'm parched. Just need a little more time to get my legs under me. Chance here? I sure could use some help."

"Chance is here. Take your time. I'll get you some water and we'll be in the conference room. Come in when you feel better. There's no rush. We're here for you."

Damian got a bottle of water and put it on the table next to where JR was sitting quietly with his eyes closed. Damian came into the conference room and sat across from me.

"Is JR all right?"

"He had a panic attack but I think he will recover."

"Does he need a doctor?"

"No. He says he will be okay."

"What's going on?"

"He didn't say but I know he was meeting with his PO."

"Okay. I don't think he should be alone. Why don't you wait with him until he feels up to sitting down with us."

Eventually Damian and JR came into the conference room, each were holding a cup of coffee Damian had an extra cup he handed to me. Damian and JR sat down next to each other on the conference table chairs near to the fireplace. I sat across from them and waited for JR to warm up and recover.

JR still looked pale and shaky. He held the coffee cup in both hands and took a sip. "Thanks. Fire feels mighty good. Man, I'm cold! Sorry for this trouble so late. I didn't know what to do and I don't have nobody else to turn to."

I spoke first. "JR, first of all, we're worried about you. Do you need some medical assistance? We would be glad to call an ambulance or take you to the ER."

"No. But thank you, Chance. I'm feeling a might better now. I need legal advice, not medical advice. I know how busy you both are and am very sorry to have to trouble you with my problems. Very sorry."

"Okay, here's the deal. We want to help you, so that's the last apology I want to hear. Whatever it is, we will see it through together. Take your time and tell us what happened."

JR slowly described what happened at the meeting with his parole officer and the threatened criminal prosecution. When he finished, he said, "I'm awful scared. I won't last in prison. I just can't go away."

"JR, look at me. you're not going anywhere. I feel responsible because I somehow got you into this mess and I am going to get you out of it. Look at me. Do you believe that?"

"Yes, Chance. I do. I'm hopin' that's true."

"Good. Now I have three questions for you. One, did Garrett ever record your conversations before today? Two, did he say how he knew you were dealing cards for me? And three, other than the weekly players, Damian, Sally and me, is there anyone else who knows you have been dealing for us?"

As I anticipated, JR's answer to all three questions was the same: "Nope."

"It's late. JR, I want you to go home and get some rest, You know I am not a criminal defense attorney. I'm going to call a criminal attorney I went to law school with, Francis Fogarty, and ask him to represent you. Francis is a former chief prosecutor in the Kings County District Attorney's Office, smart as they come and tough as nails."

JR looked up and seemed, for the first time, relieved.

"I am sure he will make himself available to meet with us tomorrow. I will text you the time we can meet tomorrow as soon as I speak to Francis. I want you to go home and get some sleep. Under no circumstances are you to discuss what happened at the probation department with anyone but us or your attorneys."

"I sure won't. My daddy taught me never miss a good chance to shut up. But, Chance, I can't pay a lawyer."

"Don't worry about it. I made this mess and I intend to clean it up."

Damian walked JR out to the front door and talked to him for a while to make sure he was OK before he left.

I went into my office and called Francis at home. I knew it was late, but criminal defense attorneys are used to clients being arrested at all times of the day and night. They are always on call, and it is always an emergency.

Francis picked up right away. I apologized for calling him so late and gave him a quick summary of the day's events. I said I thought JR would be charged the next day and if he was available, I wanted JR to sign him up before he was required to surrender. Francis asked if the client could carry the freight.

I told him not to worry, I would pay his retainer and he should send his statements to me. He suggested we meet at my office at four the next afternoon, in order to give him time to get a copy of the criminal complaint.

When I returned to the conference room, I updated Damian about Francis. "This smells. There's a stench all over it. We have to find out what's rotten. Damian, take a hard look at the PO and help Francis with any investigation he feels needs to be done."

"Got it. Thanks for helping JR out. I owe you."

"If anyone else thanks me tonight I swear I'm going to jump out the window. See you tomorrow."

CHAPTER TWENTY-SIX
A COURT FOR CRIMINALS

The next morning, Fogarty contacted the DA's office, notified them that he was representing JR and got a copy of the criminal complaint. He scanned the complaint and sent a copy to me, together with his retainer agreement and an email confirming our 4 p.m. meeting.

I made copies of the complaint so Damian and I could review it before we met with JR and Francis. JR was being charged with ten separate counts. In addition to violation of his parole, he was charged with five felonies and four misdemeanors. The felonies included promoting gambling in the first degree, money laundering, tax evasion, and racketeering, because he had crossed state lines in moving from Texas to New York for the purposes of committing a felony. The last charge was attempted bribery for attempting to give his Parole Officer a gift. The felonies carried a maximum sentence of ten years in prison.

Francis Xavier Fogarty is a bulldog in every sense of the word. He looks like a bulldog, barks like a bulldog, and bites like a bulldog. He believes, in court, if the facts are on your side, pound the facts. If the law is on your side, pound the law. And if neither the facts nor law are on your side, pound the table. Jurors love him because what you see is who he is.

Also, in any conversation outside of court, without any warning, he will say the most vile and obscene things I have ever heard an attorney say. Especially about his adversaries. Maybe it's because the nuns rapped his knuckles too many times in parochial school or because the other kids made fun of his name once too often. Whatever it was, he curses with a vengeance.

JR arrived early for the meeting. I decided not to go over the criminal complaint with him because I thought it would be better for Francis to address it and answer his questions.

JR, Damian and I were waiting in the conference room when Francis arrived. He burst in, red in the face, and stuffed into a three-piece wool suit. Without saying hello, he threw the complaint across the table and yelled, "These cocksuckers have got to be fucking kidding me! This shit doesn't pass the red face test!"

He paced back and forth and continued to yell. "In my twenty-five years as a prosecutor and defense attorney there has never, I repeat, *never*, been anyone charged with promoting gambling for playing a social card game at home. These monkey fuckers don't even try to bust the big money games they know are mobbed up and make a big rake on every hand. What the fuck, you can drive an hour in any direction to a casino where the players get raped and then comped to a shitty buffet lunch."

JR sat with his mouth wide open. He had never experienced an attorney like Francis.

"Even these dickless morons should be embarrassed. JR's been charged like fucking public enemy number one because he dealt cards to some lawyers and a judge, who never said boo to him. And violated, because he tried to give his PO a fucking Christmas present! But I have my own present for them. I'm going to shove this complaint so far up their sphincters they'll gag on it."

I couldn't help it, I started choking with laughter. Francis's obscene rants always have that effect on me. His outrage was a great relief as he said what we were all thinking, and desperately wanted to hear. He was a righteous, foul-mouthed leprechaun on a mission from God.

JR and Damian looked at me with their mouths open, not quite sure what to make of Francis. I said, "Good to see you, too, Francis, but I'm not sure cocksucker is a politically correct legal term anymore."

I told JR he was in good hands. I thought it best if he and Francis talked privately, because I might be a potential witness as the host and a player in the poker games. We left them in the conference room and Damian and I went back to our offices.

Francis called us back in about an hour later. JR looked like the weight of the world had been lifted from his shoulders. Francis said, "I had a good talk with our friend JR here. He's a good man. He signed my retainer agreement. Chance, I will send you my wire instructions so that you can pay my retainer. I'm expensive, but I'm worth it."

I told Francis I was relieved he was representing JR. I would wire the retainer first thing in the morning.

Francis continued, "Good. I love the law, but I love my summer home and boat in Montauk just as much. I have reviewed this dogshit excuse for a complaint in detail with JR. It's the same bullshit over and over again just dressed up in different counts. It doesn't mask the stink. Even these ignorant pricks know they will never get a conviction, so there must be some other reason they violated JR. Usually it's because they want to turn JR and use him as witness in another case. If he cooperates, they dismiss the criminal charges or work out a disposition, like extending his probation a few months."

"Francis, I helped make this mess and trust that you can clean it up."

"I will know soon enough what these fucking idiots want. I told JR not to worry. There is no way in hell he is going to prison for this trumped-up bullshit. We still have some time before he has to surrender. I will contact the DA and arrange for JR to go in with me to surrender late in the day tomorrow."

JR asked, "Will I have to stay in jail after I'm arrested?"

"Probably. But not for long. I'll try to have you surrender at the end of the day so, at worst, you will only be detained in that hell hole of a jail overnight, waiting for your arraignment. I know the supervising corrections officer at the jail. He is a former Marine. I will make sure that he is acquainted with your background and medical condition. He will arrange for you to get your own cell and some medication, if you need it."

"Mr. Fogarty, how can I repay you, sir?"

"First of all, call me Francis. Second, rest assured I will be paid handsomely by your patron saint over here."

"Francis, I want you to know that I didn't think I was doing anything wrong."

"JR, I don't know what the play is here, but believe me it has nothing to do with what you did or what's right or wrong. I will contact you guys when I have confirmed a time and place for JR to surrender. I've told JR, at no time is he to discuss his case with anyone other than his attorneys. That includes anyone from the DA's office, the probation department or, God forbid, anyone attending his feel good, come to God AA meetings."

Francis got up and as he was rushing out of the conference room, he said, "And Chance – for fuck's sake, find yourself a new dealer."

I told Damian to take JR to dinner at Ida Rose's and charge it to my account. JR thanked me repeatedly, saying he didn't know how he would ever be able to repay me for all my help and kindness. I told him not to worry about it. It was the least I could do after putting him in a tough spot.

A defendant has to be arraigned within forty-eight hours of his arrest. JR surrendered late the following afternoon at a local precinct house. Francis and Damian accompanied him and waited while he was printed and photographed. Because JR was charged with multiple felonies, he was remanded to the Kings County Jail until he could be arraigned.

When he came out to be transported to jail, looking pale and frightened, he was in handcuffs. He was allowed to speak briefly with Francis and Damian. Francis told him he was able to arrange for him to have his own cell. He instructed JR not to interact or talk to any other inmates or corrections offices, adding, "For the love of Christ, don't eat the bologna sandwiches they give you for dinner and breakfast."

Damian took JR's wallet, phone, watch and belt. He hugged his friend and told him to be strong. He would be there tomorrow for the arraignment.

JR's arraignment was held the next day at the Kings County Criminal Court, an old brick building with huge arched doors that looked more like a medieval castle than a courthouse. The criminal court has jurisdiction over misdemeanors and lesser crimes, but handles arraignments for all criminal cases, including the most serious felonies.

The arraignment part is jammed in the morning with families, friends and mostly bottom feeding attorneys dressed in cheap suits, colored shirts, loud ties and scuffed shoes, talking in the hall, not with their clients, but with each other. The calendars move fast.

No Assistant District Attorney wants to be responsible for a potentially dangerous criminal being cut loose because they missed the arraignment deadline. There used to be "lobster shift" arraignments in the NYC criminal courts held all night long. The lobster shift got its name because lobster fisherman go out to sea in the middle of the night to secure their lobster pots.

All-night arraignments were discontinued, ostensibly for budgetary reasons because of the high cost of staffing the courthouse throughout the night. But in truth, the judges killed it. No judge in his right mind wanted to sit on the bench all night long to assure a defendant got a speedy arraignment. Also, it was felt that a night in jail was a great learning experience for what the future holds for a felon.

Judge DiSalvo was the judge presiding over the arraignments in Courtroom AR1. He was a senior judge, with long experience. He was firm but fair and kept his calendar moving quickly. He expected the lawyers to be prepared and did not suffer fools lightly. His courtroom was the largest courtroom in the Criminal Court and could easily accommodate the frightened and defeated mass of humanity waiting for their loved ones to be brought before the judge to be arraigned.

Francis filed a Notice of Appearance on behalf of JR with the court clerk, Mary Kinkade, sitting in the dock at the front of the courtroom below the judge's bench. Francis knew Mary well from his years practicing as both an ADA and defense attorney in Kings County.

Francis chatted with Mary, asking about her family, if the prisoners had been brought in, and where JR's case was on the calendar. She told him the prisoners were on the bus and should arrive soon. JR's case was at the bottom of a long calendar, but she assured Francis she would move his case to the top of the calendar as soon as JR was in the cage, where the detained prisoners waited to be arraigned.

Francis said, "Mary, you are an angel and you are still in my will."

Mary laughed. "Much good that will do me, Francis. We both know you will never die."

On his way out of the courtroom, Francis spoke to another defense attorney he liked and respected, Brendon Steins, who had served with him in the DA's office. He asked Brendon if he knew who the ADA was who would be handling the arraignments today. He learned it was a young Black ADA named James Chamberlain. He was a Harvard undergrad and graduated from Harvard Law. Obviously, the Kings County DA's office was a not a career choice for Chamberlain but a stepping stone to get some trial experience, a few notches on his resumé and advance his political ambitions.

Brendon said the young ADA was not very experienced, very inflexible, and played things strictly by the book. Just not how things worked in the Kings County Criminal Court where 98% of the cases are disposed of by negotiating a plea. But Francis was confident that Judge DiSalvo would educate Mr. Chamberlain very quickly as to how things worked in his courtroom.

Damian and I sat on a bench outside the courtroom, waiting for the calendar to be called. I was an experienced trial lawyer who had appeared in countless federal and state courthouses throughout the state, yet I felt uneasy and disoriented sitting in this criminal court. I was out of my element.

Francis came out of the courtroom and sat down next to us, to bring us up to speed. Damian asked anxiously, "How's JR doing?"

"He's on the jailhouse express, the bus should be here soon, and I will speak to him before the arraignment. I wanted to discuss with both of you what I expect to happen today. As you know, the arraignment is just a formality. The charges are read, a plea is entered and then a bail application is made. We have a good judge. I've tried many cases before him. He's not going to have much patience with this dog shit."

"Do you know the ADA?" I asked.

"Nope. I don't know him but I'm told he's young and inexperienced and may be a bit of a prick. All of which can only help our case with this judge. You guys sit in the gallery. This shouldn't take long. And for Christ's sake, turn your phones off!"

When Francis went back into the courtroom, Mary motioned to him and signaled that JR was in the bullpen. Francis went back and showed his credentials to the guard, who unlocked the door to the caged area where the prisoners waited and let him in.

The caged room smelled of sweat and fear. Francis found JR, chained to the bench, sitting next to five other disheveled-looking inmates waiting to be arraigned. Francis looked at JR and knew immediately that he was not doing well at all. Francis shook his head and whispered, "Cocksuckers," to himself.

JR was disheveled, unwashed and sitting motionless with his head between his knees. The other prisoners in the bullpen all had their game faces and 100-mile stares on, even though they were twisted up inside, knowing they had no control, and little understanding, of what would happen to them in the courtroom.

JR couldn't hide his pain. He was broken. Francis bent down close to JR's ear so that the other prisoners couldn't hear their conversation. "JR, how are you doing?"

JR didn't look up but said with an effort, "Mr. Fogarty, I'm doing pretty poorly. I almost didn't make it. I had a bad panic attack in jail last night. The cell closed in on me, and I couldn't breathe. It lasted a mighty long time. It was almost more than I could bear. I didn't have the strength to call the guard. With no medicine and no help I was up all night sitting on the edge of the bed scared to move and afraid to sleep. Sir, I know I can't go back there."

"JR, look at me. Again, my name is Francis. You are not going back. Not now, not ever. Do you think you can stand next to me in court for just a few minutes? You won't have to say anything. I will do all the talking."

JR looked up. "Francis, I'll try."

Francis came out told Damian and me, "He's hurting but he'll be okay. But these cocksuckers better run for cover because I am looking to shoot bear."

We went into the courtroom with Francis. The jury box is reserved for attorneys waiting for their cases to be called, but Francis sat down next to us on a bench in the back of the courtroom. He had no desire to be associated with the local Criminal Court Bar.

After the armed court officer called, "All rise!" you could hear a pin drop in the courtroom. Judge DiSalvo entered the courtroom and took the bench. After the judge was seated the court officer barked "All cell phones are to be turned off! All newspapers are to be put away! There will be no talking during these court proceedings unless the judge addresses you."

As promised, Mary called JR's case first. "The People v. John Reynolds."

Francis went up to the counsel's table marked Defendant. He stayed standing and opened his trial bag. He put a copy of the complaint and a legal pad in front of him on the scratched wooden counsel's table.

JR, disheveled and still handcuffed, shuffled in slowly, led by a corrections officer. His pants were sliding down, because his belt had been taken, and one shoe kept slipping off because they had taken his laces. He was very pale and stood hunched over, next to Francis. A corrections officer stood behind him with his hand on his gun.

Francis put his hand on JR's shoulder. "This will be over soon. *Don't* say anything."

The young ADA was joined at the prosecution's counsel table by Garrett Jones, JR's probation officer. The judge looked up, saw Francis and smiled. Francis said, "Good morning, Your Honor."

"Mr. Fogarty, good to see you in my courtroom again. I was beginning to think you didn't like me anymore."

"Judge, it is always a privilege and honor to appear before you."

The judge addressed Chamberlain. He didn't acknowledge the ADA by name but said, "Are the People ready to proceed?"

"Yes, Your Honor."

"Is there a representative of the Probation Department in Court?"

"Yes, You Honor, Mr. Garrett Jones is here with me at the counsel's table."

"Mr. Fogarty, do you waive the reading?"

Francis answered, "Yes, Your Honor. We waive the reading and enter a plea of not guilty on behalf of the defendant."

The judge addressed the young ADA. "I've reviewed the complaint the People filed in detail. It appears to me that this case should be easily disposed of. I suggest that we mark this for second call, and you go out in the hall and come back with a disposition. I know you will find Mr. Fogarty very reasonable, if not amusing."

The ADA stood tall. In a loud voice, he said, "Judge, the People's only offer is as charged. We view this as a serious offense. There is no need for a second call."

There was a noticeable mummer from the attorneys in the front of the courtroom. Francis smiled. He knew what was coming.

The judge said, "Counselor, what's your name?"

"James Chamberlain."

"Mr. Chamberlain, how long have you been an Assistant District Attorney?"

"Almost one year now, Judge."

"Mr. Chamberlain, please turn around."

"Excuse me, Your Honor?"

"I said turn around."

The ADA turned around slowly to face the lawyers and spectators in the courtroom and then turned back to the judge.

"Mr. Chamberlain, I think you should apologize to the attorneys waiting in this courtroom and to me for wasting our time."

Thoroughly humiliated, the ADA plodded on. "Judge, I meant no disrespect. But my office has taken a hard position on private gambling operations, which we have found are often run by organized crime and are a cover for money laundering."

"And it's your belief that this poker game is run by a crime syndicate and is a cover for money laundering operations?"

"That is what the complaint states."

"The complaint states that a weekly poker game was held in the office of Mr. Cormac, a local attorney who employs the defendant as a clerk. Is it your contention that Mr. Cormac is a member of an organized crime syndicate?"

"No, Your Honor, the People are not suggesting that."

"Then who are members of the crime syndicate who you are asserting play in this game?"

"I don't know who the other players are, Judge."

"You don't know? But that lack of knowledge hasn't stopped you from recklessly asserting those facts as the basis of the criminal complaint, has it?"

Before the young ADA could respond, Judge DiSalvo said, "Mr. Chamberlain, you know on holidays, at my house after a big family meal, I like to take out some cards and chips and play some poker for penny ante stakes. I enjoy it, especially if I beat my brother in-law."

The lawyers in the courtroom were now laughing out loud.

"Mr. Chamberlain, do I have to worry about you raiding my game and having me arrested? Actually, in truth, I wouldn't mind if you arrested my brother-in-law."

"No, Your Honor." Then the truth came out. "Judge, this file is marked by the Chief of the Indictment Bureau *no dispositions*. I have no discretion to act here."

"You may have no discretion, but believe me you, will be held responsible. Okay, I give up. Do you want to be heard on bail?"

"Yes, Your Honor. The defendant is an addict. He is on probation for a conviction of an E Felony in Texas involving a forged instrument for the purchase of a controlled substance. He has no permanent employment, family roots or permanent residence in New York, where he has resided for only a year. He was violated for failing to comply with the conditions of his parole. In addition, he is charged with multiple additional felonies and misdemeanors. The People believe he is a flight risk and ask that bail should be set at a hundred thousand, cash or cash bond."

"Mr. Fogarty, I'm sure you would like to be heard."

"Judge, my only regret is that I have never been invited to your house for a holiday dinner or the after-dinner festivities. I'm aware, Judge, that you served our country in the Armed Forces. You should be aware that Mr. Reynolds enlisted in the Navy after graduating from high school. He trained as a Navy SEAL and honorably served his country for two tours of active combat duty overseas. I doubt that they have ROTC at Harvard, Judge, so I am confident that the assistant district attorney, or his privileged classmates, don't understand the sacrifices made by the defendant and our enlisted men in combat. JR was decorated for valor and received an honorable discharge."

Fogarty pretended to look at his notes and paused, waiting to let JR's service record sink in.

"Unfortunately, like many of our servicemen, JR suffered from a form of PTSD after his discharge. He sought and received treatment at the local VA Hospital in Texas. He was prescribed medications, including oxycodone, and like many patients, became dependent upon them. When his prescriptions expired, and the VA doctors would no longer renew them, he purchased scripts on the street in order to get the medication he needed to survive."

JR shuffled his feet but kept his head down and didn't say anything.

"He is not an addict. That mischaracterization by Mr. Chamberlain is a shameful attempt to portray the defendant as some sort of common criminal. Shame on him! JR was a disabled soldier suffering from the worst sort of pain imaginable. After his arrest, the defendant successfully completed a rehab program recommended by the court. He pled guilty and received a suspended sentence. He was placed on two years' probation with the usual conditions, including that he continue to attend AA meetings.

JR was now looking up at Francis as he spoke, and nodded.

"JR now receives VA disability benefits and moved to New York City at the suggestion of his close friend, and former platoon leader, who is in court here today. He received permission to move here, and his probation was transferred to the NYC Probation Department. He has complied with all the conditions of his probation and is employed as a clerk by Chance Cormac, a prominent attorney in Kings County. Mr. Cormac is also here in court today."

JR said under his breath, "That's the God's honest truth."

"This complaint arises from JR dealing cards at a weekly social card game held at Mr. Cormac's office. He is paid for his time and receives some tips at the end of the game. Mr. Reynolds should never have been arrested. This complaint is devoid of merit, and I am confident it will be dismissed in due course. I am requesting that the defendant be released on his own recognizance and this matter be put over for all purposes."

Judge DiSalvo looked around. "Thank you, Mr. Fogarty. Mr. Reynolds, I want to thank you for your service. Does the representative of the Probation Department wish to be heard? Has the defendant been meeting with you as required? Do you consider him a flight risk?"

Garrett Jones stood up. He looked very uncomfortable. He read word for word from notes printed on a sheet in front of him. "Judge, I am Mr. Reynolds' parole officer. Our department considers Mr. Reynolds a flight risk. Although he has been attending his monthly meetings with me, he still has no gainful employment and failed to disclose his activities in dealing cards at an illegal card game."

Garrett cleared his throat, clearly not comfortable with what he was reading. He shifted from one foot to the other as he continued to read from the prepared script. "Mr. Reynolds has also failed to report the income he earned from his gambling activities, which is a crime under state and federal law. His family and all his relatives live in Texas. He has no permanent residence in New York and there is a real risk that he will flee this court's jurisdiction-"

The Judge cut him off without even acknowledging his statement. "Mr. Jones, you can sit down. I've heard enough. Mr. Reynolds, I am releasing you on your own recognizance. There are however certain conditions for your release. You are to comply with the requirements of your parole and report to your probation officer as required. You are not to leave the State of New York without the court's express consent. You are required to continue in your treatment program which was a condition of your order of probation. I am sure you are very skilled, but your card dealing days are over. No more dealing or gambling. If you violate any of the conditions of your parole, you will be remanded. Do you understand the conditions of your release?"

Fogarty whispered to JR. JR stood up and for the first time addressed the judge. "Yes, sir, I do. Thank you, Judge."

"I am putting this matter over for all purposes to a date to be set by the clerk. Mr. Chamberlain, if I were you, I would give strong consideration to my recommendation to work out a disposition of his case. This is a Criminal Court in Kings County, not an ivory tower. Have no doubt, in the Kings County Criminal Court, I'm the king."

Francis leaned over, said a few words to JR, who was then escorted back into custody to be processed for his release.

Francis motioned for us to meet him in the hall. Once outside the courtroom, he said, "Well, that was fun. A good time was had by all except that poor excuse for an ADA. That wasn't even a fair fight. I almost felt bad for that condescending little prick. But I think the judge got his attention. Damian, take care of JR. He's a had a tough twenty four hours but I think he'll be all right. Wait for him to be released and help him get home. I'm confident I can work out an acceptable disposition with the bureau chief. My job is done here. I have to run, I'm late for another appearance."

I thanked Francis as he scurried off toward the elevators like an Irish leprechaun. Damian went back to wait for JR to be processed and released.

I took a taxi back to the office. The traffic outside the window was a blur. I was lost in thought, puzzled about why anyone would report JR for, at worst, a minor infraction of his probation.

I was confident that none of the players would have any reason to report him for dealing at the weekly game. They all liked JR. Any issue about the legality of his dealing cards for us would only come back to bite them, because they had all paid JR to deal.

I already had a headache from my morning in criminal court and this was just making it worse. JR was out and, God knows, I had paid Francis enough to solve the mystery of who the complainant was. I decided I would just trust him to figure it out.

The poker games stopped after JR's arrest. JR couldn't deal anymore and no one had any appetite to play in the game once they learned that it was the subject of a criminal investigation. JR also stopped clerking for me. I hoped there would be a quick resolution of the criminal and he would feel comfortable coming back to the office. I was worried about his well-being but was confident that Damian would keep close tabs on his friend.

I had enough drama for one day. I sat back and watched the people walking on the crowded city sidewalks. I wondered where their lives were taking them. Wherever it was, I knew exactly where I was going. It was time to get back to the office, to get some real work done on the class action.

CHAPTER TWENTY-SEVEN
A FRIENDLY LUNCH

Courtney was surprised to get a call from Jackson. Even more surprising was the fact that he invited her to have lunch with him, just the two of them. He said he was concerned about Courtney and the girls. He wanted to end the divorce quickly so they could get on with their lives. Courtney was very relieved when she got the call. She was more than happy to have lunch with Jackson.

Courtney was smart enough to call me and ask me what I thought before meeting with Jackson. I said that I had no objection to her having lunch with Jackson, if she felt comfortable being alone with him. I cautioned her not to agree to anything regarding the divorce until she had a chance to speak with me. She agreed and said she would call me after they met.

***

Courtney dropped the twins off at school and she was actually looking forward to having some time alone with Jackson so they could talk. She was hopeful that a meeting would be good for both of them. They hadn't spoken, other than in court, in a long time. She put on a plain dress and some lip gloss. She was still wearing her wedding ring.

She drove the Range Rover to meet Jackson at one of their favorite restaurants in the Village, where he had made a reservation. She parked the car at a nearby garage. When she entered the restaurant, she saw Jackson sitting in the back, at an isolated table.

She was suddenly disoriented for a minute as she walked to the back of the restaurant. She had a strange fantasy that the divorce was somehow just a bad dream. She blocked the horrible pictures on Jackson's laptop from her mind.

She was surprised to see an open bottle of their favorite Merlot on the table. Jackson stood and gave her a hug and kiss on the cheek. He said, "Thanks for coming. You look lovely. I wish this all could have been avoided. You know I still love you and the children very much."

Courtney didn't know what to say. She was touched by Jackson's kind words of affection. She said, "Jackson, I'm glad you called me. It's important we keep the lines of communication open. No matter what, we both have to be good parents and take care of our girls."

Jackson nodded. He turned off his cell phone and poured two glasses of wine, making a toast. "Here's to the best mother in the world. Here's to a happy future for all of us."

Courtney never drank in the afternoon, but she accepted the glass and made the toast by touching her glass to his. She savored the taste of their favorite wine.

They enjoyed their lunch and they spoke more openly about their marriage than they had in a long time. Jackson said that they were lucky to have such beautiful daughters and the financial ability to enjoy their lives. He assured her he would direct his attorneys to draft a very generous settlement proposal and forward it to her attorney immediately.

Before Courtney knew it, they had finished their lunch and the bottle of wine. She felt that the weight of the world had been lifted from her shoulders. She remembered why she first fell in love with Jackson and was confident he would now do the right thing. For her and for the girls.

They ordered coffee and Jackson said, "Courtney, I have to ask you one question about the divorce. Do you mind?"

Courtney, after the friendly lunch and drinking a little too much wine, was not concerned. "No, not at all."

"Do you know if someone is doing an investigation trying to find out who my clients are or what accounts I manage for them?"

Courtney was surprised. "No. Of course not. We agreed in court that your clients were none of my business. I have no desire to know who they are or what you do for them. Why? Do you think someone is doing that?"

Jackson's tone of voice suddenly became very serious. "No. But I have to make sure. You do understand it would hurt all of us if my clients felt threatened. I can't control how they might react or what they might do to protect themselves. We could lose everything. Do you understand?"

Courtney didn't really understand but said simply, "Yes."

As they left the restaurant, Jackson asked Courtney if she was good to drive home. She felt a little tipsy, but said her car was in a garage across the street and she was sure she could drive the ten minutes on local streets to pick up the twins from school and return to her apartment.

When she got in the driver's seat, she felt better than she had in a long time. She pulled out of the garage and headed uptown on Broadway. She drove to the twins' school listening to her favorite rock station and singing along to, of all things, the Beach Boys' song, "Wouldn't It Be Nice."

The twins came out, got in and buckled themselves into their car seats. Once they were belted in, Courtney clicked the child safety door locks on and pulled out into traffic to drive the two blocks to their apartment.

She had only driven one block when she saw flashing lights in her rear view mirror. She pulled the Range Rover over, to let the police car go by, unaware it had followed her from the parking garage.

It pulled up behind her car, lights still flashing. Two police officers approached her car. One came up to her window and the other stood by the back of her car. She rolled down her window. "Officer, is there a problem?"

The officer was standing sideways looking into the car, his hand on his gun, He said sharply, "Ma'am, please turn off your radio and the ignition. License and registration, please."

Courtney turned off the radio and fumbled though her tote and then the glove box, trying to locate her license, registration and insurance card. She finally found the documents and handed them to the officer. She noticed that her hands were shaking.

The officer went back to his squad car to call them in.

One of the twins asked, "Mommy, did you do something wrong? Why did the policeman stop you?"

Courtney turned in her seat to face the girls and was talking softly, reassuring them that nothing was wrong, when the officer returned. He gave her license and registration back to her and said, "Ma'am, please step out of the car."

"Why? Did I do something wrong?"

"Ma'am, I am not going to ask you again. Please step out of the car."

Courtney panicked. "I can't leave the girls alone in the car! What did I do wrong?"

"Officer Lopez here will watch the girls. They will be fine. Now, step out of the vehicle."

Courtney turned to the twins. "Girls, Mommy will be right back. Please stay in your seats." She reluctantly opened her door, got out and stood right next to the back window of the car so she could keep an eye on the girls.

The police officer pulled a device from his belt that looked like an inhaler that someone with asthma would use. It had some sort of gauge on the top. He handed the device to Courtney. "Please take a deep breath and blow into the opening."

Courtney didn't know what to do. She was frightened, confused, and still a little inebriated from the wine at lunch. She had never been stopped by the police in her life and wasn't sure if she should cooperate or not. She looked back at the girls and thought that she hadn't had that much to drink and there was nothing to worry about.

She decided the best thing to do was cooperate. What was the worst that could happen? She would be given a ticket and she could take the girls home. She blew into the device and handed it back to the officer.

The officer took a long look at the gauge and took a picture of the reading with his cell phone. He put the device back on his belt and took out a plastic card from the top pocket of his shirt. "Ma'am, please turn around and put your hands on the top of your vehicle."

Courtney froze. "What?"

"Place your hands on the top of your vehicle. You are being placed under arrest for driving while intoxicated. You have the right to remain silent. Anything you say may be used against you in a court of law. You have the right to counsel. If you can't afford counsel, it will be provided to you. Do you understand the rights that I have just read to you?"

Courtney stood next to the car in a trance. She didn't understand what was happening. She turned and put her hands on the roof of the car looking directly in the back window at the twins. She suddenly found herself standing in a busy city street with her hands on top of her car and pedestrians staring at her. She felt completely helpless and humiliated.

She pleaded with the police officer, "Please don't do this. I'm just two blocks from home, I won't drive. I can walk them home. Please, please help me. What about my girls? Please let them out of the car!"

The officer repeated, "Ma'am, calm down. Do you understand the rights I have just read to you?"

Courtney stammered, "Yes, yes I do."

"I am now going to handcuff you and search you and your vehicle for weapons. Are there any weapons or drugs on your person or in the vehicle?"

"No. Of course not."

As Courtney was searched and handcuffed, she could hear the girls starting to cry in the back seat.

"Is there anyone who can come and pick up your children?"

Courtney was now in full panic mode. In her confusion, she somehow thought the girls would be coming with her. She immediately thought of Jackson. "Yes, yes, their father can pick them up. I will give you his cell phone number. Please call him right now."

"We will call him. Now I need you to turn around and step into the back seat of the squad car."

"Fine, fine, I will. Just let me speak to my girls before I leave. I don't want them to be scared."

"Ma'am, I need you to turn around now and get into the squad car. Your husband can speak to them when he gets here."

He took Courtney by her arm with a firm grip and led her to the police car. The officer sat in the driver's seat and spoke through his handset in the police car. "She's been arrested." The last thing Courtney saw and heard were the twins, still belted in their seats, screaming, "Mommy! Mommy! Mommy!"

When Courtney was sitting in the back seat of the police car, with a caged partition in front of her and her hands still handcuffed behind her back, she could bear it no longer and broke down, sobbing uncontrollably. As the squad car did a U-turn, the last thing Courtney saw out the window as they drove away was the crying faces of her twins growing smaller and smaller.

Soon after Courtney was arrested, the police officer called Jackson.

Jackson said that he was more than happy to help anyway he could.

CHAPTER TWENTY-EIGHT
THE NEW SHERIFF

The next scheduled preliminary conference was coming up in Courtney's divorce case.

I met with Sally and Damian to find out where we were in completing discovery and when we might be in a position to discuss a settlement proposal with Courtney. I knew Judge Gonzales was strict about her discovery deadlines and I didn't want us to get on her bad side.

I've learned that once a judge sees a black hat on an attorney, it's hard to take it off. Damian said that Clay, Roy's partner, had been cooperative and had complied with all our requests. He felt we had been supplied with all the financial documents we had requested from Jackson and Checkmate.

Any confidential information had been redacted, as agreed. It was now just a matter of finalizing an asset schedule and digesting the projected income numbers for Jackson and Checkmate. Once that was done, we could compute proposed maintenance and child support payments under the state guidelines and put together a comprehensive settlement proposal.

Sally said, if she could come up for air for a few days in the class action prep, she could have most of the work done on Courtney's case before the court scheduled another conference.

"Great. I will babysit the class action. I want you guys to focus on the divorce. As my father would say, this divorce has become a bad penny that keeps showing up no matter how we try to get rid of it. Let's get this done and out the door for good."

I thought it was strange I hadn't heard anything from Courtney about her meeting with Jackson. I also had not heard anything further from Roy since our last contentious meeting on the roof. I was hoping Courtney's father had taken my advice and called off the dogs. I was sure I would see Roy in court again and was confident that he would be happy to hear that the case could soon be settled.

I called Courtney and asked her to meet with me at the office before the next court appearance. I told her we had the financial information we needed in order to start putting together a settlement proposal. She sounded distracted and very subdued. "Fine. I'll be there."

When we met, I asked her about her meeting with Jackson. She said in a subdued voice, "It was good. He wants to settle." She didn't offer anything further and I didn't feel any need to press her for more details.

Courtney had not told me, or anyone, other than Jackson, about the DWI. She had been frightened and humiliated. She wanted to put the memory of the girls crying faces in the car window out of her mind.

***

After her arrest, Jackson had picked up the girls from Courtney's car and taken them to the local precinct house, where Courtney was being processed. He spoke to the desk sergeant, who indicated that because Courtney had no prior DWI arrests, she could be released on a desk appearance ticket without any need for an arraignment or bail.

When Courtney was finally escorted out to the front of the police station, she saw the girls with Jackson and ran over to them. She dropped to her knees, broke down crying and hugged them tightly. She sobbed repeatedly, "My babies, my babies, my beautiful babies. Mommy loves you so much."

Jackson picked up copies of the desk appearance ticket and incident report from the desk sergeant and walked out of the police station with Courtney and the girls. He took them home and went with them up to their apartment.

At the door, he said, "I'm sorry you had to go through this. It's my fault. I shouldn't have ordered the wine. I don't want you to worry about anything. I will get a lawyer to take care of the DWI for you. It's not a big deal. I'll get a copy of the criminal complaint for you. We can pick up your car tomorrow. Get some rest."

Courtney said, "Thank you. Thank you so much." She hugged Jackson tightly before he left.

***

We arrived at the New York Supreme Court building on Centre Street long before Judge Gonzales's calendar was scheduled to be called.

I told Sally and Courtney I was going to look for Roy and give him the good news that we were in a position to make a settlement proposal and that I was confident that the case could now be settled. I hoped that this would calm him down and resolve any concerns he had about Jackson's clients or their investments.

Sally went into the courtroom to check in with Judge Gonzales's clerk.

I walked the hall and couldn't find Roy or his partner. Or Jackson. I thought maybe they had been delayed and decided that I would speak with Roy after the court conference.

As I walked back to Judge Gonzales's courtroom, I saw Sally standing with Courtney. Sally was frowning. "I'm glad you're back. We are not on Judge Gonzales's calendar. I know it was scheduled for today. I confirmed it on the court website last night. The court clerk doesn't know why it isn't on the calendar. She suggested we speak to the chief clerk for the matrimonial part."

I wasn't concerned. It was probably a clerical error and we had more than sufficient time before the calendar would be called. "No problem. You wait here with Courtney, and I'll go speak to the part clerk."

I went downstairs to the matrimonial clerk's office on the first floor and walked up to the tall oak counter that ran the length of the room. An assistant clerk came over and asked how she could help me.

I said, "Good morning. My name is Chance Cormac. Maybe you can help me. I'm the attorney of record for Courtney Malone, the defendant in a divorce action pending before Justice Gonzales. The case is Malone v Malone and was scheduled for a status conference today before the judge. When we went to check in with the judge's clerk, I was informed that the case is not on the calendar. Do you know any reason that the case is not on her calendar?"

The clerk typed on her computer. "I have that case right here, Mr. Cormac. The case has been transferred to Judge Monroe Granger. He will conduct the status conference this morning. His courtroom is number eight-oh-three."

Granger? I was stunned, but I didn't say anything. Of course Granger was the same corrupt judge who had presided over the Foster case that ended my career as a divorce lawyer ten years ago. I didn't understand why the case was transferred or how it was done without any notice to me or my client.

The clerk gave me a puzzled look. "Are you all right? You look confused. Is there anything else that I can do for you?"

I finally said, "I'm sorry, I'm just surprised the case was transferred. Does the portal show why?"

"Yes. The case was transferred at the direction of the Administrative Judge, Justice Dennis Donovan. I would suggest that you hurry or you will miss the calendar call."

I wasn't happy. I couldn't figure out why the judge I respected, clerked for and played poker with for so many years would transfer Courtney's case without the courtesy of calling me. I decided I would visit Judge Donovan's chambers after the appearance and ask for an explanation. I hoped it would be good, but I somehow knew better.

I rushed back up to Judge Gonzales's courtroom. Sally and Courtney were waiting anxiously outside the courtroom door because the court had started calling the calendar in my absence.

Sally said, "Where are we? They are calling the calendar."

"Our case has been transferred to a new judge. We have to go up to his courtroom on the eighth floor."

"Transferred? Why? Who is the new judge?"

"Justice Monroe Granger."

Sally suddenly realized I was talking about the same judge who had presided over the Foster case. Her face flushed with anger, and she just shook her head in disgust.

Courtney said, "Is there a problem?"

I said no but the case had been moved to another courtroom and we had to hurry. We rushed up to the eighth floor. There was no calendar posted outside Judge Granger's courtroom. When we entered the courtroom, it looked empty. Then I saw that the judge was already on the bench, hearing argument. I looked and saw Jackson sitting at the plaintiff's table. Standing next to him, already addressing the judge, was Conrad Dumbrowski. The same gunslinger who had engaged in the worst bad faith matrimonial tactics when he had represented Mr. Foster.

Roy and his partner, Clay Campbell, were not in the courtroom. It looked like this was a special calendar call scheduled by the judge just for our case. I rushed up and stood at the defendant's table. Sally and Courtney joined me.

Both Judge Granger and Dumbrowski ignored me. He continued his argument as if I wasn't there.

I interrupted Dumbrowski. In a loud voice, I said, "Good morning, Your Honor. Chance Cormac for the defendant, Mrs. Malone. Mrs. Malone is present in court today. I apologize for being late, but I received no notice that this case had been transferred to you or would be heard in this courtroom. I am also surprised that Mr. Dumbrowski is apparently representing the plaintiff. He is not the attorney of record, and I was not served with a formal notice of substitution. I appeared at Judge Gonzales's courtroom for her calendar call, as originally scheduled."

The judge was hunched over the bench and now looked ancient. Without looking up he said, "Mr. Cormac, there is a new sheriff in town. I remember you had a hard time following my rules the last time you appeared before me. I will not tolerate your tardiness or disrespect for this court. I am fining you five hundred dollars as a sanction for your failure to appear as ordered. You, not your client, are to pay that fine before you leave court today or I will hold you in contempt."

I understood immediately that the parties were different but the judge was the same. I kept silent and waited for my opportunity to address the court.

"Mr. Dumbrowski is appearing 'of counsel' to the plaintiff's attorneys of record and, as such, there is no need for a formal substitution. Now, please sit down. I am warning you, do not interrupt these proceedings again. Mr. Dumbrowski, please serve Mr. Cormac with a copy of your Order to Show Cause and proceed with your argument."

I sat down and Dumbrowski handed me a thick document captioned Order to Show Cause and Temporary Restraining Order, with extensive supporting affidavits and exhibits annexed, and then continued his argument.

I had received no notice whatsoever that Jackson's new attorney was making a motion, nor any opportunity to submit papers in opposition, yet the order to show cause and temporary restraining order had already been signed by the judge. It had been submitted to the court *ex parte*, meaning that I had no notice or opportunity to be heard before the judge ruled on it. *Ex parte* applications are only permitted in the most egregious circumstances, to prevent irreparable harm. I looked quickly at the relief granted in the Temporary Restraining Order set out on the front page of the order to show cause.

I was shocked to see Jackson had been granted temporary custody of the twins and an order of protection had been issued directing that Courtney stay away from Jackson and the twins except for supervised visitation once a week at a social services office in the presence of a case worker. She was also ordered to enter an alcohol rehabilitation program and submit urine samples to a testing agency once a week. If she failed her urine test at any time, her visitation would be suspended.

However, as upsetting as all that was, what upset me most was the first exhibit annexed to the order to show cause. It contained copies of an incident report regarding Courtney's arrest for DWI and a criminal complaint charging her with a felony DWI and endangering the welfare of a minor.

I quickly read the motion papers and half-listened as Dumbrowski finished his oral argument: "…presents a direct threat to the safety and wellbeing of the children. It is only by the grace of God that they were not seriously injured. I understand that alcoholism is an illness, but that is no excuse for putting your children in harm's way. We only hope that Mrs. Malone gets the help she so desperately needs."

Sally was staring straight at Dumbrowski.

"We were going to request Mrs. Malone be denied all visitation with the children, but Mr. Malone, to his credit, felt strongly that it was in the best interests of the children to permit supervised visitation with their mother while she gets treatment. He has helped Mrs. Malone in any way possible since her arrest. He has shown great compassion for her problems. He has been far more generous and understanding than most fathers would be under the circumstances."

The judge looked up. "Thank you, Mr. Dumbrowski. Mr. Malone, I want to commend you for your concern for your children and your wife. I am sure that this can't be easy for you. Mr. Chance, do you want to be heard? I doubt there's much you can say that would make me change my mind. You know that I am only concerned about the best interests of these young children."

I looked over at Courtney. She was crying softly. Sally was tapping her fist on the counsel's table to control her rage.

A good attorney knows there should never be any surprises in court. You should never be surprised by your adversary and certainly not by your own client withholding information about an arrest. I was blindsided by both.

There might have been a good reason why Courtney didn't tell me about the DWI but there was no good reason for the ambush by Dumbrowski and the judge. The rules in court are essentially the same as on a playground. The law requires "fair play". The American system of jurisprudence is founded on due process. A party to a lawsuit is entitled to notice and an opportunity to be heard before the court can rule on their rights. There is no greater right than a parent's custody of his or her child.

I stood and addressed the court. "Thank you, Your Honor. Again, I apologize for any inconvenience caused by my failure to appear at the calendar call. I do not believe that the sanctions you have imposed on me are appropriate under the circumstances, but I will pay the fine and pursue my remedies on another day. I stand here today at a distinct disadvantage. I am quite surprised and confused by these proceedings."

Granger had his head down writing on a pad and didn't seem to be listening to anything I had to say.

"I had no notice of the transfer of this case to Your Honor or of Mr. Dumbrowski being substituted in as the attorney of record for the plaintiff. I had no notice that there was a conference being scheduled before Your Honor this morning. I had no notice of the Order to Show Cause that was submitted to you and apparently signed *ex parte* this morning. I had no opportunity to review the motion papers, to submit opposition papers or prepare for this argument."

Dumbrowski stood up. "As you are aware, Judge, this is an emergency application."

The judge suddenly woke up. "Yes. The lives of these children were at stake."

I ignored the dog and pony show and continued, "There has been a wholesale disregard of the court rules by Mr. Dumbrowski, but much more egregious is the violation of my client's due process rights. There is no question that her constitutional rights have been violated. She had no notice of this application or an opportunity to be heard before the Order to Show Cause was signed. There has been no evidentiary hearing as to the merits of Mr. Malone's application. She has been deprived of the right to submit evidence and examine witnesses under oath."

The judge sighed and said sharply, "You are here now, Counselor. Instead of trying to avoid the issue, why don't you tell us why your client put her young children in great danger."

"I am not in a position to argue the merits of Mr. Malone's application because I have had no opportunity to even discuss this application with my client. All I can say is that Mr. Malone has repeatedly acknowledged from the beginning of this case that Mrs. Malone is a good and caring mother. She has been the primary caretaker of the children since they were born. The parties have stipulated that custody is not in dispute and that Mrs. Malone will have physical custody of the children."

I could hear Courtney continuing to cry softly.

"I am aware that Mr. Malone is away on business a great deal of the time and has no ability to provide a home or care for the children. I would ask that the court vacate the temporary restraining order that was improvidently granted on an *ex parte* basis and adjourn plaintiff's motion to another date in order to permit the defendant to submit opposition papers and be heard."

"As usual, I'm not impressed with your arguments, Mr. Cormac. I notice that you are not disputing that your client was arrested for driving while intoxicated and endangering the welfare of a minor. The minors whose welfare was endangered were her children. Her own children! You would have me put these innocent children in the backseat of a car to be driven by a mother who has an alcohol problem and was arrested for

DWI."

Courtney was shaking her head. She found the strength to say, "That's not true."

"But it is true, Mrs. Malone. You were arrested for DWI. You have shown a total disregard for your children's safety and wellbeing. Mr. Cormac, you talk about your client's rights. What about the rights of these children? My job isn't to protect the best interests of your client, it's to protect the best interests of these children. Your motion to vacate the TRO is denied. Mr. Dumbrowski, you should have a copy of the Order to Show Cause served upon the local police precinct where the defendant's residence is located and with the children's school. Mr. Cormac, will it be necessary for a police officer to accompany Mr. Malone when he takes physical custody of his children, or will your client cooperate in surrendering the children to him after court today?"

Courtney was now openly sobbing. Sally gave her some tissues and whispered some words, trying to console her.

"Your Honor, my client will fully cooperate with the court's order. I would only request that the court stay the order to show cause for forty-eight hours so that I can file an immediate appeal with the Appellate Division. We will consent to a stipulation that the defendant will not drink any alcohol in the presence of the children or transport them in her car pending the appeal."

"Mr. Cormac, your motion for a stay is denied. Mr. Malone, for the safety of your children you should make arrangements to take custody of your children immediately after these proceedings are concluded. Good day, gentlemen."

Dumbrowski said, "Thank you, Your Honor."

I didn't say anything. I didn't need to. I knew I had made the record I needed for an immediate appeal. I put the Order to Show Cause and my papers back into my file and turned to leave the courtroom.

Sally and Courtney were up ahead of me, heading toward the courtroom door. I saw Jackson out of the corner of my eye walking quickly toward Courtney and calling her name.

I motioned to the female court officer to follow me. I ran up the aisle and cut Jackson off. I squared my shoulders and stood between him and

Courtney. When the court officer arrived, I continued to look Jackson in the eye while I said, "Officer, as you just heard, the court has issued an order of protection directing my client to stay away from her husband. Mr. Malone has approached my client, without her consent, apparently attempting to provoke her to violate that order. I would ask you to direct Mr. Malone to step away from Mrs. Malone and leave the courtroom immediately."

The Court Officer put her hand on her gun. "Sir, I am going to ask you to step back and leave the courtroom immediately."

As Jackson started to speak, Dumbrowski came up behind him and put his hand on his client's shoulder. He said to the Court Officer, "There is no need for all this drama being created by Mr. Cormac. My client is simply trying to make arrangements to pick up his girls as directed by the judge."

I said, "Counselor, you are free to make those arrangements through my office. If Mr. Malone attempts to communicate with my client again, I will not hesitate to file a motion to hold him in contempt."

"Based upon the sanctions the judge imposed on you today, you should be an expert on contempt. Let's go, Mr. Malone. Mr. Cormac has a fine to pay."

I stopped to speak with Sally and Courtney in the empty hall. Courtney started to speak, and I said, "Courtney, not here, not now. We can talk at my office later today. As you can imagine, I don't like surprises. I'm not quite sure what happened in there today or why it happened. I am sure there are a lot of things you would like to explain to me."

She said, "Chance, I'm sorry, please let me explain-"

I cut her off. "Not here. Not now. I am very anxious to hear what you have to say and learn all of the facts, but there are a few things I have to take care of first. I have to pay my fine, meet with my good friend Justice Donovan and call Roy to find out exactly what the hell is going on here. I would suggest you go home right away and spend some time with the girls before Jackson comes to pick them up. Now look at me and listen carefully. I don't want you to worry about the girls. One thing I can assure you is that this order to show cause won't last half as long as it took for Judge Granger to sign it. After the girls leave, I want you to immediately come to my office so we can file the appeal."

I turned to Sally. "Okay. We have to gear up. Please order the transcript of today's hearing from the court reporter. Pay to have it expedited and emailed to us today. When you get back to the office, do some research on due process and temporary custody awards. Start putting together an emergency application to the Appellate Division to vacate the TRO."

I paid the $500 fine at the clerk's office and took the elevator up to Judge Donovan's chambers. As the Administrative Judge, his chambers were on the top floor of the courthouse and included a large, windowed office overlooking Getty Square and a separate conference room. I knew his chambers well from the many meetings we'd had together when I was his clerk and we were drafting his court opinions.

I spoke to Judge Donovan's law secretary through the intercom on the wall outside his chambers. I said it was urgent that I speak with the judge. After a few minutes, she came back on the intercom. "Chance, the judge would like to meet with you outside the courthouse. Please meet him at the bottom of the front courthouse steps in ten minutes. Does that work for you?"

I was puzzled why we couldn't meet in his chambers, but agreed to meet the judge outside as requested. I went out and waited at the bottom of the wide concrete steps leading high up to the massive front doors of the courthouse. I watched other attorneys, holding their redwell files, at various levels on the steps, talking to their clients or their adversaries. Often, more progress was made in a case on those steps outside the courthouse than in the courtroom.

The judge came out the front doors and started the long descent down the stairs. He suddenly looked old and weary as he walked very slowly, careful not to trip and fall. Without his robes, he looked just like any other aging attorney who was on the downslope of his career and tired of the game.

He stopped a number of times on different steps as he descended in order to say hello to the attorneys who had appeared before him over the years. He finally saw me, walked over and shook my hand. "Chance, good to see you. I thought it would be a nice day for a walk. Let's go over and sit in the park by St. Paul's Chapel. I like to go there sometimes just to think."

We walked in silence down Centre Street to Park Row. We strolled through the labyrinth of lower Manhattan streets that are a trip back though history. The old City Hall, the "Tweed Courthouse" and the old alehouses all looked the same as they did a hundred years ago. It's easy to imagine attorneys dressed in long overcoats and steampipe hats arriving by horse-drawn carriages at the same courthouses that still stand today to practice our profession. It is normally inspiring but today it just looked old and tainted.

St. Paul's Chapel is part of the Trinity Church and was built in 1776. It is the oldest church in Manhattan. George Washington attended services at St. Paul's the day he was inaugurated as the first president of the United States. It is a beautiful, small, brick church with a tall spire. The inside has an aisle leading to the altar, surrounded by white columns standing like guardians. Behind the altar is a massive floor to ceiling window that floods the church with light.

There is a large park in the back of the church, open to the public, and has benches under large old oak trees. It is a Garden of Eden hidden among the city skyscrapers surrounding the church. On any other day I would have enjoyed the peaceful serenity of the park and an escape from practicing law. But not today.

We sat down on a bench in a secluded part of the park. The judge gave me a tired smile. "You know you were one of my best law clerks. You were smart, hardworking and thoughtful. But more importantly, you understood that we were part of a profession that has professional responsibilities. Not only to our clients but to each other. Unfortunately, after over thirty years on the bench, I have some real doubts about our profession. I feel like my time has passed. What can I do for you, Chance?"

There were no pleasantries. "Judge, I appeared today on a matrimonial case. Malone v Malone. I represent the wife and Roy Brown's firm represents the husband. The case was originally assigned to Judge Gonzales. When I arrived at her courtroom today, the case was not on the judge's calendar. The chief clerk of the matrimonial part told me it had been transferred to Judge Granger. She said you transferred the case. I was wondering, why would you do that?"

"Malone? I don't remember that case specifically, but you know that part of my responsibilities as administrative judge is to keep the calendar moving. I reassign cases all the time. I wouldn't worry about it. Judge Granger is tough but fair."

"Judge, with all due respect, we both know better. He just sanctioned me for no reason and issued an *ex parte* order depriving my client of custody of her girls without any notice to me or a hearing. My client is devastated."

"Chance, I am sure he had his reasons. If you are aggrieved you should file an appeal."

"Judge, that's the perfect word. I am aggrieved. Very aggrieved. As you say, I am sure he had his reasons, but I think we both know they have nothing to do with justice or the merits of the case. I consider you a friend and a mentor. I deserve an explanation."

The judge folded his hands as if in prayer, looked up at the church steeple, and was silent for a long time.

He finally said, "Chance, you know I miss our poker games. I looked forward to them every week. We all did. I thought it was a shame what happened to JR. I liked him. He made some mistakes, but I thought he was on the right track and getting his life back in order. I was made aware of the criminal charges filed against him. As I am sure you appreciate they are very serious. He was charged with a number of felonies. I played in your poker game for years. Like everyone else, I paid JR to deal and gave him tips."

"Judge, I am well aware of all that, but those charges were trumped up. They're going to go away. JR did nothing wrong. And what does that have to do with my divorce case?"

"I am seventy-two years old. I have three more years on the bench before I retire. I love being a judge but the downside of sitting on the bench is that I am paid a salary as a state employee. I'm not complaining. My wife and I live a comfortable life, but I don't make a fraction of what you guys make as successful lawyers in private practice. However, there are other benefits. I work reasonable hours, have my weekends off and, best of all, when I retire in two years, I get a very healthy pension and medical benefits for myself and my wife for the rest of our lives."

"You worked hard and deserve to enjoy your retirement, but what does any of this have to do with my case being transferred?"

"You know, with those generous retirement benefits, we won't have to worry about anything. Without them we would struggle. If there was some question of judicial misconduct on my part in participating in an illegal gambling enterprise, I could lose everything. At this point in my life, I couldn't risk that. The transfer of one divorce case was a small favor to insure my family's future. It's not going to affect any of the rights of the parties. No one has been hurt."

"Judge, all I can say is I feel very sorry. Sorry because my poker game put you in this difficult position. But far more sorry because you have lost the courage and integrity that made you a good lawyer, a good judge and a good man. Ironically, we are sitting here behind St. Paul's Chapel. It was St. Paul who preached that 'the love of money is the root of all evil.' One last question: who asked you for the favor?"

"Chance, you're a smart lawyer. I'm sure you can figure that out on your own. Of course, we never had this conversation."

I got up and walked away without saying goodbye. As I looked back at him still sitting on the park bench silently looking up at the church steeple, I was reminded of a saying that my father once told me, "It's not power that corrupts, but fear of losing it."

The judge was right about one thing. I could figure out who was behind the curtain all by myself. It was time to get back to my office and call Roy.

CHAPTER TWENTY-NINE
SCORCHED EARTH

Damian had once explained to me that sometimes when his platoon was on a mission, they were ordered to employ a "scorched earth" policy, to demoralize the enemy. Scorched earth meant destroying everything that might be of value to the enemy. They would destroy homes, factories, or other buildings. They destroyed livestock and food supplies. They took no prisoners.

The earth was "scorched" because everything was burned to the ground and nothing was left standing. The ground was left black and barren. It was a hard lesson for the civilians, many of whom were just innocent bystanders in someone else's war. Sometimes lawyers use their own scorched earth tactics to win a case.

When I got back to the office, Sally was in the conference room with Courtney. I wanted to speak with them before I called Roy. I said to Sally, "Where are we?"

Sally said, "We're good. Jackson picked up the kids. Courtney told them that they would be visiting with their daddy for a few days. I got the record from the court reporter. We're finishing the motion papers to vacate the TRO."

"Great. I want to file the appeal today on an emergency basis." I said to Courtney, "Needless to say, I'm not happy. I'm not happy that we were ambushed in court today, but I'm even more unhappy because you didn't see fit to tell me about the DWI. I can't help you if we can't trust each other. I want to call Roy Brown, but first, why don't you tell me exactly what happened."

Courtney took her time and explained what happened in a shaky but determined voice. She apologized for not telling me about the DWI. She explained in detail about her lunch with Jackson and how she was arrested. She apologized again but said she was too humiliated to talk about it to anyone.

Jackson had assured her that he was handling the criminal case and that it would go away. She had trusted him to help her. She swore she would never withhold any information from me again. She was as surprised as I was about what happened in court that morning. Jackson had never said anything to her about being concerned about the children. He had even apologized to her for letting her drive home after their lunch.

Courtney said, "I'm such a fool. I trusted him! He convinced me he cared about me and the girls. It's evil what he did. I just don't understand why he is suddenly attacking me now. I thought he was anxious to get the divorce over with. I'm very frightened about what he may do next."

"Courtney, thank you for being truthful with me. Now I have a confession to make. I have not been completely truthful with you, either. I believe that the reason Jackson is trying to intimidate and frighten you is because someone has accessed his clients' accounts. It wasn't us but I know who did. As you know, Jackson's clients are very wealthy and powerful people. Our instinct is that many are world leaders. They don't want the information about their identities or their offshore accounts disclosed."

"Now it makes sense. He asked me if I knew who might be investigating him and his clients. I told him I didn't, and I have no interest in his clients."

"He's frightened. I'm certain that if the accounts Jackson manages were to be made public, it would create enormous legal and political problems for both him and his clients. He's scared and when people are scared they do desperate things. Roy came to me and asked if we were the ones who had accessed Jackson's accounts, which I assured him we weren't. He was very angry and demanded I find out who violated the NDA and court order and have them purge any records of the accounts. He said if I didn't do as he asked, he couldn't protect us. He wouldn't say who or what we needed to be to protected from. It occurred to me, based upon my first meeting with your father, that somehow, he might be involved."

"My dad? Why would he do that? I told him Jackson was cooperating and we wanted to settle."

"Unfortunately, that's not good enough for your father. He agreed to meet with me but only on the condition that our conversation would be kept strictly confidential. When we met, he admitted that he had hired a high-powered investigation firm and they had accessed Jackson's clients' accounts in violation of the order."

"Oh, God. He's going to hurt everyone."

"He doesn't see it that way. He wants Jackson to pay for his sins and thinks I am not protecting you. I told him he had violated a court order and was not helping you or the girls. I strongly urged him to reconsider, end the investigation immediately and destroy any client files in his possession. He flatly refused. He made me promise not to tell you or anyone else. In light of what happened in court, I have now decided that my duty to you as a client outweighs my promise to him. Jackson isn't interested in getting custody of the twins. I'm confident that your arrest and the custody application are intended to terrorize you so that you will demand that I find the client records and have them destroyed."

Courtney said, "My father? My father caused all this pain and suffering for me and the children? What was he thinking? I am going to see him immediately and tell him to stay out of my divorce and out of my life. I will demand he destroy any records. If he won't cooperate, I will tell Jackson what he did."

"Courtney, I understand why you would like to confront your father, but I don't think it would be helpful at this time. He is already very angry about the divorce and thinks I have been way too soft on Jackson. When he finds out about Jackson's role in having you arrested, with the children in the car, and the custody proceedings, it is unlikely he will stop his investigation or destroy the records."

"You're scaring me. What more damage can he do?"

"I believe he will threaten Jackson and his clients with what he has and do something foolish that may be impossible to unwind."

Courtney shook her head. "My children are gone! I have to speak with Jackson and make him understand that we don't want to hurt him or his clients. He'll agree the girls should come home."

"I don't think that is a good idea. Also, technically there is an order of protection prohibiting you from communicating with him. He has shown he will stop at nothing to make sure his clients are protected. If he learns your father was involved and intends to disclose the identity of his clients and their offshore accounts, I think it could be very dangerous for both you and your father."

"Dangerous? Dangerous how? Now you are really scaring me. Am I in danger? Are my children in danger?"

"I don't think so. Not right now. Jackson has made his point. He has your attention and wants our cooperation. Let's focus on getting the twins back and unwinding the judge's order. I have to decide about how best to convince your father to do the right thing."

"For my sake and the sake of my children, I hope you can."

"Before I leave you with Sally, I have just one more question for you. When you were driving the children home and the police stopped you, did the officer tell you why you were pulled over?"

"No. I asked but he wouldn't tell me. Was I wrong to get out of the car?"

"No. You did nothing wrong. Okay, you guys keep working. I want to file the motion this afternoon. I have to make a call and I will come back in later."

I took a few minutes to breathe, focus and calm down. Then I called Roy. He picked up and I said, "Good morning, Roy. I missed you in court this morning. I wanted to tell you that we were prepared to settle. Maybe you can explain to me just what is going on before we go to war."

"Chance, you know exactly what's going on. But if you are talking about what happened in court, Jackson is very concerned about Courtney's reckless behavior and the safety of the twins. We needed to retain an attorney who specializes in child neglect and custody cases to act as counsel for Jackson. I'm sure you want the twins protected."

"That's pretty good, Roy. A bit clumsy and transparent, but not bad for a beginner. I never appreciated that corporate lawyers had any skill in dissembling facts and gaslighting. Unfortunately, you need a little more practice. As my father was fond of saying, facts are stubborn things. You're on a slippery slope. You will find that you can never lie fast enough to come up with the answer to the next question asked of you. I thought you might be interested in a conversation I had with Judge Donovan this morning."

There was complete silence on the other end of the phone.

"Sorry, I can't hear you, Roy. I will take that as a yes. I met with our good friend and my former mentor because I was wondering why he transferred Courtney's case today to a new judge, who awarded Jackson temporary custody based upon a frivolous *ex parte* application. You know what he told me, Roy?"

"No."

"No? I'm pretty sure you can guess. He told me he transferred the case as a favor to someone. I know you were the one who asked for that favor. Now what I would like to know is this, why you would ask him for that favor? Why would *you* want to start a ground war in this divorce? You told me repeatedly that Jackson wants the divorce over. We're at the finish line. What's going on, Roy?"

After some time, Roy said, "The divorce doesn't matter anymore. A divorce won't solve our problems. Do what you were asked to do. Now maybe you and your client will pay some attention."

"Roy, you're making a big mistake. You can buy a judge, but you can't buy the whole legal system. People smarter and more powerful than you have tried. It ended badly for them. This will end badly for you."

Roy didn't say anything further and hung up. I sat for a few minutes wondering about what Roy had gotten himself into. Why would he risk his reputation, career and possibly his freedom to protect Jackson Malone?

That afternoon we filed an application with the Appellate Division to vacate the Temporary Restraining Order awarding temporary custody to Jackson.

The court in short order vacated the temporary order based upon the procedural issues we raised. They directed the lower court to put the case back on the calendar, permit me to submit opposition papers and hold an evidentiary hearing before any award of temporary custody was made.

Courtney was incredibly grateful to have the children back home, but the court proceedings had the desired effect on her. She was badly frightened. Frightened about her children and about her future. Her divorce had become a nightmare.

CHAPTER THIRTY
A PROPOSAL

Having finally put out the fire in the divorce case for the time being, we want back to focusing on the class action. As expected, the numerous motions to dismiss filed by the class action defendants were denied.

Sally and Damian were hard at work preparing our voluminous discovery demands. After they left for the day, I was working late at my desk, rereading portions of *Bad Blood*, to make sure I was aware of all the potential witnesses.

I was deep in thought when my cell rang and saw it was Sally. "Sally, I'm glad you called. Are we on for dinner at the office on Sunday? I have a surprise for Melody. I found a stuffed toy that looks just like Tort and I made a collar with his name on it."

"Sorry, but Melody has a play date and dinner at her friend's house." Sally sounded distracted. "If you want, I could still come over for an early dinner."

"Great. Just you and me then. I'll surprise you by cooking something different for dinner."

"Fine. No offense but everything you cook is pretty different. One condition, I get to pick the music."

"Ouch. Agreed!"

After a pause, Sally added, "Chance, I have a question for you. Were you at Melody's school today?"

"No. Was I supposed to be? Did I forget to pick her up."

"No. When I went to the school this afternoon, Melody's teacher asked to speak to me. She told me Melody had wandered off in the park at recess by herself for a few minutes. That is not a problem because the park is fenced and locked. The kids are free to wander around."

"But what…?"

"A woman, who the teacher believed was another parent, was holding Melody's hand and brought her back to the group. The teacher thanked her, and the woman said, "It's like herding kittens. Hard to keep track of them all, isn't it?"

"Okay. Was Melody scared?"

"No, not at all. That's not the problem. The woman told Melody to say hello to you. Why would she say that?"

"Say hello? Hello to *me*?"

"Yes, she asked Melody to say hello to Chance Cormac. Would you know who she is?"

"No. I have no idea. I've been to Melody's school a few times. Maybe it's one of the other parents I met."

"It could be, I guess. Maybe I'm just being overprotective. This divorce case has me spooked. See you Sunday for dinner. Thanks."

Sally came over around six. She was wearing jeans and a form-fitting red sweater that hugged her in all the right spots. I said, "Hello, beautiful."

She smiled, gave me a hug and a bottle of wine. I enjoyed the embrace and the scent I remembered so well. "Tonight, no talk about law, clients or divorces."

Sally said, "Thank God."

"Okay, this really hurts, but you get to pick the play list."

"Tonight is Bruce Hornsby and nothing but Bruce Hornsby."

I laughed. "What a great choice! I never knew you were a closet Bruce fan."

I lit a fire and we had a leisurely dinner of tacos, quesadillas and Mexican salad in the conference room.

I couldn't remember the last time we spent time together, just the two of us. We talked like an old married couple. About Melody, our lives and how we ended up where we were. We took the bottle of wine and sat next to each other on the couch, a blanket over our legs, and enjoyed the fire.

I finally said, "This is so nice. Do you know how remarkable you are? Beautiful inside and out, a perfect mother and the best paralegal in the world."

Sally laughed, taking the bottle of wine. "Oh, boy, I think you've had enough to drink."

"Sally, can I ask you a question about Melody? Tell me if I'm intruding."

"A godfather should be able to ask any questions he wants to about his goddaughter. Shoot."

"I'm wondering, do you know who Melody's father is?"

Sally sat very still for a few minutes. "No. The donor was anonymous. When Melody asks about her father, I tell her that she is a gift from God and that I am her mom *and* dad. I have often thought about what I would do if Melody decides she wants to know who her father actually is. I really don't know. All I know is, I don't want her to be hurt by knowing or not knowing."

"I'm sorry, I didn't mean to upset you. I am a strong believer that a mother's instincts are always right. I am sure you and Melody will make the right decision, if and when the time comes."

Sally took my hand. "Thank you. There is really no one else I can talk to about Melody. It means so much to me to have you in our lives."

"Sally, that night I bought Melody home from the play there were some things I wanted to discuss with you, but there was no time. You know I love both you and Melody."

"Of course. And we love you."

"You are both a big part of my life, but I want more. I want to have both of you in my life all the time. I want to be not just Melody's godfather but her real father. I want you to be my wife."

Sally didn't say anything. We embraced and kissed. I held her tight and explored her body with my hands. She said, "We shouldn't," but I knew she didn't mean it.

I undressed her slowly and saw the curves and constellation of freckles that I remembered so well. We lay on the couch and embraced for a long time, just enjoying the closeness and warmth of our bodies. We made love slowly to the sound of Hornsby's enchanting song, "Sunflower Cat / It Takes a Lot to Laugh, It Takes a Train to Cry." When we came back to earth I covered us with the blanket and neither one of us wanted to let go. I felt like I was home – safe and loved.

Sally suddenly sat up. "Oh, God! I'm late! I have to pick Melody up." She threw on her clothes and was ready to leave.

After she hugged and kissed me goodbye, I said, "Thank you. I love you. What now?"

Sally gave me another kiss. "Now, Mr. Cormac, I am going to pick up my daughter. As if my life wasn't complicated enough. One thing I know is we are going to move very slowly. See you tomorrow."

CHAPTER THIRTY-ONE
BROKEN DREAMS

Sally was up early on Monday. She liked to get a fresh start on the day before Melody got up. As a single mom, Sally enjoyed the first few moments in the morning, when she could sit and enjoy a cup of coffee and plan the day before getting on the treadmill of her personal and professional life.

She sat down on her couch and enjoyed the early morning sunlight streaming through her living room windows. She smiled and shook her head as she thought about the night before. She thought about Chance and who Melody's real father might be. She dreamed about the joy of lovemaking the night before and what it would mean to be married to a man she loved and who she knew loved her and Melody. What it would mean to Melody to have a father.

"Now what, indeed?" She laughed out loud. She was excited, confused and apprehensive. She knew she wasn't a schoolgirl anymore and realized that she and Melody could easily end up losing the good things they already had. She was lost in her thoughts when she realized that it was past time to put the day in gear. She said out loud, "Snap out of it!"

As she got up to wake Melody, she noticed out of the corner of her eye, an envelope on the floor by the front door to her apartment. The envelope was 10x12 inches and was made of an unusually shiny material.

When Sally picked up the envelope, she noticed that it had no stamps or return address on it. Printed in the center on the front of the envelope was the caption: "Malone v Malone." Nothing else.

Sally was puzzled. She couldn't figure out how the envelope was delivered without her name or address on the front. If they were some documents related to Courtney's divorce, they would have been delivered to the office. If a messenger had delivered the envelope, she would have had to buzz him in through the front door of the building.

She decided it must have been a neighbor who found the envelope in the lobby and as a favor slid it under her door.

She opened the envelope. It contained dozens of very high definition professional 8x11-inch black and white photos. At first Sally couldn't, or wouldn't, process, what she was seeing or who the photos were of. Like being hit with a brick in the back of her head, she realized all of the pictures were recent pictures of Melody.

The first one was shot from behind. It was a shot of a well-dressed woman walking with Melody in the park by Melody's school. The woman's face couldn't be seen. Melody was holding the woman's hand and it looked like they were talking as they walked toward Melody's teacher, who could be seen in the distance.

Sally realized it was the woman who told Melody to say hello to Chance! Sally was suddenly convulsed with fear. She couldn't bear to look at the other pictures but forced herself to. There were close-ups of Melody in front of their apartment house. At school. At their favorite playground, with her babysitter. Of Sally and Melody leaving the office.

Picture after picture capturing Melody's life and everywhere she went. But perhaps most disturbing of all were the last photos – Melody's room. Her bed. Her favorite stuffed animals, including the Simba toy from *The Lion King*.

Sally was hit with severe vertigo and nauseousness. She had to grab the wall to steady herself. The message was clear: your daughter is not safe. Know that we had her by the hand in the park and we can get to her anywhere and at any time.

Sally turned the now empty envelop over and dropped it on the floor. The threat was clear. "Cooperate in doing what we want in Courtney's divorce or your daughter will come to harm."

Fearing the worst, Sally raced to Melody's room. After she saw Melody still sleeping, she went to the front door, to make sure it was double locked. Her heart was racing and with a trembling she picked up her cell phone.

***

I had turned my phone off and was finishing my morning meditation. As Cat Stevens sang, "Morning has broken, like the first morning," I dreamed about the night before and how that this could be the beginning of my life as a family with Sally and Melody. The workout on the heavy bag had me punching combinations to keep beat with Charlie Watts and Bill Wyman on "Miss You," by the Stones.

It was a good start for what looked like a beautiful sunny day in Brooklyn. I said to Tort, "Are you ready for a new life? I am!"

I put his leash on and turned my phone back on. There were three calls and six texts from Sally. I knew immediately that there something was very wrong. I called Sally without listening to her messages or reading any of the texts.

She picked up, fear in her voice. "Where are you? Where the fuck are you? I've been trying to reach you! Why didn't you answer! They are threatening Melody. The pictures! Oh, God! My baby girl!"

"Sally, who? Who's threatening Melody? What pictures?"

"Jackson. Jackson's people. I don't know! I can't talk. Melody is up. I'm coming to the office with Melody. I'm coming over now! I'm frightened to death. You have to help me. Please! Please! Don't go anywhere."

She hung up before I could say another word.

I called Damian. I told him that someone had threatened Melody and Sally. I asked him to come to the office as soon as possible.

Next, I called Courtney. I was concerned that she might have received similar threats. She was surprised to hear from me so early in the morning. I apologized for disturbing her and made up an excuse that I was setting up my calendar and wanted to schedule an appointment with her. I asked casually how she and the twins were doing.

She said that everyone was fine since the girls were returned to her, and she was starting to get her life back to normal. I was relieved that she and the twins had not been threatened and saw no need to tell her about the pictures delivered to Sally. I apologized for calling so early. We set a date to meet, and I quickly got off the phone.

Damian arrived in record time. He moved through city traffic on his motorcycle at speeds faster than any subway train. We had just sat down in the conference room when Sally burst through the front door and into the conference room, carrying Melody in her arms. There was a shiny envelope in her hand. Melody was still in her pink pajamas and wore fuzzy slippers under her coat. Sally started pacing frantically, still holding Melody, too distressed to sit. Melody looked frightened and was clutching the baby Simba I had bought her for her birthday.

Sally threw the envelope on the conference room table. "Chance. What the fuck! *What the fuck!*"

I picked up the envelope and looked inside. I closed the envelope quickly, gave it to Damian and said, "Hold this for me." I wanted to make sure that Melody didn't see the pictures. I said softly To Melody, "Hello, honey. I love your slippers. Sally, why don't you put Melody down. She could go up to my apartment and play with Tort while we talk."

Sally held Melody even more tightly and moved away from me, shouting, "Don't you dare touch my daughter! She's not leaving my side. This is on you! You let this happen!"

Melody became upset and began to cry. Tort began barking loudly.

I knew I had to let Sally's storm of emotions pass so she could realize how badly she was frightening Melody. I also had to control my own surging rage. Someone had threatened the people I love.

I stepped back and took a deep breath. I said as calmly as I could, "Okay, Melody doesn't go anywhere unless you want her to. I am going to lock the front door. Damian, can you bring in some waters?"

When we came back, Sally was sitting at the conference table with Melody on her lap, talking softly to her.

I gave Sally a water and said in a soft, measured voice, "Sally, I know you want to protect Melody. We both know she shouldn't be here when we open that envelope. With your permission, here is what I would like to do. I would like to take Melody upstairs and she can play with Tort and watch TV until we figure this out. Nobody, absolutely nobody, except us, is going to come in or out of this office or my apartment. We are absolutely safe. No harm is going to come to you or Melody."

Damian gave me a slight nod and in a voice devoid of emotion, he said, "Sally, one thing I can promise you, *no one* is coming in or out of this office."

Sally took a sip of water, kissed Melody and reluctantly said, "All right."

I gently picked Melody up from Sally's lap and asked her, "Honey, can you do me a big favor and take Tort up to my apartment and watch TV for a little while so your mom and I can talk?"

Melody said, "Momma, can I go play with Tort?"

Sally, more composed, agreed. "Yes, honey, go play with Tort. We will all be right here. Tell me if you need anything."

I asked Melody, "Did you have any breakfast, honey?"

She said, with a small smile, "No. Can I have some Cheerios."

I said, "Of course. And you can let Tort lick your bowl when you are done."

"I can? Really?"

I took Melody upstairs, poured her a bowl of cereal, and made her comfortable in front of the TV under a blanket, with Tort tucked in next to her. She asked me, "Chance, is Momma mad at me?"

"No, honey, of course not. She is upset about a client of mine. We are going to talk about it. It will all be fine. I'm going downstairs. If you need anything, just call down to me or your mom."

When I returned to the office, I found Damian had taken the pictures out of the envelope and spread them out on the conference room table. As he pored over each photo, he took a picture of each one with his phone. He then put each photo in a plastic evidence sleeve. He was taking notes and putting Post-Its on each sleeve as he studied them.

Sally was sitting silently on the opposite side of the table, refusing to look at Damian or the repulsive pictures. I noticed when Damian leaned forward to take a closer look at one of the pictures of Melody, his leather motorcycle jacket was unzipped. As he leaned in, I saw the SIG Sauer nine millimeter semiautomatic pistol in a shoulder holster under his left arm. I knew Damian was licensed to carry a concealed weapon and practiced at the range but I had never seen him carry a gun before.

Although I am a believer in the rule of law, not armed combat, I realized that Damian was taking the threat to Sally and Melody very seriously and he was prepared to act accordingly. Damian noticed me focusing on the gun and, without comment, zipped up his jacket. I was glad Sally didn't see the weapon.

I sat next to Damian, and we silently examined each of the pictures carefully. I was very disturbed by the alarming number and professional quality of the pictures documenting Melody's life. This was no longer just some matrimonial tactic. These threats were very serious, and I doubted that they were being made by Roy or Jackson. I struggled to control my rage by breathing deeply. I wanted to be centered and clear in assessing the immediate risk and how best to proceed.

I didn't ask Sally any questions. I wanted her to talk when she was ready.

Finally Sally said, in a pleading, desperate voice, "Jesus Fucking Christ, they have pictures of Melody's bedroom! They were in my house! In her bedroom! How the fuck could they do that? Who the fuck are these people?"

When I tried to answer, she cut me off. "Chance, *please*, I know you love Melody. Tell me you are going to withdraw from this goddamned case. You are going to find and destroy copies of any of the documents they want. You have to unwind this fucking mess. I feel like I am going to be sick."

Sally ran to the bathroom and was ill. I looked at Damian. He sat motionless, just stroking his chin as he focused on the glossies.

When Sally came back, before I could say anything, she started speaking frantically again, "Why are they threatening my innocent child? What do we have to do with any of this? Why aren't these threats being directed at Courtney and her twins? We need to be protected. I am going to do what you always tell your clients to do – I am going to the police and the FBI."

Damian spoke for the first time. "That would be a mistake in judgment."

Sally shot him a hard look. "Damian, why the fuck not? What do you know? You don't have any kids."

He ignored the slight. "I care a great deal for you and Melody. I wouldn't let anyone hurt you. I am smarter, have better resources and am more capable than the FBI or the police. I can protect you and your daughter better than they can. More importantly, I don't answer to anyone, and I don't care who gets hurt. I am trained to eliminate threats. I give you my word, Melody will be safe."

I trusted Damian's instincts and ability but I needed time to think. If there's one thing I learned after many years of litigation, it's that the good lawyer acts, he doesn't react. I needed some time to temper my anger and crystallize my thoughts before I responded to Sally.

Finally, I said, "Sally, you know I will do anything I can to make this go away. Why don't you go upstairs to make sure Melody is all right, while Damian and I take a hard look at these pictures?"

As Sally went upstairs I was able gain some perspective about the threats being made to Courtney and Sally. I slowly realized the threats were intended for me, not them. I was the target. I was the cause of the pain to the two people I cared the most about. Whatever happened, I knew I was responsible and had to make things right.

Sally found Melody happily sitting on my bed, snuggled with Tort, their heads just poking out of the covers, watching her favorite TV show, "Bubble Guppies". Sally said, "Hey, pumpkin, how are you doing?"

"Momma, are you still mad?"

She sat next to Melody, and gave Tort a pat on the head. "No, not anymore. You know how sometimes your mom gets angry when I want you to do something? It's because I love you and want to protect you. I love Chance, too, and sometimes I get angry with him, too."

She nodded thoughtfully, giving Sally a sly look. "Can I have a cookie?"

"Okay. But first you have to give me a big hug and a kiss."

Melody gave Sally an impish grin. "I will, but only if you give me two cookies. And a glass of milk."

"You're the tough cookie." Sally laughed for the first time that morning, hugging and tickling her daughter. "You know, you're going to make a great lawyer someday." Sally gave her the two cookies and milk, telling her, "We'll only be a few minutes more. If you need anything, we're right downstairs."

When Sally returned to the conference room, Damian and I were sitting side by side at the conference table silently studying the pictures. Sally was more composed. She said, "Melody is fine," but still refused to look at me. I moved to sit next to her.

She looked up slowly and we made eye contact. "You know I will do anything to protect you and Melody. If withdrawing from this case would make this all go away, I would do it in a heartbeat. But they have made it clear they don't want me to withdraw, they want me to shut down Courtney's father and have any incriminating documents destroyed. They don't want another lawyer to represent Courtney."

Sally only looked away with a clenched jaw.

"My withdrawing doesn't change anything. We know too much. Courtney's father knows too much. A new lawyer doesn't solve their problem. We know the facts. Those facts won't disappear or become less of a threat because I close my eyes or compromise Courtney. They went at Courtney first. When that didn't work, they raised the ante by threatening the ones I love."

Sally was now listening carefully. "I'm convinced they don't want to hurt Melody or you. If they wanted to, they would have done it already. They want to get my attention. They don't know it's Courtney's father who pulled the thread. No deal we can offer them in the divorce, no matter how favorable to Jackson, will give them the protection they need."

Sally seemed deflated. She said in an even voice, "First of all, I don't ever want to hear any goddam platitudes from you about facts being stubborn, or about the law or about justice. Just tell me what we do now to make this all go away."

I replied honestly, "I don't know. Not yet. But I can assure you they have succeeded in getting my full attention. For now, I would like you and Melody to move in with me for a few weeks. Keep Melody home from school and she can sit with you in the office during the day. Either Damian or I will be here with both of you at all times."

I said to Damian, "Install the most high-tech security system and surveillance cameras inside and outside the office, my apartment and Sally's apartment, so we can monitor what's going on twenty-four seven."

"Got it. Done."

"Damian can get what you and Melody need from your apartment later. Why don't you get Melody and have her come down and sit with you at your desk. Try to keep busy. If you can, work on the class action research."

She said, "Let Melody play upstairs. She's happy where she is. I don't want her further upset by any of this. I'll tell her later that you invited us for a sleepover and we are going to be staying here for a while. I will have to trust you and Damian. If any harm comes to Melody, I will never forgive you. Never. Just don't you say anything about the good guys winning because I have already lost something inside that I will never get back."

Sally knows me too well. But, actually what I couldn't help thinking was something quite different: revenge is a dish best served cold.

After Sally went upstairs to check on Melody, I closed the door to the conference room and sat down next to Damian. "Okay, any thoughts?"

"Here are the things I don't like. First, this is a very professional surveillance op. Probably a number of photographers took pictures over a period of weeks from strategic locations and were never detected. Second, they accessed Sally's apartment and Melody's bedroom. They had to break and enter without being detected."

"What else?"

"Third, and most disturbing, see that shiny envelope the photos were delivered in? I've seen one before."

"You have? What is it?"

"It is used by couriers for select intelligence agencies like the CIA, SVR or Mossad. No fingerprints, no tracing who manufactured it or its origin. This isn't the work of some local PI working a matrimonial case. This looks like a covert government agency operation. The question is who? And why?"

I thought hard about Damian's concerns and questions. "In the end, you always have to follow the money. We know Jackson is running a sophisticated money-laundering operation for some very powerful and very dangerous people. Courtney's father poked the bear with his clumsy investigation. I originally assumed Roy's threats and attempts to coerce me were intended to hide Jackson's assets and protect him from possible criminal prosecution. But that never really made any sense to me."

"Agreed. Jackson never seemed concerned about the money."

"Exactly. From the start he was willing to be more than generous in the divorce settlement. They also know if we reported Jackson for money laundering or tax evasion, it would be of no benefit to Courtney or her children. If Jackson goes down, Courtney stands to lose as much as he does."

Damian agreed, "It's lose-lose."

"Exactly. We had no incentive or legal obligation to investigate the source of Jackson's wealth. We were looking in the wrong direction. The people who are the most threatened by this divorce, and therefore the most dangerous, are not Jackson and Checkmate, but the people whose money he is laundering. They have no interest in me or Courtney's divorce. This isn't personal. They just want to be back in the shadows and anonymous again."

"Chance, it would be a mistake to underestimate these people. In combat we always took the offensive. Always. I'm trained to attack, not defend. I would be happy to give them a wake-up call. I have the resources to push back hard. Trust me, I will get Roy's and Jackson's attention. Just give me a green light."

"Damian, there is nothing that would give me greater pleasure than to inflict some real pain on Jackson and Roy for threatening Sally and Melody. But for now I want you to stand down."

"Got it. Just tell me when."

"As soon as you install the security and surveillance systems, do a deep dive and see if you can find out who actually owns the client cryptocurrency accounts. Forget the NDA and court order. Nobody is playing by the rules anyway."

"Got it. How does this all end?"

"I have no idea, but, as I tell my clients, all divorces end, one way or the other."

CHAPTER THIRTY-TWO
SALVATION

Sally and Melody moved in. We were living together but certainly not in the way I had envisioned or wanted. Damian had secured the office but I thought it might be helpful to have JR come back to help him. They had fought countless battles together and I thought it would be smart for Damian to have some back up. Also, honestly, I needed a clerk to help with the backload of legal work that this black hole of a divorce had created.

I spoke to Damian and asked how JR was doing and if he thought JR would consider coming back to work. He said that he had not heard much from JR after the arrest. He had been meaning to call him but with all the recent drama he didn't have a chance. He said that he would reach out to him, but doubted that he would consider coming back until after the criminal case was resolved. JR had told Damian he felt very badly about his arrest and didn't want to create any more problems for me or the firm. I said I understood but he should know we could use his help and his job was waiting for him when he was ready.

What we didn't know was that JR started backsliding right after his arrest. His arrest and the time in jail had cracked the foundation that he had worked so hard to build. Something was torn and he didn't have the strength to mend the tear in his mind or his heart. He stopped attending his meetings and didn't take his medication.

As could have been predicted, without his medication and his support group, the panic attacks struck more and more often. His insomnia returned and he would wake up in the dead of night in a cold sweat and unable to breathe. When it got to the point where he was afraid to close his eyes and stopped sleeping altogether, in desperation he turned to oxycodone, the old friend he knew could keep the demons at bay. He stopped going out of his apartment, except to score more oxy.

***

When JR missed his monthly probation meeting in violation of the terms of his release, there came a knock on his door. Two officers served him with a warrant for his arrest and to search his apartment. JR watched it all happen in slow motion in an oxy haze, as if he were in a movie. Nothing happening seemed real. He was tired to the bone and had already surrendered long before he was arrested.

They handcuffed JR and one officer sat with him while the other searched the apartment. It didn't take long before they found four bottles of prescription oxy on the nightstand next to his unmade bed. Each prescription bottle had the name of someone other than JR on the label. JR was read his rights and arrested.

He said, "What took you guys so long?"

They jailed JR in the Tombs. It is an underground jail in New York County. There are no windows, no outside light and little air in the cells. Even hardened criminals can't survive underground in the Tombs for more than a few days.

JR was processed and put in a holding cell with the general population. This time there was no special treatment, no Francis Fogarty to help with this arrest or his incarceration.

As soon as the cell door closed, he was tested right away by the Hispanic and Black population, who had no love for white country boys from Texas. He welcomed the beating and didn't defend himself. As he drifted out of consciousness he smiled. This was as good a way as any to finally get some sleep. He was hoping he would never wake up.

When JR finally opened his eyes, he found himself cuffed to a hospital bed in a private room in what looked like a hospital. Next to his bed, the sun was shining through a window without any bars on it. His face and body hurt from the beating, but somehow he felt rested and at peace.

He thought, *well I'm either still dreaming or 'bout to meet my Maker.*

He saw an IV in his arm. It was then that he noticed two men sitting in the corner of the room. One of the men, dressed in an expensive suit, came over to JR's bed when he saw that JR was awake. The other man, who had special forces written all over him, was dressed in a black leather jacket, black jeans and combat boots. He stood up, and without saying anything, closed the door and stood with his back to it.

The suit said, "JR, good to see you awake. I hope you are feeling better. We were worried about you. Your treatment here has been inexcusable. The jails in this country are completely inhumane. There is more crime committed in jail than out on the street."

JR said, "I'm a bit fuzzy. Just who are you guys? Where am I? How'd I get here?"

"We are friends. You are in the jail infirmary in a room reserved for only the most important inmates. We arranged for your transfer here from the general population and for your treatment. You are receiving IV medications that should relieve your pain, anxiety and any withdrawal symptoms you may be experiencing. My name is Dimitry Kafelnikov. I am a lawyer and I have been retained to represent you. That is my associate, Igor."

"I'm a little slow. Who retained you? Do you work for Fogarty? Did Chance Cormac sign you guys up?"

"No. I don't work for Mr. Cormac or Mr. Fogarty. I have my own practice. You might say that I specialize in making problems go away. You have some influential friends who would like to help you. They would prefer to remain anonymous, but rest assured they have your best interests at heart. They can also help you with your prescription needs. They can make this all go away."

"Now, I'm real confused. How can they make this disappear? Why in the world would they want to help me?"

"How we solve your problems isn't your concern. We want to help you because you are in a position to also help us. For all that we will do for you, we need only a small favor in return. You have some special skills we would like to employ. We, of course, in addition to giving you your freedom, would pay you handsomely for your work."

JR closed his eyes. He thought he might be dreaming. When he opened them, the suit and the thug were still there.

"If you agree to help us, you will stay in this medical facility and receive the medication you so desperately need until you have recovered. You will be released as soon as you are healthy enough to function outside. Once you have done what we ask, we can make all your criminal charges, including the original probation violation, disappear. Your probation will be over. You will be generously compensated, and we will relocate you to anywhere in the world you like. You will be free to start a new life. How does that sound?"

"A little too good to be true. But what if I'm not real inclined to do you a favor?"

"That would be your choice, but I would think carefully before making that decision. If you decide not to help us, you will be returned to the general population in the Tombs. It is unlikely you will be granted bail based upon your violations of the conditions of your release and your recent probation violations. For your own good, we would make sure that you didn't have access to any illegal prescription drugs during your incarceration. In your underground cell, your panic attacks might fall on deaf ears. You would suffer in your own private hell day after day, night after night, with no end in sight. I'm not sure how long anyone could bear that."

JR looked out the window, and finally said, "I'm pretty much between a rock and a hard place. What exactly do you want me to do?"

"We will give you specific instructions in due course. First and foremost you must agree not to discuss any of this with anyone, including your friend Damian, or Chance Cormac. If you do, the deal is off and you will immediately be returned to a cell in the general prison population and your medication will be cut off. Do we have an understanding?"

JR knew he had nothing left to lose. "I believe so. We got ourselves a deal."

"Excellent! By the way, JR, I assume you can you still hit a target."

After meeting with JR, Dimitry scheduled another meeting with Jackson and Roy at a third safe house, also a few blocks from the Russian Consulate. When they arrived, they went through the same security protocols, and again were seated in another windowless room with the router on the floor and Igor at the door. Igor now carried his Glock prominently in a holster on his hip.

Dimitry came in and seemed in good spirits. He said with a smile, "Gentlemen, I have some good news. Igor feels there is no need for you to disrobe today."

Roy and Jackson sat rigidly, saying nothing.

"Comrades, please relax. We are all friends here. I'm only making a joke. But I actually do have some very good news. We have discovered who accessed our clients' accounts. Jackson, it was your father-in-law, Randolph Gault."

"*What*? Randolph? No. Are you sure?" Jackson said. "Why would he do that?"

"Apparently, you are no longer Randolph's favorite son-in-law. He was intent on hurting and embarrassing you to make you pay a high price to settle the divorce. He hired high powered investigators to investigate Checkmate and your clients."

"How did you find that out?"

"We intercepted a cell phone conversation between Courtney and her father. We have been monitoring her calls for quite some time with no success. We learned all we needed to know from a recent conversation. We discovered, as it turns out, that Chance knew who had accessed our clients' information all the time."

"What? He told me he didn't!" Roy said defensively.

"We learned that after his meeting with you, Roy, Chance rightly suspected Randolph was behind the investigation and asked to meet with him. Randolph apparently swore Chance to keep what he told him secret and admitted he'd had investigators access the information about our clients. As promised, Chance kept the information confidential. Until after Courtney's arrest, that is. Then he decided he had an obligation to inform her about her father's investigation and the threat to our clients."

Jackson asked, "You mean Courtney knows all about this, too?"

"Yes. She was not happy and wanted to confront her father immediately, however, with good reason, Chance strongly advised her to wait. Chance feared if Randolph learned Chance had broken his promise, it would provoke him to immediately use the information about our clients against you, Jackson."

"But she called her father anyway?" Jackson asked.

"I guess you know your wife. Fortunately for us, Courtney didn't take Chance's advice and we intercepted her call to her father. To her credit, Courtney begged her father to stop his investigation and to destroy any records about Checkmate or its clients. Randolph was outraged that Chance had broken his word and disclosed their conversation. He flatly refused Courtney's plea to stop the investigation and destroy the records. He told her about the money laundering and our clients."

"Doesn't he understand he is hurting his own daughter? He's too intelligent not to understand the risks. This makes no sense," Jackson said.

"He said it was clear he was the only one trying to protect Courtney. He is on a mission to hurt you, Jackson, and in the process, our clients. He believes he has his foot on your neck and he is just waiting for the right time to use the information. Are we all together, gentlemen?"

Jackson said, "He's not thinking straight. Roy, can't you talk some sense into Randolph?"

Roy just shook his head and said nothing.

Dimitry gave Roy a quizzical look and continued. "At least Randolph doesn't seem to know anything about Courtney's arrest or your attempt to gain custody. Courtney never told him. I'm sure he would not be well pleased with you, or you, Roy, if he knew you were the one who was so helpful in orchestrating her arrest and getting Jackson's case transferred to that corrupt judge."

"I did exactly what you asked, Dimitry. We got Courtney's attention," Roy said.

"That's true. Courtney's arrest and the silliness in court about granting Jackson custody, which, God knows he doesn't deserve, had its desired effect. Just not the way we anticipated. It motivated Chance to go back on his word to Randolph and tell Courtney about what Randolph had done. That, in turn, resulted in Courtney's call to her father. As we suspected, it was always about the divorce. Your divorce."

Dimity waited for a minute and went and sat down very close to Roy. "Of course, Roy, you already knew about all of this, didn't you?"

Jackson looked at Dimitry and then turned to Roy. "What? Roy, you knew about Randolph and didn't tell us? Why?"

Dimitry, now shoulder to shoulder with Roy, said, "Excellent question, Jackson. We're all interested in the answer. Why didn't you tell us, Roy?"

Roy suddenly felt nauseous and lightheaded. He struggled for air and finally said, "No. No, that's not true."

"What's not true, Roy?"

"I never knew Randolph was the one who obtained the records. Chance did tell me he knew who it was, but I swear, he refused to give me the name. I had nothing to tell you."

"Igor, Roy says that he had nothing to tell us. What do you think?"

Igor now had his hand resting on his Glock and responded to Dimitry in Russian.

Dimitry said, "Igor doesn't believe you. He's not sure you can be trusted."

"Dimitry, please. Please! I did everything you asked. Please don't hurt me!"

"Roy, do you believe in salvation? That we can be saved if we repent our sins?"

Roy hung his head and was weeping quietly.

Dimitry put his hand on Roy's shoulder. "Roy, I believe you can be saved. There may still be hope for you if we act quickly. So please, try to compose yourself and listen closely. Fortunately, I think we still have a window of opportunity to make things right. It appears that Courtney's father is still biding his time before he tries to leverage Jackson with what he has discovered. Igor is now going to eliminate the problem."

"Eliminate?" Jackson stuttered. "What do you mean, eliminate? What are you going to do to Randolph? I don't want him hurt."

Dimitry stood up. "Jackson, our patience is exhausted. We can't risk waiting any longer."

"But, Dimitry, it won't help. If Courtney knows everything, eliminating Randolph doesn't solve anything."

"Very perceptive, Jackson. I heard that you are an excellent chess player. You seem to be always thinking about all the right moves. I believe you could have been a very skilled diplomat. You are very perceptive, you realize Courtney also has to be eliminated."

Jackson jumped up and moved toward Dimitry with his fist clenched, screaming in his face, "*What? What!* You're talking about killing the mother of my children! Are you insane? I won't allow it! I'll stop you!"

Igor, in a blur, moved from the door and with one blow to Jackson's head with his gun violently knocked him to the floor before anyone realized what was happening. He stood towering over Jackson, who lay sprawled on the floor with the Glock pointed straight down at his head. Without moving a muscle, Igor spoke calmly to Dimitry in Russian.

Jackson lay silently on the floor with his hands covering his head, afraid to move. Dimitry finally responded to Igor in Russian. Igor stared down at Jackson, holstered his weapon, and went back to his position, standing by the door.

Dimitry said, "Jackson, it's best not to raise your voice. Igor has been trained to act first and ask questions later. Please get up and sit down at the table."

Jackson got up slowly and sat in the chair with his head still in his hands, rubbing the big lump on his head where he was hit with the gun.

Roy had moved as far away from Jackson as he could.

"Jackson, take a deep breath. That's it. Good. I hope Igor did not hurt you. I can understand why you might be upset. But once you think about it, you will realize this solution is a win-win for you."

Jackson continued to rub his head with both hands in silence.

"You will keep all your assets and you will have permanent custody of your children. Your father-in-law hates you. So good riddance to him. As a bonus, once my clients learn how you helped us in resolving this matter, they will be happy to have you manage their accounts again. But make no mistake. This happens whether you like it or not. If you or Roy should attempt to interfere with us, it would be a real mistake in judgment. Igor would quickly eliminate that problem as well. Am I making myself clear?"

Jackson looked at Roy, who didn't move or speak, and nodded slowly.

"Good. As Roy likes to say, now we are making real progress. Jackson, within a few days I will contact you in order for you to set up a meeting with your wife. She will have her guard up after the arrest so you must convince her you can be trusted and just want to visit her and the girls in a public place, to make peace. You will arrange to meet her for lunch around midday at a restaurant on a busy street that has outdoor dining."

"A restaurant? Where?"

"We will tell you which restaurant, the time you should meet and which table you should reserve. After you are seated, we will send you a text. Upon receipt, you will get up and take the girls inside the restaurant. They will not see anything and you can leave through the back door. Our business will be concluded and, although I have enjoyed your company immensely, there will be no need for any of us ever to see each other again or communicate in the future."

"I'll try. I don't know if I can convince her to meet with me, after the arrest."

"Jackson, don't worry, Roy is going to help you and will make sure that Courtney meets you at the appointed time and place. Roy will call Chance and convince him that you are entitled to visit your daughters and it is in everyone's interests for Courtney to meet you. Won't you, Roy?"

Roy nodded and said weakly, "What if I can't convince him?"

"Roy, pretend your life depends upon it. You have an opportunity for salvation. You can save our clients. You can save yourself."

Dimitry said something to Igor in Russian and abruptly left the room. Igor escorted Jackson and Roy out of the safe house.

Once outside, Jackson and Roy recognized the street they had come in on, but they both still felt lost.

CHAPTER THIRTY-THREE
CHECKMATE

In chess, you can make all the right moves and still lose. It's not good enough to know the game and your opponent. You can read the board, exchange the right pieces, plan the perfect endgame and still find yourself mated. One move you didn't see, or didn't make, can be the difference between winning and losing. When you are mated, you lay your king down on the board. That's always the last move.

Dimitry and Igor met with JR at his apartment the day after he was released from the prison hospital. Igor was carrying a large canvas duffle bag. Dimitry said, "JR! Good to see you! You look much better. Igor has some gifts for you!"

Igor opened the bag and handed Dimitry a week's supply of oxy in a paper bag. He took out a Russian Havoc sniper rifle, a scope and a box of shells and put them on the floor in front of JR. Igor then zipped up the duffle bag and stood with his back to the front door to Jackson's apartment.

"JR, I am sure you remember our agreement. If you are thinking about not living up to your end of the bargain, please put it out of your mind. You know what will happen. I would hate to see you back in a dark cage without your medicine."

JR looked inside the bag of oxy he held in his hand and then at the rifle on the floor. He nodded slowly.

"I will take that as a yes. Now listen carefully. I assume you are qualified to shoot with this rifle and scope. The rifle is a bolt action, which I understand was your preferred weapon as a Navy sniper. Yes? The scope is the highest quality military issue. The ordinance is 50BMG bullets. Igor tells me these bullets are unrivaled for their stopping power and accuracy. Are these adequate for you to complete your assignment?"

JR picked up the rifle and snapped the scope in place. He looked down the barrel through the scope and pulled the bolt back and forth forcefully two times as he had done so many times before when he was on a mission. "It'll do."

"Excellent. Now, I am going to give you two keys. Don't lose them.

Each key is labeled with the number of a separate apartment located in the same apartment building. The first apartment is on the top floor of the building, facing the street. Igor has confirmed that from the living room window of the top floor apartment, you will have a straight shot at a restaurant across the street. We will notify you of the date and time when you should be in that apartment. Keep these keys in a safe place. They are the only way you will be able to get into each apartment. Do you understand?"

"Yup. Don't lose the keys."

"Good. The rifle and your money will be waiting for you in two duffle bags in the top floor apartment. Jackson will be sitting at a table outdoors at the restaurant with Courtney and the children. We will text him and he will stand up and go into the restaurant with the children. This should give you a clean head shot at the target and avoid any collateral damage."

"I'll only hit the target. I won't miss."

"Perfect. After the target is down, you are to pick up the casings, put the rifle in the duffle bag and go downstairs with the rifle and the money to the ground floor apartment in the back of the building. Be sure to use the back staircase, which has an emergency exit sign, so you will not be seen. Use the second key to enter the ground floor apartment and wait for us."

"Second key. Ground floor apartment."

"When it is safe, we will come to the apartment. We will dispose of the rifle and assist you in your escape without being detected. Under no circumstances should you move until we get there. Any questions?"

"Only one. How soon we talkin' about?"

"In the next day or two. Is that a problem?"

"Nope. Doesn't much matter to me. Nothing does anymore."

"Excellent. We will see you soon."

***

When Courtney told me that Jackson had called her and invited her and the girls to lunch, I told her under no circumstances should she go.

The TRO had been vacated, but there was still an application before the court to award Jackson temporary custody. I was certain Jackson, or his people, were behind the arrests of JR and Courtney, as well as the threats to Sally and Melody. Courtney didn't know about the threats to Sally and Melody. I saw no benefit in further frightening Courtney and her daughters. Jackson had proven he simply could not be trusted.

Courtney understood my concerns, but said that Jackson had told her that his clients had gotten all their money back and the divorce was no longer a concern to them. He said he had gotten bad advice from Roy and his other lawyers and wanted to make things right. Also, the girls had been asking constantly for their father. Courtney felt, regardless of Jackson's tactics, it was wrong to deprive the girls of any relationship with their father. It's easy to say you are putting your children's interests first but it's hard to do. She was willing to overcome her anger and mistrust if that's what she had to do.

I said, "There's plenty of time for you to repair your relationship after you are divorced. If you want the girls to see their father, let him pick up the girls and return them to you after he visits. There is no need for you to be present. If we get fooled twice, shame on us. Tell him your lawyer says it's a hard no."

Courtney said she understood my concerns but she wanted to think about it. She didn't see how anything could happen if they were outside in a public place near a busy street.

I reminded Courtney that the last time she ate at a restaurant with Jackson she ended up being arrested in a very public place and her twins were taken from her.

I heard Courtney crying softly. "Chance, do you think I don't remember? Please, please I need your help. I just want to end this nightmare. For me and for the girls, I'm sorry, I have to go now."

I felt upset and angry when I got off the call. Maybe I had beaten up Courtney more than I needed to. I knew I was too personally involved. I regretted taking a case I knew I shouldn't have. I had put Sally and Melody in danger. I had been played by Roy, Dumbrowski and two judges. I took it all very personally, which is exactly what a lawyer is trained not to do.

I was just beginning to calm down and focus on how best to help

Courtney when my phone rang and I saw that Roy was calling. We hadn't spoken since our conversation after Courtney's arrest and Conrad Dumbrowski was retained.

I said, "Roy, why are you calling me?"

"Chance, thanks for taking my call. I don't know how this case went off the rails. I really don't know how it happened. It's all my fault. I realize you did nothing wrong. Jackson's clients overreacted when they thought their accounts were compromised. But fortunately, that is no longer a problem. All of those accounts have been closed and the records have been destroyed. I assure you, we can now settle this case quickly and quietly. Jackson would like to visit with the girls, with Courtney present of course, and try to make things right."

"Roy, I don't trust you any further than I can throw you. You crossed the line when you had Courtney arrested and threatened Sally. This is now very personal. I strongly suggest you stay far away from me."

"Chance, believe me, I had nothing to do with Courtney's arrest. That was all Dumbrowski's doing. Jackson was scared and made the mistake of hiring him. He's been discharged. I have no idea what you are talking about in regard to threats to Sally. I'm shocked to hear you think I would participate in that type of conduct. For God's sake, I'm an attorney."

I said, "Stop. You're just embarrassing yourself."

"I swear it's true. Anyway, the fire with the clients' accounts is out and I swear to you this divorce will end here and now. It will help a great deal if Courtney lets Jackson see the girls. She can be present. You know he will be entitled to visitation sooner or later."

"I have no reason to believe anything you say. Also, if Jackson wants to see his children, there is no reason why Courtney has to be present. But Courtney's the client. I will leave the decision up to her."

I told Courtney about my conversation with Roy. I re-emphasized how strongly I felt there was no reason for her to meet with Jackson in order for him to see the girls. We could set up a time when Jackson could have supervised visitation. I didn't want her anywhere near Jackson. I didn't trust him. Or Roy.

She said Jackson had called her again and told her he would meet her and the girls at a public restaurant where they could eat outdoors. He told her the same things Roy had said to me about ending the divorce. He assured her the Checkmate clients were no longer concerned about the documents and it was all an overreaction.

Courtney said she appreciated my concerns but she had decided the girls should be allowed to spend time with their father. She said, "Someone still has to do the right thing." She was adamant and I knew nothing I could say would dissuade her.

Finally, I said, "If you are determined to meet with him, a public place, like a restaurant, is usually a safe choice."

I insisted that she let Damian go with her. Damian could arrive early and sit in an inconspicuous location in the restaurant, where Jackson wouldn't be able to see him. If Jackson acted up, Damian could intervene.

Courtney agreed but said she didn't want Damian's presence to somehow create a confrontation with Jackson in front of the girls. I assured her he would be invisible.

I was far from happy, but I felt somewhat more comfortable with the knowledge that a meeting in a public setting, like a restaurant, normally prevented loud outbursts and threats from angry spouses. If things got ugly, I was more than confident Damian would immediately jump in and make a quick exit with Courtney and the twins.

I texted Roy that, against my advice, Courtney had agreed to have lunch with Jackson and bring the twins. I warned him, if there was any incident, I would hold him personally responsible.

Roy texted back, "Thank you. You have my word this ugly divorce will soon be over once and for all."

***

Courtney and the twins arrived early at the café nestled among the brick apartment buildings on the tree-lined Columbus Avenue. As promised, Jackson had reserved a sidewalk table near the street.

Jackson had told Courtney to dress the girls in warm outfits because, they would be eating outside. The twins had fun picking out their outfits and chose matching white Adidas sweatsuits and white sneakers. Courtney had on jeans and a black wool turtleneck. She wore her gold cross around her neck. She looked at her hand and slowly took off her wedding ring.

As the girls got dressed they were very excited and giggling. They hadn't seen their father in a few weeks, not since he had brought them home to their mother's house after the TRO was vacated.

Courtney was seated with the girls at the outside table Jackson had reserved. It was a clear cool day and the outdoor tables all had white table clothes and vases of red roses in the center. They waited for Jackson and watched the pedestrians and cars going by. The twins were excited to see their father. They giggled as they played a game to see how many dogs they could count being walked on the sidewalk past their table.

Damian was sitting inside at a table that gave him a direct view of Courtney and the children. He wore a black baseball cap, and his leather jacket with the collar pulled up. He sat at an angle that made it difficult, if not impossible, for anyone seated at Courtney's table to see him. His jacket was unzipped and he had the SIG Sauer in a shoulder holster.

Jackson was late. Courtney began to worry he would not show or that the meeting was just another ruse. Then she saw Jackson walking across the street toward them. He seemed relaxed and at ease. When he arrived, he hugged the girls and gave each one a small identical panda bear as a gift.

He asked if he could switch seats with Courtney so he could sit next to the girls. Courtney said fine, and took the seat with her back to the sidewalk and the street.

The waiter came to take their order. Jackson looked at his watch. "I only have time for a cup of coffee, but you and the girls go ahead and order lunch."

Jackson told the girls he missed them very much but hoped to have them sleep over in their own room at his apartment very soon. As the girls played with their toy bears, he told Courtney the most important thing was for them to talk. He leaned over and took Courtney's hand.

She flinched but did not remove his hand. He looked down and noticed that she was not wearing her wedding ring. "Good," he said. "Time for all this to end." Still holding her hand he thanked her for meeting with him. He said he made so many mistakes he didn't know where to begin. He began apologizing over and over again. He apologized about their separation. He said that Courtney and the girls were the best thing that had ever happened to him. He didn't deserve them.

Courtney just looked down. She didn't know what to say.

Jackson apologized about the hardship he had caused for her and the twins. He apologized for not treating her fairly and giving her the respect and appreciation she deserved as a loving wife and mother.

He told her he had never wanted to fight with her or threaten anyone. He said he had gotten very bad advice from Roy and Dumbrowski. It was his fault for letting her drink too much, causing the DWI arrest. He knew there was no truth to the allegations about her poor parenting.

Courtney took it all in without comment. She was suddenly thinking about Chance's warnings and didn't know if she could believe anything Jackson said.

He said it's no excuse, but he panicked because he was afraid of what his clients would do if their accounts were disclosed. He assured Courtney the accounts were all now closed, and the clients had resolved any concerns they had so they could now finalize their divorce, which is all he wanted to do from the beginning.

Courtney silently took her hand away.

Jackson looked Courtney in the eyes. "I'm so sorry. I hope you will find it in your heart to forgive me so I can live the rest of my life with a clear conscience. I know I don't deserve it, but I just need a chance to make things right."

Courtney suddenly felt overwhelmed with fatigue. She was too tired and too confused to think She tried to speak but broke down crying. Tears were streaming down her face.

Sophia said, "Mommy? You're crying? Are you all right?"

Seeing the tears, Damian moved his arm casually and put his hand on the SIG Sauer.

As Courtney was wiping the tears from her eyes with her napkin, Jackson looked at his watch. His phone pinged. Jackson looked at a text on his phone and said, "Girls, why don't we go to the bathroom and give Mommy a few minutes alone."

The last thing Courtney remembered as Jackson got up and took the twins by their hands to go inside the restaurant was thinking, *Maybe I can forgive him.*

The two bullets came hard and fast. The military grade ordinance exploded upon impact. The only noise was a distant pop-pop. It could have been a car backfiring. Or a rivet gun.

Blood exploded over the white tablecloth and onto the girls' white sweatshirts.

Courtney couldn't even scream.

Both head shots were perfectly on target. Jackson never knew what hit him. He was still holding his daughters' hands when his skull exploded. He hit the ground two feet from where Courtney was sitting.

Courtney saw it all, but it didn't register. It wasn't real. She had felt the violence of the bullets hitting Jackson like a sledgehammer. She froze, not comprehending what was happening or what she should do, until she finally heard the girls screaming, "Daddy! Daddy!"

Their sweatshirts and the tablecloth were splattered red with blood, like a grotesque Jackson Pollock painting. The twins were standing next to the table, struggling to hold onto Jackson's lifeless hands.

Damian knew exactly what the gunshots were. He was out of his seat with the SIG Sauer in his hand at a full sprint before Courtney could move.

He grabbed the girls and upended the table where Courtney was sitting, screaming, "Get down! Get down *now*!"

Courtney froze and didn't move.

He grabbed her and threw her down by the girls and screamed, "Stay down! Don't move!"

Crouching behind the table with Courtney and the girls, he made sure they had not been hit. He put the girls into Courtney's arms. "Don't move! Not an inch!"

Damian ran into the street and jumped in front of a moving cab. It had no choice but to stop. He opened the back door to the cab and screamed at Courtney, "Come here! Move! Now!"

He pushed the girls into the back seat with Courtney, and pointed his gun at the frightened cab driver, screaming, "Drive! Go! Go!" as he slammed the door shut.

The cab shot out into traffic with Courtney holding the twins tightly in the back seat.

Damian crouched down in the street and aimed the SIG Sauer at the window where he thought the shots might have been fired from. He waited motionless for a minute. He knew from experience, once a target had been hit, it was unlikely there would be any more shots.

Damian looked back at Jackson's lifeless body and didn't feel anything. Satisfied he was not at risk, he stood up, holstered his gun and slowly walked away, down the street. He didn't look back when he heard the sirens in the distance. He had other things on his mind.

After the head shots hit their mark, JR moved methodically, as if in a trance. As instructed, he picked up the shell casings, put the rifle in the duffle bag, and picked up the backpack containing the cash. He left the upstairs apartment where he had taken the shots through the open window and found the back staircase at the end of the hall. He took the stairs to the ground floor, located the apartment number written on the key fob and unlocked the door. He went in and locked the door behind him.

The apartment was vacant except for a metal card table and two folding chairs in the center of the living room. JR didn't turn on any lights and closed the blinds. He put the backpack and the duffle bag on the floor. He sat down on the folding chair and waited in the dark. He took two more oxys to keep the demons at bay. He heard the sirens in the street, but he wasn't worried. There would be no reason for the police to search a ground floor apartment that didn't face the street.

He was overcome with fatigue, shut his eyes and without knowing it dozed off. He woke up to the sound of a key opening the lock on the apartment door. Dimitry and Igor came in. Dimitry turned on the overhead light and sat down in the folding chair across from JR.

Igor picked up the duffle bag containing the rifle and leaned it against the wall behind Dimitry. He locked the door and stood with his back to it.

Dimitry said, "JR, why you sitting in the dark? You should be celebrating. A perfect shot. A bullseye. You win the grand prize!"

JR didn't respond.

"Your new life is about to begin. Your probation is over, and you can go anywhere in the world with $250,000 in your pocket. How does it feel to be a free man?"

JR just closed his eyes again.

"I understand. You need a little time to decompress. We have to wait until things calm down across the street anyway. That's good. It will give us some time to talk. Igor, you're not in a hurry to go anywhere, are you?"

Igor smiled and shook his head.

"Good. Igor can stay with us. JR, you never asked me why Jackson was eliminated and not Courtney. Aren't you interested in why he was the target?"

Without opening his eyes, JR said, "Nope."

"No? Well, we have some time. Let me tell you anyway. It may help your conscience, if you have any concerns that maybe Jackson didn't deserve what he got. My clients are very wealthy and powerful Russian oligarchs. Their names are not important, but suffice it to say they control vast amounts of wealth in what used to be called the Soviet Union. Of course, they could never have achieved their success without their close relationship with our president, who is their friend and silent partner. For obvious reasons, it is necessary for my clients, and the president, to hide their wealth and partnerships from the Russian people and the world. It would raise suspicions about what has been rightly described as a kleptocracy, where the wealth of the Soviet Union is just the personal piggy bank of a privileged few."

"Just not interested."

"Wait. We're getting to the good part, or in Jackson's case the bad part. He provided a valuable service in laundering money and hiding my clients' assets for many years. He was paid handsomely for his efforts. Unfortunately, he became greedy. We became aware he was stealing from us. The money laundered through the cryptocurrencies were controlled by Jackson. It permitted him to skim from our crypto accounts and it went undetected for quite some time. He ridiculed us by calling his theft of our currency Skim Milk."

JR opened his eyes. "I'm guessin' you guys deserved each other."

"Maybe. For quite some time, it was easy to deceive us, based upon the fluctuation of cryptocurrency prices from minute to minute and our inability to know exactly what trades he executed. Also, shame on us, we trusted him. We probably would have never discovered his theft if Jackson didn't decide to divorce Courtney. It was then that we took a hard look at the accounts and discovered the scheme. Do you understand, my clients were victims?"

"Got it. Victims. Can we go now?"

"Soon. Very soon this will all be over. Don't you want to know how we found out about Jackson? We learned it was Jackson's father-in-law, Randolph Gault, who accessed our clients' information. You see, Randolph never liked Jackson and wanted him to pay for his indiscretions. Ironically, Mr. Gault inadvertently did us a great favor because we would never have discovered Jackson's theft if we weren't concerned about what Gault discovered."

"He lit the fuse."

"Yes. But now that Jackson has been eliminated, Randolf is no longer a threat. Ironically we actually appreciate his efforts. He was the wake-up call. Money wasn't our biggest concern about Jackson's skimming from our clients. It was the fact that he couldn't be trusted and knew all the palace secrets. We put pressure on your boss to try to motivate him to have any evidence of my clients' accounts destroyed. Your unfortunate arrest for parole violations was part of that plan. You were just a pawn in the larger game. I hope you have recovered from your unfortunate incarceration."

JR closed his eyes again and sat dead still. He didn't look up or respond to Dimitry's question.

"Anyway, when those measures didn't succeed, we decided to end the divorce action ourselves. Divorce actions are discontinued, as a matter of law, immediately upon the death of one spouse. When we learned it was Courtney's father who accessed the client accounts to have some leverage over Jackson, we were confident, once the divorce was over, Randolph would have no further use for the information about the accounts."

"So you decided to kill the divorce."

"Well put. We actually told Jackson our solution, but with a slight twist. We told him the divorce would end with the elimination of his wife and father-in-law. He believed they were the targets. Even with that knowledge, he didn't hesitate to set up the lunch today, where he was told his wife would be murdered in front of his children. Funny how you Americans think it is us Russians who have no conscience. We could teach you a lot about family values."

"Thanks, but I already have a mom and dad."

"Once we became aware of your psychiatric problems and former drug dependency, it was easy, with the help of Roy Brown, to have you arrested for parole violations. We plied you with oxy and promised we would fix all your legal problems if you cooperated. It was an easy decision for you to make. Jackson was nothing more than a morally bankrupt thief and pedophile. Under the circumstances, we were confident you would agree to exchange his life for your freedom and sanity."

"Maybe, but I'm not proud of what I done."

"But you should be! You eliminated him and our problems. Everything worked as planned. Courtney will now receive all the marital assets and her father has no need to continue to investigate our clients or their accounts. I'm sure you realize, regardless of the threat to our clients, Jackson could no longer be trusted and would have been eliminated anyway. What is the American expression? You killed two birds with one stone?"

JR didn't look up or move. "It's been real fun talking, but can we go now?"

"Unfortunately, JR, we're still left with one problem. You. You know way too much."

JR didn't move. He was not surprised.

Dimitry motioned to Igor, who moved from the door, picked up the duffle bag containing the money and put it on the floor by the wall next to the duffle bag holding the rifle. Dimity spoke to Igor in Russian, and Igor stepped closer to JR. He drew and pointed a black Glock with a suppressor extending from its barrel at JR's head. As Igor extended his arm to assume a shooting position, someone yelled, "*Nyet!*"

Startled, Dimitry and Igor looked over and saw a silhouette of a man and an arm pointing a SIG Sauer pistol at them from inside the apartment bathroom doorway.

Damian moved his head around the door to get a clear view of the Russians. He said, "Before anyone does anything stupid, you should know the last time I was at the range I discharged ten rounds, all kill shots, in eight seconds. Whatever happens next, you both die. Dimitry, maybe you should translate for your Cossack comrade. He doesn't look too bright."

Dimitry regained his composure and smiled. "Actually, Igor speaks perfect English. So I see the Marines have arrived. JR, I didn't know you were inviting your friend to the party. I guess it was a mistake to trust you with the keys to both apartments. I see you made some copies and gave them to your friend for safekeeping."

"Heck. He's the only friend I have."

"But it doesn't really matter, Damian," Dimitry continued. "I admire your heroics, nothing that happens in this room today can save your friend. That decision has been made by people far away and far more powerful than us. His fate is etched in stone. Look at him. It would be a favor for us to put him out of his misery. Why risk your life? We would be happy to give you this bag of money for your trouble. Take it and go."

"Dimitry, there's only one thing I am sure of. I'm trained to kill and prepared to die. I live by a code you and your trained monkey could never understand. It's not just me, but every SEAL we served with. Rest assured, JR's life is worth more to me than your life or a bag of money."

Igor still kept the Glock pointed at JR's head.

"Dimitry, I'm not quite sure I have your gorilla's attention. Maybe he's willing to die for the hammer and sickle, but there are some other things you should be concerned about. You live on 37th Street in Georgetown. Your wife Tatiana is thirty-four years old and teaches public school at the Ross Elementary School. She goes to yoga classes on Tuesdays and Thursdays and likes to run alone on the tow path by the Potomac River in Georgetown. Not a good idea, by the way, with the homeless problem in DC."

"Are you... are you *threatening* my wife?"

"This isn't a threat. SEALs don't make threats, they act. It's information you should consider to help you make some important decisions for you and your family. Now where was I? That's right. Your children, Gregor and Sasha, are eight and ten years old. Good looking boys. They both attend private school at the Sidwell Friends School. On sunny days they like to walk to school and back home together. It's about ten minute walk and they have to cross two busy intersections. Sometimes they are not as careful as they should be and cross against the light. Here's the last thing you should be aware of. Before I was deployed, I was trained that it might be necessary to eliminate the family of your enemy to achieve an objective. I know you understand this concept because you threatened Sally and Melody."

Dimitry regained his composure. "Damian, sometimes the hero still dies. Maybe neither you or JR will leave this room alive."

"Maybe. Maybe not. But the former members of my platoon, JR's comrades, know everything about you, your family and your threats to kill JR. Whether or not JR or I survive, they have their marching orders. Do I have your attention now?"

Dimitry looked stricken, but nodded.

"Good, because my boss taught me you have to get someone's attention before you can negotiate. I know you are a skilled fixer. So let's fix this. Now I'm going to tell you how this can be a win-win situation. Neither JR nor Chance, or I give a fuck about your clients, your corrupt president, Russia, or money laundering. The divorce is over, and Jackson has been eliminated. Any threat died with him. Agreed?"

Dimitry said nothing. But he was now listening to every word.

"JR would never disclose what he knows or that he pulled the trigger. He would die in jail. This is how it works. JR leaves, with the money, and you never hear from him or me again. If we are safe, you and your family are safe, and your clients are safe."

Dimitry started to speak, but Damian held up his hand. "Wait, before you say anything, there is one other thing you should be aware of. I think you'll like this because you are an expert in trade craft. Do you see the phone on my belt? It recorded and transmitted, everything you said to JR in this room today to five separate encrypted sites. You were very eloquent in putting the noose around your president's neck. Tell your SVR goons not to even try to locate the recordings."

Dimitry was at a loss for words. He knew there was no end game that worked for him.

"If anyone attempts to breach any of the sites, or, of course, if anything happens to JR or me, or Chance or Sally or her daughter, the recording will be immediately publicized and you and your family will never be safe. Not here, not in Russia. Igor doesn't look smart enough to actually understand English. You should translate all this for your dimwitted companion, because what happens to you, happens to him."

Dimitry was silent for a few moments. Then he said something in Russian to Igor.

Igor lowered his gun.

Dimitry said, "Damian, maybe you should come work for me. We have a deal, but we never expect to hear from you or JR again. We expect you will make sure Courtney's father destroys all evidence of our clients' accounts. Is that understood?"

Damian nodded. "Understood."

Igor picked up the duffle bag holding the rifle. He and Dimitry walked out the door. They left the backpack with the money on the floor.

After the Russians left, Damian locked the door and holstered his weapon. He sat down on the folding chair next to JR and put his hand on JR's shoulder. He bent over and looked JR in the eyes. "JR, talk to me. Are you all right?"

The shooting, the threat to his life, and the effects of the oxy had left JR broken and numb. He said, "Damian, thank you. You saved my life. But, ya know, maybe it ain't worth savin'."

"Our mission was always to live to fight another day. No SEAL gets left behind. I'm here for you today and tomorrow even if tomorrow is harder than today."

CHAPTER THIRTY-FOUR
THE HARD FACTS

Facing facts is not an easy thing to do. Some facts are not only stubborn, but they are cold and hard to swallow. In some cases there are no winners. Courtney's divorce was such a case. Everyone lost. Courtney lost her husband. The twins lost their father. Damian lost his friend and, of course, immediately after the shooting, I lost Sally and Melody.

Sally, with good reason, had been shaken to the core by the threats to Melody. She lost all faith and trust in me. I wasn't surprised when she resigned.

We talk occasionally and I still see Melody on holidays and special occasions. I'm still her godfather but it's not the same. The dream of a life together is once again, what it always was, just a fantasy.

I often find Tort sleeping with his head on the baby Simba toy Melody left behind. It is a reminder of what we both have lost, the two people who matter most to me.

Damian informed me all the crypto in the offshore accounts owned by Jackson, Checkmate, and Roy Brown were lost. Lost to the ether. The crypto logarithms and passwords created by Jackson were buried with him.

Roy wasn't upset about Jackson's death. It was the best possible solution to his problem with the Russians. Jackson was just another greedy client who thought he was smarter than anyone else. Roy wasn't concerned about clients, other than the Russians, who lost their accounts but was devastated by the loss of his own wealth and his dream life. He tried desperately to recover the hidden crypto treasure but never succeeded. He didn't blame Jackson, he blamed me. He went to Jackson's funeral and consoled Courtney and the girls. After all, if nothing else, he was a professional.

Damian still works as my trusted investigator and IT expert. He's never talked to me directly about what happened the day when Jackson was shot. The only thing he said to me was, "Tell Sally she and Melody have nothing to worry about."

I understood why they were now safe when I received an encrypted copy of the recording Damian had made of Dimitry's conversation with JR in the apartment after the shooting. I don't know if Jackson deserved to die but I was relieved Courtney and the girls were now safe.

As Roy had promised me, the divorce was over. Just not the way he thought. Courtney, as the surviving spouse, inherited all of Jackson's assets and was the beneficiary of a large life insurance policy insuring Jackson's life.

Randolph had succeeded, and his daughter had gotten not just her fair share, but everything. There was no need for any further investigation by Randolph Gault of Jackson's clients or their accounts. When you win everything there is nothing left to fight for. But I had to make sure.

I called Courtney's father. "Randolph, this is Chance Cormac." When there was no response, I said, "I just want to say I'm sorry to hear about Jackson's death."

"Really? You're sorry about Jackson? What you should be sorry about is that you almost got my daughter and her children killed."

"I regret Courtney met with Jackson. I strongly recommended she should not meet with him. I regret what happened."

"You're got a lot of regrets, don't you? Well, you know what we all regret? We regret you ever got involved in this case. Fortunately it had a happy ending. Jackson was a criminal and he got what he deserved."

"As you are aware, many people were threatened by Jackson's clients because of your investigation. I believe they are dangerous people. I assume, now that the divorce is over, you have no need to continue your investigation or keep any of Jackson's clients' documents."

"I was never interested in Jackson's clients. Courtney got everything she deserved, thanks to me. I've called off the dogs and told them to destroy any client documents."

"Good. I'm happy to hear that."

"Chance, now I want you to do me a favor."

"Okay, what is it?"

"Lose my phone number and lose Courtney's phone number."

When Randolph hung up I was confident Sally and Melody were out of harm's way. I just hoped I could eventually convince Sally that they were safe.

JR disappeared after the shooting. Damian says he has not heard from him and doesn't know where he is. If he does know, I don't think he would tell me. I know he would want to protect his friend and protect me. Damian was not the least bit concerned by the shooting and Jackson's death. He believed Jackson was the enemy and was dangerous.

I was gratified when Damian finally agreed to take the LSAT exam and started applying to evening programs at law schools in the City. I wrote a strong letter of recommendation and am confident, with his skills and background, he will be accepted into the law school of his choice. Damian will make an excellent lawyer. Eventually he will make an even better partner.

The poker games are a thing of the past. I no longer have any relationship with Roy or the Judge. That bridge was burned forever. Gus and Spencer invited me to join them in a new weekly game they wanted to start, but I have lost any desire to gamble. I spend most nights in the office reviewing and drafting legal documents. I have dedicated my life to my law practice and count my days in increments of billable hours.

Of course, I suppose the Russians did win. But in my mind, they only got back what belonged to them to begin with. They have no further interest in Courtney, Randolph or me. I think Roy only narrowly dodged a bullet.

Back in DC, Dimitry was told by the Russian ambassador that the president wanted him to personally thank Dimitry for his efforts and fine work. Dimitry knew the president's gratitude was worth more than any gift he could receive.

Roy and his firm have never referred another case to me, not that I would have accepted any new work from them anyway. I didn't see or hear from Roy after the shooting. He contacted my class action clients, who had asked him for a reference, and told them, since he had recommended me, he felt ethically bound to inform them about my participation in an illegal gambling operation. He sent them a copy of the criminal complaint filed in JR's case.

Soon after, I got a call from Dylan. He said he had reviewed the criminal complaint with his general counsel. They were very pleased with my work, but they thought the optics would not be good if I continued as the lead attorney in a class action based upon criminal fraud.

I thanked Dylan for calling me personally and told him I understood completely and would cooperate in having a new firm substituted in. I thought I would be upset about losing a big case but for some reason I only felt relieved. It was time to start over.

About six months after Jackson's death and the discontinuance of Courtney's divorce action, I was walking down the steps of the US District Court for the Southern District of Manhattan located in Getty Square. I had completed a pre-motion conference with the judge in a new case.

The courthouse has massive columns in front and so many stairs, it takes a lifetime to reach the street. Walking down the stairs I had time to reflect on my day in court and feel proud about the privilege of appearing before some of the most respected and honorable federal jurists in the nation.

Deep in thought, I looked up and saw Roy on the steps below me. He was chatting with a client and some litigators from his firm. I looked away, but when he saw me, he excused himself from his group and walked up the steep stone stairs to talk to me. I kept my head down when he approached. He said, "Chance, I think we should talk."

I looked down at him. "We have nothing to say to one another. Now, if you will excuse me."

As I started to walk away, he grabbed my arm. "I thought you might like to know Courtney is doing well. We are helping her, and her father, with her financial planning and putting her life back together after Jackson's tragic death. She forgives you for putting her and the twins in danger and causing them such pain and hardship. She speaks to Sally from time to time. I heard Sally no longer works for you. That's a shame. She's a real talent."

I stopped and took a deep, breath. "Roy, before you say anything else, you should think about protecting yourself."

Roy raised his voice. "Why should I protect myself? What can you do to me? You are lucky you are still practicing law. You don't have any hand left to play. Your problem, Chance, is that you think you live on some higher moral plane than the rest of us with your meditation, holier than thou attitude and silly platitudes. Wake up. Look who you hurt – your client and her family. And you hurt Sally and Melody."

Without looking up I repeated, "Roy, I still think you should protect yourself."

He replied, "Why do you keeping saying that? There's nothing you can do to hurt me."

I said, "Roy, you don't understand. You should really protect yourself. Right now."

Before he could respond, I looked down at him, focused and threw a perfect right cross that connected with his left temple. Roy went down hard on the stone steps and rolled down another three steps, where he lay unconscious.

The litigators from his firm saw Roy fall and started screaming at me, "Don't move!" as they ran over to where I was standing.

They bent down to help Roy, who was still out cold. They yelled for help from two court officers standing in front of the courthouse.

I didn't move a muscle or say a word.

The court officers ran down the steps from the courthouse and separated me from the other lawyers. They had not seen what happened but saw Roy on the ground and were soon informed about how he got there. Roy slowly regained consciousness. There was a large egg on the side of his head where I hit him and a cut on the back of his head, but otherwise he seemed to be recovering. One of the court officers asked me what happened. I said, "I hit him. It was a right cross."

The court officers asked Roy if he wanted to have me arrested. He looked up at me. "Don't bother. By the time I am done with him I will own his firm, live in his house and he will be working for me for the rest of his life."

I smiled. I was suddenly at peace. I had thrown a perfect knockout punch. It was the pure combination of mind and body I had been practicing for so long. It was the best thing I had done in a long time.

And no one saw it coming.

CHAPTER THIRTY-FIVE
THE MISSING FACTS

It turned out the Russian safe houses weren't quite as safe as Dimitry believed. The houses where the meetings with Roy and Jackson took place were under active surveillance by Homeland Security. All their meetings and conversations were intercepted and recorded. Although the transcripts of these meetings have been classified and every page is captioned "Top Secret," one morning when I arrived at the office, I found copies of the transcripts sitting on my desk.

I called Damian and asked if he knew anything about the transcripts. There was a long silence before he replied, "What transcripts?"

I read the transcripts twice and shredded them. No good could come out of being in possession of top secret documents. The encrypted recording of Dimitry made by Damian on his phone in the apartment has been downloaded to a disk drive and is in my bank safe deposit box.

Between what I learned from the transcripts of the meetings in the safe houses and the encrypted recording Damian made of Dimitry's conversation with JR I was able to fill in all the blanks.

I was not surprised by Jackson's conduct or that of some ruthless Russian oligarchs who did only what was expedient. I was shocked, however, by the extent of Roy's participation in a criminal scheme that resulted in his client's death. I knew I couldn't use the classified documents for any purpose to hold Roy accountable but was confident the government was fully informed and would act at the appropriate time. As Damian says, it's what you don't see coming that can hurt you the most.

Roy did file a grievance against me. The complaint was based on my alleged unprofessional conduct in assaulting him and for engaging in criminal conduct by running an illegal gambling game. I retained Francis Fogarty to represent me before the grievance committee. He told me the gambling complaint was more of the same silly shit, but the assault would probably cost me a suspension of my law license for at least six months. He asked me, "Was it worth it?"

"Without a doubt."

"So, why did you only hit him once?"

Francis wanted to demand a hearing and file a cross grievance against Roy. He was itching to cross examine Roy under oath. "He won't know what fucking day of the week it is when I am done with him."

He wasn't happy when I directed him not to contest the grievance. I acted unprofessionally and there was no defense. When my license to practice law was suspended for six months, I thought it was more than fair.

EPILOGUE

"Yesterday's weirdness is tomorrow's reason why."
~ *Hunter Thompson*

These are all the facts. I believe them to be true, but I know there is always more than one version of the truth. It has been helpful to write everything down. It has given me a purpose during the months since my suspension. More importantly, it's been an opportunity to reflect upon my mistakes.

I have learned some hard lessons about what happens when you don't follow your good instincts. I took a case I shouldn't have for the wrong reasons.

I have also learned a lesson in humility. My father said, "Pride goes before a fall." Arrogance can blind you. It makes you think you can control the world with just skill and good intentions. You think you have a better hand than you do because you fool yourself into believing you can play it better than anyone else. You end up betting against the odds.

My boxing coach taught me when you let your guard down that's when you get knocked down. Then you have only two choices. Get up or stay down. I have never been one to stop a fight. When the bell rings again, I am going to come out punching.

Yesterday in the mail, I got a small package wrapped in plain brown wrapping paper with no return address. When I opened the package, I laughed out loud for the first time in a long while. It was Courtney's autographed copy of *The Curse of Lono*.

Inside the front cover, above Hunter's signature, she had written: "Thank you. Your friend Courtney."

ABOUT THE AUTHOR

Richard A. Danzig is an attorney, author and artist who lives in Ridgefield, Connecticut with his wife, who is his biggest fan and toughest critic. In addition to *Facts Are Stubborn Things*, Richard's second Chance Cormac novel *Punch Line* will be published soon. In addition to his legal thrillers, Richard has also written two children's books. Richard's literary website is richardadanzigauthor.com. His artwork can be viewed at richarddanzig.com.

ACKNOWLEDGEMENTS

Writing a first novel is a lot like learning to ride a bike. It looks easy until you lose your balance and fall on your head.

I wish to thank the people who helped me pedal down the road. First and foremost, I need to thank my gifted editors, Kieran Devaney and Barbara Ellis, who seemed to understand the characters in my book better than I did.

I also want to thank my wife for her help and support in letting me live in the world of Chance Cormac for much longer than I anticipated. I appreciate the comments and support of my friends and relatives, who were kind enough to say how much they enjoyed my book even if they didn't read it.

MUSIC AND LYRICS

"Romeo and Juliet' Music and Lyrics by Mark Knopfler. (1981)

"When The Levee Breaks" Music and Lyrics by Joe McCoy and Memphis Minnie. (1927)

"Kow Kow Calculator" Music and Lyrics by Steve Miller (1969)

Made in United States
Orlando, FL
27 March 2025